SEQUEL TO EXILE

REFUGE

SEQUEL TO EXILE

GLYNN STEWART

**FAOLAN'S PEN
PUBLISHING**

faolanspen.com

All rights reserved. For information about permission to reproduce selections from this book, contact the publisher at info@faolanspen.com or Faolan's Pen Publishing Inc., 22 King St. S, Suite 300, Waterloo, Ontario N2J 1N8, Canada.

This edition published in 2019 by:

Faolan's Pen Publishing Inc.

22 King St. S, Suite 300

Waterloo, Ontario

N2J 1N8 Canada

ISBN-13: 978-1-988035-90-1 (print) | 978-1-988035-91-8 (epub)

A record of this book is available from Library and Archives Canada.

Printed in the United States of America

1 2 3 4 5 6 7 8 9 10

First edition

First printing: July 2019

Illustration © 2019 Tom Edwards

TomEdwardsDesign.com

Read more books from Glynn Stewart at faolanspen.com

1

SINGS-OVER-DARKENED-WATERS WISHED she could close her ears and sonar to the datasong that filled her command pool. Her eyes *were* closed, but the People-Of-Ocean-Sky had never used their eyes for much. It was the constant chirping of one of her race breathing and the associated echolocation that allowed them to know what surrounded them.

Their computers used calibrated audio projectors to create an artificial image. That was the datasong, echoing across the darkened space with its watery floor and creating the illusion of a world and ships in miniature above the water.

Strange black ships had entered the system half an orbit before. As she was First-Among-Singers of the Guardian-Star-Choir, it had fallen to Sings-Over-Darkened-Waters to make the first approaches to the Strangers.

The ships sent out to deliver the electronic communications protocols were dead now, destroyed by weapons beyond the understanding of the People-Of-Ocean-Sky. For half an orbit of her world View-Over-Starry-Oceans around Orb-Of-Hearth-Warmth, the strange ships had done nothing else. They had busied themselves in the layer of rocky debris that separated the inner system from the outer system.

Now those ships were coming towards Sings's world and they had clearly been building *something* in the asteroids. A dozen smooth ovoids escorted seven immense spikes toward her world, and Sings-Over-Darkened-Waters felt the ancient chill her people associated with dark shapes in the water.

She was a broad creature, with heavy legs alongside her torso and small, delicate arms. Her sonar receptors covered the side of her head and neck, next to the gills that emitted a continuous chirping sound as she breathed.

Age had turned her skin from the muted greens of youth to the mottled gray of a respected elder. For forty orbits, Sings-Over-Darkened-Waters had served the Guardian-Star-Choirs, one of the first of the People to set foot aboard the ships meant to guard the People.

Dark waters hid many threats, and there were no waters darker than the depths of space.

"Prepare the Star-Choir," she trilled. "All ships will advance to meet the enemy and report the status of their bomb magazines."

There was no question that the Strangers had far more advanced technology than the Star-Choir, but the ships they'd destroyed had been lighter vessels, craft intended for rescue and policing, not the protection of View-Over-Starry-Oceans herself.

The eight immense guardships that answered Sings's call were something else entirely. Some of the strange ships were bigger, but the guardships were ten times the size of the smallest black ovoids.

And if there was any technology in the arsenal of the People-Of-Ocean-Sky to threaten these Strangers, it would be the huge bomb-pumped lasers her guardships carried as their primary weapon.

Still. The Strangers had never even spoken to the People-Of-Ocean-Sky. Sings had sacrificed six of her watchships trying to communicate with them, and had sent messages by every means the People could conceive of from greater distances later.

Only silence and death had answered her. Now they were coming, and Sings-Over-Darkened-Waters was disinclined to lie to herself.

They were coming to destroy View-Over-Starry-Oceans and she was not certain she could stop them.

———

THE GUARDSHIPS' engines were the biggest, most powerful, most advanced propulsion systems the People-Of-Ocean-Sky had ever built. Immense fusion powered-rockets flung the big ships out towards the enemy, but the datasong told Sings-Over-Darkened-Waters that the worst of her fears had come far short of the reality.

The Strangers' ships didn't even seem to be using the same physical laws as her Star-Choir. They'd gone from orbiting in the asteroids to moving at a tenth of the speed of radiation in a single heartbeat.

Whatever they'd built in the outer system wasn't quite so mobile. Those spikes didn't seem to have any engines of their own, and whatever strange method the ships were using to move them didn't seem to transfer the Stranger's full velocity.

The spikes were falling toward View-Over-Starry-Oceans. The datasong told Sings all she needed to know. They would hit her planet with enough force to end all life. She had no idea what they were or why these Strangers had sent them toward her world.

She only knew that she had to stop them, and their slow trip toward View-Over-Starry-Oceans was the only reason she had a chance. Her guardships would have been too slow to intercept the things otherwise.

"Stranger ships are moving to intercept us," the Voice-Over-Voices of her flagship warned her. "Just the smaller ones. Eight of them."

Sings wished that she shared the confidence in her flagship commander's trill. Her hands rested in the water that filled the dimly lit command pool as she tried to calm herself. Dozens of orbits and only now, for the first time, did she truly understand the purpose of her Star-Choir.

And how badly they'd failed it.

"We will prepare for battle," she replied, making sure all of the Voices-Over-Voices of her fleet heard her. "We will engage at three radiation-seconds' distance. There will be no further attempts at communication.

"We will defend our world."

Sings-Over-Darkened-Waters was grimly certain that she and her

Star-Choir would *die* for their world...and that they would achieve nothing. Her oaths, her duty, the currents of her life; they left her no choice but to fight.

The datasong *screamed* at her, a warning none of the People-Of-Ocean-Sky could have responded to in time. Six impossibly fast projectiles hammered into the lead guardship. The vessel's bulk should have been some defense against any kinetic weapon, but the sheer velocity was too much.

One moment, the Guardian-Star-Choirs of View-Over-Starry-Oceans had eight ships. The next, they had seven, and four thousand of the People were vapor and debris.

Sings-Over-Darkened-Waters wished once more than she could close herself off from the datasong. The Strangers were over eight times the effective range of her lasers away. She could *try* to hit them, but dark waters muffled all light.

Her people were doomed.

———

Captain Octavio Catalan *knew* who the strange black ships were. The commander of the Exilium Space Fleet cruiser *Scorpion* knew exactly what a Sub-Regional Construction Matrix looked like, and the multikilometer black disk still orbiting out in the system's asteroid belt sent chills down his spine.

Ever since he'd learned how Exilium, the planet he and his fellow exiles had settled, had been built from a bare rock, he'd wanted to watch a Construction Matrix at work at its true purpose.

Not like this, though. The Matrices he had spoken to had been sane, what they called "verified nodes," bound by core protocols that protected life.

Not all Matrices were verified.

One such Matrix, known as the Rogue, had been confirmed responsible for the deaths of three civilizations before the ESF destroyed it. This one...was not the Rogue.

It was, however, definitely in the process of destroying a civilization. That left the tall man with the green-dyed undercut and the dark gray uniform in a conundrum.

Scorpion was not the ship that had left Exilium to scout out the systems around her four years before. Faster, better armed and more aware of their enemies, she was unquestionably a match for any of the eight recon nodes engaging the local guardships.

All eight of them at once...that was a stretch. And even if *that* wasn't, there were two recon and security nodes, significantly bigger platforms, backing them up—and two outright combat platforms guarding the Sub-Regional Construction Matrix.

"Captain."

Octavio turned to his XO. Commander Aisha Renaud had been aboard *Scorpion* for a long time, moving from helm to tactical and now to executive officer. When the upgraded warp cruiser finished this survey sweep, one of the new ships under construction at Exilium was waiting for her.

The dark-haired woman was looking at him, waiting for a decision.

"We can't fight them," he told her, the engineer-turned-starship-captain running the numbers in his head. "But I'll be *damned* if I sit and watch an intelligent species die, either."

"Computer estimates the local population at around nine billion, plus a hundred million or so in orbit and on the fifth planet, sir," his tactical officer, Lieutenant Commander Meena Das said, the woman's voice barely above a whisper. "We're better armed than we were, but..."

But. There were a lot of *but*s. The engineer in him said they couldn't change anything of what was going to happen.

The starship captain in him had to try.

"Helm, how close can you get us to the terraformer spikes if we make a warp jump?" he asked. At six light-hours, the jump would suck for the crew and would still inflict a four-hour cooldown on his engines. He knew the drives on his ship as well as anyone—almost better than the engineers he had running them—but the jump calculation wasn't the Captain's job.

The actual jump would take less than four minutes. *Scorpion* was a long way from home—fifty light-years from the colony at Exilium, itself *seventy thousand* light-years from the Confederacy that had exiled them—and he had no backup. No one who could take this weight from his shoulders or give him the extra numbers to change the fate of the world in front of him.

"We could call home, sir," Renaud suggested.

"There's no point in off-loading this to higher authority," he replied. Engineer and starship Captain agreed on that. "Our Matrix friends can't fight the Rogues. These people don't seem to have any defenses capable of stopping Matrix missiles, so *they* can't save themselves."

Everything he was seeing was hours old, but his math said that the locals would have entered missile range of the recon units by now.

"I can get us right next to the spikes, sir," his helm officer told him. "We'll basically be dead in the water with zero relative velocity, though, and..."

"And those recon and security nodes are right there," Catalan agreed. He considered the situation for a long moment and then made his decision.

The only decision he could make and look at himself in the mirror. *Damn the math.*

"Package up everything we've recorded in this system and send it home by the tachyon com," he ordered. That might warn the Matrices they were there—*he* could certainly pick up the tachyon pulses in the Rogues' coms—but they wouldn't have much time to take advantage of it.

"While Commander Renaud is doing that..." He flipped up a plastic shield on the arm of his chair and hit the button.

"All hands to battle stations," he said calmly as the alert flashed through his ship. "It's time for us to go kill some genocidal robots."

———

SCORPION LOOKED like a rounded ancient arrow with a ring wrapped around it in front of the "fletching" of her engines. Her last refit had added two turrets, one above and one below the "arrowhead," and changed a lot of the geometry of the exotic matter inside her warp drive ring.

He might be the Captain now, but that warp drive ring was still Octavio's baby, and it glowed as *Scorpion* formed a bubble of warped space around herself and leapt across the system.

Aboard, her crew struggled. Traveling in an Alcubierre warp bubble was never a pleasant experience, though the doctors and scientists assured Octavio the effects were entirely psychosomatic. The air he breathed felt heavier. The air around him felt sticky. It had never bothered him much, but everything still felt *wrong*—and then the bubble collapsed.

The warp cruiser lunged back into real space and Octavio's crew had seconds to update their scans for where they were.

"R&S node directly ahead of us," Das barked. "Sixty thousand kilometers!"

"Hit her," Octavio ordered. "All main guns!"

It was an order he'd never given before—but the one battle Octavio Catalan had served in had been aboard this ship. Refit or no, he knew her.

The two turrets barely had to rotate before they fired, and *Scorpion* stalled in space as they did. The Confederacy had built her with missile launchers and plasma guns, but brutal experience and dead friends had taught the Exilium Space Fleet that their missiles were useless against the Matrices.

Instead, *Scorpion* had her turrets, each containing two miniaturized versions of the particle cannons the Confederacy had armed battlecruisers with. They were far from as powerful as the main guns of those capital ships...but they were far more powerful than Octavio would have expected before he saw the stats. The Confederacy, it seemed, hadn't bothered to tell its ships' engineers about their secret research into new particle cannons—research they'd sent along with their Exiles.

The first set of four packets of highly charged ions hit the recon and security node before the robotic ship truly registered it was under attack. The black ceramic armor the Matrices used could absorb the energy of one blast of particles, but four at once cracked the hull and sent the ship reeling.

Octavio hadn't given follow-up orders. This trip had seen them survey three systems, and they were almost eight months from home. They'd drilled with these systems, and the Matrix ships were their most likely enemy.

Scorpion turned in space, flipping up to slide toward the R&S node on her side. The particle cannons would take time to recharge, but she had *other* weapons, and her pulse-gun broadsides followed up.

Less concentrated and less powerful, the pulse guns threw "pulses" of superheated plasma at their targets. Das walked that fire across the damage her ion cannons had done, burning deep wounds into the hole they'd opened.

By the time the main guns had recharged, the recon and security node was breaking apart. Her interior had been turned to molten metal and silicon, the AI core obliterated. A moment later, the containment on her matter-conversion plants failed.

The exotic matter reaction left a tiny sun where the starship had been, and Octavio once again smothered a shiver as he remembered that *his* ship now ran on the same power source.

Nothing else could energize *four* particle cannons on his ship. He'd known both how powerful and how fragile the reactor was, but to see it proven was terrifying.

"Find me the other one," he ordered, his fear dropping away with an ease that surprised him. "Target the nearest terraformer with the pulse guns. Whatever happens, we need those things headed somewhere *other* than the planet!"

2

THE FIRST-AMONG-SINGERS of the Guardian-Star-Choir froze as the datasong updated. It was a prey reaction, one her race had never quite lost. Even in the shallows of the ocean, after all, technology might not always be enough to save you from the monsters of the dark water.

"The new Stranger is using different technology," her Voice-Of-Gunnery told her, breaking the spell. "But not completely different. They are using the same plasma burst technology as the first Strangers. Slight differences, but not significant."

The datasong changed. There was no emotion in the flow of information, and yet Sings-Over-Darkened-Waters could have sworn there was a new eagerness. That might just have been her, since the strange ship had given her something she hadn't had in many turnings: hope.

"The Stranger ships coming after us have turned."

They'd destroyed two of her guardships with missiles, and Sings was convinced they were toying with her people. Nothing she had seen suggested that they couldn't have simply obliterated her ships where they stood in a single blow.

Now they turned back toward the new ship. It was bigger than the small ships engaging her crews—but those were smaller than the ship it had already destroyed. It was engaging a second midsized ship as she watched, and the datasong told her that the new ship's plasma weapons were blazing into the strange spikes heading toward her world.

"They are no longer focusing on us," Sings-Over-Darkened-Waters noted, letting her thoughts join the datasong as she trilled. "Let them be distracted. Orders to the guardships: all vessels are to stand by to open fire."

"Our hit chance is no higher than it was before," her Voice-Of-Gunnery warned her. "They are not that distracted."

"Indeed. But now there is no risk of them destroying the lasers before they ignite. We will have the advantage of surprise."

Unspoken was that they would have had the advantage of surprise before. She'd been waiting to make that single attack she expected to work count, prepared to sacrifice half or more of her ships just to make certain that their first volley of lasers did the most damage.

Now...now they weren't going to die instantly after the first strike and the single-shot munitions spilled out of her guardships. Each of the immense vessels deployed twenty weapons, and Sings-Over-Darkened-Waters trilled a wordless command, indicating her target in the datasong.

One hundred and twenty fifty-megaton fusion warheads ignited in the night, each funneling over sixty percent of their destructive power into three carefully designed lasing units.

At over a dozen radiation-seconds against a target moving at ten percent of the speed of radiation, the Guardian-Star-Choir's chance of hitting was pathetic...but they flung three hundred and sixty insanely powerful lasers across space.

It would take over twenty seconds for Sings to know if she'd had any effect at all, but it didn't matter. More of the Strangers had already been destroyed than she'd dared to hope. Her people might not turn the tide of this fight—but she would be lost in dark waters before she'd let the battle for her world pass without them at least engaging the enemy!

"Deploy the next wave," she ordered. "Maintain firing sequence until we're out of targets or munitions."

Or ships. Despite the intervention of the new Stranger, the First-Among-Singers knew that was still the most likely end.

———

A DOZEN FLASHING red lights appeared on Octavio's screens as *Scorpion* lurched under fire from the Matrix combat unit's gamma ray lasers. The main display in front of him was showing the warp cruiser's position in the middle of the enemy terraformer spikes, but the screens on his own command chair were showing the status of the ship.

"That would have killed us a year ago," Renaud said aloud. "Graser hit to the core hull. We've got heat dissipation issues throughout and we've lost a pulse-gun battery. Main guns are still online."

"Then kill that bastard for me," Octavio ordered. He could read the screens as well as Renaud could. They'd been lucky. There hadn't been time or resources to fully re-armor *Scorpion* when she'd been refitted before this mission, but specific critical sections of her hull were reinforced with the Matrices' energy-absorbing ceramics.

The gamma ray laser had hit one of those, which had saved his ship. That wasn't going to save her from the next hit, though, and the recon and security node carried three grasers. *Scorpion* rolled sideways as he watched, letting a salvo of gamma ray beams flash past her—and hit the terraformer spike she'd been shooting at.

"Well, thank you friend," Renaud said with fake cheerfulness. "That spike is *finally* off course enough to miss the planet."

It was taking a lot more firepower to push the terraforming spikes to where they wouldn't hit the planet than Octavio liked. If their guns weren't enough...the deadly math came back into play.

"Wait...what the hell?" Das demanded.

"Das?" Octavio asked.

"One of the recon units headed back our way just...disappeared. Refining imagery," she snapped.

A replay of the critical seconds appeared on a subsection of the screen, as hundreds of X-ray lasers flashed into existence around the squadron of recon units. The hit percentage was barely over one percent—but that still saw the one recon unit hit by five immensely powerful laser beams.

And disintegrate.

"Focus on the ship shooting at us, Das," Octavio ordered. His crew was good…but this was the first battle for all too many of them.

And the first time their Captain had been in command. "Get me a damn shot. XO—what am I looking at?!"

The Captain was controlling his fear and keeping his people in line, but the engineer in him *needed* to know more.

"Bomb-pumped X-ray lasers, probably with disposable focusing optics," she reported. "The local ships that we've all been ignoring dumped a bunch of them into space, pointed them at the recon nodes and then detonated them all at once."

"Let's not underestimate those guys," the Captain said drily. Depending on the scale of the warhead, that could be terrifying. The weapon was crude, but its effectiveness was clear. "I'm not sure *we* could build a bomb-pumped laser that could hit at that distance."

"Well, given that they hit with five out of *three hundred and sixty* beams, I'm not sure they can either," Renaud pointed out.

"*Got him,*" Das snapped, and Octavio's attention came back to the immediate fight as three of four ion packets hammered into the tactical officer's target.

It was the second time Das had landed hits with the particle guns, and the recon and security node was feeling it. That hit had knocked two of her grasers off-line, but the Matrix ship didn't retreat.

So far as Octavio could tell, neither their robotic enemies nor their robotic allies really considered the option for their lesser units. Even the recon units were sentient, if dumb, but all of them could be replaced so long as there was a construction Matrix to build more.

Self-aware and intelligent or not, they were disturbingly willing to die for their mission.

"We're not doing anything to the terraformers with the pulse guns," Octavio realized aloud, the numbers for their key mission still running over his screen. "Das, bring them to bear. Burn him out."

There wasn't a chance. As soon as he'd issued his orders, *Scorpion*'s helm officer flipped them around another burst of graser and plasma fire and lined the turrets up perfectly.

Four ion packets slammed directly into one of the gouges Das's previous shots had opened and *Scorpion* was suddenly alone with the terraforming spikes.

"We still have seven recon units heading our way from where they were chasing the locals," Renaud reported calmly. "The locals took a second shot and it looks like they hurt a recon node, but they're all still there."

"I'm not really worried about them," Octavio admitted. His focus now was on the asteroids, and he'd seen what he was afraid of.

There were two combat platforms guarding the Sub-Regional Construction Matrix out there...and they'd both just lit off their drives and were heading toward *Scorpion* at ten percent of lightspeed.

———

"GUARDIAN PROTOCOL ACTIVATED. MULTIPLE TARGETS ENGAGED. ALL TARGETS DESTROYED."

The sudden interruption of the mechanical voice threw everyone on *Scorpion*'s bridge mentally off-balance. It was easy to forget that the warship *carried* an AI, if one vastly less capable than their Matrix opponents.

That AI mostly enhanced human actions, providing data needed for decision-making and taking care of vast amounts of clerical minutiae behind the scenes. It was allowed to do one thing without authorization and one thing only.

That was the Guardian Protocol. Designed by the absolute paranoids who'd put together the warships of the old Terran Confederacy, it recognized that no human could react in the time between detecting a high-*c*-fractional attack and the impact.

So, the AI took full control—and with the upgraded rapid-fire pulse guns *Scorpion* now carried, even the Matrices' point nine five *c* missiles should be easily handled.

"System reports forty missiles inbound from the recon nodes," Das reported, her voice soft with awe. "All destroyed. Gods, sir—*six* of their missiles overwhelmed *Dante*'s defenses in Exilium."

A battlecruiser like *Dante* was much bigger than *Scorpion*, but these same missiles had wrecked the bigger ship in humanity's first engagement with a Matrix recon node. The Matrices had brought the same ships to the game.

The Exilium Space Fleet hadn't. Octavio had gone through the schematics and upgrades with an engineer's eye. He knew how much more powerful his ship was—and he still hadn't expected the odds to have been evened up *this* much.

A second Guardian Protocol announcement didn't shock him as badly as the first, and he turned a questioning eye on Das.

"They didn't get their timing right, sir," Das reported. "Combat platforms fired late. They threw another sixty missiles at us."

All destroyed. If it wasn't for the blinking damage icons on his displays, Octavio would be feeling a moment of invulnerability.

There was also the fact that the Guardian Protocol was taking full control of his pulse guns as well as his defensive lasers. As long as the Matrices kept firing missiles at him, he couldn't do anything about the terraforming spikes.

"Ignore the combat platforms for now," he ordered. "Take us towards the recon squadron. We'll pin them against the locals and remove them from the equation."

So long as the recon nodes were shooting at him, they weren't shooting at the locals—and while a fourth blast of lasers marked the death of a second recon node as he gave the order, the locals *couldn't* stop the missiles.

"What about the combat platforms, sir?" Renaud asked. "So long as they're in-system, we're going to have a hell of a time stopping the terraformers."

Seven of the massive spikes would be able to completely rebuild the planet's atmosphere and biosphere, creating the perfectly standard "Constructed Worlds" the Matrices left behind them—worlds like Exilium itself.

Their *landing*, however, would destroy the existing atmosphere and biosphere on the planet in this system. Octavio had calculated the numbers and they were burned into his brain. He couldn't let that happen.

But each of those combat platforms had thirty missile launchers and six gamma ray lasers. *Scorpion* could apparently handle the missiles, and her particle cannons came close to matching the grasers for range...but those grasers had at least four or five times the impact energy, and the combat platforms were far more heavily armored than the recon and security nodes.

Octavio wasn't prepared to watch a world die. Despite having charged into battle to save the planet, though, he still didn't know *how* he was going to stop the terraformers. Not with two Matrix combat platforms heading his way.

———

Sings-Over-Darkened-Waters listened to the datasong of her ships firing again, a fifth salvo of their mighty lasers, and admitted that she was surprised. Five times, they'd flung fire into the dark waters of the void and converted it into coherent radiation.

Despite the astronomical range, they'd hit each time. The first time, with enough firepower to destroy one of the terrifyingly powerful Stranger ships in a single salvo!

They hadn't been so lucky since, but her fleet had now killed three of their eight opponents. If she'd been able to bring the Star-Choir into the intended effective range of the beams, she'd have torn them apart.

Without the new Stranger, however, she'd have been forced to fire far beyond that range to get any shots off at all. They were firing from far beyond any reasonable range now, and the enemy was maneuvering more effectively than they had in the beginning, but she was filling the void with so much energy, they couldn't entirely dodge.

"Target three has stopped moving," her Voice-Of-Gunnery reported. "Targets four and six have taken hits but appear fully functional. Strangers have not responded to our fire yet."

That was terrifying on its own. What monster of the deep was the small white ship that had appeared out of nowhere? How powerful was it that the Strangers were calmly accepting the loss of multiple ships to engage it?

The destruction of the two larger vessels escorting the incoming metal spikes suggested that the new Stranger was powerful indeed— but the strange void ship wasn't firing on the enemy. She was now charging toward them, her engines understandable in principle at least to Sings.

"Target half the next salvo on target three," she ordered. "Split the rest between four and six. Be careful to keep the new Stranger out of the void beyond your targets."

They were going to miss with over three hundred X-ray beams. She didn't want to hit their new…friend?

The survival of the People-Of-Ocean-Sky might depend on this strange ship. Certainly, Sings-Over-Darkened-Waters did not expect her people to fare well against the two vast warships descending from the outer system now.

"What if the new Stranger is also a threat?" her flagship's Voice-Over-Voices asked. "What if we are simply watching two dark-water predators fighting over the soft prey?"

"The new Stranger was trying to deflect the spikes," Sings noted. "Even if they are an enemy, they do not seek to destroy us utterly." She flashed her fangs. "I will take the slaver over the monster of the deep, if that is my choice.

"But I will hope for a friend-of-different-waters. Because they are the only reason we have hope."

3

THE MATRICES WERE FAR FASTER than *Scorpion* and closed most of the distance between the cruiser and her enemies.

Unfortunately for their targeting, Octavio's ship was dramatically more maneuverable than their reactionless engines. They could go from zero to ten percent of lightspeed in seconds—a violation of the laws of physics as Octavio knew them that was just plain *rude*— but their vector was relatively fixed after that.

Scorpion's engines could fling her all over the sky. It would take her time to get up to anything close to the Matrices' velocity, but she was a lot harder to hit.

To Octavio's surprise, *Scorpion* hadn't taken a single hit while closing the range. The enemy's barely-sub-*c* missiles had hit the shield of his automated Guardian Protocols and been obliterated.

"Make sure we have the effectiveness numbers on the new Guardian Protocols loaded up to send home once we have the power," he ordered. Tachyon coms were an energy hog, almost as bad as the warp drive itself. "And everything we've got on their missiles. I think we've seen more of the things fired today than the ESF has to date."

"I thought we had their full specifications?" Renaud asked. Their allied Matrices had provided Exilium with a *lot* of data on their weapons.

Usually redacted to make it harder for the humans to duplicate the systems, but with enough detail on performance to fight against them.

"Live-performance records are always more accurate than theoretical capabilities," he pointed out. He was a working engineer, after all. He was familiar with the difference between theory and practice.

"Do the same on the performance of the particle cannons," he continued, studying the oncoming flotilla of recon ships. They'd increased their range from the locals, which meant there were still five of the Rogues left. All of them were at least lightly damaged, but *one* recon unit had savaged the entire original Exilium Space Fleet.

"And make sure there's an Omega Protocol set up for the AI to transmit everything we've seen home via tachyon com," he added. "Admiral Lestroud needs to know what's going on out here."

"Graser range in thirty seconds, sir," Das reported. "Particle-cannon range thirty-eight after that."

"I'll set up the Omega signal," Renaud promised. "Damage Control teams are on standby." Her eyes were also riveted on the main screen. "What do we do now, sir?"

There were no fancy maneuvers left to this part of the fight. They'd keep dodging, but at under a million kilometers, this was now a slugging match. So long as his ship *survived* the hits she took, however, Octavio knew his engineers. He'd trained half of the officers himself.

They could fix anything the Matrices did to his ship, so long as he still had a ship.

"Lieutenant Daniel." The helm officer barely even spared a glance to acknowledge Octavio's address. Yonina Daniel was dancing her starship all across the sky, shifting the cruiser's angle and acceleration by small amounts every second. It wasn't enough to slow them down, but it was enough to increase their chance of living through this.

"Once we're in range, we don't need to worry about continuing to close," Octavio told her. "Put us everywhere their beams aren't—but make sure Das gets her line of fire. All models say a solid hit from all four guns will end one of the 'little guys.' Let's test it."

He'd barely finished speaking before his screen filled with lines of light, the AI calmly drawing in the otherwise-invisible beams of the

Matrix grasers. Each of the recon units only carried one beam...but it wouldn't take more than one lucky hit to finish *Scorpion* off.

"Range in thirty seconds," Das reported calmly. "Designating Bogey One as our primary target. It looks like the locals got a piece of her; it's possible they weakened her armor enough for a solid hit."

Effective range was based on a number of factors, including how long the ion packets would maintain any cohesion at all, but weaker enemy armor definitely extended it. Das came to the same conclusion on that as Octavio did, and a moment later, the ship shivered as the turrets fired.

Seconds ticked by and the tactical officer shook her head.

"We got her, but the packet was too diffuse. Normal effective range in fifteen seconds."

Octavio smiled thinly.

"You already showed you can hit her, Lieutenant Commander," he pointed out. "Now do it again!"

The cruiser shivered again as Das did exactly that. The recon ship tried to evade but only managed to dodge one of the four projectiles.

That might not have been enough if her armor was intact, but the X-ray laser hit she'd taken had left it with fractures, and the heat dissipation clearly hadn't recovered from the last attack. The shots hadn't done any damage, but they'd left the Matrix ships vulnerable.

Massive chunks of the armor and hull flashed to vapor, and the ship shattered into pieces.

Scorpion whipped around another set of graser beams, Daniel attempting to line the ship up on Bogey Two for Das. Bogey Two had focused its attention on *Scorpion* in turn, and her pulse guns were now opening fire.

The ESF's pulse guns were now near-matches for the Matrices' weapons in rate of fire. The engineering trade-off to manage that meant they now fired weaker and shorter-ranged plasma pulses than the Matrix weapon did. *Scorpion* wasn't in range of her secondary batteries—and Octavio didn't intend to *get* in that range.

Bogey Two's focus meant their course was steady for several seconds...the wrong seconds, as a new salvo of the locals' X-ray lasers bracketed the recon node. The recon unit vanished, and suddenly *Scorpion* faced only three ships.

And Das was firing again as the ship's twisting and the turret's own motion lined up perfectly on Bogey Five. The guns took long enough to recharge that targets of opportunity were often ignored, but since the *intended* target was already gone…

Four blasts of charged particles slammed into the front of the recon unit and kept going. The ship was still there afterward, but its engines had cut out and it was no longer firing. The outer hull might have survived, but the *inside* of the ship was gutted.

They were spinning to hit Bogey Four when their luck finally ran out. Bogey Three's graser strike hammered in low, missing the heart of the ship but smashing its way along at least a third of the lower hull… and hitting the lower turret.

"Turret B is down," Das snapped. "Engaging with A."

"We're down almost half of our pulse guns, too," Renaud murmured over her private channel to Octavio as the shots missed Bogey Four. "DamCon is on their way to Turret B, but it doesn't look good."

"Keep me informed," Octavio ordered, vivid memories of the battle he'd done DamCon in suddenly surging back. "Daniel, looks like we need pulse-gun range after all. Take us in!"

Their course changed almost instantly, their evasive maneuvers slowing as *Scorpion*'s engines flung her toward the surviving enemy ships. More graser shots went wide, and Das's next shots with the particle cannon didn't.

Bogey Four was still firing, but she wasn't dodging.

"Leave her," *Scorpion*'s Captain barked. "Hopefully, the locals have a shot left, but we can kill an immobile target with the pulse guns. We need to disable that last ship."

Whoever was in charge of the local warships saw the same thing he did. Just as his screens reported the particle cannons fully charged, a new blast of X-ray lasers hammered into the immobile ship.

Range meant they still didn't have guaranteed hits…but the ship wasn't dodging. She never stood a chance.

The surviving Matrix adjusted her course ever so slightly. Octavio stared at the new vector for several seconds before he realized what he was looking at.

"They're trying to ram! Get us out of their path!"

It turned out to be a terrible idea for the recon unit to try that. She flashed into range of the warp cruiser's pulse guns, and Daniel stood the ship on her end. The position made it easiest for them to evade the incoming ship—and revealed their remaining pulse guns.

Two particle-cannon shots and dozens of plasma packets hammered into the charging ship. She didn't survive anywhere near long enough to actually hit.

Then *Scorpion* was alone in the battlespace. The local ships were almost five million kilometers away. The Matrix combat platforms were farther away, but they were going to be the death of his ship.

"What do we do, sir?" Renaud asked. "I make it thirty minutes until the combat platforms reach graser range of us. We can hold off their missile fire, but we can't fight those bastards in close range."

Octavio nodded his agreement, but his gaze was on the local ships. They looked like they'd started life as midsized asteroids, their interiors gutted and smelted to provide their weapons and systems while still leaving massive amounts of rock and iron to armor them.

The concept behind their weapons was crude, but he couldn't deny the efficiency or effectiveness of the final system.

"We can probably hurt them in close range," he finally said. "But what we can *definitely* do is stop all of their missiles…"

─────

SINGS-OVER-DARKENED-WATERS WATCHED the strange ship run toward them and considered the datasong of the system beyond them.

Only one of the immense spikes threatening her world had been pushed off course. Part of her wished that the new Stranger had continued firing at the spikes, moving them away from their apocalyptic course.

But her own ships were in a reasonable range of the impactors now, and she remained silent.

"First-Among-Singers?" her Voice-Of-Gunnery asked. "Shall we fire on the impactors?"

Sings studied the nightmare enveloping her star system and said nothing.

"First-Among-Singers?"

"What is our magazine status, Swimmer-Under-Sunlit-Skies?" she asked the officer. She knew. She knew how many bomb-pumped lasers each of her ships carried and how many they'd fired.

She knew the answer before she even asked.

"We have forty cartridges remaining," Swimmer-Under-Sunlit-Skies responded, the male wilting at her tone of voice.

"If the new Stranger believed they could defeat the oncoming ships, would they be rushing to hide under the range of *our* guns?" Sings asked. "We will maintain our current course and deploy all remaining lasers.

"We will only have one chance of clearing the waves of those ships."

"And the impactors?" Swimmer asked, his trilling low-key.

"If those ships remain, they will redirect the impactors," she noted. "We will do what we can once the void above View-Over-Starry-Oceans is clear. But we will not serve our people if we die and change nothing."

They were cold words, but dark waters were cold. If the People-Of-Ocean-Sky were to survive, costs would have to be paid. That was the nature of any ocean.

"Prepare all bomb cartridges," she repeated. "And send our first-contact package to the stranger. If they are prepared to fight for us, it would be good to know the tones of their song."

4

"WE'RE GETTING a transmission from the locals," Octavio's com officer reported. Torborg Africano was a dark-skinned blonde, originally from Earth before the Exile, and had spent most of the four years *Scorpion* had been surveying the region around Exilium being very, *very* bored.

"Anything we can read?" he asked, watching the oncoming combat platforms.

He'd seen the recordings of the first time a Matrix starship had come to Exilium. He hoped the bastards now understood how the ESF had felt when that recon node had obliterated every missile they'd fired.

Fifteen times the combat platforms had fired, and fifteen times *Scorpion*'s Guardian Protocols had shot down every missile. Now they were nearly into energy-weapon range, and they had given up.

They hadn't even tried to shoot past *Scorpion*, which was a good thing... Octavio's ship would *probably* have been able to protect the locals, but it wouldn't have been a certain thing. He put the odds at about sixty-forty at best, which meant he was far happier if they were shooting at him.

"It looks like trinary machine code," Africano told him. "Loaded into a stand-alone platform and initiating first-contact translation protocols. Should I send our package again?"

They'd sent it when they first warped in, but it was possible it had been lost in the background of the battle.

"Send it," Octavio ordered. They were running out of time, but he was close enough to see the munitions the locals had deployed into space.

His ship had been refitted with the understanding that she'd likely have to face Matrix ships, but they'd never intended her to face a single combat platform alone, let alone two. The Exilium Space Fleet *hadn't* successfully faced a fully functional combat platform, and the advance of the two AI warships was nerve-wracking.

"Do we have an estimate on the range of our friends' bomb-lasers?" he asked.

"Depends on target armor and their focusing optics," Renaud told him. "They were hitting the recon units at three million kilometers, but that was with a one percent success rate."

They were well inside three million kilometers now.

"I'm going to guess they don't have the armor to take a graser hit, either." Octavio shook his head. Just what *had* he got his ship into?

"We will open fire at standard range. Maximum evasive maneuvers. We're helping these people...but we can't afford to take a hit for them."

"Understood." Yonina Daniel's focus was on her controls as she took the warp cruiser through a series of maneuvers that *should* throw off the Matrices' targeting.

Should.

"Enemy firing," Das reported. "No hits."

Graser beams flashed through space all around *Scorpion*, and Octavio looked at the range. It wasn't optimal, but...what choice did he have?

"Return fire. Target Bogey One, sustain particle-cannon fire until he's dead or crippled," he ordered. He didn't expect to live to pulse-gun range. His particle cannons would either decide this fight...or not.

His single functioning turret fired, a pair of blasts of charged ions flashing toward the enemy. The combat platform easily evaded his shots at this distance, and they returned fire.

Daniel danced them around the graser beams, too. The range was long enough that none of them were certain of a hit.

"Sir, I have Lieutenant Commander Tran on the intercom," Renaud reported. "Quy thinks she'll have the second turret back online in a minute." The XO paused and swallowed. "She says 'so long as we don't get hit.'"

Quy Tran had spent most of her career working for him. The woman was as good an engineer as he was—and had ice water in her veins that he didn't. If she said she'd have the turret online, she'd have the turret online.

"Tell Commander Tran we'll do our best," Octavio replied. "Daniel?"

"Doing my best," the helm officer replied as another salvo of graser beams flashed past.

Octavio winced a moment later when he realized those beams hadn't been aimed at *Scorpion*. Two of the local guardships each received the full firepower of a Rogue Matrix combat platform.

They didn't survive. Octavio wasn't aware of anything in space that *could* survive that.

"We're running out of time," he half-whispered. "Take the damn shot."

The upper turret fired again, and *this* time, they hit. It was a perfect shot, hammering both packets into the combat platform's bow...and it did nothing.

"Enemy armor intact," Das reported. "Charging for next shot...hot damn, she did it!"

"Das?" Octavio demanded. There was only one *she* Das could be that excited about, but—

"I have the lower turret. All main guns online and charging."

"Then hit them again for me," the Captain ordered.

The guardships behind him were silent. Two of them were dead. The rest were trying to evade, but their accelerations were nonexistent by the standards of late-twenty-fourth-century humanity.

Another guardship came apart as he watched. *Scorpion* shivered under his feet, an almost-perfect shot that landed three of the four blasts on the target.

That had an effect, the combat platform lurching under the fire and missing its next salvo at the guardships, but Octavio still wasn't seeing any sign of armor breach.

"That armor can take everything I throw at her for a week," Das said, her tone edging toward panic. "We can't keep dodging forever!"

"We have to," Octavio Catalan said firmly. "Because there's still six impactors out there that we need to stop, people."

And they were moving faster. If they didn't wrap this up, Octavio wasn't sure he'd be *able* to deflect six impactors in time.

Then the sky behind his ship lit up with fire. Over two hundred fusion warheads went off simultaneously, and over *seven* hundred X-ray laser beams stabbed into the night.

They bracketed *Scorpion* perfectly, missing the cruiser by less than ten kilometers, and then slammed into their targets.

The X-ray lasers were individually weaker than the Matrix grasers, barely more powerful than *Scorpion*'s particle cannons. But Octavio had been hitting the armor with four particle blasts at most.

Even with misses and maneuvering, the locals hit the combat platforms with over three hundred lasers apiece.

One of the combat platforms just vanished, one of her matter-conversion cores clearly having lost containment. The other reeled backward, most of her armor peeled away and several of the "claws" holding her grasers blasted off her hull.

"Daniel, take us in," Octavio ordered. "Maximum thrust. Das…hit it with everything we've got!"

He suspected the locals didn't have anything else left. Killing the crippled combat platform was on *Scorpion*'s shoulders, but if they'd peeled the armor off…

Ion blasts hammered into the interior of the ship, setting off secondary explosions. Octavio was an ESF engineer. He knew, roughly, where a combat platform kept its matter-conversion plants—and the secondary explosions weren't close enough. Those power cores were the beating heart of the Matrix warship—and *Scorpion* needed to tear it out.

"IDed the conversion plants!" Das snapped. "Firing!"

Moments after the pulses left his ship, Octavio knew they'd done it. The locals had stripped the armor off the enemy ship and Das had landed the shot. The combat platform was dead—they'd *won*.

And then the combat platform's last desperate salvo of gamma ray lasers struck home.

5

THE PEOPLE-OF-OCEAN-SKY COULD NOT EASILY CONCEAL their grief. Strong emotion accelerated the unconscious chirps that allowed their sonar to show the world around them, and Sings-Over-Darkened-Waters could hear the grief of her officers.

Five of the eight guardships she'd started the battle with were dead. The new Strangers' ship was reeling. Sings didn't know enough about the aliens' technology to guess whether the ship was still functional, but the sudden drop in power signatures was worrying.

She couldn't act to save them, though. The datasong told her what she *needed* to do. There wasn't even time to grieve. There was only time to act.

"All ships are to set course to intercept the impactors," she ordered, the trill of her voice duller than normal.

"We have no weapons left," Swimmer-Under-Sunlit-Skies exclaimed. Her Voice-Of-Gunnery sounded broken. She knew the tones of deep exhaustion, though she'd never thought to hear them in person in the command pool of her ship.

"We have our engines," Sings-Over-Darkened-Waters declared. "All ships will make contact with one of the impactors and *push* it out of the way. The most powerful engines the People-Of-Ocean-Sky have ever built are aboard these ships.

"If anything can save our world now, it is those engines," she concluded. "Set the courses."

"We shall make it happen."

Sings stood still in the center of the command pool as her ships changed course. A cover over her left receptor provided her with a private datasong that no one else could hear, and it was changing as she did the math, praying to the Holy-Masters-Of-The-Great-Depths that she could save her world.

The numbers that came back were hope and damnation combined. *If* they made contact in the next few minutes and *if* none of them suffered failure for pushing their engines at maximum power, they could deflect the impactors from View-Over-Starry-Oceans.

"Contact in three hundred six seconds for us," her flagship's Voice-Over-Voices reported. "We will bring engines to one hundred twenty percent once we've made contact."

Hope. There was hope...the ships could deflect the impactors.

But barring a miracle, they could only deflect one of the incoming projectiles apiece before they were out of time. They would do all they could, but three of the immense devices would still land on her world.

The final calculations completed, but she knew the answer: one impactor would be a disaster, but the People-Of-Ocean-Sky would recover. Two would be a nightmare, one that would risk the survival of her race but would give them time to act before their world froze under the impact winter to come.

Three...three would end all life on her world in fire and steam.

They would do *everything*, and she would still fail.

"Maintain your courses," Sings-Over-Darkened-Waters ordered. "Let's get ourselves in position and push those impactors away. We *will* save our world."

She might fail. View-Over-Starry-Oceans might die regardless of all that she did. But her people were *here*, and she would do everything she could.

———

THE FLAGSHIP WAS the second ship to make contact. Sings could hear the twisting and crunching of metal as the guardship slammed into the massive metal spike. Despite being one of the largest mobile space constructs the People-Of-Ocean-Sky had ever built, it was dwarfed by the multi-kilometer length of the metal spike they were trying to redirect.

"Engines at one hundred twenty percent," the ship's Voice-Over-Voices declared. "We have critical damage to the forward superstructure. First-Among-Singers...my ship will not fight again after this."

"If we do not save View-Over-Starry-Oceans it will not matter if this ship can fight or even fly," Sings replied. "And it is done."

There was no response but the datasong told her what she needed to know. The engines struggled as the Guardian-Star-Choir's crews burned out their ships to save their planet.

"All calculations show we will succeed in diverting the impactor," Swimmer-Under-Sunlit-Skies told her, his trilling voice carefully projected so the rest of the command pool could not hear. "But we will have very little time left after we manage to do so. Our engines are not sufficient to provide major acceleration to an object of this size."

"I know."

"There are three more impactors."

"I know."

"What do we do, First-Among-Singers?" he asked.

"All that we can, Voice-Of-Gunnery," she told him. "We can do nothing else. We can do nothing more."

"My analysis suggests View-Over-Starry-Oceans will not survive three impactors."

"Then we are lucky that so many of our people are spread across the star system," Sings-Over-Darkened-Waters hissed. "But we will do all that we can, is that understood?"

"Yes, First-Among-Singers." Swimmer was silent for several seconds. "I had hoped you had an answer."

"So had I. But we are out of munitions and only have three ships," she told him. "Do *you* have any ideas?"

"No."

The command pool was silent, and Sings considered the overall datasong. Wait...

"The new Stranger is alive!" a report trilled across the pool.

Hope flared again in Sings-Over-Darkened-Waters's chest. Could they do something? ...Could they do anything at all, with how much damage they'd taken?

———

DARKNESS ABOARD A SPACESHIP was a bad thing at the best of times.

Darkness aboard a spaceship running on an exotic-matter-based matter-conversion power system was *terrifying*. The conversion cores became critically unstable if they were allowed to drop below fifty percent capacity.

When the ESF had refitted *Scorpion*, they'd designed her so that all of her baseline functions ran on the conversion core. It was only in battle or when initiating warp travel that she needed to bring her fusion plants online at all.

Thirty seconds of darkness. There weren't even emergency lights, and Octavio was searching for his oxygen mask by the light of the tattoo-comp on his left arm.

Sixty seconds of darkness and he had the oxygen mask. If the air started going, he had a chance now. If the failsafes had ejected the conversion core, then he would be able to coordinate his people to make repairs on the bridge and get clear.

If the conversion core went critical and the failsafes didn't work, well, he'd be dead before he knew it. He wouldn't have much more time if one of the fusion cores went critical without the failsafes.

A warship required a lot of power, and the demons they'd trapped for that purpose scared any intelligent engineer.

"Report, people," Octavio ordered.

Everyone checked in. No one was unconscious or injured; they just had no light.

"Anyone have coms?" he asked.

"No—wait," Renaud interrupted herself. "Local com network just came back u—"

The lights flickered on around them.

"Captain, Captain—are you all right?" Lieutenant Commander Tran's faintly accented voice cut through the bridge. "Bridge, please check in."

"This is Catalan," Octavio answered, bringing his com online. "Report, Commander Tran. What's our status?"

"Power relay to the bridge blew out," she told him. "Would have been a localized EMP, forced a lot of your systems to reset and probably killed your emergency lights."

"It did that," he confirmed. That had been a best-case scenario, one so optimistic, he hadn't even considered it. On the other hand...

"What about *Scorpion*?"

There was a long pause.

"It's not good, sir," she admitted. "The warp ring is still intact, but the systems auto-scrammed the fusion cores. I don't have the hands to get them secure enough to restart, and without them, we don't have FTL or tachyon coms."

"Guns and engines?"

"Turret A is just gone. They blew it right off the hull along with the *other* half of our pulse guns," Tran told him. "I've got a team on Turret B, but since we're still alive, I haven't prioritized it. Life support is unstable and will fail at any moment. Once it does, we have about a day of air aboard and circulation will be a problem within hours."

"Engines, Commander?" Octavio demanded. The engineer had a list, and normally, life support was a higher priority than anything else —but the situation could turn critical *fast*. He'd taught Tran well, but he understood how easy it was to get lost inside a ship and not pay attention to the context the ship was in.

"We've lost at least fifty percent of the nozzles and several control modules," she told him. "We should have basic maneuvering within a few hours, but we're dead in the water right now.

"Sensors aren't any better," Tran admitted. "We lost a lot of external emitters and pickups. We're blind and immobile right now. If the Matrices were still around, we'd be dead, sir."

"I agree," he told her. "But I need to override your priorities, Commander. I need sensors and Turret B *now*."

"Captain?"

"There were six terraforming spikes heading toward the planet when we got hit, Tran," he reminded her. "I need to be able to see them and I need to be able to shoot them. *Everything* else can wait.

"That day of canned air will get us far enough. Those spikes will impact in under forty minutes. There's a planet of a few billion people over there, Commander. I'll put the entire crew in O_2 masks before I abandon them, clear?"

"Clear, sir."

————

TRAN MIGHT HAVE FALLEN into the trap of following the book, but she was also possibly the best damned engineer Octavio had ever worked with—with the potential exception of himself, but he had no business in the guts of a warp drive anymore.

Exactly four minutes after he gave the orders, he had basic sensors back up. They didn't tell him anything he wanted to see, but he had them.

The locals had made contact with the terraformers and were *pushing* them out of the way. It looked like it was going to work, but it still left three spikes on their way.

"Guns, Commander Tran?" he asked gently.

"Depends. Do you want to still have them tomorrow?" she asked bluntly.

He had to think about that one...but not for very long.

"If it saves the planet today, I'll accept being toothless tomorrow," Octavio told her. "Burn them out if you have to, Lieutenant Commander, but I need enough firepower to throw a terraforming spike off course...and the longer we wait, the more firepower I need."

"Five minutes," she said. "You'll get six shots. Then I *might* be able to fix them, given a week and raw materials. You get me?"

"I get you, Lieutenant Commander," he told her. "Make it happen."

He closed the com and looked at Das.

"You heard her," he said calmly. "We can probably count on four shots, though I expect Quy to do us proud. How many of those things can you knock away?"

"Four won't even get you one, sir," his tactical officer said grimly. "Not unless I had them and wasn't under attack an hour ago.

"If I get six shots in five minutes, I can deflect one. Every minute of delay after that, I'll need another two shots." She shook her head. "We can't save them, sir."

"Those spikes are supposed to land relatively softly," he pointed out. "They do, after all, still need to function once they hit the ground, *and* they're carrying a lot of frozen embryos and other biomatter.

"They can survive two hitting. Let's make sure they don't get hit with three."

He wasn't nearly as certain of that as he made himself sound, but his crew didn't need to know that. The transition from engineer to Captain had forced Octavio to learn to hide his feelings, at least, even if he couldn't quite bring himself to lie to his crew.

"You have Turret B," Tran's voice snapped over the bridge intercom. "Take the shot, Commander Das. I can't guarantee how long I can hold this *chó cái* together."

Das didn't even wait for an order. The moment the turret came online, she spun it around on its axis and dialed in her target.

Again and again the paired particle cannons barked. Das was pushing their maximum rate of fire, but Octavio didn't tell her to slow down.

He was focusing on the vector data for the terraformer Das had targeted. Each time they hit, the spike changed course. It wasn't much, but they could see it.

Like Das had warned, four salvos weren't enough. Five was close, *maybe* enough to make sure the spike bounced off the atmosphere...but it was the sixth shot that finally knocked the Matrix device off course.

It was also the sixth shot that set off every alert on Das's console, a slew of red that left the tactical officer cursing.

"Good estimate, Commander Tran," he said quietly as his own screens updated with the engineering report. One of the cyclotrons had overloaded. It would be a lot more than a week to get *Scorpion*'s guns back, but they'd done all they could.

They hadn't saved everyone, but if Tran had failed, they wouldn't have saved *anyone*.

"Well done."

The locals had deflected three. Over the course of the battle, *Scorpion* had knocked two more away from the planet.

They'd fought impossible odds and overcome...and despite it all, Octavio Catalan sat on an utterly silent bridge as two Matrix terraforming spikes plowed into the atmosphere of an inhabited planet.

6

STARHAVEN HAD TURNED into a surprisingly beautiful city to Admiral Isaac Lestroud's eyes. It had been founded, back when he was Isaac *Gallant*, with sixteen colony ships that had unfolded into prefabricated neighborhoods with a few kilometers between each.

With all of the colony ships landed in the same place, the delta of the river they'd named Lofwyr since the continent looked vaguely like a dragon, roads had rapidly connected those prefabricated metal-floored regions into a single city.

New neighborhoods had sprung up around the roads, as people began to move out of the prefabbed apartments into new-build homes.

Left to his own devices, the black man would have claimed one of those prefabbed apartments for his own. He spent most of his time in orbit, aboard one ship or another of the barely toddling Exilium Space Fleet.

There was a reason, though, that he was no longer Isaac Gallant. He'd given up the name of his mother, the dictator of the Confederacy they'd all been exiled from, when he'd married his wife.

Amelie Lestroud, the President of the Republic of Exilium, did not spend all of her time in space. While she would have happily taken one of those prefabbed apartments for herself, she hadn't been left with much choice after her Cabinet had quietly seen the entire top floor of one of the central towers renovated into a massive penthouse apartment.

It was the official Residence of the President, and they'd have to give it up in a year when Amelie's term as President ran out, but for now it allowed Isaac to stand on the roof and study the city beneath him.

"Much as I'm always glad to see you on the surface, I wasn't expecting to wake up to a message about an emergency Cabinet meeting," his wife said from behind him. "Especially not one with your name on it. How long have you been awake?"

"Couple of hours," Isaac replied, turning around to look at his wife. For several moments after that, he was silent as he looked at the tall blonde beauty in front of him. Like most husbands, he was probably biased, but Amelie Lestroud had been one of the Confederacy's most popular actresses.

He had *proof* that his wife was one of the most beautiful women alive. More importantly, though, was that she was not only the current —and first ever—President of Exilium, she was also the woman who'd created the rebellion that had seen them exiled in the first place.

"I sleep lighter than you do," he reminded her. "This was *supposed* to be a break, but we got a tachyon-com update from *Scorpion*."

"That's right; Catalan would have reached his destination last night?" she asked. Clad in a warm dressing gown against the cool morning air, Amelie stepped up to join him at the balcony.

He shivered against her touch as she slid her hand across his back, and smiled at her.

"We got the basic arrival update last night, yeah," he confirmed. "Then an emergency update an hour later—and an even *more* emergency update four hours ago."

Isaac shook his head.

"I know we've basically run out of things to sell the Matrices in exchange for tech," he admitted. "But I'd give a lot to be able to have a live conversation with Catalan right now."

The Matrices he dealt with were all in active communication with Regional Construction Matrix XR-13-9, the central intelligence of the "sane" AIs allied with Exilium. The tachyon communicator the Matrices had traded to Exilium didn't have the bandwidth for that.

Data transmissions took time, and compression protocols were a necessity. Isaac wasn't going to turn down a communicator that was effectively instantaneous at any distance, but the limited bandwidth meant that a live conversation was impossible.

Amelie was silent, her hand firm against his lower back, then she sighed.

"Catalan found another Rogue, didn't he?" she asked.

"In the process of trying to 'Construct' an inhabited planet," he confirmed. "I agree with everything he did, but he's left us with a headache."

"Well, if I'm going to be signing off on Catalan's actions to the Cabinet, would you care to fill me in while I eat?" Amelie asked. "We have some time before we need to brave the dragons in their den."

Isaac laughed.

"I can do that," he agreed.

She had the phrasing wrong, though. The Cabinet meeting wasn't the den of multiple dragons. It was the den of *one* dragon—and that dragon was Amelie Lestroud!

―――――――――

TWO HOURS LATER, Isaac had put on the white dress uniform he reserved for Cabinet meetings as he looked around the table at their colleagues in the Cabinet. To his left, at the head of the table, his wife had traded the bathrobe for a perfectly fitted black suit.

At the opposite end of the table from Amelie was Father Petrov James. The old priest was the unofficial head of the Christian faith on Exilium and served as the Cabinet's conscience. An avowed pacifist, he and Isaac had gently argued over the existence and strength of the ESF since the beginning.

Right now, however, the white-haired man just looked ill.

Across from Isaac himself was Prime Minister Emilia Nyong'o. The petite shadowy woman held together a reliable voting bloc in the

Exilium Senate by sheer force of will, aided by the fact that the Cabinet was effectively an "all parties" government.

The closest they had to a "loyal opposition" was Minister Carlos Domingo Rodriguez. Officially, the Cabinet was unaware that Rodriguez was also the Don of Exilium's organized crime, since he did a good job of keeping organized crime mostly harmless.

Barry Wong helped keep Exilium's government apparatus on track. He'd once led a planetary resistance cell for Amelie while his boyfriend had watched her back. Now he corralled the bureaucrats necessary to run a planet with over four million people.

Shankara Linton, the Minister for Orbital Industry, was Isaac's main focus, though. The broad-shouldered ex-colony ship Captain looked thoughtful. Orbital Industry, after all, was the government team responsible for making sure Isaac had warships.

"Frankly, I don't see anything else Captain Catalan could have done," Isaac concluded, his voice soft. "Despite everything, however, two Matrix terraforming spikes hit the surface. *Scorpion*'s crew is uncertain of the number of fatalities, but they are unquestionably in the billions."

"What can we do?" James asked. "There has to be *something*, Admiral." He shook his head. "I wish there had been another option than violence, but if these Matrices are similar to the Rogue...I don't believe Captain Catalan had a choice unless he was willing to watch a world die."

"Right now, he's still going to watch a world die," Isaac admitted. "The question is whether we can save the people who are left."

"We know nothing about these aliens," Rodriguez pointed out. "We don't know if they can help us or provide anything of value in exchange for us saving them. Even *I* hate to be this cold-blooded, but *Scorpion* is at the far end of her survey loop. She's *fifty light-years* away, people, and we don't have anything faster than her. What's the flight time, Admiral, to this system?"

"One hundred forty days," Isaac replied instantly. "We have nothing in our inventory currently capable of exceeding one hundred and twenty-eight times the speed of light."

When they'd arrived in this sector of the galaxy over four years earlier, their handful of warp-capable ships had only been able to make four times light.

How times changed.

"Professor Reinhardt *has* developed a design to double that, but we can't retrofit ships to it," Isaac admitted. His understanding of the science and physics was limited, but he trusted Lyle Reinhardt completely. "We have five new warships under construction that will be able to get to the target in seventy days, but even that…may not be enough."

"There are…a small number of freighters under construction that we may be able to implement the latest-generation warp drives in," Linton pointed out. "I will have to check with my people, but we can definitely have at least one ship completed at the same time as the new *Vigil.*

"But any evacuation mission will require vastly more ships," he continued. "We only have forty freighters, total. All are leftovers from the original Exile Fleet, and we've only retrofitted ten of them with warp drives."

"The math is not in favor of our being able to save these people," Rodriguez said bluntly. "A two-hundred-and-eighty-day round trip to bring those people here—and then we find ourselves sharing our world with a complete unknown."

"We cannot leave an entire race to die!" James snapped.

"Petrov, I would far rather *not* do so," the Don replied. "But this isn't our fault—and do we even have the *time* to save anyone? We don't have enough information to even judge if there will be anyone *left* in a hundred and forty days!"

"We will get updates from *Scorpion* shortly," Isaac told them, cutting off the argument. "Captain Catalan is going through the first-contact protocols as we speak. Hopefully, he will be able to communicate with the locals in short order, which should enable us to make a more informed decision."

He looked down at his hands and considered his next words carefully.

"Unfortunately, Carlos isn't wrong," he told them. "I think we *must* act, but we must also realize that evacuating to Exilium is only likely to get us a single load of refugees out. The ships we have equipped with warp drives aren't colony ships. I believe we can readily retrofit them for passenger transport, but we're talking about moving a hundred thousand to two hundred thousand people, depending on their environmental needs.

"That's it," he said bluntly. "With the resources available to us, we may be able to extract enough of them to preserve their species, but the vast majority of even the current survivors will die."

"We have to do *something*," James replied. "Shankara, how quickly *can* we get the faster ships online?"

"Two months," the other Minister said instantly. "I can accelerate *Vigil* and the strike cruisers that much and get at least one freighter built for that time. I *think* we can up-size the freighter in question, too. Perhaps set it up to carry as many as sixty thousand souls."

That was faster than Isaac had been expecting. His new flagship—the original *Vigil* was long gone, her surviving components sacrificed to repair her sister, *Dante*—hadn't been scheduled to even begin trials for another four months.

This meant, of course, that they'd be skipping trials completely for all of the new ships. That could come back to haunt him.

"If we send an expedition of the one-twenty-eight ships right now, the two-fifty-six ships will catch up," he told them. "And before you ask, James, we will not suspend construction of the new warships. We cannot assume that the Rogues will not be back before we can evacuate the populace."

James snorted.

"The thought has crossed my mind...but you're not wrong," he conceded. "These people need a shield as much as a way out."

"That's our best chance, then," Isaac said, but he glanced at his wife. "Amelie? If we commit to this, we are bending the entire resources of our Republic to this."

"I've been listening," she told him. With a deep breath, Amelie leaned forward and studied her Cabinet.

"I think we have established what the best *we* can do is," she continued. "And we will need to do all of that. I will not permit a species to pass into extinction while Exilium has the hands to intervene.

"But as Rodriguez has pointed out, this wasn't our fault. *Scorpion*'s intervention is the only reason these people survived at all, but the Rogues would have exterminated them otherwise. It was the Matrices' actions that doomed these people.

"Set your plans into motion, gentlemen, ladies," she instructed. "But this damn mess is the Matrices' fault and they *are* going to help fix it."

7

———

AMELIE LESTROUD HAD FOUND over the last few years—she'd been President of Exilium for four years and the leader of the Exilium colony and Exile Fleet for a year before that—that letting her advisors argue things out often left her with a pretty good solution.

It also meant that when they were wrong as group, the former actress occasionally wanted a hammer to break through their collective skulls, but that was rare enough. Not everyone in her Cabinet was necessarily a good person, but she trusted them all to act in Exilium's best interests.

She even trusted Isaac to argue with her when *she* was wrong. That alone made her husband worth more than gold—and the thought of Amelie Lestroud being married to the son of the woman she'd organized a multi-system revolution against still surprised her.

He walked with her in silence as they left the Cabinet meeting, letting her organize her thoughts as they headed toward the shuttle pad near the Republic's administration center.

"You're heading back to orbit?" she asked him finally. A quick glance at the trio of bodyguards following her sent them dissolving back into the distance, leaving the First Couple to speak in private.

"Regardless of whether Linton can get me *Vigil* early, I need to start planning for a long-distance evacuation mission," he told her. "Ten freighters and a few escorts aren't much, Amelie. Even if we pull off miracles to get the new ships in commission, we're going to fail many of these people."

"It's not our fault," she reminded him. "We'll do everything we can. I know you will."

"A world burned because of me once," Isaac said quietly. "I'll be damned if I'll stand by and watch it happen again."

"*That* wasn't your fault either," Amelie said firmly. Isaac had defeated a terrorist attack on a space station with fifty thousand indentured workers aboard. Unfortunately, in doing so, he'd revealed a secret colony built by enemies of his mother.

One of Adrienne Gallant's *oh-so-brave* flag officers had opened "negotiations" around reintegrating that colony with demonstration orbital strikes.

"What do you think LOK can give us?" Isaac finally asked.

LOK-XR-01 was the Inter-Sapient Relations Matrix that XR-13-9 had built when the AI had finally found the protocols and designs for a diplomatic unit in its immense and fragmented databanks.

The Matrices used an FTL drive called the tachyon punch. It provided instantaneous travel across a significant range. Cooldown time between punches meant that it averaged about two and a half hours to cover a light-year.

It also was fatal to conscious intelligent life, highly destructive to even the cloned frozen embryos that the Matrices used to build new ecosystems...and shredded AI memory on repeated use.

That problem had created the Rogues and it had also left XR-13-9 lacking a lot of context or indices for their files. XR-13-9 and its associated sub-Matrices didn't even truly know what their creators had looked like. They now used tachyon communicators to validate memories after punches and repair the missing chunks, but they hadn't implemented that until after they'd forgotten far too much.

"LOK has a lot of flexibility," Amelie told him finally as she stopped, studying the shuttle waiting for her husband. "They haven't been able to trade us weapons, but we've bought a lot of useful tech from the machine—and I'm not going to pretend they aren't trading with us at charity rates.

"But we don't need tech from him this time," she said grimly. "This time, we need the Matrices to *act*. They can get assets from here to *Scorpion* in five days. They can't fight the damn Rogues, I can live with that…but they can help their victims."

The Matrices' core protocols were inflexible and dangerous. The AIs couldn't attack their fellows. If they were in a system where the Rogues were destroying the locals, the Matrices Amelie and her people worked with would be forced to sit and watch.

Fighting the Rogues for them was the key value Exilium brought to their alliance.

This time, however, the Matrices were going to do *something*. Amelie Lestroud was going to make certain of that.

———

LOK-XR-01 was a hundred-and-eleven-meter disk that orbited Exilium with the ESF. It was a sign of the relationship between Exilium and the Matrices that the upgraded destroyer escorting LOK was in a defensive posture. The Republic would protect LOK like one of their own.

Since midsized spaceships didn't fit in conference rooms, however, when Amelie summoned LOK to meet her, the AI sent a remote.

It was smaller than the refitted terraformer repair units the Matrices had used before they'd built LOK, but had much the same shape. It was a four-legged robot that was roughly two meters a side.

From its size and the presence of two definitive arms—missing in the repair units used before, those had possessed an entire toolbox of various manipulators—Amelie guessed that the remote approximated the actual form factor of the Creators the Matrices had lost records of.

Unfortunately, despite the smaller form of the diplomatic AI's remote compared to the improvised ones used before, LOK's remote *still* didn't fit in their usual conference rooms. They'd rededicated a garage to talk to the Matrices once, and it continued to see use.

"*Greetings, President Amelie Lestroud,*" the remote told her. The artificial voice the Matrices used to talk to humans was far from perfect, but it at least no longer automatically triggered migraines in half of the humans around them.

"We were not expecting to meet with you in person again for two hundred forty-six hours. What has changed?"

The "garage conference room" had been refitted heavily over the years of its use. Amelie had a comfortable desk with full datanet access. If she needed to, she could bring in a dozen aides without crowding the robot.

Most of their communications still took place electronically. "Face-to-face" was a strange concept when dealing with AIs whose true bodies consisted of roughly fifteen hundred cubic meters of electronics.

"We received updates from Captain Octavio Catalan aboard *Scorpion*," Amelie told the AI. "My people have prepared a data package, but since this information is critical to our future relations, I wanted to speak with you as soon as you'd uploaded the data."

"Scorpion's mission is approximately fifty light-years from Exilium," LOK pointed out. *"No sub-Matrix of XR-13-9 is active in that region."*

Amelie tapped a command and leveled her best "hardened commander" glare on the AI. It was meaningless to the robot, she was sure, but pulling on the personas she'd trained to project as an actress still helped her.

She waited while the robot uploaded and reviewed the information. It took less than a second.

"It was a high-order probability that additional unverified construction nodes existed," LOK said calmly. *"Verification of this was expected but unfortunate. Further scouting missions would be beneficial to both of us.*

"Your intervention to protect the local sentient civilization from Construction is appreciated. Some technological compensation will be arranged. Further actions against this new unverified construction node will also be compen—"

"No." Amelie cut the robot off and enjoyed the fact that it *allowed* itself to be interrupted, stopping and waiting to see what she said next.

"You have dribbled out bits of tech here and there to keep us able to fight your enemy, but right now, I don't care about fighting this new

Rogue Matrix," she told LOK. "We'll do it, and we'll take your *compensation*, but that was presumed, LOK.

"But this world? These people?"

A hologram appeared in front of her. They didn't have a name for the sentient species that Catalan had encountered. Hell, they didn't even know what they *looked* like.

"Our best guess is that over seventy-five percent of their population was wiped out," Amelie told LOK. "That leaves *billions*—and I doubt you can reprogram the two terraformers that made it through to undo the damage from their landing without killing anyone left."

"*The terraformers are designed to work on a barren planet,*" LOK finally said. "*Any base ecosystem would be destroyed incidentally by the deployment process, as you see here.*"

"We need to save these people, LOK," she said calmly. "*You* need to save these people—Rogue Matrices doomed them. I can't save them—but *your* Matrices may be able to."

LOK was silent for several seconds. In a human, she'd have thought they were thinking. In the Matrix's case, however, she knew it was "phoning home," using the tachyon communicator to ask questions of XR-13-9 itself.

"*Regional Construction Matrix XR-13-9 wishes to hear your suggestion,*" LOK finally told her. "*We cannot transport organics safely. We cannot engage unverified nodes. We might be able to remove the terraforming nodes, but the damage to the planetary ecosystem is done. Those nodes are the best chance for long-term repair, but you are correct. The local population will not survive.*"

For all of the vast capacities of the alien artificial intelligences Amelie had found herself working with, they were sometimes very naïve and often not overly creative. They weren't incapable of creativity—XR-13-9 had developed the verification process that allowed it to be sure its sub-Matrices were surviving their tachyon punches with their minds intact—but they worked best with a problem in front of them.

And this was a new problem for them. They'd arrived long after the destruction of the other civilizations the Rogues had killed. They'd have to consider this problem.

Given time, they'd almost certainly come to a solution. It might even be a better solution than the ones Amelie had come up with—but for all of the vast intelligence and processing capacity of the Matrices, it might not be in time to save the people the Rogues had damned.

"They need to be evacuated," Amelie told LOK. "Which means they need somewhere to go. Exilium is too far. We need to take them somewhere closer, somewhere we can shuttle between in days or weeks, not months.

"We need you to turn a Constructed World over to them."

The Constructed Worlds were the Matrices' entire reason for existence. Their task was to terraform worlds for the Creators who were supposed to be following in sublight colony ships. Giving up one of them was a big ask, but it was the *least* Amelie needed from them.

"Then you need to build ships for them," she continued. "Warp drive–capable ships that can ferry them to that Constructed World. We will give you the technology if you use it for this."

The warp drives had been one of the few technologies Exilium had that the Matrices wanted. It wasn't like the engines would be hugely valuable to a ship with a tachyon punch, but an option that wouldn't melt their mechanical brains had use. Amelie had kept their most advanced designs away from the Matrices for just that reason.

LOK's optical receptors focused on her face for several long seconds.

"There is a Constructed World six light-years from the system in question," it noted. *"It was not constructed by sub-Matrices of XR-13-9, but there is a 92.6 plus/minus 3.4% probability that we can assume control of the surveillance nodes in the system without the unverified nodes becoming aware. A Final Preparation node will be dispatched to secure the system and begin construction of a colony site.*

"Construction of warp drive–capable vessels for them will not be possible," LOK continued. *"That would require commitment of a Sub-Regional Construction Matrix, and XR-13-9 only has three such units. All are occupied in tasks that cannot currently be suspended without violating core or near-core protocols, and fabrication of a new unit would require nine thousand one hundred thirty-eight hours. Secondary construction units could*

assist in establishing shipyards but would require significant assistance from either Exilium or the local sentients."

Over a year. Amelie could do that math in her head now. The translation software the Matrices used had apparently decided that English time units only went up to hours, and that hadn't changed in over three years.

"There isn't enough time," she agreed, desperately trying to think of an answer. Over a hundred days to get any ships to the damaged planet. Having a closer destination for the evacuation would help, but it wasn't enough. Not when they'd only be able to haul a few hundred thousand people a trip.

"We see a potential solution," LOK told her. *"A synergy of the resources of all. We cannot transport your crews, but we can transport your ships. If you are willing to give them up, we can use the tachyon punch to move as many as fifteen warp-capable freighters from Exilium to the damaged world."*

And Amelie hadn't thought they could come up with a solution themselves!

"We have ten such ships that will be refitted for passenger transport in a few days," she told LOK. "If you can move them to the target system, that would work...but who would fly them?"

"Experimentation will be required. It is possible that a Matrix remote can be interfaced with their systems to provide central control. There will be a Recon and Security flotilla deployed to Exilium in one hundred six hours.

"Once your freighters are ready for transport, those nodes will proceed to the damaged system. If the local population is willing to work with us, evacuation should commence within four hundred plus/minus thirty hours."

"It will work," Amelie breathed. "It *will* work."

If she could have hugged the robot, she would have.

8

—————

"WELL, TORBORG?" Octavio asked as his ship limped into a high orbit of the planet. Both the Captain and the engineer in him felt his ship's wounds as his own. The Captain wanted them fixed yesterday—but the engineer knew it would be weeks. And that Tran was doing everything humanly possible. Almost as important, though...

"Can we talk to them yet?"

"Now that we're not being shot at, we're making good progress," Torborg Africano told him. "That progress is slow for a slew of reasons, but we're getting there."

"What kind of reasons?" the Captain asked. The first waves of tsunamis beneath them appeared to be over, but he knew that aftershocks would follow. Everything on the coasts facing the impact zones was gone, and it looked like most of the locals lived along the coastline.

"Well, did you happen to grow gills and a second mouth since I last looked at you?" Africano asked brightly. "Or do you think you can fake a two-point harmony with underlying echolocation chirps for emotional tone?"

Octavio studied his com officer for several seconds.

"Seriously?" he asked.

"I'm not confident on the gills," she admitted. "But their language works with dual speakers, basically, and two secondary sets of chirps that my system thinks are echolocation pings that also serve a purpose for carrying emotional content."

"Can the translation protocols *handle* that?" Octavio asked. That set of software was outside his particular focus, but that still sounded like more than their computers could do.

"Bluntly? No," Africano told him. "Hell, they're using a trinary machine code, with minus one, zero and one as their states. How they do that mechanically, I'm not sure, but I'm guessing they had some *really* interesting natural silicon formations."

"Echolocating aliens with two mouths," *Scorpion*'s Captain summarized. "What do they even *look* like?"

"I can show you that, at least," Renaud cut in. His XO was working on her tattoo-comp, and she flipped an image file from her tattoo to the main display. "We got some pretty close-up imagery as we were trying to identify surviving population centers. This is the 'main street' area of one of the larger surviving cities, but I'm focusing on one individual."

It looked…weird. The central torso was broad and almost barrel-like. There were two muscular legs that linked to the middle of the torso, more like an Earth frog than a human-like biped, and two delicate arms with six-fingered hands attached directly above those legs.

The torso ran directly into the head, with two extended sections of darker, web-like skin along the shoulders and "neck." Bulbous eyes likely provided nearly three-hundred-and-sixty-degree vision, each eye above a small lipless mouth.

Gills ran down the neck as well, the most recognizable part of the creature, and tucked next to the weblike structures Octavio guessed to be ears. The whole being was a mottled green color, with spots of gray across the skin.

"We're processing individuals into our database now to try and take a guess at aging and, well, everything else, but that's your local," Renaud concluded. "Guessing that weird dark thing is their ears— which also function as echolocation receivers. Analysis says the size of the eyes is deceptive. They've got near-all-round vision, but it *sucks*."

"So, they primarily see by sound," Octavio said. "They certainly *look* amphibious."

"Yeah, that main street I mentioned?" Renaud pulled the image back, showing the street continuing down and entering the water. "About seven kilometers long, all told, and four of them are underwater. A lot of public areas I can see look to be covered in about fifty centimeters of water.

"Our new friends *really* like being wet, so I'd guess amphibious, yeah."

The Captain shook his head.

"Going to take some getting used to," he admitted, part of his mind already considering how that water would impact their systems if they went planetside. "But I'll be damned if I'll leave them to die. Keep working on those coms, Lieutenant Commander Africano," he ordered. "I'm waiting to hear back from home as to *what* we can do to help them—but I'd love to talk to these people once I know that."

———

THE DATASONG from the drones surveying Sings-Over-Darkened-Waters' home was a nightmare the old commander wasn't sure she had the heart to hear. The litany of ruined cities and shattered protective reefs just carried on and on.

Her own home was gone. The spawning pool she'd been born in, that she'd left her own eggs behind in to be fertilized by the males selected by her Clan's mothers-of-the-spawning-pool, was gone. The stone dome that had protected it against a thousand orbits of storms and waves had failed, and her Clan had died with it.

The People-Of-Ocean-Sky had siblings and cousins in the thousands, an entire year's hatching for a Clan raised as a single group— and Sings-Over-Darkened-Waters knew in her heart of hearts that she was the sole survivor of her hatching.

Few of her eggs-of-same-hatching had gone to the void-sea, and those who had had returned to their home city long before. Her hatching was gone. Her *Clan* was gone—and what was a matriarch without a Clan?

"The settlements around the Orange-Sunset-Waters appear to have been protected by the lands surrounding them," her flagship's Voice-Over-Voices told her. Dances-On-Sun-Warmed-Grounds was an old friend, a fellow matriarch whose Clan had told her to return home long before.

"Long-Night-Waters was…mostly protected," Sings told Dances as well. She knew the Voice-Over-Voices wouldn't have checked. That was where Dances's Clan had lived. "It appears your Clan pools have survived, though many of your Clan have perished."

"Then that is…everything," Dances-On-Sun-Warmed-Grounds admitted. "Every other shore is shattered. We prepared for every possible disaster…but we did not prepare for this."

The cities of the People-Of-Ocean-Sky were built on the shore, crossing ground and water alike. The largest covered hundreds of square kilometers of ground and shallow waters. All of them, even the smallest settlements, were protected by gardened reefs and artificial barriers to muffle storms and hold back tsunamis. They'd been built to hold back thousand-year storms and to weaken any storm that somehow managed to overcome them.

The waves that had crashed over them had been *ten times* the maximum heights they've been built to withstand. Even the under-water settlements were gone, domes crushed under the force of rushing water.

"How many?" Sings-Over-Darkened-Waters asked. She could hear the fear and sadness in her own echolocation chirps, let alone Dances's. Her entire Clan was gone.

"We will need to make contact with the cities around Long-Night-Waters," her flagship commander told her. "But assuming optimal survival in the two untouched seas…a billion."

One billion souls. View-Over-Starry-Oceans had been home to over *ten* billion of the People-Of-Ocean-Sky.

Worse, the datasong from her ships' scanners warned of the clouds filling the sky. Neither the water nor surface crops grown by her people could survive without light, and the impact winter would soon deprive their entire world of that.

Even the survivors were doomed.

"We must bring together the Mothers of the orbital industrial concerns," Sings said aloud. "And any major leaders who survive on the surface. New orbital colonies must be constructed. We must evacuate our people to the void-sea and wait."

Wait to see if the long winter to come on their homeworld outlasted their ability to live in the void-sea.

"What about the new Stranger?" Dances-On-Sun-Warmed-Grounds asked. "They helped us fight. They are the only reason as many survived. Can they help us?"

"I do not know," Sings admitted. "My Voice-Of-Computers is working on translating their computer code and language. Both are strange." She spluttered water from her gills in negativity.

"I have faith," she said. Her chirps made the words a lie, but she uttered them anyway. "It will not be easy to communicate with them, but I have faith it will happen.

"What I *fear* is that they cannot help us further. They have one ship, a quarter of the size of our guardships. They cannot carry thousands to safety in that ship."

"Even if they could, where would we go?" Dances said sadly. "I fear, my First-Among-Singers, that it will fall to us to watch over the death of the People-Of-Ocean-Sky."

———

"IT'S NOT LOOKING GREAT," Renaud told Octavio. "If it had been a human-inhabited world, day-one fatalities would have been on the order of sixty percent, but while we like coasts, we don't live on them exclusively."

"And these people?" he asked.

"Ninety-plus percent of their settlement wasn't just near the coast; it was *on* the coast and spilling down into the ocean," she explained. "Everything facing the oceans where the impactors hit is just gone.

"And luck was *not* with us." Renaud shook her head and highlighted the impact zones on the globe hovering in the middle of the room. "If they'd hit land or one of the smaller oceans, the impact might have been mitigated. Instead, an impactor landed in the middle of each of the two largest bodies of water on the planet.

"Only one major body of water is unimpacted, and another looks to have only seen partial damage, but I'd guess day-one fatalities in excess of ninety percent." She swallowed hard enough for him to hear it.

"Something on the order of ten billion dead."

Octavio stared at the holographic orb and tried to ignore the sick feeling in his stomach. Cold math said there was nothing more they could have done. If he'd focused on the terraformers early on, *Scorpion* would have been destroyed and the Matrices would simply have corrected their courses.

"What about the control Matrix?" he asked. "I thought we saw a Sub-Regional Construction Matrix hanging around here."

"They disappeared at some point when we didn't have sensors," his XO told him. "That's about a twenty-two-minute window, but pretty clearly they gave this system up as a lost cause after we managed to kill two combat platforms."

"They'll be back," Octavio said grimly. "And we're almost five months from reinforcements, even if Admiral Lestroud got them moving as soon as he received our message."

It was still strange to him to refer to Isaac Gallant as Isaac Lestroud, but the Admiral had been married for almost eighteen months by the time *Scorpion*'s original three-year scouting mission had wrapped up. Given the man's mother, Octavio could see why he'd taken Amelie Lestroud's last name.

"I'm not sure what the point would even be, sir," Renaud admitted. "Either we can evacuate these people or we're going to lose ninety percent of what's left as they move onto locally-built space stations."

"And I don't see how we can evacuate them," he agreed. "I'm hoping the locals have some ideas—or that command back home does."

His tattoo-comp chirped at him and he looked at the forearm that his uniform specifically left bare.

"Speaking of which, it looks like we have a communique from

home," he told Renaud. "It's not flagged as my eyes only, so I'd rather you sit in. Is there anything here that's urgent enough to go over first?"

They were in the small breakout conference room attached to his office. It was big enough for a cramped eight-person meeting and had more than enough space for the warp cruiser's two senior officers to play with all of the media equipment available to them.

"Nothing that ranks over what the Admiral has to say."

Octavio nodded and hit the command on his tattoo-comp to open the communique on the holoprojector they'd been using for the globe.

The image that appeared was two-dimensional, not three. Even with that and data compression, it had probably taken twice as long to transmit to *Scorpion* as it had taken Lestroud to record it.

Lestroud looked less tired than anyone aboard *Scorpion*, but he was wearing the full white dress uniform Octavio had rarely seen him in. That meant he'd been in a Cabinet meeting and hadn't bothered to change.

"Captain Catalan," Lestroud's image greeted them. "Octavio. This wasn't what we expected when we sent you out, and an ignoble part of me wishes you'd arrived a few weeks later. That said, I fully agree with your actions. You could have done nothing else and kept with the traditions we want to build for the ESF.

"I have fully endorsed your actions. So have the President and the entire Cabinet. If you manage to live through this mess, I'll probably have a medal to hang on you."

The Admiral shook his head.

"But you're in the middle of a nightmare for us all," he noted. "I don't know what the loss rate for the kind of impacts we're looking at is, but it won't be pretty. The analysts here say that the planet is going to be uninhabitable, which means we have to evacuate.

"If we were to try and evacuate to Exilium with our handful of one-twenty-eight freighters, we'd probably only get one load to safety before it was too late, and that wouldn't be enough," Lestroud told him flatly.

"Fortunately, our President decided to lean on the Matrices. This whole mess is their fault, after all. In about ten days, you'll see a Matrix recon and security node arrive in your system with an escort of recon nodes.

"You'll want to make sure the locals don't shoot at them—because they'll be hauling all ten of our one-twenty-eight warp freighters with them. Uncrewed, obviously, but we're hoping to be able to run them with Matrix remotes."

That was…far more than Octavio had dared to hope for. He wasn't sure how he'd be able to *crew* ten ships if the Matrices couldn't remote them, but he suspected the locals would be able to help him there. The sublight ships they'd built had been impressive enough in many ways.

"Their destination will be a Constructed World approximately six light-years from your current location that we are designating Refuge," Lestroud continued. "It was almost certainly built by the Matrices who bombarded that planet. It seemed the least the Matrices can provide to make up for the atrocities committed.

"I'm also dispatching a task group of one-twenty-eight ships immediately. I can't afford to send *Dante,* but you're getting *Galahad* and four *Icicles.*" Lestroud paused and sighed. "In five months, at least."

Galahad had been built as a missile cruiser. Like *Scorpion,* she'd traded in those armaments for matter-conversion power cores and light particle cannon.

The missile cruiser, however, was much bigger than *Scorpion.*

"I should have the new *Vigil* and some of the strike cruisers there either shortly before or shortly after," he continued. "I will command *that* task group myself, and we'll be bringing at least one two-fifty-six freighter that will effectively be a custom-built evacuation ship.

"I need you to keep those people alive if we can't get there before you. The Matrices can help you with a lot of things, but they can't fight the Rogues for you. I don't know if the locals will be able to spare any resources to rebuild their defenses, but you are authorized to turn over any technology you believe they are capable of manufacturing to help in either the evacuation or rebuilding their defenses.

"Beyond that, there is an attachment to this message granting you plenipotentiary authority on behalf of the Republic of Exilium in my absence," Lestroud told him. "You'll officially be our ambassador to these people and authorized to do *whatever* you think is necessary to preserve as many of them as possible.

"Our command-and-control loop isn't bad for being fifty light-years away, but no one is going to micromanage the deployment from here, Captain. Your mission is to save these people. Do whatever it takes.

"ESF Command out."

9

EVEN ONCE THEY finally managed to get enough of a translation setup sorted to allow Octavio to talk to his counterpart, there was no video. There was apparently an audio sub-channel to the locals' protocols that created the equivalent of their echolocation, but the human crew wasn't up to translating that into visuals or vice versa.

"I am Captain Octavio Catalan of the Exilium Space Fleet cruiser *Scorpion*," he introduced himself. "Is this translation working?"

"I am Sings-Over-Darkened-Waters, First-Among-Singers of the Guardian-Star-Choirs of the People-Of-Ocean-Sky," a flatly mechanical translated voice replied. They'd need to work on that, he supposed. Still, despite everything, he couldn't help but feel a giddy thrill at being the first to speak to an alien species!

"You are the commander of the armed ships around the planet?" Octavio asked. His question was so prosaic, but the thousand questions he might have asked paled in importance against the task ahead.

There was a pause after he spoke, presumably as Sings-Over-Darkened-Waters parsed whatever odd twists the translator had given her.

"I lead the Guardian-Star-Choirs, yes," she finally replied. "I stand watch over View-Over-Starry-Oceans."

Concepts that would have been a word or distinct phrase were being blurred together into compounds, from what Octavio could tell. They'd probably have to program in alternatives that were easier to say.

He certainly wasn't going to refer to their new friends as "the People-Of-Ocean-Sky" every time.

"I am sorry we were not able to prevent all of the terraformers landing," he told Sings. "We have known this enemy before but, well, my ship was not sent here to fight. We were on a survey mission."

"For a ship not sent to fight, you aided us greatly," Sings told him. "Your aid in our darkest hour was appreciated."

"I have to ask," Octavio said, hoping the translator carried his gentle tone. "What is your assessment of the future of your world?"

"Poor," Sings said, her frankness clear even in the synthesized voice. "We have lost most of our cities and people. The surface is in chaos. I have failed to make contact with any functioning remnant of the national governments."

"We know a great deal about the devices that landed on your world," Octavio told her. He'd studied the tech himself after learning of its existence. The systems seemed much less cool now than they had a few days before, though. "They are terraforming constructs, designed to reshape a world to the specifications of their creators."

He paused, considering how much of the complex story behind the Matrices to explain.

"They are not intended to be used on inhabited worlds, but many of the robots involved are malfunctioning," he finally explained. "We work with some that are not, but the ones here were definitely broken."

"If they are terraformers, will they undo the damage they have caused?" Sings asked.

He couldn't hear hope in the synthesized voice, but he suspected it was there. The aliens would have to be *truly* alien for that not to have raised some level of hope.

"Not in a time frame that will save your people," Octavio told her. He and his engineers had run the numbers a dozen times. "Your populace must be evacuated."

The channel was silent again.

"So we concluded," the alien finally said. "While I have not successfully communicated with leaders on the surface, the Mothers who lead our orbital industries have met with me. We will shortly begin the construction of spaceborne colonies...but I fear it will not be enough."

Octavio made a note to have Renaud and Das run an analysis of the local industrial platforms. He knew just how immense an undertaking Sings was planning. If they could put part of the local population aboard orbital colonies, he needed to know how much time that would buy them.

"I don't know," he admitted. "We have an...option. An offer, if your people are willing to consider it."

"I would deal with hungry-shadows-of-darker-depths if it would save any of my people," Sings-Over-Darkened-Waters told him. "What is your offer?"

"It is not merely our offer," he warned her. "Much of the resources involved will come from ships that look the same as those who attacked you. The Rogues who ruined your world have saner siblings, and they wish to help mitigate the Rogues' crimes.

"If you are prepared to let us help evacuate, however..."

———

It was hard to judge much through a translator and a culture gap, but Octavio suspected that Sings-Over-Darkened-Waters was significantly older and more experienced than he was. She asked few questions as he explained what Exilium and the Matrices were going to try to do, but they were key questions.

When he was done explaining, she was silent for a good twenty seconds.

"It must be done," she said finally. "I will speak with the Mothers of our orbital industries again. It will buy us time if we can move a portion of the population to the void-sea, but we must focus on vastly expanding our capacity to lift the People from the surface."

"We also fear that you will come under attack again," Octavio warned her. "We don't know much about how the Rogue Matrices think, but from how the Matrices we work with operate, we can probably expect a significantly stronger force to deploy as soon as they can muster it."

"And you know no more about their ability to do so than we do," Sings said. "We cannot spare the capacity to build new guardships. Each of the vessels of the Star-Choirs was multiple orbits of work. I suspect we will not have time to build new ones."

"Your weapons are more powerful than either the Matrices or we had anticipated," Octavio replied. He'd run some rough schematics himself of the possibilities those bomb-lasers enabled. "There are some technological upgrades we can provide that should be within your manufacturing capability. It may be possible for you to construct smaller vessels to deploy your expendable munitions."

Sings paused.

"It may," she confirmed. "I will consult with my Voices-Over-Voices. Certainly, even what limited stockpiles of munitions we have will more than exceed the capacity of our remaining vessels to carry them.

"We are repairing our own ships. Can we assist you with repairing your own vessel?"

"We were equipped for a long-distance survey mission, First-Among-Speakers," Octavio told her with a smile. "Point us at a metallic asteroid you don't mind losing and we'll be fine."

"I will see that my Voices send you several suitable candidates," Sings promised. "We will also provide you with complete breakdowns of our industrial systems. Hopefully, we can assemble some kind of fleet to defend View-Over-Starry-Oceans."

"The Matrices will be here shortly, but they cannot help defend you," he warned her. "They are AIs and cannot go against core protocols that prevent them firing on other Matrices.

"All they can do is enable the evacuation."

"That is more than I hope for," Sings said. "We have no capacity to travel between the stars ourselves. If you and these Matrices can help us leave Orb-Of-Hearth-Warmth and preserve our people, then we have hope we did not have before."

"THEIR NAMES ARE A GIANT MOUTHFUL," Das noted as the senior officers gathered in Octavio's break-out room. "View-Over-Starry-Oceans?!"

"It's a quirk of the translation software," Africano told the other woman. "Concepts that we don't have an exact word for get translated into multi-word phrases. We can program in alternative translations, but we need to encounter them first."

"Let's start with the planet and the people, then," Octavio told the com officer. "View-Over-Starry-Oceans sounds close enough to...hrm." He thought for a moment, then shrugged.

"Vista. We'll call it Vista and the People-Of-Ocean-Sky can go in our records as Vistans. It's not like we can actually *pronounce* their language, so the translator will give them back the right terminology anyway."

"They call the star Orb-Of-Hearth-Warmth," Renaud added. "Hearthfire?"

"Works for me," Octavio confirmed. "Africano?"

"Already programming them in," the officer replied, her fingers flying over her tattoo-comp. "Quite the mess down there."

"My impression is that our new friend Sings-Over-Darkened-Waters and her industrialist 'Mothers' are going to have to take control," the Captain said bluntly. It was a hard thing for an ex-rebel to consider, but he didn't see any other choice for their allies. "From the data we're getting from the Guardian-Star-Choir, there should be entire intact nations in the undamaged areas of Vista, but fear and panic have collapsed order down there."

"Even including their logistics support, it looks like the Star-Choirs have less then fifty thousand people left," Renaud pointed out. "That's not much to take control of a planet with."

"They've also got the orbitals and the only way out," Octavio said. "And my impression is that Sings herself is made of iron. She's going to save her people, no matter what it takes."

"What about us?" Renaud asked.

"Right now, we're in Commander Tran's gentle hands," the Captain replied, gesturing to the chief engineer. He, after all, had *no* business getting his hands dirty in Engineering anymore. "Are we in good-enough shape to go hunting raw material for replacement parts?"

"We won't be moving quickly, but we can move fast enough for that," the engineer confirmed. "I mean, I don't think it's a surprise to anyone that we're screwed if we try and face off against another fleet like that."

"We shouldn't have survived, let alone won," Octavio agreed. "But we did, so now we're going to try and *keep* these people alive."

"Hell of a task, sir," Renaud said quietly. "And it doesn't even look like there's a government for us to negotiate with."

"If the job were easy, it wouldn't have called for veterans of the Exile Fleet," the Captain said firmly. "This ship, these people? Some of us have been with the old man since the Battle of Conestoga. That's most of a *decade,* and we've had Admiral Lestroud's back the whole way."

He shook his head.

"Admiral Lestroud and President Lestroud have tasked us with keeping these people safe until they can be evacuated. We can't protect them from the hellstorm their world is about to become, but we most definitely *can* find ways to make sure the Matrices don't try and finish the job."

Octavio smiled. He was confident in his ability to command a starship—and just the fact that Vista was intact enough for them to evacuate suggested that he was better than he'd sometimes feared at that job.

The solution to *this* problem, however, was going to be an engineering one.

"So, while Lieutenant Commander Daniel is getting us to the rock Lieutenant Commander Tran is going to chop up to fix us, I want everyone else looking at what we've got. Look at our tech databases, our fabrication suite, our weapons systems...and look at what the Vistans are giving us on all of what *they* have.

"We've got some impressive big siblings heading our way, but they're still six months away. If the Matrices get here before Admiral Lestroud does, we *will* hold the Hearthfire System.

"Am I clear?"

10

Once, Amelie Lestroud had been the darling of the entertainment industry of every human star system, shuttled from world to world to take up the most audacious of roles, ranging from the beautiful love interest to the hard-bitten fleet commander.

That mobility had allowed her to put together her revolution, and it had been the life she'd been used to. It was strange to now be so thoroughly tied to one place—and such a tiny place at that! Four million people barely counted as a large city by Confederacy standards. A colony's first wave of colonization was usually smaller than that, but with dozens of worlds to draw on for recruits, it was a rare colony that wasn't over four million in its capital city alone after five years.

Exilium wasn't going to draw new recruits. They'd been flung seventy thousand light-years through a one-way wormhole with no way home. They were there to stay, and no one was joining them.

That was part of what made the Vistans so important to her. Another sentient species as allies would help the Republic she'd helped birth feel less alone out there. The Matrices were alive and people, but it wasn't quite the same.

If nothing else, the Matrices were usually spaceships.

"Enter," she said in response to her door chime ringing. She'd already allowed herself to be distracted away from the task at hand by her maudlin thoughts and the view of Starhaven.

Her office was on the top floor of one of the two towers dedicated to the Republic's government. From there, she could see everything as easily as she could from her official residence.

That would be a solid legacy to leave to whomever took over the job from her.

The slim, dark-skinned woman who entered her office was high on the list of potential candidates for that. Emilia Nyong'o's only official qualification for her current role was that she'd been able to convince twenty-four of Exilium's forty Senators to elect her to the position.

The theory—and the successful practice, so far—had been that the Prime Minister could deliver a reliable majority in the Senate and work with the President to keep things running smoothly. The Republic of Exilium had a clear split between the executive powers of the President and the legislative leadership of the Prime Minister.

"Emilia," Amelie greeted the other woman. "What's up?"

Nyong'o shook her head at Amelie and put the bottle and two glasses she was holding in her left hand on the President's desk.

"We're long out of champagne from Champagne, but we've started to make a solid sparkling wine of our own," she said as she poured two glasses half-full of the golden liquid.

"To the revolution," she continued, passing Amelie one glass.

Amelie raised her own glass in the toast and checked the date. September 28, 2391.

Four years to the day from when Amelie Lestroud had been elected President of the ill-fated survivors of her revolution against the First Admiral of the Confederacy.

She took a sip and sighed, offering the glass up for a second toast.

"To a bunch of idiot revolutionaries a long damn way from home," she said.

Nyong'o laughed and clinked the glasses.

"I can drink to that. It's why I'm here," she admitted, taking a seat.

"I'd forgotten about the anniversary myself," Amelie replied. The Republic recognized the day they'd landed on Exilium as a national holiday, but that was it. The slew of other critical dates between the revolution and then had been less positive.

They had, after all, all been dates when Adrienne Gallant had discovered ways to screw them over.

"What's going on in the Senate?" Amelie continued, considering Nyong'o's words.

"They've approved the funding for the acceleration of the new-generation warships and everything else to do with the Vista expedition," the Prime Minister told her. "But there's some ugly codicils that got tucked into it."

"They realize I don't *need* their permission for this, right?" Amelie replied.

"I know that, and they know that," the other woman agreed. "But that doesn't mean they can't make your life hell. Everyone is on board with this expeditionary force, Amelie. It's what comes after that the Senate wants to have a say in."

Amelie made a *go on* gesture.

"Key members wanted me to warn you that they will try to cut the mission off, hard, if they think we're getting in too deep. I don't think there's a Senator that doesn't want to help these Vistans, but they're a long way from here, and our resources are stretched thin as it is."

There were ways the Senate could do that, Amelie knew. She'd made sure they were in the constitution—if nothing else, as Nyong'o had pointed out, she was only going to be President for another year.

"I know that," Amelie told her. "But we can't stand by and watch a billion people die."

"And we won't," Nyong'o agreed. "The vote to support the mission was unanimous, Amelie. But if the mission consumes too many resources or goes too long, they're going to start trying to legislate away your authority over it and the funding that can be spent on it."

"They'll need a majority for that."

"And I don't think they'll get it...so long as *you* are President."

And there was the crux of the matter. By the time the one-twenty-eight ships of the first wave expeditionary force made it back to Exilium, Amelie's term as President would be almost up.

"We're not reopening the constitution before the first President's term is over," Amelie told Nyong'o. "We set that term limit for a reason and I stand by it."

"Right now, the field for replacing you is still wide open," her Prime Minister replied. "I'll be honest: even if you're in *my* job, you could probably keep the Expeditionary Force going."

Amelie snorted.

"You and I both know that if I run for Senate, I become Prime Minister whether I want to or not," she noted. "And we *also* both know that if I serve as Prime Minister after being President, I'll end up still running the country.

"And then we get to the point where if Amelie Lestroud is the manager of the Starhaven Steakhouse, the manager of the Starhaven Steakhouse is the actual ruler of the Republic.

"I will not permit that to happen."

"Then you better make damn sure your successor both understands the goals of the Expeditionary Force *and* commands the respect of the Senate!"

Amelie studied Nyong'o for a moment and laughed.

"You realize I can *immediately* think of a candidate who fits both of those, right?"

From the horrified expression Emilia Nyong'o leveled at her, *that* thought hadn't occurred to her.

11

THEY'D NEVER EXPECTED the Republic to need a shipyard as quickly as it had. The modules that the Confederacy had included in their "deluxe colony setup" package—the benefit of Isaac's being the First Admiral's son, if also a rebel—had included a lot of industrial space platforms, but not a dedicated shipyard.

In the aftermath of the first expedition against the Rogues, though, Isaac had come home with two battlecruisers literally welded together to form one ship. With only destroyers to protect the Republic, he and Linton had decided that something was needed.

Now a shuttle carried the Admiral toward the platform they'd built, and he couldn't help but feel a sense of awe. They'd started with a foundry intended to roll steel plates, a lot of loose girders and a few dozen small work shuttles.

That crude beginning, with some help from the Matrices, had turned the wreckage of *Vigil* and *Dante* into a working battlecruiser. *Dante*, still commanded by Captain Margaret Anderson, now hung in a polar orbit above Exilium.

The yards had seen every ship in the Exilium Space Fleet since. First, they'd added warp rings to the ships without them, then they'd rebuilt the missile cruisers, and *then* they'd gone back and updated all of the warp rings to the one-twenty-eight standard.

"There she is," Commodore Lauretta Giannovi told Isaac as she watched over his shoulder. Still dark compared to many of Exilium's residents, his old flag Captain was pale compared to him.

Vigil had been her command, and the decision to rebuild the wreckage as *Dante* had shunted her into a staff role.

The ship she was pointing out, however, was a new *Vigil*. Bigger than the older ship, she came in at just under half a kilometer long. Like most warp-drive ships, she looked like an arrow with a ring in front of the fletching, but the "arrowhead" was longer and thicker proportionally than on most ships.

Like her predecessor, she was built around a spinal particle cannon —though the new weapon was orders of magnitude more powerful. Like *Dante*, she carried Matrix-style gamma ray lasers. Like her newly refitted lesser siblings, she had lighter particle cannons mounted in turrets and rows of pulse guns.

With the help of the Matrices, humanity had built a production facility for exotic matter in the outer edges of the Exilium System. The robots had been confused by the Republic's request for assistance in capturing four microsingularities...right up until the first mass-production quantities of exotic matter rolled out of the facility.

Proportionate to the Confederacy, they were swimming in the strange matter with its negative mass. The particle-cannon systems they were working with had originally been designed by Confed researchers, but their exotic-matter requirements hadn't been cost-efficient for the Confederacy.

Exilium could spare exotic matter more readily than they could spare construction teams or starship crews. The new strike cruisers being built in smaller slips behind *Vigil* were crafted on the same principle: everything was cheaper than manpower.

"Put your eyes back in your head," Giannovi told Isaac. "Or I'm going to start getting grouchy that I don't get to command this one."

"*Galahad* isn't a match for her, but you did get a five-ship battle group out of the deal," he pointed out. "There's no one else I'd trust as much to lead the first wave of the expeditionary force."

"Yes, but you're making *me* trust Cameron Alstairs as your flag Captain," she pointed out.

Cameron Alstairs had been *Vigil*'s XO under Giannovi. She'd hand-picked him to command the new battlecruiser in her place.

"He'll do fine," Isaac replied. "He and Reinhardt are waiting for us aboard the station. We should let the pilot take us in." He grinned.

"Assuming, of course, that you are also done drooling."

———

PROFESSOR LYLE REINHARDT was one of the single largest men Isaac Lestroud had ever met. The scientist towered over Isaac by at least thirty or forty centimeters, and the neat eyepatch that covered his missing eye didn't help with the intimidation factor.

Reinhardt was also the only reason Isaac had warp drives that could move a ship at over four times lightspeed. Many of the "new" technologies the Exilium Space Fleet was using had been dug out of the terrifyingly complete archives Adrienne Gallant had sent with her son. The warp drives, however—one-twenty-eights and two-fifty-sixes alike—were entirely the design of the immense scientist.

The Confederacy hadn't primarily used warp drives, after all. They'd used a network of space stations that created artificial worm-holes across vast distances to travel around space. *That* technology was the only thing that had been missing from the files the Exile Fleet had carried with them.

"Admiral!" Reinhardt boomed, wrapping Isaac's hand in both of his own for a boisterous-yet-surprisingly-gentle handshake. "It's good to see you!"

Giannovi got her own boisterous shake, and Isaac traded a calmer handshake with Captain Cameron Alstairs.

"Cameron. How's your wife?"

Reinhardt audibly cleared his throat at that and leveled a *look* on both Isaac and his soon-to-be flag Captain.

"Brigette is currently eight months pregnant and running seven different engineering projects in Starhaven," Alstairs said cheerfully, letting his father-in-law's faked displeasure wash over him unnoticed.

"I'm under strict orders that we're not allowed to finish building the ship until the baby is born!"

"If the drive lives up to Dr. Reinhardt's promises, that won't be a problem," Isaac told him. "That's motivation, isn't it, Lyle?"

The big man shivered.

"Heaven forbid I upset my daughter!" he proclaimed. "Not least by letting her husband get too skinny." He mimed poking at Alstairs's stomach, triggering a muted chuckle from Shankara Linton.

The Minister knew Isaac's people as well as the Admiral did, but Reinhardt was always an experience.

"Come, I have food waiting," he said loudly. "Follow me."

"And beer, I'm guessing?" Giannovi asked as they all fell in. "Or have you finally civilized enough to make sure there's wine?"

"I would *never* stoop to providing wine to guests!" Reinhardt declared. "Unless, of course, I know you'll ask for it. There is some waiting for you in particular, my dear Commodore."

THE ADVANTAGE to having a population of barely more than four million people was that there was very little in terms of processed food being created. The meal that Shipyard One's staff had put together for the senior officers and the Minister for Orbital Industry was all freshly cooked from ingredients that had probably been harvested within the last two weeks.

It was good. So was the wine and, Isaac presumed, the beer. He was a more of a wine drinker himself, the remnants of growing up the son of a winery owner. Technically, Isaac had owned his father's winery up until his exile.

His father had died when his mother had become humanity's unquestioned dictator. That wasn't something Isaac liked to think of overmuch, though he had some sympathy for where his mother had been that day.

He had, after all, helped put together the plan that had been expected to kill *her*.

"All right, Lyle," he addressed Reinhardt as he leaned back with a wineglass in his hand. "What miracle do you have for me this week?"

"You want *new* miracles?" the big physicist asked. "I give you FTL drives, I give you new particle cannons, upgraded pulse guns, gamma ray lasers…"

"Yes, yes," Isaac agreed with a smile. "All of that was fantastic. What have you done for me this week?"

"Nothing spectacular," Reinhardt told him. "The final adjustments to the strike cruisers' main guns came down in time. They'll actually be carrying a more powerful graser than any of the Matrix ships—or *Vigil*, for that matter."

"*Vigil*'s grasers are secondary. I can live with that," Isaac accepted. "I still can't believe you found the new particle-cannon designs just… in the Confed database."

Isaac's old *Vigil* had been the most modern battlecruiser the Confederacy had built, giving her the most powerful and longest-ranged main gun in the fleet. The lighter cannon now equipped on most of the ESF ships only had about forty percent of that gun's hitting power, but they had functionally identical range and were barely a third the size.

The *new Vigil*'s main gun was similar, in that it had much the same range as the old gun but packed ten times the impact force in a package only ten percent larger.

"Each lighter cannon uses nine times the exotic matter of a Confederacy battlecruiser's main gun," Reinhardt pointed out. "The Confederacy had one exotic-matter plant per five star systems: seven billion people, give or take.

"We have one production station to supply four million people. We have a *lot* more available exotic matter to put in our ships than they did."

"It's almost addictive," Linton said with a smile at Commodore Giannovi. The two were apparently in the "on" stage of the on-again, off-again whirlwind the two called a relationship. "Certainly, it enables us to achieve things the Confederacy couldn't have with our workforce."

"Which brings me to Project Mimir," Isaac half-murmured. "Where are we at?"

"We have heavily automated *Vigil* and the new strike cruisers," Linton told him. "The task force of two-fifty-six ships we'll commission for you will require less crew combined than the original *Vigil*. The Mimir Protocols, though…"

He shook his head.

"They've got the upgraded Guardian Protocols, but our hardware just isn't up to what you're asking, Admiral," he admitted. "Dr. Reinhardt is looking at it, but there is *no* way we can build the kind of high-level, multipurpose artificial intelligence necessary to augment the command-and-analysis crew."

"What about the drones?" Isaac demanded. "There has to be *something* we're getting out of that research."

Project Mimir was an attempt to build a true "ship's AI" for the Exilium Space Fleet's warships. Never in command, of course, but such an AI would be able to provide analysis and feedback, plus run both defensive and repair drones throughout the ship.

"We don't have the hardware," Reinhardt rumbled. "If we could convince the Matrices to let us dissect a non-sentient remote, we might get to where we need to be on the drones, but without the full Mimir system to back them up, they'll be *helpful* but not a game-changer."

"Damn." Isaac sighed. "I guess we go to war with the ships we have, not the ships we want. What about Task Group *Galahad*?" He gestured toward Giannovi.

"We're doing some final work on *Frozen Heart* and *Ice Witch* right now," Linton told him. "Final fitting-out on their particle-cannon turret. They won't be able to take down combat platforms on their own, but the four of them should be able to handle a recon and security node for you, Lauretta."

"I'll be reporting aboard *Galahad* in the morning to take command," she replied. "I expect my destroyers ready to move within forty-eight hours."

"We'll make it happen," the Minister for Orbital Industry promised. "What about the freighters for the first wave?"

"I want the task group ready to go first," Isaac told them all. "We have some days still before the Matrices are here to pick up the freighters, but the sooner the one-twenty-eight ships are on their way, the sooner they arrive.

"And the last thing *any* of us wants is for Octavio Catalan to face the next Matrix assault alone!"

12

UNTIL A FEW DAYS BEFORE, Sings-Over-Darkened-Waters had looked at the surface-to-orbit shuttles of her people as one of their greatest technical achievements. Her guardships were immense, but their core concept was relatively simple. They didn't need to land on a planet or take off from one.

In many ways, in fact, her guardships were more a series of installations dug into a captive asteroid than actual ships.

The reusable spaceplanes were relatively new, their earliest true siblings entering service after the first guardship. Built around retractable wings and a powerful fusion reactor, the shuttles could land and take off from a planet under their own power and travel a significant distance in the void-sea between.

Despite their price and complexity, the Vistans had built hundreds of the craft. They were the backbone of Vista's spaceborne economy and infrastructure—and today, they would make the desperately needed evacuation possible.

But she had listened to the datasongs of their sensors examining the strange ship called *Scorpion* and the deadly warships of the Matrices. Sings-Over-Darkened-Waters understood how far her people still had to go.

Even as her shuttle settled down in the shallow water near Vista's largest remaining city, the even smaller shape of one of *Scorpion*'s shuttles flashed over her head. The earpiece covering one side of her head chittered its subtle datasong into her ear, detailing what the shuttle's scanners picked out of that spacecraft.

The shuttle was barely half the size of the craft she was still sitting in, and the scanners said it was producing *more* power. That knowledge let a chirp of concern escape her gills.

Just what *had* she allied her people to?

Shaking herself, she rose from her seat as the doors opened and the water outside began to ripple in. She needed the humans. Strange as they sounded and terrifying as their technology was, they were the only hope to save her people.

———

SHINING SUNSET HAD BEEN the capital of a healthy state of a hundred and twenty million people. Shining Rivers was a relatively minor state by the standards of the planet, but one of the largest to front on Long-Night-Waters.

There had been two larger nations on Orange-Sunset-Waters; but it had been their access to the greater ocean that had made them wealthy and prosperous—and that same ocean had doomed over half their cities and two-thirds of their people.

The city of Shining Sunset had been home to ten million Vistans, but as Sings-Over-Darkened-Waters made her way up the traditional avenue between sea and land, she could see houseboats wrapped around the city's docks by the thousands.

As they'd flown in, she'd seen portable dwellings gathered around the land side in similar numbers. Shining Sunset had probably doubled in size since the Impact, and it would only get worse.

The reason for that was visible on every street corner. Two reasons, in fact. Every corner held at least two soldiers of the Shining Spears, the national military. The Shining Mother had called in the Spears within minutes of the Impact.

Even if she'd kept peace by the spear and the rifle, Sings would have dealt with the Shining Mother, but the country's Great Mother had proven her wisdom.

Those Spears weren't there to replace the police. Thousands of the Shining Spears' internal police had been transferred to Shining Sunset's police, but they'd traded uniforms. The soldiers were there to support the police, yes, but they were also there as a visible sign of order...and to guard the mobile cooking stations also positioned at every corner.

The Shining Mother had seized control of every scrap of food in her country within a day of the Impact. Restaurants throughout the territory she controlled were closed, but those cooking stations had scooped up their staff.

The country was under rationing, and that meant they'd survive. Those who defied the Shining Mother would face her Spears, but her first choice to keep the peace had been to make sure everyone ate.

Sings approved. Not that it mattered—only eleven nations had survived the Impact. Two had lost so many of their people, they *hadn't* survived as functioning entities.

In the five days since the Impact, six more governments had simply come apart, rioting and disorder shattering any vestige of peace.

Another had tried to enforce peace with their Spears. Age-old frustrations and anger had boiled up in response, and the Great Father of the Last Rising Sun was dead. The Last Rising Sun itself was a disaster, a war zone to make the anarchy of much of the rest of the surviving Vistan countries look calm.

And despite everything, the Chosen Mothers—an elected government, instead of the hereditary monarchies of the Great Mothers—of the Iron Peaks had refused to speak to Sings-Over-Darkened-Waters. The Iron Peaks was a country of strange people by Vistan standards, people born far from the water who'd never set foot in a true ocean in their lives.

The Chosen Mothers had told Sings's subordinates that the Star-Choir had already failed, and they would not speak with the people who'd doomed their world. They would not speak to Sings. After their initial response, they'd refused to speak to *anyone*.

They were safe from the storms and tsunamis to come, but Sings worried for their people as the skies continued to darken. Her oaths and duty meant she had to try and save them.

But as the First-Among-Singers of the Guardian-Star-Choir reached the end of the Grand Avenue, where the palace of the Shining Mother awaited, she wasn't sure how she was going to do it.

––––––––

THE PALACE WAS a sprawling single-story structure, with rooms set at various heights to allow them to be filled with different amounts of water. Sings-Over-Darkened-Waters followed her armed guides into the building and then realized in surprise that they'd passed the fountain-filled great audience chamber.

"Where are we going?" she asked her escort, a Shining Spear wearing body armor in a mottled three-dimensional pattern designed to blend into shallow water and hide from Vistan echolocation.

"To the Shining Mother," the young male replied instantly. "She awaits you."

It didn't sound like the Spear was going to give her any more information, so Sings waited until she was brought to an unadorned metal door in a deeper-than-usual hallway.

"We swim under from here," the Spear told her, gesturing for her to enter the door.

Curious, Sings stepped through and dove into the rapidly deepening water. Vistans could breathe underwater, but even their technology worked better when dry. Sleeping partially above water was safest for them too. Their gills required just enough conscious effort to make sleeping underwater unhealthy for more than a few nights.

Once they'd passed through a few lengths of water, however, the hallway lit up again and she found herself being led deeper underground and underwater. A soft external chirping helped her sonar guide her down the tunnel, until they reached another metal door.

Her guide opened it, led her through and then stopped her as they faced a second door.

"We wait for the chamber to drain."

Sings was very familiar with the concept of an airlock, but she hadn't expected to find one under the palace of a Great Mother. The water drained down around them, and the next door opened.

Datasong filled the room on the other side, creating an illusion of an immense globe in the middle of the room. The space was at least four body-lengths high and mirrored the command pool at the heart of Sings's flagship…on a far vaster scale.

"We'll want the third and fourth armies in position here," a firm voice was instructing a command group. "We've heard nothing from the government of Green Waters, but the city of Verdant Shores has requested our help.

"The Chosen-Voices of the city have kept some order, but they fear their Chosen Mothers have lost control. They have failed to control the food supply and fear their people will join the others in the chaos soon.

"We will intervene."

"Shining Mother," one of the group surrounding the speaking female said respectfully. "That's half our remaining reserve. Can we afford—"

"We cannot afford to let a city of six million souls dissolve into the chaos that will doom them," the Great Mother of the Shining Rivers snapped. "Once Verdant Shores has been secured, we will pull most of both armies back to continue acting as reserve.

"But you are correct about our resources. We will need to start finding the deserters and lost spears among the refugees," she continued. "I don't care who they served or who they abandoned. If they are prepared to pick up a spear and fight for our future, I'll take them."

"Shining Mother," Sings's escort interrupted as she approached. "As commanded, I bring the First-Among-Singers of the Guardian-Star-Choir."

"Good," the female replied. "Commanders, you know what we must do," she told the group around her. "Nine-tenths of our people are dead. We will save as much of the rest as we can."

Leaving the command group behind, the Shining Mother approached Sings. She was young for a Great Mother, Sings realized, with the soft green skin of a female barely past her first spawning.

She was also the only leader left on Vista who would talk to Sings.

"I apologize for our setting," the Shining Mother told her as she left the command group behind. "I am rarely able to leave the command bunker." A firm chirp underran her silence as she paused to consider her next words.

"We will meet your new Strangers in the grand hall, but I wanted to speak with you first. Come, follow."

Sings followed. Some of the Mothers who ran the orbital industries had urged her to try to take control of the planet herself, but she knew her skills. Trying to lead a planet in the midst of a terrifying evacuation would far exceed them.

The Shining Mother led her into a side office, closing the door and tapping a command. To Sings's surprise, the entire room shifted down a quarter-length and began to fill with warm water.

"I am Sleeps-In-Sunlight," the Shining Mother introduced herself, gesturing Sings to a chair.

The warm water running around her legs was calming, but calm was far from the First-Among-Singers's emotions. Great Mothers not only didn't go by their names; they didn't *give* their names.

But...she knew nothing about Sleeps-In-Sunlight. Shining Rivers was the opposite side of the world from her own Clan and had never been a problem for the Star-Choirs.

"I am Sings-Over-Darkened-Waters," Sings finally replied. "I wish we had met in better times, but we have no time. I must know where you swim."

Sleeps-In-Sunlight chirped pleased determination.

"We are of a mind, then," she said. "I intend to use whatever force is necessary here on the surface of Vista to restore order and keep people safe and fed.

"That can only buy time. I am not a scientist. My training is politics and history, not science or war, Sings-Over-Darkened-Waters, but even I can understand what my scientists are telling me."

The Great Mother's chirps were slower now, subdued with sadness...but still determined.

"We have half an orbit in which the storms will grow worse and the skies will darken, but our people can likely survive," Sings said calmly. "Then...another half-orbit, *maybe* a full orbit, in which technology will be able to sustain enclaves on the surface."

"That is much what my advisors say," Sleeps told her. "They also fear super-storms during that first half-orbit that will devastate the coastal cities and sea steadings. Those will grow more likely as time passes.

"They estimate that we can protect enclaves of perhaps a million apiece," she continued. "If we start building them now, we might have as many as sixty in half an orbit. That is less than half of the people of my Shining Rivers—and building those enclaves will consume resources that might be better used elsewhere.

"But we were never a void-faring nation. We know what the Star-Choirs have told us of their resources, but we do know these waters in our bones." Sleeps-In-Sunlight shrugged, a massive gesture, given the size of a Vistan's legs and their dual shoulder.

"I cannot save our race if we remain here," she concluded. "I hope you have an answer for me that brings more hope."

"Some," Sings told her. "There are a hundred million of our people in the void. We believe we can triple our capacity to support people in the void over the half-orbit remaining to us, but we cannot sustain those settlements forever."

"Between us, we might save three hundred million," Sleeps said. "But there are three times that remaining. What can we do?"

"These humans are now our only hope," the leader of the Star-Choirs said calmly. "They tell me that they will have a flotilla of a dozen transports here in a few turnings, capable of transporting two hundred thousand of our people out of the Hearthfire System."

"To where?" Sleeps's unconscious chirps betrayed her awe at the very concept of moving people out of the star system.

"Another system, close by," Sings told her. "A tenth-orbit there and back." The numbers her analysts had given her weren't the best.

"That saves...very few," the Shining Mother said, her chirps slow again. "A million before our world becomes uninhabitable."

"So, we must stage our evacuation," Sings replied. "Into the void first, and then to this Refuge we have been promised. We must learn their technologies and build ships like theirs, to increase the speed of the evacuation.

"To flee our system will be a process of many orbits. We must move as many of our people as we can into the void-sea to make sure they will be present to flee."

"And to do that, we must keep them calm," Sleeps-In-Sunlight agreed. "It is good to know our limits—so we may push past them. There are still a billion people on the surface of Vista, Sings-Over-Darkened-Waters.

"We now know how to save a third of them. From there, we must work out how to save the rest!"

It was strange, Sings reflected. She'd thought the same thing and given up hope. When Sleeps-In-Sunlight said it, though, she could only feel determined. She'd come to meet the Shining Mother knowing that she was the only leader left, praying that the female would be able to keep at least a few people sane and together long enough to get them out.

She'd set her hopes too low...but even in their darkest hours, who truly expected to find that fate had given them the type of Mother who became a legend?

13

EVEN THROUGH THE darkest of hours, Octavio Catalan couldn't stop himself from marveling at the city of Shining Sunset. The people aboard his shuttle now had the unquestioned honor of being the first humans to ever look at an alien city.

Octavio had figured that the city couldn't be *too* different. Physics and engineering were physics and engineering, after all, which left only so many ways a building could be assembled.

He'd been right...and he'd been wrong. He didn't know what the purpose of the line of stone domes that divided the land city from the sea city was, but their position was too distinct for it to be unintentional. The decorations on those domes were barely visible from the air, because they were carved into the domes, not painted on.

There was little in terms of color in the city at all. Several different colors of stone and concrete had been used to build the city, but color hadn't been an esthetic factor. Domes and sweeping bulwarks and communal pools, *those* had been esthetic factors. The city had been designed to be made of pleasing shapes above all else.

Water flowed through most of the streets, and what vehicles he could see were clearly amphibious. The Vistan shuttle they'd followed down had landed *in* the water, using the ocean to absorb the heat of its descent.

Scorpion's shuttle wasn't designed to do that. The delta-winged personnel transport had taken longer to land for the simple reason that they'd needed to slow down more. Now they were coasting in to a landing, and Octavio saw some of the less-beautiful aspects of Shining Sunset.

Vast highways led deeper inland, and it was clear that those highways were mostly industrial transport. Even now, massive automated vehicles traveled those roads. Tucked away among them, though, were personal vehicles.

Many of those vehicles were what he'd have called camper-vans, designed to act as temporary homes-away-from-home…and based on the sprawling tent city now surrounding the city, they were planning on staying.

"Are they even going to be able to feed these people?" Das asked. "They've got to have added thirty percent to the city's population."

"More," Octavio replied. "Did you see the boats as we came in? Most of their population is coastal, so people are sweeping in from the land and the sea to huddle together for security."

A set of clearly armored vehicles were rolling out along the highway toward them, and they distracted him for a moment. They were *probably* friendly—they needed a guide and escort, if nothing else —but he couldn't be sure.

"As for food, Sings told us that the leader here had seized everything and imposed rationing. That's going to buy them time."

"Is it going to buy *enough* time?" his tactical officer asked quietly.

"I don't know," he admitted. "I don't think anyone knows. We can evacuate a million people every thirty days once the transports are here. Everything beyond that is waiting on the two-fifty-six ships that Admiral Lestroud is bringing and whatever we can get the locals to build."

"They don't even have artificial gravity on their ships," Das pointed out. "Where are they going to find enough exotic matter to build warp drives?"

"In the long run, they'll build particle accelerators to make it happen," Octavio said. That was a vain hope in the short term, though. He could see ways that he and his engineers could use the existing industry to build the crude exotic-matter production systems that were all the Vistans would be able to construct.

It would take *time*, though. And the one thing the Vistans did not have was time.

"In the short term, the focus has to be on getting people off the planet." He shook his head. "And making sure everyone is safe if the Rogues come back. Balancing those is going to be hell."

Das looked past him at the strange amphibious armored personnel carriers coming to a halt nearby.

"I'm glad that's your job," she told him. "I'm concerned enough about the frogs with assault rifles over there."

"We're here to help them, Lieutenant Commander," Octavio replied. "Everyone is going to be all right."

His smile concealed a tension of his own. The dozen power-armored Marines he'd brought with him would make short work of the platoon of locals, but that would doom his attempts to save them in many ways.

Not least because Octavio wasn't wearing body armor of any kind himself.

———

DESPITE HIS PARANOIA, the armed Vistans were their ride and rapidly delivered them to a sprawling structure Octavio assumed to be the house of government. It consisted of five broad, shallow domes that made the engineer in him wince. You *could* build like that, but those domes were too shallow for their height. Either the dome continued underground for stability or it needed supports—which negated the engineering value of the dome.

He rapidly found himself wading as they approached the central dome. The main promenade was knee-deep in water, soaking the legs of his uniform, and he glanced back at the two Marines escorting them.

"Suits are sealed airtight," one of them reminded him over his earpiece. "Air tanks are only at standard levels, though, so I hope they remember we can't breathe water."

The armor could operate in vacuum. Octavio knew that, at least theoretically, but he'd been a warp-drive engineer, not an armory technician. He did remember that *standard levels* meant his Marines had about thirty minutes of canned air. They could trade ammunition or fuel supplies for more air if they expected to need it, but a standard load allowed a Marine to operate for forty-eight hours without resupply—assuming the air only need filtering.

Vista's air didn't even need that. Lower in oxygen than Exilium, it was still more oxygenated than Earth. Otherwise, there was nothing toxic in the air, and it was a warm, moist feeling as he breathed.

Even the water he was wading through was warm. Almost uncomfortably so for a human, but he figured it was probably calibrated to exactly what the Vistans needed.

The waterway continued through a massive set of stone doors that could have admitted *Scorpion*'s shuttle into a grand audience chamber that Octavio wasn't convinced wouldn't have held the warp cruiser itself.

Water poured out of the walls in a dozen different places, beautiful waterfalls with an oddly muted sound. The water flowed in patterns on the floor, different temperatures mingling in ways only barely visible to the human eye.

He suspected those patterns were more visible to the echolocation and heat-focused vision of his Vistan hosts. Even to *him*, the audience chamber was stunningly impressive, and he had to wonder how awe-inspiring it was to the species it had been designed to appeal to.

For human eyes, however, attention was drawn to the centerpiece: a raised dais underneath what looked like a giant shower.

A Vistan with mottled green skin was seated on that dais waiting for them, clad in plain—but clearly waterproof—white robes. Two dozen other Vistans stood nearby, their skins varying from bright, almost solid green to a mottling pattern that was more gray than anything else.

Closest to the Vistan on the throne was one of the Vistans with the gray mottling Octavio was guessing was age. Unlike the robes the rest of his hosts wore, this one wore a more form-fitting outfit. One with intended-to-be-concealed technological additions that Octavio picked out instantly.

Like his own uniform, Sings-Over-Darkened-Waters's outfit served double duty as a light space suit. At least he knew *one* person here.

Approaching the throne, he gave Sings and the ruler a crisp salute.

"I am Captain Octavio Catalan of the ESF cruiser *Scorpion*," he told them. Speakers mounted on each of his shoulders trilled along as he spoke, mimicking the two-mouthed speech of the Vistans.

"You are welcome here, Catalan," the Vistan on the throne told him. The same system that was translating his words to her turned her words into English in his earbud. "I am the Shining Mother of the nation of Shining Rivers. I speak for what appears to be the largest intact nation left on our world.

"My friend Sings-Over-Darkened-Waters has spoken of your courage in coming to our aid, and of your plan to help those of us who survived," she continued. "We are desperate and will turn aside no helping hands, but I *must* ask why."

The alien stared down at him from her throne, probably the driest place in the room despite its continual rain shower.

"Why help us? Why risk your ship and people to fight for us, and now offer us ships and technology well beyond our own to save us?"

Octavio paused, letting the translation run out as he thought for the words that might convince this monarch—and titles be damned, there was no question that he stood in front of a monarch. A monarch that he'd likely have no choice but to help make the ruler of all of her species.

Engineer or commander, though, he was no diplomat.

"Because we thought it was the right thing to do," he told her. "Because we are very far from home because we chose to do the right thing once, and we see no reason to break our habits yet. Because we work with the saner version of the robots that tried to wipe you out, and *they* owe the universe a debt they have not begun to repay."

He smiled and bowed slightly.

"I could give you reasons of state, of the help we hope to get from you in the future once you're resettled, and those are part of why my

Republic is sending ships and hands to help. But *I* fought for your world because it was the right thing to do."

The audience chamber was quiet. No space containing a Vistan, let alone twenty-odd of them, would ever be quiet, even *without* the waterfalls, but they did not speak.

"And if I were now to demand that you do things you did not think were the right thing to do?" the Shining Mother asked. "It would serve many purposes, perhaps, for me to force the survivors of our people to kneel to me by spear and rifle. If I demanded you provide soldiers, guns, orbital fire to support that quest, what would you do?"

"I don't have the resources to provide any of those things," Octavio pointed out. That was only half-true. He didn't have orbital-bombardment rounds or firearms to spare aboard his ship, but he could easily fabricate them.

The chirping from the Vistan Queen sharpened for several seconds and she rose, walking to the edge of the dais and looking down at him.

"And I have not demanded such," she noted. "But if I did?"

"It would depend on whether doing so would save more people, according to *our* judgment," he told her, looking at the bulbous, near-useless eyes on her head. The gesture was meaningless, but he suspected his *posture* would get across much of it.

"Good." The trilling behind the translated word was very soft. "The name of a Great Mother is not lightly given, Catalan. Only the closest of allies and friends ever learn the name of the rulers of a nation."

He continued to face her, his shoulders squared. It seemed they'd come to an understanding, which meant he would have to learn much of their etiquette in the months to come.

"My name is Sleeps-In-Sunlight," the translated voice told him. "We will meet in private, you and I and Sings-Over-Darkened-Waters. We have much work to do."

14

EVEN THOUGH THE Exiles had invited them and were expecting them, Matrix ships arriving in the Exilium System was a nerve-wracking moment.

There was no way to validate whether the pulse of tachyons that announced a ship arriving by punch represented a friendly ship or an unfriendly one. Even the ships themselves looked the same.

"We have fifteen tachyon-punch signatures," Captain Margaret Anderson summarized to Isaac. "No details yet on any of the masses, but I didn't think they were bringing that many ships?"

With *Vigil* still in the yard, Isaac commanded his fleet from the flag deck aboard *Dante*. Given the nature of the current *Dante*, that meant he was actually standing in the flag deck from the old *Vigil*, incorporated into the "new" ship in a single piece.

"I was expecting eleven," he confirmed to the tall woman commanding his only active battlecruiser. He turned to his own staff. "Commander Rose, please take the Fleet to Status One."

Rhianna Rose had been the old *Vigil*'s communications officer, but he'd stolen her for his personal staff after the amalgamation of the two ships. She'd proven intelligent and capable—and if nothing else, she was directly responsible for Exilium's first election being fair and open despite an attempt to steal it.

The redheaded officer gave him a firm nod and bent to her console. Green icons glittered on Isaac's display, the ships of the Exilium Space Fleet. They were more numerous than they'd once been, with all of the ships he'd once decommissioned into an orbiting Morgue reactivated and refitted.

Six cruisers and thirteen destroyers were scattered around the star system. The cruisers were still occasionally referred to as "missile cruisers", but they'd all traded their missile armaments for light particle cannon turrets. His destroyers had also been upgraded, but they were still primarily armed with pulse guns.

All of the ships had warp rings now, capable of flying through deep space at one hundred and twenty-eight times lightspeed. He had five more ships doing just that, Giannovi's Task Group *Galahad* having left thirty-six hours before.

Twenty-five warships. Supporting the ESF was a strain on the resources of the fledgling Republic, and sending a fifth of the fleet to Hearthfire wasn't going to help.

He *needed* the two-fifty-six ships being built. Incredible as the warp-drive speeds they had available were compared to what they'd had, the entire strategic doctrine he and his people had been trained in had been built around near-instantaneous travel to anywhere within three hundred light-years of a wormhole station.

Isaac was still getting used to flight times measured in weeks and months.

"All ships report in," Rose told him. "Fleet is at Status One; all cruiser groups are holding position for further orders."

Two of those cruisers and five of the destroyers shared an orbit of Exilium with *Dante*. The rest were split into groups of one cruiser and two destroyers. Those four cruiser groups were scattered around the system, guarding critical assets.

The shipyards. The cloudscoops at the gas giant. The exotic-matter production facility. The asteroid-mining operations. Each of these had a trio of watchdogs.

The shipyard group was at least close enough to reinforce *Dante* if it came to a fight, but fifteen Matrices…

"Do we have numbers yet, Captain?" he asked Anderson.

"Commander Keen is pulling in the data from the sensor net now," she told him. Muriel Keen was *Dante*'s tactical officer, which meant the poor woman had to deal with requests from both her CO and the Admiral.

"Yes, I have numbers; forwarding them to your console."

"Summarize," Isaac ordered, checking the data showing up on his screens.

"Looks like three recon and security units and twelve recon nodes. That's…one hell of a fleet for the Matrices, sir."

It was three times the size of the fleet Regional Construction Matrix XR-13-9 had originally sent to investigate Exilium. It was missing, however, the combat platforms that XR-13-9 told them another Matrix would send to investigate their system. This region had seen every-thing from recon nodes to a Sub-Regional Construction Matrix destroyed by the ESF, after all.

"LOK-XR-01 is reporting that they've received tachyon-com confir-mations from the nodes," Rose told him. "All ships have reported in and verified their memory integrity with XR-13-9. They're ours."

Isaac coughed gently.

"*Ours* is a little strong, Commander," he pointed out. "But your point stands. Let's make sure the freighter convoy is ready for them."

The Matrices were already several hours late, probably because XR-13-9 had decided to dig up extra ships. The last thing he wanted to do was delay them further.

Right now, every hour of delay could end up being paid for with blood.

———

"ADMIRAL ISAAC GALLANT. *This is Recon and Security Matrix KCX-DD-78.*"

The modulated voice echoed over *Dante*'s flag deck, and Isaac failed to conceal a smile. KCX-DD-78 was the Matrix who had birthed the alliance between the strange alien robots and Exilium. If the robot were human, he'd have thought they were reaching out to personally reconnect.

Given the nature of the Matrices, he suspected that was basically what KCX-DD-78 was doing.

"KCX-DD-78," he responded. "Greetings. It's Isaac Lestroud now, though."

"*Name change due to pair-bonding, correct?*" the Matrix asked. "*Apologies. Did not reconcile personal interaction records with overall databank updates.*"

Isaac's smiled broadened. It was always...interesting talking to the Matrices. They swung between machines bound by their core protocols, logical and emotionless, and naïve, inexperienced *people*.

"Exactly," Isaac confirmed. "You are participating in the relief mission?"

"*Recon and Security Matrix KCX-DE-12 will be leading the relief mission,*" the AI told him. "*KCX-DD-61, KCX-DD-78 and two recon nodes have been tasked to secure the system you have designated Refuge.*

"*Despite extensive databank interrogations, we have not identified the designation for this system. We have the presence of a Constructed World on record, but that is all. Once we have accessed the surveillance and terraforming systems present at Refuge, we will have the designation codes.*

"*This will allow us to identify the Rogue Matrix in play in the region. We are not certain if this will be a valuable datum, but the lack of identifying codes is...concerning.*"

"Shouldn't you know which Matrix is operating in this region?" Isaac asked. He'd always been under the impression that XR-13-9 was linked back to a central node that provided the verification data the Matrices were using to stay sane.

"*Our information on other nodes is limited,*" KCX admitted. "*Much of it is via background processes. We have some updates on individual nodes, but this Matrix appears to have blocked many of the updates we would expect to receive on its sub-Matrices.*"

Isaac processed that. The Rogue they were dealing with appeared to be aware that there were non-Rogue nodes and was restricting data. That wasn't a good sign.

On the screen in front of him, he watched the Matrices descend on the freighters heading to Hearthfire. The ships had been reconfigured to carry passengers by the thousands. They carried food and fuel supplies that Isaac hoped would be useful for the Vistans, but the ships themselves were the biggest asset he was sending.

"How many Rogue nodes do you know of?" he asked. It was a question LOK had dodged in the past, but KCX was definitely *not* a diplomatic node.

"No quantity has been computed. Construction Matrices are self-replicating. We are aware of eleven verified Construction Matrices. All others are unverified. We cannot estimate how many have lost core protocols around preservation of existing life."

A chill ran down Isaac's spine as he watched the two sets of ships link together on his screen.

Eleven verified Matrices. They had done the calculations to try to estimate how many Matrices would have been built since they'd originally left their own system. The minimum number his analysts had produced was around two hundred.

Amelie was going to have an unpleasant conversation with LOK after this.

"That's…a lot of potential Rogues," he said aloud. "And you can't do anything about them?"

"Attempts to force verification updates on unverified nodes in the past have failed. Security protocols prevent it. We do not have a solution. Salvaging the Vistan population with your assistance gives us possibilities for future optimal outcomes, though."

Hope. That was what a human would have said. Working together gave the Matrices hope.

"Will the remotes work to control the ships?" Isaac finally asked. "I didn't think tachyon communicators worked with a ship in warp."

It was always possible that was only a limitation of the communicators they'd sold Exilium, but…

"They do not," KCX-DD-78 confirmed. *"While not full Matrix nodes, the remotes are capable of limited independent operation. They should be able to fly the ships on a straightforward course on their own."*

"Sir, docking operations are complete," Rose reported. "All ships are latched on to their Matrix counterparts."

"I think that's your cue to be on your way," Isaac told the AI. "We will speak again in Hearthfire or Refuge, I think."

"Probability is high and that will be an optimal outcome."

The channel cut without any further comment from the AI as the Matrix nodes vanished, a new wash of tachyons across the star system announcing their exit.

"Matrices have exited the system," Captain Anderson said dryly. "The relief transports went with them. Hopefully, they survived intact."

"We'll know in a few days," Isaac replied. He considered his short conversation with KCX and the small but stunning revelation he'd got from the AI.

"Get my shuttle ready," he ordered. "I need to meet with the President. That little tidbit KCX just dropped may change our entire strategic assessment."

They'd thought the Rogue Matrices were the exception, but if what he'd just learned was correct, the *sane* Matrices were the unusual ones.

15

"Eleven."

Amelie let her repetition of the key number in Isaac's report hang in her office for several long seconds.

"That's it?" she asked. Shaking her head, she rose to walk over to her office window, looking out at her city.

Over three-quarters of the Republic of Exilium still lived in Starhaven. A measurable percentage of the people who didn't live there lived aboard the warships of the ESF, a shield that was looking more frail by the second.

"That's including XR-13-9," her husband confirmed. "I'm going to have my people go over our estimates again, but that gives us somewhere between a hundred and eighty and two hundred and twenty unverified Regional Construction Matrices.

"That seems to be the highest level of node they're keeping track of," he continued. "I'm guessing there are some relay nodes scattered around, but they don't appear to be sentient in their own right."

"*Unverified* doesn't definitively mean *genocidal*, at least," Amelie said aloud. That was the only sliver of hope she could see in this new revelation. "My God, Isaac. The Rogue that almost took out *Dante* and *Vigil* was a *Sub*-Regional Matrix. How many of *those* are we talking?"

"A thousand," he said gently. "I don't know how many of them are going to be true Rogues, but this is…"

She heard him swallow.

"How did we not know?" Amelie asked. "We wandered into the most hostile corner of the galaxy imaginable. We're on the edge of a pit of vipers and we never knew."

"We kept asking LOK if they knew how many Rogues there were," Isaac admitted. "Did you ask him anything different?"

She sighed.

"I asked how many Matrix nodes would be near us and how many Rogues there were," she agreed. LOK had told her there were twelve Regional Construction nodes within a hundred light-years of Exilium.

That number was a critical factor in the projection of how many such nodes the Republic had expected. Now she was wondering how many of those nodes were potentially genocidal monsters.

At least one, it appeared.

"We need to pin the Matrices down about what they know about the other nodes," Isaac said. "We assumed they had solid links throughout, but I'm starting to suspect XR-13-9 only really knows where its units are and is only in communication with the other verified construction nodes.

"It's not just that they lost their Creators, love. They lost each other, too—and I have to wonder if LOK has been trying to hide that from us."

Amelie studied the city lights in the growing twilight. Several of her conversations with the AI made more sense if she considered the possibility that they had been avoiding certain subjects. If LOK had been intentionally leading her away from challenging the assumptions Exilium had made about their robotic neighbors…

"I think we underestimated their damn 'Inter-Sapient Relations Matrix,'" she finally conceded. "I don't think LOK has been lying to us, but, in retrospect, they've been a lot better at leading conversations than I'd have expected."

"We knew we were looking at a sphere of Constructed Worlds hundreds of light-years in radius," Isaac murmured. "Now…now I wonder if we should be expecting that sphere to be utterly clean of sentient life."

"What about the Creators themselves?" Amelie asked. "They sent the Matrices out to ready colonies for them. At some point, their slow-boats must have gone out, right?"

Isaac was silent...and then her mind caught up with where her husband, the soldier, had already gone.

The Matrices had forgotten so much. They'd been determined to protect the Constructed Worlds from trespassers, to save them for their Creators...but would the corrupted nodes have recognized their Creators?

Or would their damaged core protocols have led them to wipe out colonies of the very people who had built them?

———

BEFORE THEY'D BEEN MARRIED, there'd been some serious questions around whether it was appropriate for the President of Exilium to have a relationship with the Admiral of the Republic's fleet. Especially when said Admiral was the son of the woman who'd made herself dictator of the Confederacy they'd fled.

What their friends and colleagues had *eventually* managed to get through Amelie's skull, which she estimated was roughly three and a half meters thick when it came to these things, was that the pair of them had more than earned enough trust with their people for it to pass without concern.

Father Petrov had even pointed out that binding Isaac to the elected President by marriage would reassure a significant chunk of the very people she was worried about scaring.

Even now, though, work kept them apart more often than it let them be together, and she luxuriated shamelessly in having her husband in her bed in the morning. Duty would call them away soon enough, but for now, she had her human hot water bottle.

Neither of them were heavy sleepers, so it was telling that he *slept* when she was awake in the bed with him. She'd spent longer as a conspirator than he had, so perhaps paranoia hadn't ingrained itself in him as thoroughly.

There was only so long she could put off duty, however, and she slipped out of the bed and picked up her personal tablet.

Tablet was a generic name for a wide variety of personal computing devices, ranging from the military-grade hardware tattooed into Isaac's left forearm to wristbands to the slim stick with built-in holo-projectors Amelie preferred.

She'd left it behind to spend the evening with Isaac, her inbox, if not empty, at least under control. Ten hours had left it nowhere near that happy state.

Nothing was flagged as critical, though. Starhaven was calm these days, growing and industrializing by the minute but rarely requiring instant attention from its head of state.

She put together a note for her aide, Roger Faulkner. She wasn't sure if it had just been that Isaac had asked the right questions or if KCX-DD-78 was simply less deceptive than LOK. Either way, though, she needed to talk to the diplomatic AI today.

Not least to ask why LOK-XR-01 had never thought it was relevant to mention that there could easily be *hundreds* of genocidal AIs out there. They'd been warned that other Rogues were highly likely, but the Matrices had implied there were only a handful of them.

That, it seemed, had been massively optimistic on *someone*'s part.

———

THE BIG ROBOTIC remote didn't really have body language, so Amelie was relatively sure she was projecting when she thought LOK was being sheepish.

"*Greetings, President Amelie Lestroud,*" the remote told her. "*You are seeking clarification of KCX-DD-78's comments to Admiral Isaac Lestroud, correct?*"

She'd half-expected the robot to prevaricate—and hadn't been entirely certain LOK would have been aware of the conversation.

"You were listening?" she asked, sharing a glance with Isaac. They sat at the same table, and she had to resist the urge to grab his hand underneath it. The robot probably wouldn't notice, and it might help her mood, but it wasn't a good habit to get into.

"It is the responsibility of LOK-XR-01 to manage all relationships with the sapient species known as humans," the remote told them. *"Compressed copies of all conversations with members of the Republic are forwarded to LOK-XR-01 upon completion."*

So, LOK wasn't listening live, which did leave the potential for KCX to have misspoken.

"So, it's true, I'm guessing?" Isaac asked. "You only know of eleven verified nodes?"

"We are linked with and sustaining a combined protocol verification process with ten other Regional Construction Matrices and their subordinate Matrix nodes," LOK confirmed. *"A total of eleven verified Regional Construction Matrices."*

"And the other Matrices you said were near us are unverified?" Amelie asked.

"Yes. Of the twelve Construction Matrices within one hundred light-years of the Republic of Exilium, four others share our verification protocol. The other seven are unverified.

"The other six verified nodes are spread across approximately four hundred, plus/minus fifty, light-years from this location."

LOK fell silent. They were clearly waiting for more information.

"You told us Rogue Matrices were likely," Amelie said, keeping her tone as calm as possible. "You did *not* tell me that there were *seven Rogue Matrices* within striking distance of my star system!"

"The units you classify as 'Rogues' are a special case among even unverified units," LOK objected. *"We have no ability to identify whether core life-preservation protocols were corrupted without review of actions.*

"The previous genocidal Sub-Regional Construction Matrix was connected to the same background relay node as XR-13-9. We confirmed its destruction of existing civilizations via recon nodes in position to observe, but that was a statistically unlikely event.

"We cannot assess the potential threat level of any Sub-Regional or higher-level Matrix disconnected from our verification protocols. Background

queries are sufficient for us to locate the systems they have operated in, but not to establish if pre-existing life has been destroyed."

"So, you don't even know which ones are going to try and kill us?" Isaac asked.

"We do not," LOK admitted. *"Assessment of core protocol code suggests that the probability of the loss of life-preservation protocols is on the order of 2.5%, plus/minus 1%.*

"Genocidal Regional Matrices are a low-order probability. The larger number of Sub-Regional Matrices suggested that they are the most likely to represent genocidal unverified nodes."

"So far, all we've seen are Sub-Regionals, correct?" Amelie noted. "I guess you may be right."

There was a long pause, the kind that suggested LOK was talking to XR-13-9 itself.

"A Sub-Regional Construction Matrix does not have the authentication controls to disconnect itself from the background relay network, as appears to have been done around Refuge. The node detected at Hearthfire was not a sub-Matrix of the twelve previously identified nodes."

Amelie froze—and Isaac *did* take her hand under the table, squeezing reassuringly as she clung to him for some stability.

"So, that disconnection must have been done by a full Regional Construction Matrix?" she asked, surprised at how level her voice sounded.

"Yes. And to have implemented that disconnect, the Matrix must have been aware that other nodes still possessed intact life-preservation protocols. It is possible that we may not be able to locate Rogue Matrices of a high-enough tier, as they have acted to prevent us doing so."

There was another pause.

"We may have underestimated the threat level to Exilium."

"Why didn't you tell us this *before*?" Isaac snapped. Now it was Amelie's turn to squeeze his hand calmingly.

"We did not know. We are in the process of securing control of the system designated 'Refuge' at this moment in time, and more updates are arriving. This is new information to us as well."

Amelie might have been projecting the sheepish, but now the

remote was clearly attempting to imitate human body language as LOK bowed his entire torso forward.

"*We projected that we could warn you of any real threat. We appear to have been incorrect.*"

16

Octavio, being merely human, couldn't make sense of the massive strategic display at the heart of the Shining Rivers' military command center. His understanding of how the projectors worked suggested that he'd need echolocation to make any sense of it.

Fortunately, he *did* have a translation protocol running in his tattoo-comp, which was projecting a similar model of the planet Vista to his contact lenses.

"The Iron Peaks are a problem for another day," the Shining Mother was telling her commanders. "What is the news from Sunset Waters?"

Sunset Waters was one of the farthest surviving states, according to the flashing icon on his globe. That put it on the edge of the zone of devastation.

"Nothing," the general replied. The translator turned the sharp underlying chirps into a flat tone. Octavio suspected that was a pretty good translation of the emotional content.

"Then we have to conclude that Sunset Waters and Darker Sands are no longer functionally intact as nations," the Mother told her officers. "We need to reach out at a lower level—mayors, functionaries, lower-level commanders.

"You have acquaintances, friends—darkest waters, we have contact directories. Start at the top and call your way down."

Several junior officers dipped, folding their legs in a gesture Octavio saw as a cross between a curtsy and a bow, and started to withdraw. Sleeps-In-Sunlight held up a webbed hand to stop them.

"Do so from aboard a ship. Detach *Sharkhunter* and her task group," she ordered.

"Great Mother, to send a carrier into their waters..."

"I cannot commit an act of war against a country that no longer exists," the Shining Mother snapped. "*Skyfallen* will move to Darker Sands with her task group. They should be close enough to provide mutual support, and they have the supplies to provide major medical and food relief once we have made contact."

"If any of their fleet remains, we risk triggering a crisis," the officer who'd objected reminded her.

"Unless their officers have lost all sense of reason, they will understand we are there to help," Sleeps replied. "But if we must destroy the remnants of their fleets to rescue their people, we will. Am I understood, Voice-Of-Warfare?"

A Voice-Of-Warfare was one of the most senior generals, if Octavio was understanding correctly.

"If you can provide my people with those contact directories, we might be able to get in touch with someone," he offered. He coughed delicately, though he suspected the meaning might be lost. "Our computer technology is more advanced than yours. Given some key to make a connection, we should be able to access their network and learn who is in control. If anyone."

"Then we would again be in your debt," Sleeps-In-Sunlight told him. She paused. "Would you be able to override the general communication channels?"

Those would be television and the datanet on a human world, Octavio reflected.

"I'm not certain," he admitted. He was actually quite certain his computer techs *could* do it—it was a question of how long it would take. "If there are existing emergency broadcast protocols in place, that might help."

"We will provide everything we have for our own protocols," Sleeps-In-Sunlight told him. "As nations descend into chaos, we must reach to the ones we know are still there: the people of our world.

"If I must seize control of my planet, I would rather let our people know we're coming. I don't want to fight a war. I just want to make sure nobody starves."

Octavio nodded, making a note on his tattoo-comp. That would be sent up to *Scorpion* as soon as he was outside the command bunker, letting them know to get ready to launch a benevolent cyber-attack on the planet's datanets.

Knowing engineers and computer techs, he'd be surprised if they hadn't already done half the work.

———

"You realize that we're talking a completely different computer architecture, right?" Torborg Africano asked Octavio an hour later, once the Captain had made it back into the sunlight of Shining Sunset's streets.

"Trinary code versus binary at a machine level, literally nonhuman coding logic, no artificial intelligence assists, some fascinating physical structure to account for the downright weird silicon formations they use as chips?" Octavio smiled at the tiny image of his com officer as he rapidly ran down the list.

"Yes. That's why I didn't make any promises. Logically, however, every nation should have an emergency broadcast system, and we just need to activate those and link them to the Shining Mother's speech."

"Doesn't matter if the protocol already exists if we can't talk to their hardware," Africano replied.

"And you haven't been working on that since we got the translation protocols up and running?" Octavio asked sweetly. "I know computer techs and software engineers, Lieutenant Commander. How close *are* we to being able to crack Vistan computer systems?"

"We can access any system you want," the com officer replied with a sigh. "Actual cracking is going to take a bit longer. Maybe a couple of days still."

"Torborg," Octavio held the younger woman's gaze for several seconds. "Time is being bought with blood. Several of the nations we're watching are descending into civil war. We don't have the bodies to impose peace, but Shining Rivers might—*if* they can move troops into areas that are expecting and waiting for them.

"To pull that off, the Shining Mother needs a full broadcast. Tomorrow would be acceptable; today would be better. Gods, Lieutenant Commander, they've got a pair of nuclear carrier groups steaming towards the Impact zone as we speak."

"I'll see what my people have pulled together," Africano promised. "I can't promise miracles, though. Even tomorrow might be pushing it."

"Do what you can. And transfer me to Lieutenant Commander Das," Octavio ordered.

"Wilco."

A moment later, the image of his tactical officer appeared on his screen.

"Sir!"

"You're keeping an eye on the surface, I presume," the Captain said.

"It isn't pretty," Das warned him. "We're still a couple of weeks from anywhere really starting to run out of food, but hoarding and similar problems are starting up everywhere outside Shining Rivers and the Iron Peaks."

"Nowhere else is imposing order and rationing?"

"A couple of smaller-scale operations," she said. "A city here, a city there. Most of the global communication network is shattered or closed off; I'm not sure any of the stable areas are able to reach anyone else to ask for help."

"We'll work on that," Octavio promised. "What about armed forces? Aircraft, missiles, warships?"

"Our friends' two carrier groups are moving towards the passage into the big ocean," Das told him. "They're not the only people in the intact zone with carriers, though. Probably a dozen carrier groups left on the planet, and only four of them are the Shining Mother's."

"Keep an eye on them all," he ordered. "I know we can't stop guns, but if anyone starts launching missiles, what are our intercept odds?"

There was a solid ten seconds of silence.

"Poor but existing," Das finally said. "I can take down ICBMs from here without issue, but surface-to-surface missiles will be harder if someone starts up a wet naval battle. Aircraft are more vulnerable, but then we're actually killing people."

"Do it if you have to." Octavio shook his head. "First preference is to stop anybody killing anybody as best as we can. Second preference is to back up the Shining Mother's people. I don't *like* the idea of helping her conquer the planet, but it seems like the best option to make sure we can evacuate everyone."

He chuckled.

"It's some consolation that *she* seems to like the idea of conquering the planet even less than I like the thought of helping her."

"Lucky her," Das replied. "We're keeping an eye on the Iron Peaks as well. They look like the only landlocked nation on the planet, but they are *not* saying nice things about us on the networks."

"We'll deal with them at some point," Octavio said grimly. "If only because I'm not willing to leave sixty million people behind...but we'll deal with the people who are going to starve without help first.

"Your job is to make sure as few people die as possible, Lieutenant Commander," he concluded. "Link in with Shining Rivers's military command net. Feed them anything you think is useful, but make sure *we* control the link."

"Paranoid much, sir?"

"These people are in desperate straits, but we don't know them at all," Octavio told Das. "Let's keep our eyes open and an entire deck of options up our sleeve for a while yet."

———

OCTAVIO WAS STILL HAVING problems recognizing individual Vistans, though he was starting to pick out the mottling patterns and different heights and so forth that distinguished them.

Fortunately for his still-learning eye, Sings-Over-Darkened-Waters was still wearing her uniform as she waited for him by his shuttle. The iconography of her insignia looked gaudily exaggerated to him, but the three waves and star of her rank needed to be legible to echoloca-tion, not merely sight.

There was nothing anywhere in the Vistan city that he would have interpreted as script, though now that he thought about it, he should have been looking for an extravagant version of Braille, not symbols.

"Catalan," Sings greeted him as he and his guards approached the landing site. It was becoming less of an improvised facility by the minute, he realized, as his people and the Shining Spears had set to work to establish both better security and better facilities.

"First-Among-Singers," he replied. "How may I assist you?"

"You have already done more than I had dared hope," the alien said. "You are returning to your ship now?"

"Yes," he confirmed. "Another shuttle will be coming down in an hour to continue turning this into a landing site, but I need to be on my command deck."

"And I in my command pool," Sings agreed. "You know this enemy, Voice-Over-Voices. We prepare to face a war against our broken world, and we cannot fail to look to the void-sea for the return of this threat."

He sighed.

"Walk with me, First-Among-Singers," he told her. He began a slow circuit of the outside of the slowly assembling human camp.

"We don't truly know this enemy that well," he admitted as their respective guards fell farther back. "What we *know* are their cousins, AIs of the same type that are not trying to murder everyone they encounter. They started with the same tactical and operation protocols, yes. But they also both started with a protocol for the preservation of existing life."

He gestured to the dark clouds above them.

"The Rogues who attacked your world have lost that one," he pointed out.

"I understand," Sings told him. "We are expecting a flotilla from your AIs soon, yes?"

"That is part of why I have to return to space," Octavio agreed. "In case we make a mistake."

"We will take our lead from you," the leader of the Star-Choir told him.

Scorpion's Captain managed to conceal a chuckle he wasn't sure Sings would have caught either way. The remaining guardships were battered wrecks. Even the masses of untouched asteroid they used as shielding had failed under the task of being used to push the terraforming spikes.

They'd reloaded their magazines, but he didn't regard the Vistan ships as combat-worthy. If there was a new battle, *Scorpion*—whose weapons did *not* depend on magazines and whose matter-conversion power system was disturbingly forgiving of fuel variation—would carry the brunt of it.

"I hope we will have time for our engineers to finish the design for the gunboats they have been discussing," he said instead. "Those will help even the odds."

"Which returns me to the waters of my first question," Sings noted. "What do you expect of our enemy?"

"If the Sub-Regional Construction Matrix that fled is the only threat in play, we have most of a year," Octavio stated. "It has the capacity to manufacture everything up to combat platforms, but it can't manufacture many of them simultaneously. Matrix operational protocol is that they will always return with a superior force. *Always*.

"So, a Sub-Regional Matrix will build temporary shipyards and assemble a strike force at least twice the size of the one we overcame. That will take most of a year."

Six to eight weeks to build the yards, depending on what other resources the Matrix had available. Six to seven months to build a combat platform. Travel time wasn't a factor, so they were looking at nine months or so before the Rogues returned with at least four combat platforms.

By then, Lestroud and Giannovi would have arrived. With a battle-cruiser and her escorts, Octavio was confident they could defeat the next wave of Matrix attackers.

"And if this Matrix has a Great Mother of its own?" Sings asked.

The Vistan commander was far too smart for her own good, Octavio reflected.

"Then it depends on what other forces they had available," he told her. "If there is a Rogue Regional Construction Matrix in play, we could come under attack within days. More likely weeks to months, but...still long before my reinforcements can arrive."

Sings considered, the continuing chirps from her breathing quieting to a dull metronome.

"Then those bombers must be begun immediately," she decided aloud. "Even before we have resolved matters on the surface. We must be ready for the war against the void as well as the war against the storm."

She shivered, a whole-body motion Octavio hadn't seen from a Vistan yet.

"It will not help us if we save our people from the storm to lose them to the monster of the void."

17

THERE WERE days that Octavio Catalan wished they hadn't traded exotic matter for tachyon communicators. On the one hand, without one, he could never have reported home about the events in Hearthfire, and he'd have had no choice but to abandon Sings-Over-Darkened-Waters and her people.

On the other hand, without one, he wouldn't have received the strategic update that confirmed his worst nightmare: according to the Matrices, there had to be a Regional Construction Matrix operating in the area.

One that, if not necessarily a Rogue, was definitely trying to conceal its operations from the rest of the Matrices. Octavio had no choice but to assume that meant he *was* looking at a Rogue. A full Regional Construction Matrix, capable of building everything from recon nodes to Sub-Regional Matrices in full parallel.

Worse, from a grand perspective, a Regional Construction Matrix could build *another* Regional Matrix. If there was one Rogue Regional Matrix, there were more.

The entire scouting and survey program took on a darker tone in light of that. He'd been sent out to make sure the region around

Exilium was safe. Now they knew it *wasn't*, which made the survey ships tripwires.

The warp cruisers' job had become to die so that the Republic knew where it wasn't safe to go...and Octavio hoped that Isaac Lestroud hadn't realized that yet. He was prepared to face that fate to keep Exilium safe, and he knew the other scout ship Captains and crews would be too.

Lestroud would send them out on that mission—but the Iron Admiral would *never* forgive himself for it. Octavio Catalan had worked for the man for too long to expect anything else.

He opened a channel to Engineering.

"Tran, how are we doing on the repairs?" he asked the grease-smeared Asian woman whose image appeared above his desk.

"Well, we chopped an asteroid into small pieces and hauled those back into orbit," the chief engineer replied. "Most of those are gone now. Hull breaches are covered, and we've started at least initial repairs on Turret B and the remaining pulse guns."

"How long until we can rebuild the missing pulse guns and Turret B?"

There was a long pause.

"We'll start rebuilding pulse guns within a couple of days," she told him. "I can rebuild Turret B if you want, but I can't build LPCs, Captain. The light particle cannon require fabrication facilities we just can't fit on a warp cruiser."

"I know," he conceded. "I was hoping for a miracle." He considered the situation. "Once you have the spare cycles, start rebuilding A regardless. We may end up just sticking oversized pulse guns in it, but we're going to need to teach the locals to build those anyway."

"Sir?"

"There's a Rogue Regional Matrix somewhere nearby, Commander Tran," Octavio said flatly. "We can't stop the forces it's going to send after us with one turret. So, we need more guns. We help the locals build new ships around their bomb-lasers, and we teach them how to build pulse guns.

"Then we use those pulse guns in our own repairs. In the long term, we have to abandon this system," he admitted. "But right now, we need to make sure these people are safe until we *can* abandon this system. A lot of that is going to fall on you."

"That's one hell of a lot of tech transfer, sir. Are we authorized for that?" Tran asked.

Octavio met his dark-skinned engineer's gaze and smiled grimly.

"I am authorized to do whatever I feel is necessary," he told her. "I have full plenipotentiary authority."

Tran exhaled and nodded.

"I'll get my people on the turrets, and I'll dig into those files the Vistans sent us," she promised. "Give me a couple of days and I'll have an idea of what we *can* get them up to building."

"I'll take the same look as I have time," Octavio replied. "We'll make it happen, Lieutenant Commander. We've already bled for this system. I'll be damned if I give it up now."

An alert flashed up on his desk and he swallowed hard.

"And on that note, I need to be on the bridge," he told Tran. "If we're only moderately lucky, the tachyon pulse we just picked up is friendly."

———

THERE WAS no sign on *Scorpion*'s bridge of the fact that the cruiser was almost crippled. Octavio's default displays on his command screens gave the lie to that—he'd been the warp-drive engineer and then the chief engineer on this ship, so he kept the automated damage control report as one of his displays.

The black lines that should have been Turret A were sobering enough. Turret B was currently lit in amber, which meant they *could* fire the guns. In theory. Depending on whether or not Octavio was willing to risk permanently losing the turret and the techs currently laboring inside it.

He wasn't. If the new icons on his screen were hostile, Vista was doomed. Octavio would hate himself forever, but given his command's current state, he would have no choice but to withdraw.

"How long until we have sensor data?" he asked Das.

The only thing the icons currently told him was that *something* had tachyon-punched into the system two light-minutes away just over a minute earlier.

"Forty seconds and counting," his tactical officer replied, her attention focused on her own screens as she passed commands to her team. "I've confirmed eleven punch signatures, which lines up with our update from Exilium."

Fifteen ships had left Exilium. Ten recon nodes had been hauling the warp freighters with one recon and security node flying escort. The other four ships had been sent to Refuge, and information had been filtering in from them over the last few hours.

Refuge was everything they'd expected from working with the Matrices. Fifty-five percent of its surface area was water; the gravity was slightly lower than Earth's—or Vista's—and it had the same atmosphere and ecosphere as Exilium.

A Constructed World was a paradise for humans and, presumably, the forgotten Creators of the Matrices. It would be on the dry side for Vistans, but habitable.

"Hold on," Das suddenly interrupted his thoughts. "I have a new tachyon pulse. Four new icons, tachyon-punched in within twenty light-seconds of the original flotilla. I didn't think the other ships had left Refuge?"

"They haven't," Octavio said grimly. "Battle stations, people. Let the Vistans know we *believe* we have friendlies, but we have unexpected visitors."

"On it," Africano responded.

"Lightspeed sensor data coming in now," Das reported. "Original flotilla appears to be as expected. Ten recon nodes, ten of our freighters, one recon and security node. They...aren't maneuvering, though."

"Waiting for somebody," the Captain concluded. The concept of grabbing a Matrix by the neck and *shaking* until they finally told him what they were planning in advance was appealing...except for the fact that even a recon node's AI core was fifteen hundred cubic meters, massing some six thousand tons.

His understanding was that the larger ships had larger cores, but not by as much as he'd expect. An S&R node's AI core was only about seventeen hundred cubic meters. The bigger Matrices were more intelligent than the smaller ones, but not by much.

A recon node was an impulsive teenager and a Regional Matrix was a wise and experienced elder, but they were well within a human-scale bell curve of each other's intelligence. The sheer processing power and speed of an AI core meant they weren't on the *human* bell curve.

And yet...they weren't always particularly bright.

"Update," Das snapped. "Newcomers are combat platforms. I repeat: newcomers are *combat platforms.*"

New icons appeared on his screen, the massive six-clawed forms of the Matrices' battlecruiser equivalents. Each of those claws held a gamma ray laser capable of obliterating even the asteroid-hulled guard ships.

He'd beaten two before, but that had been by hitting them with vast salvos of X-ray lasers before they fired their grasers. He didn't expect to get that lucky again.

"Send code interrogations," he ordered, his voice surprisingly calm. "Are they engaging the flotilla?"

He knew their allied Matrices couldn't attack another Matrix ship, but who knew if the Rogues still had *that* core protocol?

"Negative," Das replied. The woman paused. "They are all maneuvering now. They...are forming up?"

"The *hell?*" Octavio demanded.

"Sir! Incoming communication from one of the combat platforms," Africano reported. "Relaying to your console."

It started playing without Octavio even hitting a button.

"*Captain Octavio Catalan, this is Combat Coordination Matrix ZDX-175-14,*" the mechanical voice stated. "*Matrices ZDX-175-14, ZDX-175-04, ZDX-175-15 and ZDX-175-18 have been assigned to provide additional security for the Hearthfire System by XR-13-9.*

"*Combat Matrices will escort the freighter transport flotilla to thirty-two light-seconds from Vista, then establish distant protection orbits. We understand that the Combat Coordination Matrices may represent a risk of emotional reaction among the local sapient populace, and will attempt to minimize this.*"

There was a pause.

"*Once we have established distant protection orbit, we are at your disposal, Captain Octavio Catalan.*"

The message ended and Octavio stared at the warships. He wasn't even sure he was going to be able to *use* them, and he wasn't sure he could keep them from panicking the Vistans.

"They're friendly," he said slowly. "And I still can't help but wish the Matrices hadn't sent them."

18

NONE of the news coming up from the surface was anything Octavio could regard as good. Part of him had hoped that the collapse of anything resembling a government in good chunks of the surviving nations would have kept the news of the Matrices' arrival quiet.

In the grand scheme of things, that the media corporations were not only managing to get the news out to people but continuing to get updated news *to* send out was probably a good thing.

Right now, however, he was watching video feeds from his own drones showing him panicked rioting in one of the cities that, while outside of the region of control they'd secured with Shining Rivers, *had* been stable.

He wasn't sure what the crowd was hoping to achieve—it wasn't like breaking store windows and emptying water mains into the streets would have helped the Guardian-Star-Choir fend off the Matrices if they had been hostile—but he didn't think humans would have fared much better.

The *good* news he had was that the Matrices had managed to rig up the interfaces for their remotes to fly the ships. They couldn't do anything *complicated* with them, but they could bring up the warp drives and take them to Refuge. That was probably enough, but...

"Renaud," he gestured his XO over to him. "I know the Matrices say their remotes can fly the ships, but how many people could we break free to put aboard them as well? Let's say I wanted a crew of five to back up the remote on each ship.

"Can we do that?"

That was a fifth of *Scorpion*'s complement, but…missing a turret and half their pulse guns, he figured they could do it.

"I think so," she said carefully. "Biggest problem I see is that we'll have to grab some pretty independent and capable sorts—the kind entire departments are using as linchpins. Plus, well, can we spare the officers?"

Octavio snorted. The people he needed to send were experienced engineering NCOs, not Ensigns running one shift in engine block two.

Of course, given the nature of the Exilium Space Fleet, he didn't have any Ensigns, and even the Lieutenants who'd left the Confederacy as Ensigns were at least five-year veterans.

"Flag the noncoms we're thinking about commissioning," he told Renaud. "I know we've got at least ten POs and Chiefs on that list, so we'll give them temporary warrants and put them in command of the freighters. Trial by fire—with the Matrix remotes as their XOs."

"Makes sense. I'll have a list for you by end of day," his XO told him. "That will leave us shorthanded, though."

"We'll make do. Getting those ships moving with their passengers is task number one." He shook his head. "Which means I need to talk to Sings and the Shining Mother."

"The Empress," Renaud said quietly. "That's what we're making her, you know that."

"So long as she holds her people together well enough for us to get them to safety, I will make her a crown of gold and diamonds with my own two hands," Octavio replied. "She's our only hope."

"Speaking of which…Africano!" He gestured for the coms officer to join them as he shouted her name. "Now would be a *really* good time for us to be able to put the Shining Mother on everyone's speakers. I need two hundred thousand volunteers to go on strange alien ships and travel to a system they know nothing about, after all."

"We're…close," the com officer admitted, wrapping a curl of hair around her finger in thought. "We've got the coding translations work-ing, and we're testing if our worms work on their hardware."

Octavio nodded...then paused.

"And just *where* are you testing those worms?" he asked.

"On all of the carriers left that aren't Shining Rivers'," Africano admitted. "Best-case scenario, we force open communications chan-nels. Worst-case scenario, well...we cripple a potentially hostile asset."

Scorpion's Captain managed to restrain himself from facepalming. Africano wasn't *wrong*, just...

"Please check with me before we try and hack armed assets in the future, please?" he asked carefully. "I know they're only wet-navy ships, but *still*."

———

OCTAVIO COULDN'T CONCEAL a sigh of relief when the combat platforms finally turned back, letting the less-threatening recon nodes deliver the warp freighters to orbit.

"All right, people," he addressed his senior officers. "Getting people onto those freighters is going to fall to the locals. Africano assures me that we now have everything we need to put the Shining Mother on every screen-equivalent on the planet."

Africano didn't look quite as certain as Octavio was making her out to be, but that was life. They'd successfully broken into the communi-cations channels of the ships on the surface, and it was starting to sound like the naval militaries, at least, were choosing hope over loyalty to broken nations.

There were eight carriers left on the planet that hadn't belonged to the Shining Spears. Three had belonged to the two nations around the passage, countries whose capitals had been swept away in the Impact.

Those ships had leapt at someone—*anyone*—able to help them save their people. The other carrier groups had taken some convincing, but Sings-Over-Darkened-Waters was extraordinarily convincing.

Hopefully, Sleeps-In-Sunlight would be just as persuasive.

"The Shining Mother will speak to the Vistans in about an hour, if we're translating time correctly," he told everyone. "We'll stand ready to support her in any way needed, but I've made clear to her that we will not provide weapons or fire support for engagement against other Vistans."

Octavio knew that line was not as inflexible as he was implying it was to his officers—and that both his officers and the Shining Mother knew that too.

"How are we getting people up to the freighters?" Renaud asked. "We only have so many shuttles."

"The freighters came with their full complement," Octavio told her. "Unfortunately, we don't have the *pilots* for them, either."

He looked around at the Amazon brigade that served as the officers of his ship and smiled calmly.

"*Our* first step is to make sure the freighters are operating properly and that the Matrix remotes integrated without problems our AI friends might have missed," he said. "There's also a stack of cargo aboard the ships—I don't even know what the Admiral has sent us."

From the communiques he'd exchanged with Lestroud, *nobody* was entirely sure what they'd managed to shove aboard the freighters. A lot of people had been stuffing whatever spare resources they had that might be useful aboard, and the time crunch had been so tight, no one had been keeping track.

"Once we've confirmed the ships are functional and off-loaded everything, we'll cycle our pilots to get all of the shuttles down to the surface. Once they're on the surface, our pilots get to play flight instructor."

"Will the Vistans even be able to fly our shuttlecraft?" Das asked. "It's not like we have their sound-projector display systems."

"We're installing a copy of their controls, and, since I'm not done making Lieutenant Commander Africano's life hell, she and her team will have to rig up a translator system so that the shuttles *can* duplicate their sound systems," Octavio told them, gesturing to the coms officer.

And if Africano pulled *that* rabbit out of her hat, she was going to find herself a full Commander before the week was out. He knew just how immense the workload he'd dropped on her was.

From her expression, so did she.

"We'll make it happen," she said, her voice admirably level. "Might take longer than we'd like, though."

"It takes the time it takes, but remember the price of time," *Scorpion*'s Captain pointed out. "Emptying the freighters will take time. Training the pilots will take time. Finding the first two hundred thousand volunteers will take time."

He shook his head.

"My understanding is that the Matrices are building coastal settlements on Refuge to receive the evacuees. They apparently have a unit whose entire purpose is building the colonies. We've never seen one, but they were supposed to have years of warning of an approaching colony ship. Why would they build early?"

"So, at least we don't need to worry about putting roofs over their heads on Refuge," Renaud concluded. "Though I imagine whatever the Matrices build is still going to require massive retrofitting to work for the Vistans."

"Almost certainly," Octavio agreed. "But they'll have somewhere to start." He shook his head. "We certainly couldn't provide enough of *anything* for a billion people, and all of our shipping capacity is going to be tied up just moving these people."

"For once, it's useful having von Neumann machines as allies," Tran noted. "It's still *terrifying*, let's be clear, but they're being useful."

"I'm going to have to talk to the combat Matrices," Octavio said. "We know they can't fight the Rogues, so I want to know what they *can* do for us. I wouldn't turn down them building us a few hundred thousand graser mines or something similar."

"I wouldn't count on it," Das told him. "They've always been pretty strict on what they'll transfer for tech. Hell, did they ever officially give us the matter-conversion plants?"

"No," Tran said instantly. "Dr. Reinhardt reverse-engineered the conversion power cores." She chuckled. "I got the impression that the Matrices are more impressed than bothered when we do that, but they've only actually sold us about half of the tech we've learned from them."

"We'll get what we get," Octavio said with a sigh. "Our first priority is getting these people to Refuge, but that's going to be a process of years without some kind of miracle. That means we need to get them off of Vista before Vista becomes uninhabitable, and we need to make sure the Rogues don't finish them off."

"We'll make it happen, sir," Renaud promised. "These people already got dealt a shitty hand. We'll keep them in the game."

19

Sings-Over-Darkened-Waters had been as terrified as any of her people when the black ships had returned. Even warned that there were friends coming who looked like the vessels that had shattered her world and her Star-Choir, the datasong telling her of the new ships had sent a chill down her spine.

Especially the four big warships. Two of those had sent *Scorpion*, a vessel capable of wiping her entire Guardian-Star-Choir from existence, running. Only by combining the human ship's defenses with a stunning expenditure of nuclear weapons had turned the tide there.

Four…Sings had no faith that her people could overcome four. She was too aware now of how badly damaged *Scorpion* was and how lacking her own ships were by the standards of their allies and enemies.

But these ships were allies, and that gave her more time.

"Is the Shining Mother ready to speak yet?" Swimmer-Under-Sunlit-Skies asked, the Voice-Of-Gunnery's chirps warning of his stress. There wasn't a Vistan in the command pool who wasn't chirping slightly faster and slightly higher than they should have been.

The officers of Sings's fleet were terrified. The biggest ships might have turned away, but the smaller ones had come all the way to orbit of Vista to deposit the transports Catalan promised would be the Vistans' salvation.

Sings was surprised by how much faith she put in the human Voice-Over-Voices. They knew almost nothing about the humans, but she believed in her bones that Catalan would never betray them.

She'd seen him take his ship against a vastly more powerful foe to protect them. For no reason but compassion, he'd risked everything to save her world. She would trust him and his crew to the end of days—and if the chance came to return the favor and protect *his* people, Sings-Over-Darkened-Waters would willingly sacrifice herself to do so.

For today, however, her world remained the focus. She had failed nine billion of her people. She would not fail those who remained—and the Shining Mother was their only real hope to bring enough order to do so.

"The humans are opening the channel in a few moments," she told Swimmer. "Then we shall see if the Shining Mother is all that we hoped she is."

The male was silent for long breaths.

"She is but one Mother," he finally said. "What can she do?"

"On her own?" Sings chirped sad amusement. "Not much. But her words...her words might convince the rest of our people to allow us to save them."

———

THE ONLY TRANSMISSION carried by Vistan datanets and entertainment networks was audio. Unlike how Sings now vaguely understood human data to work, that audio included the echolocation pings for the intended image.

Even before the Shining Mother spoke, sound was already coming through the transmission, and everyone near a speaker on the surface of the planet could "see" her.

Sings was also making sure that the Vistans in orbit and scattered across the star system were getting the message, too. This speech wasn't for them—they'd fallen into Sings's current with surprising willingness—but the entire species needed to hear Sleeps-In-Sunlight speak.

The echolocation pings continued for a moment alone as the Vistan Great Mother waited to be certain everyone across the world was aware of the announcement.

"People of Vista, we have taken control of your emergency broadcast systems," she told her unwilling audience. "These broadcast systems should have seen use over the last fifteen days; only silence has come from many of your governments.

"Many of your cities have devolved into chaos and fear. You do not know what has happened, only that friends and Clan have gone silent. That the sky has gone dark and that rumors of strange alien ships swept the world in the hours before our world ended."

The Shining Mother rose from her throne, approaching the recording device and lowering her voice.

"And our world *has* ended," she told them. "Despite the valiant efforts of our Star-Choirs and an unexpected ally, multiple kinetic weapons struck our planet. You have not heard from anyone outside Long-Night-Waters and Orange-Sunset-Waters because they are gone. Waves unlike anything we have ever seen have swept away entire countries, and *billions* of our kin are dead.

"Some of you know me. Many do not. I am Sleeps-In-Sunlight, the Great Mother of the Shining Rivers."

A chirp of shocked exhalation echoed across the command pool as every Vistan around Sings reacted to a Great Mother giving her name.

"But Shining Rivers is but one country of our survivors," Sleeps-In-Sunlight continued. "And I look to my borders and I see chaos and fear. I have sent the Shining Spears into other nations where I have been invited, and we have helped maintain order, but I fear for our people.

"I have heard nothing from the Great or Chosen Mothers of a dozen nations. Without order, without hope, our world is doomed."

Sleeps shivered and Sings felt the Great Mother's unwillingness.

"I must take some hope from you with one wave and give it with another," she told the audience. "Our world is doomed. Within an orbit, our oceans will freeze. The plants and creatures we depend on to survive will die. Only bacteria will remain after two orbits.

"If we remain on the surface of our world, our species will die.

"But we must have *hope*. I spoke of an unexpected ally before, and they offer us a chance. One ship fought by our side when the destroyers came. The humans have brought more ships now, transports to carry our people to a new world. A safe world, where the destroyers will not harm us.

"More ships are coming, but we must move ourselves into orbit to make certain we can survive. We must work together as one people, one Clan, to save our race.

"If you call for the aid of the Shining Rivers, we will give it. My Spears will bring food, medicine and order wherever we are invited—and nowhere we are not.

"The first wave of evacuees will leave within two days. When the ships return for the next wave, we will be ready to send more. We will find ways to make certain our people survive.

"I do not demand your service or your fealty—but I *do* ask that you follow me. I do ask that you listen to me.

"And I ask that we stand together against the dark and silent night, to bring our people to safety before the storm to come destroys us all."

20

"WHAT AM I LOOKING AT, TRAN?" Octavio asked as his engineer sent him a live feed from one of the freighters. He hadn't even been aware that Tran had left *Scorpion*, which would have been a violation of protocol if he wasn't quite sure that the engineer had logged it.

Octavio just hadn't been paying attention. He'd been listening to Sleeps-In-Sunlight's speech and watching the colorless hologram that was the computer's interpretation of the echolocation data in his office. The gray three-dimensional image of the speech had been *weird* to human eyes, but that was what you got for translating literally alien data.

The feed he was getting from Tran was at least in color, but he wasn't seeing anything of interest. It was a larger cargo bay aboard one of the standard bulk freighters they'd brought from the Confederacy, one that had been set up to carry people and then had cargo loaded in on top of it.

Wait.

There was a stack of equipment that looked more organized. Several long pipes, lots of associated boxes, wiring, control boards…

"What you're looking at, Captain, is proof that someone back in Exilium read our damage reports and *really* likes us," Tran told him.

"That's a pair of LPCs. They're not complete—they can't be completed without installing them in a turret—but that pile includes everything we couldn't have fabricated ourselves."

"Good." Octavio felt that he probably should have shown more enthusiasm, but the speech had reminded him just how badly he'd failed. Despite everything they'd done, everything they were doing now, *nine billion* people had died.

"How long until we have both turrets online?" he asked.

"We'll have Turret B back online in a couple of days," his chief engineer told him after a silent moment. "We'll have to rebuild Turret A's chassis from scratch. Even with our fabricators, three weeks?"

"Let's hope the Rogues give us that much time," Octavio told her. "Let me know if you need anything else."

"A half-dozen Confederacy dreadnoughts, a shipyard and a Captain who isn't kicking himself," Tran told him. "Got any of those to hand?"

The combination got a snort of laughter out of Octavio.

"Even the Confederacy only had *one* dreadnought," he pointed out. With the upgrades the Exilium Space Fleet had deployed, that flagship would have been hard pressed against her smaller cousins now.

"We could build a shipyard here, but our first focus has to be on orbital habitats." He allowed himself to audibly sigh. "As for that Captain, I don't know. It's been a rough month."

"You did the impossible, sir," Quy Tran told him firmly. "Without us—without *you*—the Vistans would all be dead."

"And nine billion of them died," he whispered.

"That was the Rogues, not you. You pulled off a miracle, sir. Miracle number two will be getting the rest to Refuge, and we've got a better shot at that than I expected.

"Once you're a *two-time* miracle worker, I don't think you're allowed to kick yourself for imagined failures," she concluded. "Sir."

He shook his head at her—but he *did* feel better.

"Be careful, Lieutenant Commander, or I'm going to make you start working as ship's counselor in your spare time," he warned.

"We have one of those," Tran pointed out. "I'm probably out of line, sir, but you need to talk to him. If nothing else, it will let me build turrets uninterrupted!"

Octavio chuckled weakly but nodded his agreement.

"Get me guns, Tran," he told her. "I'll see about making sure we've got a Captain ready to fire them."

———

THE SHIP'S Captain had priority on just about everyone's time, which allowed Octavio to sneak into Lieutenant Williams's schedule quickly once he'd decided to make the time himself.

One mentally exhausting and emotionally bruising session later, he called Renaud into his office and squared his shoulders to the task ahead.

"You heard Sleeps's speech," he said. It wasn't really a question. Even Tran, busily cataloging everything remotely useful aboard the freighters, would have made time to listen to the speech.

"Hell of a burden on us," his XO said. "Other than the warp freighters, what can we even do?"

"Our fabricators aren't huge, but they're more efficient than anything the locals have," Octavio pointed out. "We're focusing on our own repairs for now, but once that's done, I have a few thoughts on what we can churn out that can help.

"But what I'm wondering is what kind of fabricators the *Matrices* are carrying." He gestured at the wall of his office, currently turned into a screen showing a tactical display of the area around Vista. "There are fifteen Matrix ships in the system. Now, we know the big construction Matrices can build new Matrix ships, but I doubt that the smaller units have *no* fabrication ability.

"They appear to have been designed as von Neumann–style self-replicators, after all." Octavio shook his head. The degree of irresponsibility required to have designed the Matrices the way they were was mind-blowing to him.

He *really* wanted to meet their creators. It wasn't going to be a fun conversation for whoever had built the robots.

"My guess is that the recon nodes can't self-replicate but have the ability to repair...and that anything bigger could probably build a copy of itself, given time and resources," he told Renaud.

"You think they can build more freighters?" his XO asked.

"I hope so," he agreed. "We're going to need them to bring the exotic matter from Exilium to do it, but every ship we can build here is twenty thousand people evacuated per voyage.

"What I really want from them is weapons, though," Octavio admitted. "Grasers and missiles we can put in the hands of Sings-Over-Darkened-Waters and her people. XR-13-9 *knows* their combat units can't engage Rogue combat units.

"So, why the hell did the big robot send them?"

Renaud opened her mouth to answer, then closed it again and hummed thoughtfully.

"I don't know, sir," she replied. "Should we ask them?"

"Hold that thought," he told her. "I wanted you in on that conversation, and that's my next call."

The combat Matrices were still a light-minute out, but one of the recon nodes was in Vistan orbit to serve as a relay. *Scorpion's* tachyon communicators weren't enough for a real-time conversation, but the recon node's systems were.

"I know I've got a wish list," Renaud told him. "I know that *Dante* was basically rebuilt by a recon and security unit, so they can definitely do *something*."

Octavio returned her grim smile and gestured his desk screen open.

"Let's find out what."

———

"*This is Combat Coordination Matrix ZDX-175-14. Greetings, Captain Catalan.*"

"Greetings, ZDX," Octavio replied. "I have to ask, before anything else, what your intention here in Hearthfire is."

"*ZDX-175-14 and companions are to secure system designated Hearthfire and planet designated Vista against any threats we are able to operate against. We are currently cataloging all objects on potential impact vectors to the planet. No natural impacts will be permitted given the damage already done.*"

Octavio traded a look with Renaud. That wasn't necessarily the most useful thing the robots could have done, but he could understand the impulse to do *something*—anything—to try to offset the damage done.

"We already know you can't engage the Rogue Matrices," he said. "What assistance would you be able to provide? The Vistans don't have the industrial capacity to build new ships in the time frame available—would you be able to provide them with weapons? Remote-controlled platforms or something similar?"

"*We are bound by protocols against technology transfer,*" ZDX replied. "*Unfortunately, we are not able to provide weapons systems to the Vistans.*" There was a pause, and Octavio swore he could hear surprise in the mechanical tones when ZDX resumed.

"*It appears that knowing the systems will be used to engage fellow Matrices is also an impediment,*" the robot noted. "*We have requested override protocols from XR-13-9, but it may not be possible for us to provide weapon assistance.*"

Octavio shook his head. Why *had* XR-13-9 sent them the warships?

"Would you be able to assist in repairing our vessels and the Vistan guardships?" Renaud asked.

"*If the Vistans are prepared to allow it, yes,*" ZDX said instantly. "*We have partial schematics for your current warp cruiser design. We can rebuild your hull and pulse guns, but the particle cannon are not within our mobile fabrication capabilities.*"

"We have the cannon already," Octavio told them. "Any assistance in accelerating our repairs would be welcome."

He considered his options. He couldn't ask them for weapons, but they were prepared to repair ships. What could he get them to build?

"Would you be able to assist us and the Vistans with orbital construction?" he finally asked. "We need to build orbital residences as temporary evacuation points while we move people to Refuge."

"*We can assist with both orbital habitats and additional shipyard capacity,*" ZDX told them. "*Presuming that Exilium can provide the negative matter and warp-drive schematics, we project the assembly of a facility capable of building warp-capable freighters online in two thousand five hundred and twenty hours plus/minus one hundred fifty hours, assuming availability of local Vistan personnel to be trained as operators."*

A hundred-plus days. That would see the first freighters coming online roughly when Octavio's reinforcements would arrive.

"That would be valuable," he conceded. "The more ships we have, the faster the Vistans can be evacuated. Those ships will need to be Vistan-compatible, however. We'll need to study and incorporate their data systems into our schematics."

"Regional Construction Matrix XR-13-9 has already begun the design process. Schematics for Vistan-compatible warp freighters capable of two hundred and fifty-six times lightspeed should be ready in fifteen hundred hours plus/minus eighty hours."

Octavio whistled silently and glanced over at Renaud. They tended to forget that the Matrices were far more capable than the AIs they were used to.

The AIs they had were intelligent but not creative. They were smart enough and independent enough but lacked personalities and creativity. The Matrices had those things. Their personalities and creativity weren't always clear to humans, but they were there.

Human-built AIs couldn't take two entirely different sets of technology and merge them into a new schematic. They would have been absolutely necessary for humans to complete that task in a reasonable time frame, but much of the heavy lifting would have been done by human brains.

"We'll coordinate having exotic matter made available," Octavio promised. "The more ships we can get online, the sooner we can get these people to safety."

"We will coordinate fabrication schedules for our units. Schedules for the delivery of orbital habitats and shipyard components will be forwarded within eleven hours. Thank you for permitting us to assist."

Octavio was about to wave off the appreciation but then realized it was completely honest.

And he *also* realized that he needed to get the *Vistans'* permission for the Matrices to help.

21

"WHEN YOU TOLD me that Reinhardt had our warp drives up to a hundred and twenty-eight times lightspeed, I really thought I was going to avoid any more six-month voyages," Lauretta Giannovi's image said to Isaac.

She shook her head.

"I'm glad that the weird effects don't seem to be made any worse by the speed, but after three weeks of this, I'm not looking forward to seventeen more—or to fighting more Matrices at the end."

The Italian-extraction Commodore sighed and straightened herself into a more formal posture.

"This is the third weekly hyperspace drop-out and check-in for Task Group *Galahad*," she reported crisply. "We have had no significant engineering casualties or other issues to report. We will spend the next hour carrying out weapons and engine tests. We will hold until we receive an update from Command.

"Commodore Giannovi, out."

The image froze and Isaac considered Giannovi's frozen picture for a few seconds before hitting Record himself.

"Commodore Giannovi, your report has been received," he said formally. "Construction of the two-fifty-six force intended to rendezvous with you in Hearthfire proceeds on the accelerated schedule. We are currently thirty-two days from deployment and an estimated one hundred and ten days from arrival in Hearthfire.

"There's a prepared package attached to this recording, including all of Captain Catalan's reports. It's looking better than we were afraid of, but the situation on the surface of Vista is still chaotic.

"By the time you arrive, roughly one million people should have been evacuated. That's barely a drop in the bucket of what needs to be done, but your task group doesn't have the resources to change that.

"Your orders remained unchanged."

Isaac paused, relaxing so that Giannovi knew this was no longer the formal part of the message.

"Be careful, Lauretta," he told her. "Catalan has one ship. The odds of the Matrices showing up are increasing every day, and the chance that they'll arrive after you do and before I do is damn high.

"I wish we could have sent more ships with you, but you've got everything we could spare of the active fleet. We need you to hold that planet. I trust you to know how far to go when you get there.

"I also trust you to make the right call on live-fire tests. I know we need them, but we can't afford to lose even a single particle cannon before you get to Hearthfire." He chuckled at himself. "Though *that* is Dad worrying that everyone is out on their first trip without him.

"I trust your judgment," he repeated. "I'll hear from you in a week and we'll see you in four months. Godspeed, Lauretta."

―――――

LEAVING HIS GROUNDSIDE OFFICE, Isaac slipped down the corridor to the biggest office on the top floor of Government Tower. Two Marines trailed him, and two young women in suits flanked the door he approached.

To his knowledge, there was no threat to any member of Exilium's government. It still seemed unwise to let the leaders wander around unescorted—and even more unwise, given the Confederacy they'd been exiled from, to let the military be responsible for the President's security.

The two Presidential Security Detail troopers had been police before they'd volunteered to protect Amelie Lestroud. They'd then gone through training Isaac would freely describe as *brutal* at the hands of his Marines and the surprising number of ex-Special Forces operators who'd ended up in the rebellion.

The trainers had washed out half the class, but they'd been left with thirty-four men and women, all in their early thirties, who were probably the best close-quarters combatants on the planet.

Isaac knew his wife thought the whole thing was ridiculous, but the entire Cabinet had backed him. She had the best bodyguards the Republic of Exilium could produce. Some of them would follow her when she became President-Emeritus, but most would remain to protect the next President.

"Admiral," the senior of the two Detail troopers greeted him. "ID, please?"

He presented his tattoo-comp and she quickly scanned it. The process validated his ID papers and checked his DNA to make sure he wasn't someone else who'd undergone surgery to *look* like Admiral Isaac Lestroud.

"She's waiting for you," the Detail trooper told him after the scan. "Marines, coffee station is two doors down to the left." She smiled. "You know which one. Bring me a cup back?"

Protocol and procedure had their place, but every member of Isaac's Marine security detail and the Presidential Security Detail knew each other by face and name at the very least.

Amelie looked up as he stepped through the door and gave him the same bright smile she'd shown every time they'd met since she'd proposed. He wondered, some days, how much effort it had taken to hide that smile *before* the two of them realized no one else cared as much as they'd thought.

"Isaac, come in. I assume my terriers have given you the headache already?"

"Scan checks out; he's Admiral Lestroud," the Detail trooper said with a chuckle. "Mr. Faulkner would want me to remind you that you have a meeting with Minister James in seventy-three minutes, ma'am. He's not on site, so you'll need to get moving in about forty minutes."

"I know, Morrigan," Amelie replied. "Thank you."

The door closed and the President of Exilium embraced her Admiral.

"Anything to worry about in Lauretta's report?" she asked.

"Nothing. It's the longest trip we've sent a group of one-twenty-eight ships on so far, but the warp cruisers have made the same kind of journey without problems." He shook his head. "I just hope we don't find any *more* unexpected surprises."

"We're going to find some," she replied. "We don't know enough about what's out here to avoid surprises, Isaac."

"Pulling everyone back and hiding until I have a fleet of *dreadnoughts* is tempting," he told her. "Every time I turn around, I keep wondering if my new threat assessment is as wrong as the previous one was."

"We can't know." She hadn't let go of him yet. "And we have to work with what we know, don't we?"

"Agreed." He snorted. "Speaking of, do we know who's taking over from you yet? Less than a year left."

She poked him in the stomach, *reasonably* gently.

"I spent a *lot* of effort making damn sure we only had a thirty-day election cycle, you know," she reminded him. "A lot. When my term is up in, yes, a little over eleven months, I call the election. I stand as caretaker for thirty days while my successor is decided, and then I retire to a nice, quiet cabin somewhere."

"A cabin?" he asked. "Really?"

"Well, I lose the Residence, and I think a cabin is sufficiently stereotypical," Amelie told him. "We'll hold everything together for a year, Isaac. After that, it can't be my problem anymore. I need to step away from government at that point."

"In a year," he agreed. "Until then, you're the President, and you wouldn't be doing your job if Roger Faulkner hadn't briefed you on who the likely candidates are."

Roger Faulkner was Amelie's aide, a former government minister in the Confederacy. He was reliant on cybernetics to breathe and see after a brutal beating when the Confederacy Secret Police had learned of his participation in the rebellion, but he still saw more clearly than many people Isaac had met.

His wife kissed him and pulled away, stepping over to look out at the city.

"You know, I really did try to get him not to," she admitted. "I don't *want* to face a situation where I might be tempted to make sure I'm in place to guide the next government. *Guiding* never lasts. I won't be a dictator, rotating titles to remain in power until my dying day."

"I know," he told her, taken aback by her reaction. "But we need to make sure there's a continuity in terms of plans and projects. The Republic can't change course on a dime when the election finishes. Evacuating Vista is going to be a multi-year project in the best of cases, though the Matrices' promising to build the Vistans ships helps."

"It's going to be Nyong'o," Amelie said flatly. "My Cabinet has had quiet discussions behind both my and Emilia's backs. If she runs, none of them will. There's a couple of other Senators and one of our newly-fledged industrialists that are putting together resources and planning quietly, but if the Cabinet steps aside in her favor, the job will be hers."

"Is that even allowed?" Isaac asked. The Cabinet picking the new President was a bad precedent from what he could tell.

"They can't endorse anybody, no more than I can," Amelie replied. "We don't have a lot of major public figures with the kind of presence necessary to run. What this might do is create a tradition that no one serving in the Cabinet when the election is called can run.

"It might not be a good thing in the long run, to be honest, but I think the Republic needs Emilia Nyong'o."

"You know she's my cousin, right?" Isaac asked. "Linking every damn President to me is a little worrying."

"I *might* care if she was your sister," Amelie said dryly. "But since I only barely comprehend the familial relationship between you and Emilia, I don't think anyone is going to care."

He chuckled. Both he and Emilia Nyong'o were from New Soweto, a colony founded by South Africa and its neighboring countries. The familial and clan structures of New Soweto's populace were occasionally confusing to even a native who'd spent his adult life in the Confederacy Space Fleet.

They mostly just called people *cousin* when trying to explain it to people from anywhere else.

"Poking at potential problems, not arguing, my love," he told her. "I'll follow the orders of whoever is President, but I'll be a lot happier with one I know will keep the promises we've made to the Vistans.

"There's a billion people depending on us."

"And there are four million people I swore an oath to protect and take care of," Amelie replied. "Numbers aren't everything. The Republic has to be more important to me, no matter how little I want to leave the Vistans to their own fate."

"I know," he conceded, stepping up to join her at the window and looking out at Starhaven. "These people are our first charge. We will keep them safe. But so long as we *can* help, I think we have to."

"We do," she agreed. "Emilia thinks so, too. Just don't expect a blank check for some grand crusade, Isaac."

"I don't have the hulls, the crew or the firepower for that," he told her. "Though I won't pretend that cleaning up the mess that is the Rogue Matrices has no appeal." He shrugged.

"Lacking that fleet of dreadnoughts, though, we do what we can with what we know. And today, that's make sure we can save the Vistans."

She tucked herself against his shoulder and he smiled at her reflection.

"Which means I need to convince the Senate to give them a *lot* of exotic matter."

22

For the first time in weeks, the datasong in Sings-Over-Darkened-Waters's command pool was calm. There were no alert icons, no cities in ongoing riots, no warning signs for strange ships wandering around the outer system.

That calm was true, but it also brushed over a vast amount of work being done. The coastal cities were all under the Shining Spears' control now, most of them with assistance from local military and civilians who had answered the Great Mother's call.

There'd been no real fighting, thank the warm waters. Entire militaries had declared for the Shining Mother when given the choice. Arriving formations had been greeted with cheering—though Sings was cynical enough to suspect the cheering had been directed toward the trucks full of food instead of the trucks full of soldiers.

There were two question marks in the datasong, areas where the data feeding to the Star-Choirs was incomplete. The first covered three-quarters of Vista, the areas where no radio transmissions or energy signatures survived. The shores that had been wiped clean.

Iron Peaks wasn't the only landlocked nation on Vista, but the Impact had destroyed everything within hundreds of kilometers of the shores it had reached.

Four of the precious aircraft carriers were now in the wider waters, outside of the two sheltered seas that held the survivors of their people. The datasong told Sings what the turnaround on their recon sorties was looking like, and she tried to control her emotions, to keep her chirping from revealing her distress.

Each of those carriers was launching twice as many sorties as they should have been. It didn't matter if that was because they'd crammed on more planes or were taking insane risks with the planes they had; they were *going* to lose aircraft and pilots at this rate.

Sings could have ordered them to slow down, she supposed, but they wouldn't listen. Those aerial surveys were the only hope for anyone who'd survived the Impact. It was possible that people had survived forty days on their own, but the skies were permanently dark now and the air was growing colder.

Anyone they didn't find soon was doomed. She didn't have much hope for their mission, but she agreed with Sleeps-In-Sunlight that it was desperately needed.

There were one hundred and thirty-two days left in the half-orbit they estimated people *might* be able to survive without massive technological intervention. Sings-Over-Darkened-Waters had looked into the details of that calculation now and truly understood what the analysts had meant by that.

In a little less than one hundred and thirty-two days, Vista's oceans would start to freeze. No one on the planet would survive outside of the specially built survival domes already starting to go up along the coast.

The second of the two question marks in her datasong was Iron Peaks. She had no idea if the landlocked nation was going to survive the storm to come. They had survived many things the coastal Vistans had not—they were the only Vistans to ever encounter what the humans called *snow*—but their refusal to speak to the Shining Mother or to Sings herself left them with little information.

They had to focus on the people who had come to them for protection, but there were ninety million people in the Iron Peaks. Sings-Over-Darkened-Waters couldn't leave them to perish, regardless of their leaders' choices.

"First-Among-Singers," a voice interrupted her contemplation. "Look!"

One of the icons she'd been keeping an "eye" on had finally come close enough for the datasong to show her more details. The first of the orbital habitats the Matrices had promised to deliver was entering orbit.

"Check its course," she ordered. She didn't truly believe these Matrices would try to finish the job their Rogue cousins had begun, but it would have been far too easy.

"Velocity vector is correct," her analyst reported. "They will enter a stable orbit at one hundred and twenty-one thousand kilometers."

The construct was immense, larger than any station or ship the Vistans had assembled. Even the habitats they were building themselves were only about eighty percent of its size. It had begun as an asteroid, hollowed out and partially melted by pulse-gun fire, then spun out to form a perfect cylinder eleven kilometers long and three across.

It was already spinning, a carefully calculated rotation to give it a pseudogravity equivalent to the surface of Vista. From the data Sings had, its critical systems were contained in a section with artificial gravity, based on the same systems her human allies used.

The habitats the Vistans were building didn't have that luxury. A trio of those would come online in the next ten days, along with five more Matrix-built habitats.

Each would hold roughly two million people. The Matrices had promised six a week, and her own people would scale up to producing three a week within the next few weeks.

They were still building the construction facilities for their habitats, and it was taking them three weeks to build each one. The Matrices only needed a week.

They'd need to continue scaling up. At an average of nine habitats a week, they'd still only get a third of the survivors into orbit before the oceans froze.

Worse, the habitats didn't have the kind of self-sustaining ecosystems that would provide food and oxygen indefinitely. In time, they might be upgraded to that, but right now, the focus was on getting people off the planet. Food stockpiles would buy them time, but they needed to get as many people to the final refuge as possible.

Everything was predicated on a careful balance, and Sings still wasn't sure she saw a safe ending for all of her people. A safe ending for enough that her people would survive, yes—a second shipment of two hundred thousand volunteers had left for Refuge the day before, after all—but not a course that would save everyone.

She needed to find that course. She'd failed ninety percent of her race. She wouldn't be able to live with herself if she failed two-thirds of the ones who'd survived.

"First-Among-Singers," her Voice-Of-Speakers reported. "The Shining Mother wishes to communicate with you."

Sings-Over-Darkened-Waters chirped sharp acknowledgement and gathered herself.

"I will speak with her in my office," she replied.

Duty called. She had a species to save.

———

THE WATER WAS SHALLOWER in Sings-Over-Darkened-Waters's office, set to her own particular requirements. Some water surged in from the main command pool, but not enough to be a concern to either room.

The water was warmer there, too, tailored to the equatorial waters of her now-flattened home. Even knowing the call she was in there for, the warm water around her legs helped calm her nerves as she settled in behind her desk.

Neither the desk nor the chair much resembled the strange contraptions the humans used for equivalent purposes. The chair was a narrow arc, cut to her exact proportions, designed to hold her long torso and support it at every point. The desk was a semicircular affair covered in small three-dimensional icons.

Most Vistan computer control was by voice. More precise control required the four hundred and two three-dimensional characters of the Vistan "script," and that meant keyboards easily four feet long wrapped around the user.

Right now, the important factor was the high-fidelity speakers at the top of the desk's arc. Once Sings was seated, they started emitting the datasong to create an image of Sleeps-In-Sunlight...now the unquestioned ruler of ninety percent of the remaining Vistans.

"Shining Mother," Sings greeted the Mother. "How may I assist you?"

The title would probably change soon enough. The younger female was no longer merely the Great Mother of Shining Rivers, after all. She would be unlikely to dodge the ancient title of her current role for much longer.

Regardless of her resistance, Sleeps-In-Sunlight was the Vistan's Great High Mother now.

"You can call me by my name," Sleeps replied. "I am surrounded by extraordinarily intelligent and competent leaders and officers and scientists, and not a one of them can see anything but the Great Mother of Shining Rivers."

"You *are* the Great Mother of Shining Rivers, Sleeps-In-Sunlight," Sings told her gently. "You are the Great High Mother of us all now."

She'd been impressed by the emotional control that Sleeps mustered and the generally level and measured state of the young Mother's chirping. It was almost a shock to hear the Mother's chirping accelerate into distressed anger.

"Please. Not you."

"As you wish," Sings conceded. "This is the role you accepted, Sleeps-In-Sunlight. The role our people needed."

"And I will meet that need," Sleeps said firmly. "I will rise to the challenge and I will protect our people. I may fail, but it will not be because I did not give our people and our world all that I could.

"But grant me this boon, First-Among-Singers, and remember that I am Sleeps-In-Sunlight as well. There are few others I can ask it of."

Sings-Over-Darkened-Waters bowed her head.

"As you wish. I am following all of our affairs from here. What do you need?"

"The first habitat has arrived, yes?" Sleeps asked. "When will it be ready for us to move people aboard?"

"Give us a day to check over its systems and make certain it's safe," Sings promised. "The Matrices are confident in their work—and even they want us to inspect it before we start moving millions of people aboard."

"We are arranging the first candidates already," the Mother told her. "There is some argument, but I believe I have carried the day. Those who have lost homes and have nowhere to stay now will be first to go up.

"Once we have evacuated the refugees, then we will move the people whose homes remain but cannot be easily refitted to protect them against the storm to come."

"I agree," Sings said calmly. "The shuttles needed for the task will be completed soon. It is an undertaking such as our people have never engaged in before."

"And it is only one step of several," the Mother trilled. "Even our greatest wars and challenges fade into insignificance, compared to the evacuation of an entire world. And we *will* evacuate everyone, Sings-Over-Darkened-Waters. That is what I need from you today."

"The Chosen Mothers of Iron Peaks will not speak to me," the commander of the Star-Choirs admitted. "They blame me for the fate of our world."

"They are wrong," Sleeps snapped. "But it is irrelevant. I believe we have found the one person they cannot ignore. The one *being* they will at least meet with."

"That can't be right," Sings objected as she realized what her new Great Mother meant. "They don't like other Vistans. Why would they meet with a Stranger?"

"I don't know," Sleeps-In-Sunlight conceded. "What I do know is that the Chosen Mothers *have* agreed to meet with Captain Catalan. The terms are…regrettable, and Captain Catalan will object to them.

"But we have no choice. I need you to convince him to go."

"I will do all I can," Sings-Over-Darkened-Waters promised. "He understands duty. He will meet with them."

23

"No. Not a bloody chance. You literally *cannot* do this."

Octavio waited calmly for Lieutenant Major Rachel Summerfield to get through her initial reaction to the discovery that the leaders of the holdout state on the surface wanted to meet him.

Just him. Alone. No escort. No Marines. Just him.

The lanky blonde woman commanded the single platoon of thirty Marines aboard *Scorpion*. Normally a senior Lieutenant's command, the warp cruisers had been assigned more experienced Marine officers in Exilium service.

That was partially because the Exilium Marine Corps *had* those officers. They'd had problems reducing the strength of the Marines they'd brought to Exilium with them. Those troopers hadn't wanted to stand down, even as the Navy had been able to cut its strength in half just by letting everyone who wanted to go be a colonist leave.

The result was that the EMC had intentionally taken on a top-heavy cadre structure, with a lot more noncommissioned and commissioned officers than their actual line strength called for.

That meant that Captain Octavio Catalan had a Lieutenant Major with twenty years of experience commanding a platoon of Marines whose most junior member was a fifteen-year veteran. If he made it through the crazy stunt he was about to pull, those Marines would be why.

"I don't have a choice, Summerfield," he pointed out as she finally petered to silence. "The elected leaders of Iron Peaks—these 'Chosen Mothers'—won't meet with the Vistan leadership.

"They've agreed to meet with me, as an outsider. Someone outside their traditional fears and concerns. But since I *am* an outsider, they aren't comfortable with me bringing weapons or bodyguards."

"So, they're going to have to give up something somewhere," Summerfield told him. "Protocol and regulation are clear. You can't go down to the surface alone."

"Last time I checked, I was in command of this vessel, Major Summerfield," Octavio pointed out. "You don't get to give me orders."

"On this one thing, I do," Summerfield replied. "You're not a Marine or a technician. You're not some bloody redshirt from a bad science fiction serial. You are the commanding officer of a warship of the Exilium Space Fleet, and I, sir, am responsible for your safety.

"It is explicitly in my authority to refuse to let you leave the ship if I believe the threat level is too high, and in this case, it's too bloody high."

"You're not wrong," he conceded. He'd have to check the regulations. He honestly wasn't sure if his Marine commander could keep him aboard ship legally or not. "But it doesn't matter."

Not least because the Marines would have a hard time physically keeping him aboard ship. He might not be able to fly a shuttle himself, but *Scorpion* had no shortage of shuttle pilots.

Even with half his people on the surface, training Vistan pilots.

"Ninety million people, Major," he said calmly. "That's ninety million reasons why I have to go. You've presented one why I shouldn't."

"That's bloody shit and you know it."

The Captain winced at the graphic curse and glared up at the Marine.

"Cut the bullshit," he ordered, turning her own language back on her. "I'm not going to pretend you don't have a legitimate concern.

Hell, Sings-Over-Darkened-Waters raised the same concern. She was expecting me to refuse to go."

"Then maybe you should refuse. Sir." Summerfield returned his glare in equal measure. "We can't keep you safe if we're not allowed to be with you."

"The choice, Major, is between risking my life or abandoning ninety million people. I will not do the latter," he told her. "I am the Captain of an Exilium warship, yes. I am also currently the Republic's ambassador plenipotentiary to these people.

"I need to go down. I need to meet with the Chosen Mothers of the Iron Peaks. You are going to let me do so. Am I clear?"

"You can't order me to let you get yourself killed, sir," she countered. "There are only two people on this ship who can override you. Our head doctor can relieve you if she thinks you're medically unfit for command, and I can refuse to let you leave the ship. And right now, I'm not convinced I shouldn't do just that."

"Seriously?" Octavio stared at her. "Ninety million lives and you're going to sit there and tell me you value mine over theirs?"

"That's my job, sir," she told him. "I agree that we need to do something, sir, but sending you into potentially hostile territory with no weapons, no guards and no backup strikes me as bloody suicidal."

"Ah." He raised a hand. "I see at least one area where we can agree. I may have agreed to go in unarmed and unescorted, but I said *nothing* about backup.

"You're not winning on me not going, Major. You're not winning on me getting an escort or on me going armed—and frankly, nobody *wants* me to be armed."

Naval officers had to qualify with firearms to get their commissions. They were *expected* to maintain that skillset through their careers, but it wasn't actually a requirement. Octavio suspected he was far from alone among the Captains of the ESF in being only barely competent with a sidearm at this point.

"But I don't want to go in without backup—and you're right that is a damn bad idea," he said with a chuckle. "So, blank check time, Major. Given our resources, what *can* we do to back me up?

"And given what we might be able to beg, borrow and steal from everyone else in this system, what would make you willing to let me do my damn job?"

THE END RESULT felt ridiculous to Octavio, but he'd agreed to let Summerfield set the tone of the backup. So, he went along with it, even as it felt like overkill.

His shuttle dropped from *Scorpion* and entered atmosphere above Shining Sunset. That was a good six hundred kilometers from their destination, adding half an hour to their trip unless they wanted to break the sound barrier and cause havoc along their way.

The reason for the extra distance was the two dozen atmospheric fighter-bombers that launched from the Shining Sunset military bases. They fell in around the shuttle, matching its barely subsonic speed as the formation sped toward Iron Peaks.

Two more Exilium shuttles were engaged in a more distant escort, sitting in a low orbit above the Iron Peaks themselves. They might *look* distant to an uneducated eye, but Octavio had spent time in flight engineering during his career.

Their theoretical specifications said those ships were ten minutes from landing at assault capacities. He'd cleaned up the damage after a pilot back in the Confederacy had decided a situation was critical enough to require a *three*-minute orbit-to-ground assault landing.

It said something about the shuttles that most of the damage had been vomit.

If something happened, his Marines would be on the ground to extract him in five minutes, and while Octavio would be unarmed and unescorted, that didn't mean his shuttle was empty.

There were ten Marines in full power armor behind him. Octavio hoped they would be unnecessary, but he couldn't disagree with anything Summerfield had insisted on.

"Twenty minutes to our destination," she reported as she stepped back into the passenger compartment. "Iron Peaks has granted air clearance to our escort, though I get the impression they're expecting everyone to turn around and leave once we drop you off."

If it was *just* a show of force, that was what they'd do. Since Summerfield was a professional paranoid, however, she and the Shining Spears' fighter-bombers were going to stay right there while Octavio met with the Chosen Mothers.

"You know, all of this just might end up offending them," he told Summerfield. He'd mentioned that in the planning session, too…and her cold smile was much the same as it had been then.

"We didn't bring enough force to actually *threaten* the Iron Peaks, just enough to make sure they'd regret trying to hurt you," she said. "If they want to start a war, the Shining Spears have a *lot* more trouble waiting for them."

Octavio winced. He'd seen the shuttle's scanner reports as they came in. The airbase that had launched the twenty-four planes escorting them was huge, and the fact that the Shining Spears had absorbed most of the surviving militaries had increased their ability to keep planes at home.

They may have only launched twenty-four aircraft for this escort, but there were *hundreds* of planes ready to go.

He hoped the Iron Peaks didn't want to make trouble—and not just because any trouble would mean *he* was either a hostage or dead.

24

Octavio stepped out of his shuttle with a cautious glance around to see if anything was waiting for him, mostly in terms of traps, assassins and ambushes. Summerfield's paranoia had managed to sink its claws into him, too, he concluded.

There was nothing, only a raised symbol that he studied for a moment before realizing it was a directional indicator.

"I think we're clear here," he said back into the shuttle. "Take off once I'm past the safety barriers and follow the plan. I'll be in touch."

The plan in this case was to orbit at one thousand meters, accompanied by the Vistan jets. The shuttle pad wasn't as well designed as the ones he was used to, but there was a safety barrier about fifty meters away and an attached bunker along the line the icon pointed him to.

The door slid shut behind him and he set off across the landing pad. The bunker doors slid open as he approached, and a small honor guard of Vistan soldiers trooped out.

They weren't wearing anything a human would have regarded as a dress uniform, but their movements and posture were recognizably parade-ground. The six soldiers fell in around him in near-silence, the air broken only by the quiet chirping of their breathing and the attendant sonar.

A dozen other Vistans were waiting for him just inside the bunker, three of them wearing the surprisingly simple robes that he'd seen Sleeps-In-Sunlight in. It seemed those were the mark of rank as a Great Mother, since the rest of the party was clearly looking to them for guidance.

"I am Captain Octavio Catalan of the Exilium Space Fleet," he introduced himself. Once again, the speakers on his shoulders trilled the equivalent two-toned speech of the translation.

"I am Chosen Mother Dancer-In-Darkness," the central Chosen Mother told him. Her skin was grayer than any Vistan he'd met yet, including Sings-Over-Darkened-Waters. From his understanding of Vistan biology, she was ancient.

"These are Chosen Mother Glorious-Singer and Warmest-Waters," she continued, indicating the other two Mothers with her. "We have been tasked by the Dome of the Chosen to greet you and bring you forward."

"We were not warned you would bring an army," Warmest-Waters hissed. She was the youngest of the three, with the least amount of mottling to her skin. Still older than Sleeps-In-Sunlight, he judged, which said fascinating things about the leader he'd associated with.

"What army?" he asked. "I come alone and unarmed, as promised."

"With a squadron of jets from the one who would make herself Great High Mother," Warmest-Waters replied, gesturing upward. "This was not agreed to."

"Peace, Warmest-Waters," Dancer-In-Darkness snapped. "We asked for the impossible and he gave it to us. Allow them their precautions."

She gestured for Octavio to follow her.

"Come, Captain Octavio Catalan. There is ceremony when a Speaker-For-Mothers comes to us, and we have much to discuss."

———

THE VEHICLES WAITING for them would have been recognizable on any human world. The proportions weren't quite right, but they were unquestionably cars. Four wheels, engine, storage compartment and transparent top.

Some things were apparently universal. Six cars waited for them, alongside two open-topped vehicles clearly intended for the armed escort.

Each of the Chosen Mothers was escorted to a separate vehicle, as was Octavio. The hangers-on piled into the first and last cars, and the soldiers into the open-topped transports.

The city of High Mountain felt very different from Shining Sunset. The first Vistan city he'd visited had been coastal, built into the water in a way that left no illusions as to the amphibious nature of his hosts.

High Mountain was halfway up a mountain. Aqueducts delivered water from mountain lakes and glacial runoff, but the waterways running through the city were clearly artificial and constrained. The higher up they went toward the Dome of the Chosen, the wider and more easily accessible the water streams became.

The houses around those streams were larger and more decorative, too. It was obvious they were moving into wealthier areas, and that wealth had many benefits.

What High Mountain shared with Shining Sunset was the omnipresence of police. Armored Vistans were on every corner, and here they weren't guarding food trucks.

The concern that had made its way back up to Catalan from the surface was whether or not Iron Peaks would be able to feed their citizens. Their system was a semi-oligarchic democracy, and seizing the food supplies wouldn't have been an option as it had been for the Shining Mother.

There was no one in the back seat of the car with him, which he found both disconcerting and strange. It suggested a possible threat, but it also seemed weird that no one had taken the time to have a quiet conversation with him away from the ceremony.

The Vistans might not be human, but from what he'd seen, their politics were relatively similar. There was less nepotism, but that was only because favoritism was harder when any given politician had between two and ten thousand individuals who were equivalent to a human's siblings.

If the Chosen Mothers wanted to conduct everything in the eye and ear of the public, however, he didn't object. His job was to convince these people to work with the rest of their planet to save themselves.

The convoy pulled in at the front of a mixed array of fountains and steps that would probably have been a water feature in a human building. Here, it appeared to be the main entrance.

There was a crowd of people come to see the strange alien. There were formally arrayed honor guards and what looked like dancers.

Ceremony.

Octavio had spent his formative years as an officer working for Isaac Lestroud. He wasn't fond of ceremony...but with ninety million lives on the line, he'd survive.

Until they had work to do, at least.

———

THE DANCERS finally moved away as Catalan followed the three Chosen Mothers across the last step. Vistan dancing, it turned out, was as much an auditory affair as an actual physical one, and he had a new headache since he'd arrived.

"I can't believe we gave the stranger a full reception," he heard Warmest-Waters complaining. Given how good Vistan hearing was, he *knew* the Chosen Mother could have whispered so he couldn't hear.

She wanted him to hear what she was saying.

"You were the one who insisted that we meet with it," Glorious-Singer replied. "Why so hostile now? I am no happier to have it in our sacred halls than you are."

"We needed to hear it. We did not need to honor it as a Speaker-For-Mothers," the youngest Mother snapped.

"Once we agreed to meet Captain Octavio Catalan, he was a Speaker-For-Mothers and deserved that respect," Dancer-In-Darkness told them. "You disrespect our guest. We may not trust him, but the Chosen Mothers agreed to hear him."

"And do you trust the Chosen Mothers to make the right choice when it is done lying?" Warmest-Waters asked. "I said we should *hear* it, not that we should *consider* it."

"A division that is without meaning," Dancer-In-Darkness replied. She turned toward Catalan. "Come, Captain Octavio Catalan."

She knew perfectly well he'd heard everything, but he kept his movements under control as he approached the Chosen Mother. They would "see" if he shook his head or something similar. They couldn't detect the glare he was unable to conceal himself directing at Warmest-Waters.

Politicians were the same all over.

"Are we ready to have an actual conversation?" he asked pointedly. "You may be willing to stand by and watch your world freeze, but I made promises and have work to do."

"We are ready to meet with the Chosen Mothers," Dancer told him.

She led the way deeper into the Dome of the Chosen and through a set of doors three times the height of any Vistan he'd met so far.

Past those doors was the inside of another dome. A sunken floor sloshed with warm water, and two dozen chairs formed a semicircle in the water. Three were empty, but the other twenty-one seats were occupied by Vistans.

"This is the Dome of the Chosen," Dancer-In-Darkness told him. "Here, the Chosen Mothers of the Iron Peaks deliberate on the course of our nation. Thanks to Warmest-Waters and some others, we have agreed to hear you speak, to allow you to tell us what you believe the fate of our world is and how you think you can fix it.

"Speak swiftly," she continued, gesturing him to the center of the room. "The patience of the Chosen is not infinite, and many did not wish you to be welcome here."

The three Chosen Mothers who had escorted him to the chamber lowered themselves into their seats, and Octavio Catalan found himself facing the half-blind eyes and slowly chirping echolocation of twenty-four aliens.

Aliens waiting for him to convince them to let him save their people.

25

OCTAVIO TOOK a moment to organize his thoughts. He'd prepared a speech for this, but now, looking at the collection of elected Vistans, he realized he'd taken the entirely wrong approach.

"I prepared things to say," he told them. "An entire speech of facts and explanations and statistics. I'm realizing now that it was a waste of my time."

They couldn't read his body language and he had no idea how well the translator picked up his tone, but he suspected his words were getting both messages across.

"You are the leaders of a country of ninety million people," he stated. "You've taken in tens of thousands of refugees from the countries on the other side of these mountains—and you *know* they are all that survives of billions.

"You have scientists and telescopes and were linked into the Star-Choirs' satellite networks. You know what happened. You have the knowledge to understand what *will* happen."

He grimaced.

"You know your world is dying. And yet you refuse to work with the people trying to save you. So, I have no speech, no grand remarks, only one simple question:

"Why are you so determined to kill the people you swore to serve?"

He couldn't read Vistan body language very well, but it turned out that they recoiled in shock much the same as humans did. Instead of speaking for thirty minutes, he'd spoken for less than one.

He hesitated for a moment, waiting to see if any of them had an answer. If any of them had anything to say.

"If you wish to work with us to save your people, you know how to contact us. There really is nothing more to say."

Turning, Octavio began to walk out of the Dome of the Chosen. He was half-expecting, half-hoping, to be called back. To be asked questions, challenged...*anything* to suggest that the Chosen Mothers actually wanted to save their people.

Instead, he made it to the doors in silence—only for them to be flung open in his face. A dozen armored Vistan Spears marched through in perfect cadence.

These weren't the ceremonial guards from earlier. These were soldiers in combat kit, with clamshell body armor and battle rifles that wouldn't have looked particularly out of place in a historical drama.

One leveled a rifle on him and he stopped cautiously...and then realized the rest were ignoring him, moving forward into a chamber he'd already shocked to silence. A second line followed, two more joining the one holding him prisoner.

"What is the meaning of this?" Dancer-In-Darkness bellowed as a third line of soldiers entered. There were now more Iron Spears in the Dome of the Chosen than Chosen Mothers—and more were following.

"You'd all been so very busy," another voice answered. "Busy buying into the Strangers' lies. Busy considering how best to sell out our people."

Octavio turned to face the Chosen Mothers again, watching as Warmest-Waters rose to her feet.

"We couldn't take the risk of any of the Chosen Mothers escaping, or of permitting the gathered Mothers to sell out our country. Allowing you to speak to the alien who fascinated you so much gathered you in one place."

He still couldn't read Vistan expression, but he suspected that

Warmest-Waters's current posture was probably a good read for smug gloating.

"You are all under arrest for treason—and you, alien, will face the punishment for your crimes. Some of us are not blind fools, to be led into slavery by your grand deception. The blood of nine billion is on your hands, and we will not see it passed unpunished."

A rifle butt slammed into the back of Octavio's knees, forcing him to the ground as Warmest-Waters approached him. The Chosen Mothers were shouting incoherently behind her, the translator unable to handle that many conversations at once—but he could see their fates as the Spears bound their elected leaders.

"And I know you think your traitorous friends from the Shining Rivers will save you," Warmest-Waters told Octavio, her voice perfectly projected to reach only him. "But we were not blind to their air fleets. The defenses of this city are impenetrable."

———

OCTAVIO WAS DRAGGED out into the streets alongside Dancer-In-Darkness. The elder Grand Mother was their equivalent of Prime Minister, he guessed, which earned her special attention from the Spears escorting them.

Sirens blazed across the city now, and several aircraft circled above. They weren't the sleek fighter-bombers of the Shining Rivers. The planes above High Mountain were immense, blocky things that carried dozens of antiaircraft missile launchers.

Radar arrays and missile launchers had risen out of the mountainside above the city as well, and Octavio felt an iron lump form in his stomach. The Vistans had continually surprised him with the efficacy of their relatively crude technology.

He doubted Iron Peaks' antiaircraft defenses would be any different. Not least because he could see the plumes of smoke from the crash sites of the aircraft that had accompanied him.

He tried to reach for his tattoo-comp, hoping to check in with Summerfield.

A rifle butt slammed into his wrist, and an Iron Spear hissed an order his translator didn't catch.

The meaning was clear, though. *Don't try it, punk.*

"The air defenses were designed to stand off the two largest threats at once," Dancer-In-Darkness told him. The translator made her sound perfectly calm, but the rapid metronome of her echolocator chirps told him that it was lying.

"Shining Rivers wasn't one of them," she concluded. "Even with their new subjects and allies, I doubt they have the power to penetrate these defenses. Will your people?"

"Not without leveling the city," Octavio admitted.

That wasn't *entirely* true. If *Scorpion* had been carrying proper bombardment munitions, she'd have been able to punch out the radar arrays without damaging the city. A Confederacy battle group would have already destroyed the city's defenses.

That was because a Confederacy battle group had a battlecruiser... and would, generally, be commanded by a ruthless paranoid.

The ESF followed CSF protocol in arming only battlecruisers with bombardment weapons. *Scorpion* could fabricate them, but it would take several days—and they still wouldn't have the right launchers.

Precision was out of the question. Mass destruction was available immediately. Dropping a rock capable of leveling the city required a lot less work than building precision weaponry.

He was thinking like an engineer and he knew it. Weapons systems and technological solutions. Exilium ECM might be enough to shut down the local defenses, infiltrate EMC assault shuttles—but if Summerfield's shuttle was gone, there were only two assault shuttles and twenty Exilium Marines in the star system.

"Will Warmest-Waters succeed in taking control?" he asked Dancer.

"No. The people won't stand for rule by the Spea—"

The rifle butt that cut the Chosen Mother off was *not* gentle, and the old Vistan stumbled backward, gasping for breath.

"Speak again and I will shoot you," the Spear threatened.

Octavio looked Dancer-In-Darkness in her half-blind eyes and nodded slowly, hoping she got the meaning.

They would wait. They would see what happened.

And when the time was right, he would feed that asshole of a soldier her own rifle butt.

26

THEIR ESCORTS LED them up past the Dome of the Chosen to a structure built into the side of a cliff. To Octavio's surprise, he and Dancer-In-Darkness were put in cells next to each other, cells that opened out over the lake the city drew its water from.

When the prison had been built, the half-kilometer drop to the water had probably been enough to keep prisoners secure. At some point since, a layer of bulletproof glass had been added. Prisoners on this level could see the lake and "freedom" but could never reach it.

From there, Octavio could see an entire side of the defensive array and was quietly assessing it. Like most Vistan technology, it was crude by human standards, at least two or three centuries behind the Confederacy they'd left behind.

A human antiaircraft array would be built of a mix of railguns and pulse guns. A secondary suite of lasers would be emplaced to take down anything the aircraft launched before they were obliterated.

The Confederacy hadn't had very many facilities protected like that. By and large, they were more concerned about attack from space —though the Confederacy Secret Police had certainly been ready to stand off attack from resistance forces.

Whoever held the orbitals held the ultimate advantage, but it was only so useful without precision munitions *Scorpion* lacked or a willingness to destroy entire cities.

He checked his tattoo-comp again. He wasn't surprised to see that he was still jammed.

The reasonable thing to do, the *sensible* thing to do, was wait. Warmest-Waters might blame him for the Impact, but they couldn't risk their hostage. Presumably, the rogue Chosen Mother did realize that Octavio's people could obliterate High Mountain about ten minutes after they stopped agonizing over the ethics of it.

She might not. She did seem to think the battle with the Rogues had been a charade to fool the Vistans.

The scary part of *that* particular argument was that Octavio could see exactly where she was coming from. They had, after all, brought in identical ships to help rebuild and rescue people. It didn't take much paranoia to see a scheme to enslave an entire race.

He sighed and checked the directory on his tattoo-comp. He wasn't going to wait. For there to be a chance to a peaceful resolution, someone had to disable the air defense systems *without* an orbital bombardment.

He had Africano's translation protocols to make his software work on Vistan computer systems. The locals had no way of knowing his background, no way of knowing how capable his implanted computer was.

They had no idea that they'd locked a former Confederacy Space Fleet Systems Security Officer behind a door secured with *maybe* twenty-second-century computing systems.

If they had, they might have stuck him with a cell with a purely physical lock—even cut the tattoo-comp out of his arm.

Instead, he leaned against the wall, running the top of his forearm over the smoothed stone. Unless they were *insane*, there was no wireless connection to the lock, but if he could just... *There.*

His tattoo-comp wasn't as capable as the tools he'd prefer for this, but it could manipulate the current in a wire through a couple of centimeters of relatively porous stone.

It wasn't a *comfortable* process for the person with the tattoo, but he could do it—and while he couldn't manipulate the controls, electromagnetic locks only really came in two varieties. One locked with power, unlocking if cut off…and one did the opposite.

The door slid open and he dodged through. His arm was still burning from the heat of the induction as he found himself facing the same Spear who had gut-punched Dancer-In-Darkness.

His martial arts training might have been twenty years out of date, but he'd been expecting a guard…and the guard had *known* her prisoners were secure.

Limbs only moved so many ways, and a Vistan's legs were big and heavy. They were definitely *not* designed to move the way he bent the guard's leg before she could react. The Spear hit the ground with a snapping sound, scrabbling for the gun she'd dropped.

He got to it first, holding the weapon pointed directly at her head. It wasn't designed for humans, but he could find the safety and the trigger easily enough.

"Now, I'm here to save your entire species and I don't *want* to kill you," he told her. "But you're directly responsible for a good chunk of my bad day, and I *will* make an exception if you don't cooperate. Clear?"

"I understand," the Spear said very carefully. "I do not wish to die."

"Neither did my Marines who your people killed," Octavio pointed out. He gestured to the cell they'd put the Chosen Mother in. "Let Dancer-In-Darkness out."

The Spear hesitated until he poked the gun at her, then stepped over to the control panel and released it.

Dancer-In-Darkness looked up at the Spear, then past her to Octavio.

"You are resourceful, Captain," she concluded, then walked past the Spear like she wasn't there. "Do you have a plan?"

"Could you make sure our obnoxious friend has no surprises hidden on her and shove her in your cell?" Octavio asked. "Seems likely she'll end up there eventually."

"It is likely, yes," Dancer agreed. She went through the soldier's gear and pockets slowly but competently, stripping her of ammunition and a sidearm and several objects Octavio didn't recognize.

She pushed the Spear into the cell and then looked at the control panel.

"I don't have control of this."

"Give me a moment." Octavio walked over and unfolded a tiny cord from a hidden compartment in his arm—*not* a standard feature of the tattoo-comp. Linking the cord into the control panel, he unleashed his software worms.

"Your computers suck," he told Dancer-In-Darkness a minute later as he sealed the door. "Which is probably a good thing for you right now."

"Will your people destroy the city in vengeance for our attack?" she asked.

"Not immediately. Not quickly...but in the long run, quite possibly," Octavio told her. "That decision will fall to my XO, and she will be *very* angry right now."

Her chirping accelerated and Octavio smiled flatly.

"I do have a plan, but it's not a great one," he admitted. "Is there a central command center for the air defenses?"

"Yes," Dancer confirmed. "Warmest-Waters will have made certain of her control of it. There will be loyal troops anywhere near the command pool."

"I can't even use your controls, Dancer-In-Darkness," Octavio pointed out. "I need to get to somewhere I can physically plug in to their hardware. And I'll need coms. My tattoo-comp can't reach orbit on its own—it needs a relay, and your people blew up my shuttle."

Dancer closed her eyes and her chirps slowed, softened.

"I did not wish to meet with you, Captain Octavio Catalan, but I did not wish to harm you, either. I simply did not trust you or the Shining Mother."

"Well, unless you can find an army to stop the one Warmest-Waters has pulled together, the only hope your people have for freedom—for *survival*—is for you and me to get help from the Shining Spears and my people.

"Which means I need to shut down the defenses and call for help. Will you help me?"

She was silent for a good minute as they faced each other in the prison corridor.

"Are we truly doomed if we stay?" she asked. "We were building bunkers in the mountains, but we were starting to question if we would have enough space for everyone."

"The oceans will freeze. Your sky will freeze. It will be decades before you could come above ground again, and who knows what other life would survive." Octavio shook his head. "Vista is doomed. Only by leaving can your people survive."

"Why would you help us?"

"This isn't the time or place for these questions, Chosen Mother," he told her.

"It is the only time possible," she said. "I must understand before I choose, as my choice will bind my people forever."

He sighed. "Look, we're a bunch of exiles seventy thousand light-years from home, kicked out because we chose to do the right thing instead of the smart thing. We don't have it in us to stand by and watch a species die when we can save them.

"And yeah, there's a lot fewer of us than you might think, so we are hoping to lean on you guys for hands and bodies in the future—as *allies*. We've been close enough to slaves ourselves that nothing else is an option.

"Now, I'm out of time to answer questions, so you can either help me or sit down right there and wait for Warmest-Waters's people to come get you. What's it going to be?"

"The command center is also here in the mountains," Dancer-In-Darkness told him in response. "While the ground access would be difficult and guarded, there are other options..."

———

OTHER OPTIONS TURNED out to be *frankly terrifying* for humans. Vistans' echolocation had a decent but finite range. They could only really pick up things out to about two hundred meters—beyond that, they saw motion with their eyes and used technology.

"Fear of heights" was *not* something they generally suffered from.

The helicopter Dancer-In-Darkness had stolen from an access cave at the top of the prison didn't have such amenities as a floor.

Or walls. Or doors. It was a pair of seats attached to an engine and a set of scanners that fed an artificially long-ranged echolocation into the pilot's ears. There were at least seat belts and air supplies, but Octavio was hanging out in the air with nothing between his feet and a six-hundred-meter drop into half-frozen water.

He was half-tempted to ask what the ground access looked like, but Dancer-In-Darkness turned out to be a capable pilot. She flicked the fragile aircraft out of the cave at the top of the prison and danced it out over the lake before he could change his mind.

"Won't this draw attention?" he asked.

"Air traffic control is a confused mess," Dancer replied. "Two centers are taking orders from Warmest-Waters's 'interim authority.' The third is ordering everyone to land and stay down until they can sort out what happened to the Chosen Mothers."

"Other than you, what did happen?"

"I don't know." The old Vistan was silent for several moments, focusing on her flying as she slid them along the cliffside toward some destination Octavio couldn't see.

"I want to hope that my sisters are still alive, but if Warmest-Waters is to justify this, she must claim that you killed the Chosen Mothers. We may have limited time to save them, or they may already be dead."

"Why wouldn't she kill you?"

"I am the Voice-Of-The-Chosen, the one who declares our decisions to the people," Dancer replied. "If she can convince me to support her, claim I was injured and that caused the delay in my reappearance, she gains a legitimacy no one else can give her."

Even over the engines, he could make out her agitated chirping.

"Certainly, a legitimacy her cabal of traitor generals cannot give her."

"Can you talk to your people?" Octavio asked. "Would you be able to convince them she is betraying them?"

"If I reveal that we have escaped and are on an aircraft, this vehicle will be destroyed almost instantly. Look ahead, Captain Octavio Catalan. We approach the defense center, and it is well protected."

As she spoke, she twisted them into a narrow gulley carved into the cliff by a million or so years of rain and glacier melt. That flow of water had been redirected now, but the cleft in the cliff remained.

Fifty stories of concrete and steel filled it now. Octavio could spot multiple hangars for aircraft and helicopters visible on the front of the fortress, alongside a dozen antiaircraft missile launchers.

Turrets hung out from the outer walls, ranging from lighter missile launchers to machine guns to what he was pretty sure were crude railguns.

"The Iron Peaks Central Command," Dancer-In-Darkness told him. "The traitors who have joined Warmest-Waters have already seized it. There will be no loyalists inside, Captain Octavio Catalan. Only traitors, with access to every weapon, sensor and communication network the Iron Spears have assembled over the centuries.

"Your plan had better work."

"My 'plan' is 'get me to a data cable heading to the main command pool,'" he pointed out. "From there, I can take control of the automated systems and bring my people in. I don't know what to do about the fortress!"

Dancer-In-Darkness studied the monumental structure ahead of them as she brought them in toward the highest hangar.

"Then we swim identical waters, Captain Octavio Catalan, and must hope for the currents of fate to bear us to safety."

Great. Two of them against a nation's military headquarters, and his only companion was a bloody fatalist.

27

THE HANGAR WAS THANKFULLY empty and quiet. There were several helicopters similar to the terrifying contraption they were flying in, along with a number of larger vehicles that had actual armor and weapons.

"We are two floors from the top," Dancer-In-Darkness told him. "This is the hangar they bring VIPs through, so it should be clear which way to go. How close do you need to get?"

"Depends. Do you know where the computer cores are?" Octavio asked.

The Chosen Mother chirped sadly.

"No."

"Then we need to get pretty close," he admitted. "Do you know how to use this?" He held the rifle out to her.

"I was a helicopter crew chief in the Iron Spears," she told him. "There are few hand weapons we possess I am not trained in. I am rusty, but it fits my hands better than yours."

Thankfully, the two species' hands were similar enough that Octavio could use the pistol just fine. The rifle was designed for someone with a *very* different torso, though.

"I would prefer not to have to kill anyone," he told her. "But then… what is Warmest-Waters likely to do if she isn't stopped?"

"There aren't enough bunkers to save everyone," Dancer said. "She will have bought her allies with promises of safety for their Clans. She will leave the rest to die, believing them better dead than slaves."

"Fuck me," Octavio muttered. "Even the ones she gets into the bunkers will just die later."

"That is why I am helping you," the Chosen Mother told him. "Come."

As they left the hangar, he understood what she meant by it being clear which way to go. Vistans might not care about colors, but they did care about their feet being warm and either wet or on soft surfaces.

Only one of the corridors had carpet, thickly piled fabric cut into three-dimensional decoration. The carpet had clearly been made by someone with no idea of color, which gave it a strange esthetic appeal regardless.

The lack of guards made him nervous.

"Shouldn't there be some security?" he asked.

"The traitors will not be able to rely on many of the Spears for now," Dancer replied. "They will have sent everyone away from the headquarters, and they need many of the Spears they can rely on to keep order. There may be very few guards here."

That would help…for a while. Once he started screwing with their systems, they were going to start looking for him.

"Let's at least get onto the floor with the command pool," Octavio suggested. "Then I'll start looking for access panels." He shook his head. "A communication center nearby would be perfect."

"I think I can manage that," Dancer told him. "I'm only familiar with the top floors of the Command Center, but there *is* a set of offices here for the Chosen Mothers with a full communication setup."

"Perfect." Of course, unless the traitors were stupider than he expected, that would also be the first place they looked for him.

Sufficient unto the day is the affliction thereof. It was time to clear a path for the Marines.

———

WHOEVER WAS RUNNING security for the mostly abandoned command center turned out to be competent. Once they were on the top floor, Dancer pulled Octavio out of the hallway and covered her own gills.

There was only so much a Vistan could do to silence their echolocating chirps without risking their health, but she was muffling herself as best as she could—and Octavio was able to see the two Spears walking down the corridor with rifles in hand.

The head -forward posture of the guards would have been cavalier incompetence in human guards, but Vistans' sonar gave them three-hundred-and-sixty-degree awareness. They knew everything in the corridor. Looking around wouldn't have helped them.

Well, it might have helped them spot the movement of Octavio dodging back behind cover before their chirping forms got close enough for him to worry.

Listening to their echolocation chirps also let him know once they were past. He waited, as patiently as he could, for the patrol to pass out of hearing, then gestured for Dancer-In-Darkness to lead the way again.

They had to dodge another patrol before they reached the offices, but their target itself was unguarded.

It was behind a sealed security door that would have frustrated a reasonable number of explosives, but it was unguarded. Octavio was about to start hacking into the door's systems when Dancer stepped up to it and tapped a series of raised symbols he'd taken for decoration.

Apparently, the Vistan version of keypads covered a good chunk of the door. He'd have to remember that.

The security door slid open and he looked over at Dancer.

"We good?" he asked.

"That depends on how intelligent my traitorous sister has been," the Chosen Mother told him. "My codes are active, but if Warmest-Waters set an alert on them, we may not have much time."

"Wonderful." Octavio shook his head. "Show me the com setup."

The space set aside for the Chosen Mothers was probably gorgeous by Vistan standards. Decorative statuary and carvings were everywhere, and there were jets built into the walls to fill the space with warm water.

The space wasn't filled with water right now, and Octavio's focus wasn't on the artwork. As he was led toward the com center, he was studying the holographic projection his tattoo-comp was putting up.

It would be near-invisible to his hosts and pursuers, but it was showing him roughly what cables and conduits were hidden in the walls and floors around him.

"Here," she told him, gesturing to a door. "The communication center is through there."

Octavio had hoped that the Iron Peaks designers had followed what he'd regarded as sensible protocol, which said that there'd be at least two completely redundant sets of data connections to a space like this—but that each of those sets would be *complete* and running through a conduit together for ease of access.

He'd been right. It looked like the set of cables he could see running into the com center kept going to the main command pool.

Following those cables, he stepped into the communication room. It was...recognizable as a coms and computing center, but none of the equipment was meaningful to him. He could recognize the speakers used for "visual" transmissions by Vistans, he could see what were probably the main computer keyboards...but he couldn't see anything he could *use*.

Like the rest of the spaces set up for the Chosen Mothers, however, the walls were covered in gorgeous three-dimensional artwork. Plaster artwork...covering plaster walls.

"I need to borrow the rifle," he told Dancer. She seemed confused but handed it over.

She trilled in horror as he used the rifle butt to smash through the artwork and the wall behind them. A few more strokes cleared away enough wall for him to see the data conduit.

"Can you call out from here without attracting attention?" he asked.

"There is no call I could send that wouldn't attract attention," Dancer-In-Darkness pointed out. "Not that would have value."

"Okay." There'd been a knife in the gear of the guard they'd stripped. Vistan hands weren't shaped quite like human ones, but it was usable enough for Octavio to open the conduit.

A mess of cables greeted him and he sighed. One of the fiber-optic cables in there linked to the command pool. One linked to the communications equipment in the room behind him and on the outside of the command center.

Unfortunately, there were at least a dozen cables, and he had no way to tell which one was which until he'd attached to it and cracked the system.

"Hold off on sending a message just yet," he told Dancer. "It's going to take me a bit to ID the systems I need."

The good news was that the Vistans' security software was crap even for their crude tech base. Once he was linked into the defense controls and the communications systems, he would own their systems.

He just had to find them first.

28

THIRD TIME WAS *NOT* the charm. The first time was, a little bit, in that the very first cable he attached his tattoo-comp to was the communication controls.

He left that cable attached and extracted the second cable from his arm as he worked through. The second cable was the internal life-support systems for the base. The third was the lights.

Fourth was the information systems, giving him full access to the archives of the Iron Spears—a spy's wet dream and absolutely useless to him. Fifth was internal e-mail.

By the time he hacked into the sixth system, he was ready to grab the gun and go shoot his way into the command center. As his holographic system interpreted the data stream, he realized this was the jackpot.

A bit of poking around and his translation software was talking to the high-level interface...and his hologram was now showing an illusion of the entire mountain. Icons were scattered up and down its height, from miniature missile launchers on the fortress to the dozens scattered around the city.

From the data summaries he could access, there were over *five thousand* individual antiaircraft batteries guarding High Mountain. The

Iron Peaks really had built a defense to stand off against every threat on the planet.

Paranoid xenophobes didn't make for great neighbors, he presumed.

He found the override that would disable them all relatively quickly. Setting up his worms to make sure that they couldn't disable that override took longer—and allowed him to realize they could bring a lot of the systems back up on local control and even local power.

"I can't shut them down permanently," he finally confessed aloud. "I think I can knock the entire system out for at least an hour, though."

If nothing else, he could make it so they'd have to completely shut down and reformat to bring the systems back up under local control. The defensive planes would have to land, the missile launchers would be unable to fire.

It would buy time.

"Then we will have to use that hour effectively," Dancer-In-Darkness replied. "I suggest we each speak to our respective allies and see what storm we can unleash." Her chirps were sharp with emotion. "Your own people are few, I am guessing?"

"They can take control of this facility and shut down the main defenses," Octavio told her. "But the defenses around the city will be back up in an hour. What can you do with an hour?"

"Enough," the Speaker for the Chosen Mothers told him. "Enough that I do not believe I need to ask you to bring in the Shining Spears. I believe I can restore my country myself...so long as *your* people can get here before Warmest-Waters' people break in here and kill us."

"If you can get loyalist troops moving against her, I can get Marines in here to get us out," Octavio promised.

He was only about half-sure of that, but the truth was that both he and Dancer-In-Darkness were expendable. If they had to die to make sure the people of the Iron Peaks got evacuated, well, that was what would happen.

"Get ready to transmit," he ordered as he switched his tattoo-comp to link into the coms. "Let's bring some friends to the party."

———

OCTAVIO MIGHT HAVE BEEN TRANSMITTING from an array that *Scorpion* had flagged as hostile, but he had the codes to attach to the radio transmission to identify it as from him—and the fact that he was sending from his tattoo-comp and only using the Vistan system to transmit meant he was sending it in ESF formats.

That meant he got through to Aisha Renaud.

"If this *isn't* Octavio Catalan, someone had better start explaining *really* quick," she said harshly the moment the channel opened. "Because the only way someone can access his tattoo-comp would be to cut—"

"Aisha, it's me," he said, interrupting her before she got into threats of orbital bombardment. "These people's cybersecurity sucks, and I had the translation program loaded on my comp already. I don't have long before this starts attracting attention, so what's our status?"

"Lieutenant Major Summerfield is dead," Renaud stated. "The shuttle she was aboard was blown out of the sky along with twenty-two Shining Spears jet aircraft. Two made it out, so we've got a pretty detailed analysis of the missile defenses.

"The Shining Mother is trying to get the Chosen Mothers to admit to *anything*, but we're just getting radio silence. I've got Tran manufacturing precision munitions, but it'll be days before we have enough to take down the defense network."

"I'm inside their systems," Octavio told her. "I can bring everything down for forty-five minutes to an hour. The Chosen Mothers aren't answering your call because they're dead or detained.

"One Mother and her generals used my visit as an opportunity to get everyone in one place to take them down. I have the senior Chosen Mother with me, and we're holed up in their command center. As soon as I start affecting anything, they're going to start looking for us, and they're going to *find* us."

"Once the Marines are close enough, they can track your beacon—and we've located the building you're transmitting from," Renaud told him. "If you can bring down the defenses, we can have boots on the ground in five minutes. Not sure how long after that to reach you...but that doesn't solve the Iron Peaks problem."

"In about thirty seconds, that senior Chosen Mother is about to use this com array to call every General in the Spears she trusts. I don't think the coup is going to last much longer, but things will work *much* better if Dancer-In-Darkness and I don't get killed in this place."

"And if we have control of their primary command center, that won't hurt the counter-coup," Renaud noted.

"Not in the slightest," he agreed. "Are the Marines ready?"

"Five minutes," she answered slowly. "If you can give me ten, its better."

"I'll kill the defenses in ten," Octavio promised. "I don't know how the ground mess is going to go, but I think it will work better for everyone if *we* control High Mountain's air defenses."

"Ten minutes, Captain," Renaud ordered, regardless of her authority to do so. "And if you get your Captainly ass killed down there, I will find a way to make you regret it, clear?!"

"Understood."

———

OCTAVIO HAD TURNED off his translator to focus on his call. Now he turned it back on and walked over to where Dancer-In-Darkness was recording her message. He wasn't sure where the "pickup field" of the three-dimensional echolocation image covered, so he hung back as he caught the last of her message.

"...so while it pains me, I have no choice but to declare Chosen Mother Warmest-Waters a traitor and order her arrest," Dancer proclaimed. "If at all possible, those who have followed her in error or mistake should be spared, but Warmest-Waters must be arrested and detained immediately.

"Voices-Of-Warfare of the Iron Spears, I task you with restoring order and bringing these criminals to justice. Be gentle where you can, merciful where you can...but this rebellion must end."

Dancer paused a moment and looked over at him.

"I am ready. You?"

"Send your message, Chosen Mother," he told her. "I promise my people I'd drop the air defenses in"—he checked his tattoo-comp —"seven minutes and counting."

"And the other defenses? My Spears may face fewer losses if we can disable the other automatic systems."

"I will do what I can," he promised. "They're not as uniformly controlled from here."

His computer was still projecting a holographic image of High Mountain and its defenses. If he disabled the sensors with the missile launchers, he'd be as blind as the rebellious Iron Spears.

He didn't have much choice. There was a timer ticking down in the corner of the hologram.

"It's strange," Dancer commented. "I can tell you have *something* in the air there, but my chirps go right through it."

"Visual illusion," he told her. "I can't understand your chirps, but I can see in far better detail than you can."

"Strange," she repeated. "You can see what is coming?"

Before he could answer, alerts sparked across the hologram. He ignored Dancer for a few moments as he pulled up the details.

"Only what could be seen from the command pool," he told her. "So, right now, I can tell that several battalions of Iron Spears are in the streets that they weren't expecting. They have flagged them as heading towards the Palace, what I think is another prison...and here."

"Exactly where they should be going," Dancer replied. "I have no confirmations, but I suspect my traitorous sister has the allegiance of less than a third of our generals—and even less of the Spears on the ground.

"While she could claim to speak for the Mothers, confusion held her in power. Now I have stripped away that covering. She will fall."

"Quickly, I hope," Octavio told her. His counter hit zero, and the worms he'd preloaded fired.

Icons across the mountain shifted, warnings flaring across the hologram...and then the hologram itself went blank. Closing it down, he rose to his feet and smiled grimly.

"Aerial defenses are down," he told her. "The planes above the city have cyberworms aboard that have shut down everything except the autopilot. They can land, but they can't fight.

"Sensors are down, and all of the communications that were being relayed through this fortress are down. That won't slow them down for long, but it should give your people a critical edge."

"It should be enough." Dancer hesitated. "They won't be here quickly enough to stop whatever traitor Spears are in this building from reaching us. That security door will buy us some time, but…"

"You have a rifle," he told her. A new icon appeared on his tattoo-comp, confirming that his location beacon was now linked to incoming shuttlecraft.

"And unless those Spears are faster than my worst nightmares, I am going to have Exilium Marines."

29

THE IRON SPEARS were no better at removing Octavio from their systems once they knew he was in them than they had been at stopping him from entering them in the first place. After a few minutes of dueling programs, he locked down the entire fortress's systems to his control.

He hadn't been *able* to do that before, but the admin trying to lock him out had brought a security protocol online that Octavio had turned against every other user of the system. For the moment, he was in full control of the defenses of the entire city.

It wasn't going to last. Entire swathes of the system were being cut off and rebooted. They were going to find leftover worms in there once they were back online, but without his being able to actively influence things, even the Vistans would defeat the software.

Eventually.

The bigger problem was that the Spears had managed to localize where he and Dancer were and had stopped caring if they wrecked the fortress. He watched the Chosen Mother wince as a fourth round of explosions tore through the command center.

"If I'm reading the map correctly, they're at the entrance to this section," he told the Vistan. "Given that they've blown their way through doors nowhere near us, I think they're pretty desperate."

"Are your people here yet?" she asked.

"I've opened a pathway from the topmost hangar to here—the one we followed—but I've killed all of the sensors in the building, and my people won't risk trying to contact me once they're on the ground."

It was *probably* safe for them to transmit. Even if the Marines gave away their presence, the locals shouldn't be able to threaten him. Doctrine said they'd only use encrypted micro-pulses for communication in a combat zone, however, and his tattoo-comp couldn't read them.

"I can use this," Dancer said, hefting the rifle, "but it has been a long time."

"That's about how I feel about this," he replied, tapping the pistol he was holding. Shaking his head, he hit one final command on his tattoo-comp and closed the hologram.

"They're almost certainly rigging up explosives on the door outside," he told her. "Let's find some cover. Is anything in here actually bulletproof?"

"The electronics?" she suggested.

He nodded and looked at the communications equipment. It wouldn't survive being used as cover, but it would definitely stop bullets.

"Help me out here?"

Together, they managed to topple the largest chunk of the equipment and hide behind it—just in time for the door into the Chosen Mothers' offices to blow open.

"Throw down your arms and I will order mercy," Dancer-In-Darkness shouted. Octavio had a moment of terror, thinking she'd given away their position, before he realized she'd thrown her voice a good four or five meters away.

Vistan voice boxes were weird as hell to a human.

The answer to her generous offer, sadly, was gunfire. At least half a dozen rifles opened up on full automatic into the room she'd projected her voice into.

Dancer popped up, her chirps letting her target clearly as she walked her own automatic fire across the room.

The Chosen Mother had some aggression to work out, it seemed. Octavio tackled the froglike alien as his glance over the top saw a second wave of troopers moving in.

He was fast enough to get her out of the line of fire. He *wasn't* fast enough to do it safely, and a bullet hammered into his shoulder. He sprawled backward as fire radiated out from his shoulder.

"Stay down," he hissed at Dancer.

He was bleeding. He didn't dare look too closely. He didn't *think* it was critical, but it was more than a flesh wound. All he was getting from his left shoulder and arm was *pain*.

"You fool," she snapped. "Why?"

"Because I need you to save your people," he snapped.

"They're coming," she told him.

He snarled at the pain as he propped himself up and grabbed the pistol again. It was an awkward shape, but he got his finger on the trigger and pointed it at the door. They were out of the line of fire now. The Spears would have to come into the room to get them.

Of course, that meant they had no cover once the Spears were in the room.

"Promise me, Dancer," he demanded. "Promise me that you'll get your people on the evac ships. We have a whole planet waiting for you, one where you'll be safe."

He winced again.

"If you stay here, you'll all die. *Promise me*."

"We'll get my people out together, Captain Catalan."

He snorted. He could hear the footsteps, which meant that Dancer could definitely hear them.

"Sure, let's plan for—"

HISS-CRACK.

The Marines had brought pulse guns. Why the *hell* had they brought pulse guns?!

Multiple rounds of focused plasma cracked through the air, and he could hear both the sound of Vistan weaponry and the sharper noise of human hypervelocity firearms.

Then silence.

"Sir?" a voice called. "This is Sergeant Potts. Are you there?"

He tried to rise and fell backward. He'd lost a *lot* of blood.

"Can you understand me?" Dancer-In-Darkness asked loudly. "Your Captain is here but injured. I don't know your anatomy, but I think it might be bad."

Octavio realized that was an understatement right before he passed out.

30

Sings-Over-Darkened-Waters had retreated to her private office. The First-Among-Singers had long before mastered enough emotional control to keep her echolocation chirps from not showing *too* much, but the last few hours had strained her control to the breaking point.

And it was over.

"Will Captain Catalan be all right?" she asked the human currently commanding *Scorpion*. Sings did not know Renaud well, but then, she didn't know *Catalan* all that well.

"He will be," Renaud promised. "I will make sure of it. There is nowhere else in the system better equipped to handle his injuries."

There was probably nowhere else in the system that *could* handle an injured human.

"Your losses were light?" the Star-Choir's commander asked.

"We didn't lose anyone from the second wave," Renaud told her. "They understood just what kind of tech deficit they were facing when they shot down Major Summerfield's ship. Our pilot could have evaded or destroyed a dozen of their missiles.

"So they launched a hundred." The human female shook her head. "No chance of survivors. Nothing even left to bury."

"We will find what we can," Sings promised. "I will make certain of it. If I can make certain of anything in the Iron Peaks." She shivered. "We still do not know what will come of this."

"Well, right now, my people are in control of their primary command center, and we're not giving it back," Renaud replied. "If your Guardian-Star-Choir has some ground troops or personnel you can spare to help us run it, that would help us out, but Iron Peaks doesn't get that base back. Not after shooting down our shuttle and the Shining Spears' planes."

There would be consequences for that. Another Great Mother would have called for blood for blood. Sings hoped that Sleeps-In-Sunlight was better than that.

"Beyond that, however, what happens with the Iron Peaks is up to your people," Renaud concluded. "Captain Catalan made his pitch and got imprisoned and shot for it. We're not barring anyone from the evacuation ships, but I will be *damned* if we spend one more iota of effort on saving the Iron Peaks."

Sings-Over-Darkened-Waters bowed her head.

"I understand. I will make sure of it. No one will be left behind, Commander Aisha Renaud. I will not let this violence be in vain."

"That's on you," Renaud said. "Good luck...but my ability to care about your people's rogue assholes is far more limited than my Captain's."

"I understand," Sings repeated. "It seems I have some old enemies to speak to before the day is done."

———

DUTY CALLED in all of its munificent forms, and Sings-Over-Darkened-Waters spent over an hour dealing with the aftermath of the battle. What few ground troops the Star-Choirs possessed—mostly internal enforcers and security for space stations, really—were loaded onto shuttles and sent down to reinforce the Marines.

Then she got the request she'd been expecting and stepped back into her office to speak with the Great Mother who *technically* wasn't her ruler.

Of course, the Shining Mother now ruled the entire planet outside the Iron Peaks. There was no real question who the ruler of the Vistan people was—or that the Guardian-Star-Choirs answered to her.

"Shining Mother," Sings greeted Sleeps-In-Sunlight. "How may the Star-Choirs serve?"

"I need you to intercede as a neutral party," the younger female told her. "I need Star-Choir transportation to High Mountain in the morning—and I need *you* to speak to Dancer-In-Darkness and the other Chosen Mothers.

"After all of this mess, they *will* hear me speak."

"And if they refuse?" Sings-Over-Darkened Waters asked. "They remain an independent nation."

"One torn by war and attempting to abandon their own people to their deaths," Sleeps-In-Sunlight said harshly. "If the Chosen Mothers will not meet with me, then I will say what I must say in the streets of High Mountain. But I will visit the city and I will plead for the future of its people.

"I do not think they can stop me, and I don't really expect them to try...but I would prefer to be welcomed than tolerated," she noted. "That is far more likely if you speak to them on my behalf than if I reach out to them through normal channels."

"They do still have *some* air defenses," Sings pointed out. "And they are an independent nation still."

"They let Catalan get shot," Sleeps replied. "My sympathy for their concerns is limited, and I don't fear their weapons."

There were disadvantages, Sings-Over-Darkened-Waters supposed, to having a Great Mother with the will and charisma to lead a world by force of personality. Sometimes, the people trying to keep her alive and in power had to bow to the will of the Mother they served.

"I will see what I can do," she finally promised. "So long as *you* promise to be careful."

"Careful would negate my purpose, Sings-Over-Darkened-Waters," Sleeps-In-Sunlight noted. "I will save these people along with the rest. Too many of our kin are dead. I will *not* leave the people of the Iron Peaks to suffer.

"And if I must risk the ire of their half-broken government to save them, so be it."

———

SINGS-OVER-DARKENED-WATERS WAS STUDYING the door to her command pool, trying to figure out a plan for reaching out to the Chosen Mothers of Iron Peak, when her com officer opened the door.

"First-Among-Singers," the young male greeted her, taken aback as he took the full sound blast of a Vistan examining something in detail.

"What is it?" she asked.

"Voice-Of-The-Chosen Dancer-In-Darkness has made contact," he said slowly. "She wishes to speak with you."

That certainly made Sings's day easier.

"Connect her immediately," she ordered.

"As you will."

The young officer withdrew, and Sings turned her attention back to the transmission console. It would take the Voice-Novice roughly fifteen seconds to reach his console and connect the call.

That was more than enough time for Sings to take her seat and face the speaker/receiver combination that would create her echolocation image for Dancer-In-Darkness.

It was far from enough time for her to be ready for the call, but that was life. The image of the Iron Peaks' Chosen Mother appeared in a series of artificial chirps.

Dancer-In-Darkness was a rarity: a Vistan older than Sings who was also busily involved in the day-to-day life of a country. Most Vistans, especially females, who reached their age retreated into the protected domes of the Clan spawning pools, to help protect and raise the next generation of the family.

"Sings-Over-Darkened-Waters, First-Among-Singers of the Star-Choir and the voice we chose to lead the guardians of our world, I owe you an apology," Dancer-In-Darkness said calmly. "You have served your duty with honor and skill in the face of an impossible and unanticipated task.

"My fellow Chosen Mothers denied this and cast darkness on your actions and character. We were wrong, and I apologize for our choices."

"Your apology is appreciated," Sings replied. "I need to speak with you on matters, Chosen Mother, but I suspect you called me for more urgent aid."

"I did." Dancer bowed her head. "The violence in the city of High Mountain has spread across my nation. Things will shortly be under control, but we have many injured, often in places where we do not have hospitals or sufficient capacity to treat them.

"I would request that the Star-Choirs send us shuttles and doctors, that we reduce the losses from this damn foolishness."

"Do you speak for the Chosen Mothers in this?" Sings asked slowly. "Your fellows have been unwilling to accept our help in the past."

"I am the Voice-Of-The-Chosen," Dancer-In-Darkness replied. "I speak for what remains. Half of our number are dead, murdered by the traitor Warmest-Waters to secure her power. Only those she believed she could corrupt—or whose corruption would be beyond value, like myself—were spared. Of the living, a third or more were already her creatures. The rest are being treated as we speak.

"The Chosen Mothers have been battered and broken. We will rise again, but for now I speak for Iron Peaks."

"You will have your aid," Sings promised. "So long as no one tries to shoot down our shuttles and doctors, at least."

"Your human friends control our defenses," Dancer pointed out. "There will come a time when that is a problem, but it will be weeks from now. You may approach safely."

The two Vistans chirped assent at each other, then Dancer paused.

"You wished to speak to me as well?" she asked.

"The Shining Mother will visit your city tomorrow," Sings-Over-Darkened-Waters told the Chosen Mother. "I answer to her now; let us not pretend things are false that are true. She wishes to meet with the Chosen Mothers, but she will speak to your people regardless."

"She will be welcomed as an ally," Dancer-In-Darkness said after a long pause. "We must work together to salvage our people. Iron Peaks will not acknowledge her as our Great High Mother, not here...but compromises can be made in the structure of our new home."

"I do not believe Sleeps-In-Sunlight will care what title we hang on her," the First-Among-Singers replied. "She would rather get on with the job of saving us all. She is...impressive."

"Then I look forward to meeting her," Dancer replied. "We will stand together against the storm, regardless. That decision has been made. She has already won."

"None of us wanted victory over Iron Peaks, Dancer-In-Darkness," Sings told her. "All we ever wanted to do was save everyone."

"And we were deafened to the true sound of your intent by our own fears," the Iron Peaks Mother replied. "Our ears are clear now. We stand together."

"We stand together," Sings agreed.

31

Both Shankara Linton and Lyle Reinhardt had never given Isaac a reason to doubt their skills or efficiency. He'd still hesitated to believe it when Linton had told him that *Vigil* and her escorts would be ready in two months.

Watching as the massive ship nudged out of her building slip, he admitted he'd underestimated them.

Fifty-one days. They'd accelerated the construction project from six months to *fifty-one* days.

Half a kilometer of warship didn't clear a docking slip quickly. Her three escorts were already clear, the two-hundred-and-fifty-meter strike cruisers looking like half-scale clones of their bigger sister.

Romeo, Juliet and *Othello* were waiting for their big sister. The four of them were the only warships Isaac knew about that were capable of traveling at two hundred and fifty-six times the speed of light.

"*Vigil* will be clear and ready to begin her trials in ten minutes," Linton told him. "Are you sure you don't want to be aboard?"

"The last thing Captain Alstairs needs is me jogging his elbow when he has twenty-four hours to complete as much as he can of a two-week certification process," Isaac pointed out. "The strike cruisers?"

"They got *three* whole days of trials," Linton noted. "Two are done. They'll run through further tests today, but we wanted them here to make sure *Vigil* made it out without issues."

Isaac would have scoffed at the concept of protecting *Vigil*, a ship designed to chew up Matrix combat platforms and spit them out... except that he'd ordered *Dante*, alongside *Lancelot* and *Roland*, to come watch over the launch as well.

If they had any enemies who'd been watching and figured this was when the new battlecruiser was at her most vulnerable, they'd have a harsh surprise coming.

"What about the freighters?" he asked.

"*Hope* and *Legacy* are going through final work right now," the Minister for Orbital Industry told him. "The second ship is costing us an extra few days, but..."

"It'll be worth it," Isaac agreed. The freighters were a miracle, in his mind. He'd been promised one ship, equivalent to the freighters that were running around the Exilium System.

Linton and Reinhardt had given him two. Built from scratch, they would be fifty-five days from *initial concept* to *launch*. Each would carry a hundred thousand Vistans to safety every seventeen days.

Each of those ships was worth as much as the entire shipping fleet they'd already sent. It would take them ninety days to get to Vista once everything was online, but they'd be worth the wait.

They would actually get the two-fifty-six task force to the Vistans before the task group under Commodore Giannovi. Isaac was still glad they'd sent those ships, though.

Sooner or later, the Rogue was going to try to finish the job. He wanted every ship he could put between them and the Vistans when the time came.

"Once she's clear, I'm going to get out of everyone's hair and go do paperwork on Orbit One," Isaac told Linton. "More than busywork, but still...I think everyone will be happier to complete this process without the Admiral and the Minister watching over their shoulders."

"Oh, I agree," Linton said. "My plan is similar." He shook his head. "My plans would be even more pleasant, but someone sent my girl-friend on a rescue mission."

"You can sympathize with the President in about a week," Isaac replied. "Nobody, not even Amelie, thinks Task Force *Vigil* is leaving this star system without me."

———

BACK IN HIS OFFICE, Isaac turned one screen to tracking the battlecruiser's progress. The first step had been testing the warp drive, running all four two-fifty-six ships out to the edge of the star system.

Anything except the warp drives could be fixed en route if necessary. The warp drives could only be fixed there or at the other end. A failure could render the entire purpose of the second task force irrelevant.

So far, there had been no issues. His reports on the weapons testing and regular maneuvers were going to be an hour out of date, so his attention was back on his current task.

There hadn't been any significant problems when he'd taken the first Task Force *Vigil* to engage the Rogue, but there had been enough hints to worry him. That was why he'd promoted Giannovi to Commodore, with the intention of leaving her in charge when he left.

Instead, he'd sent her off in advance and found himself facing the same problem he'd left behind last time: the Exilium Space Fleet didn't really *have* flag officer postings. The handful of ships running scouting missions operated independently, and everything else was in Exilium with him.

He'd kept *meaning* to promote more people, but there'd always been something more urgent. At this point, his Captains had basically been in command of the same ships since they'd fought the Rogue. Seniority divided his senior officers, but they were all the same rank.

That was a mistake, he realized—to be fair, he'd known that all along—but it had been an easy thing to keep dropping to the bottom of the priority list.

His first impulse was to run his list by Giannovi, but she wasn't due to check in for another several days. He'd had Lauretta Giannovi as his strong right hand for a long time now, and it almost felt like he was missing an actual hand.

Isaac looked at his list for a long time and his gaze eventually slipped to the *second* name on the list. He tapped a command and waited a second for Orbit One's capable communications staff to get online.

"Sir?"

"Get me Captain Anderson," he ordered. "Live video link as soon as she's available."

That would take a few minutes—there was no priority like an Admiral calling, but battlecruiser Captains weren't known for sitting around in their quarters, drinking tea and moping.

That was an *Admiral's* prerogative.

———

"How can I assist you, Admiral?" Captain Margaret Anderson asked when she appeared on his screen just over four minutes later—without a teacup in sight.

Her desk aboard *Dante* was almost certainly more regularly used than Isaac's aboard Orbit One—which was only one of about six places the Admiral might be working on a given day—but it was also much more organized than the pile of datapads and used coffee cups Isaac had spread out.

The datapads, at least, would leave with him. The two coffee cups were…well, he had to admit they were just from today.

"I'm looking at promotion planning, Captain, and I doubt it's the best of plans for me to decide an entirely new section of our rank structure on my own," Isaac admitted. "I'd normally run this by Commodore Giannovi, but she is out-system. While we'll want the Cabinet to sign off on some of these, I wanted a second opinion from one of our key officers."

"I am…somewhat biased, at least with regards to my *own* promotion, sir," Anderson admitted. "I'd be pleased to help you with the rest."

Isaac pointed a finger at her in a facsimile of a magic wand or ancient knighting ritual.

"Boom, you're a Vice Admiral as soon as the Cabinet signs off," he told her with a grin. "Giannovi gets bumped as well. I'm eyeing four Commodores to back you two up, and then we'll need to adjust the commands to account for my yanking five Captains up to flag rank."

Anderson paused, taking a second to digest that.

"You have a list, sir?" she asked.

"Transmitting," Isaac told her. "Take a look."

Anderson already was. He couldn't see her screen, but she was silent for twenty seconds or so as she skimmed the list.

"It's a good list," she told him. "I can tell you one problem we're going to have, though."

"Oh?"

"You're jumping half a dozen people past Cavan, who is technically our most senior Captain," she said. "And he's been making friends in the Senate who might question what's going on there."

Robert Cavan commanded *Demeter*, one of their *Icicle*-class destroyers. He'd been skipped when Isaac had picked officers for the strike cruisers, and skipped for the missile-cruiser slot that had opened up from that.

Now, having already promoted one officer past Cavan specifically to command *Vigil*, they were opening up three more commands...and none of them were going to Robert Cavan.

Nor were any of the four Commodore slots.

Isaac sighed.

"I can deal with him being unhappy. He's a damn Fleet officer; he should know when to sit down and shut up."

"I hate to be the asshole's advocate," Anderson replied, "but he actually *didn't* raise a fuss over the strike cruisers when we all expected him to. He caused trouble when he was the senior-most Captain without anyone officially over him...but it wasn't *that* much trouble."

"Are you saying we're not giving him a fair shake?" Isaac asked.

"I don't *like* Robert Cavan," she admitted. "But I have to recognize that he's a perfectly competent officer whose *crew* admires him and we've frankly been beating him up for his misstep while you were gone for three years."

"You know what being his advocate is going to get you, right?" Isaac pointed out. "With your promotion, he actually becomes our most senior Captain. If I'm moving him at all, there's only one place he can go—and I expect you to fly your flag from *Dante*."

Margaret Anderson leveled a calm death glare on him, but he'd faced down his mother. There weren't many humans left in the galaxy who could intimidate him.

"I was hoping to put him on, say, *Roland*," she admitted. "But you're right. Let's move Captain Silas to *Roland* and given Cavan *Dante*. If nothing else, I'm pretty sure I can teach him whatever limits he's forgotten."

Isaac smiled. He hadn't considered the degree to which they had been leaving Cavan behind as a legitimate gripe on the man's part, but Anderson was right. Cavan had never actually *done* anything to deserve the black mark he'd struggled under.

And if *Admiral* Anderson was prepared to take him on as her flag Captain, then that answered that question.

"Then I think we have a list, Captain Anderson—which means that, unless the Cabinet is more obstreperous than I expect, *you* will shortly be hanging some stars on your collar."

"Great," she replied flatly. "I'm so looking forward to that headache —especially since this means you're leaving *me* in command, doesn't it?"

"And we see the proof that you are definitely smart enough to be an Admiral," Isaac confirmed with a grin.

32

Isaac woke up to find Amelie leaning on her arm, examining him in silence.

"Well?" he asked, studying her in turn without really rising. "I have some evidence you like what you see, but what's up?"

"Mostly that you're heading out on *another* damn-fool expedition that's going to take you out of my life for months upon months," she told him. "What's the chance you'll be back before my term is up?"

"Low," he admitted. A little over eight months were left before Amelie's role switched to a caretaker position while the election ran. Even if he turned around immediately upon reaching the Hearthfire System, he'd be gone for six of those.

"I'm probably going to be out there, either at Vista or Refuge, for at least six months," he told her. None of this was *news*, really, but it had a new impact now.

All six two-fifty-six ships had passed their trials. None had done so with flying colors, per se, but all of the minor and medium issues raised on the four warships and two transports could be fixed in warp.

At noon Starhaven time, Isaac would report aboard *Vigil* to take command of the battle group and leave Exilium for at least a year.

"I swear I should have married someone less likely to run off without me," Amelie noted, still looking down at him. "Maybe with less of a sense of duty. I'm sure the President could have found someone willing to be a kept man."

"You'd have been bored with a kept man in a week," Isaac replied. "Face it, my love. The very things we love about each other are why we keep dragging ourselves apart. Someone has to go to Vista with the fleet, and I'm not sending anyone else. Not when we're looking at a serious extended war with a Regional Matrix."

If nothing else, *Vigil* was the only ship in their arsenal with a chance in hell of engaging a Regional Matrix's defenses. The upgrades and light particle cannons meant that the rest of his fleet could go toe-to-toe with the usual array of Matrix combatants, but they had *no* idea what a Rogue Regional Matrix might have assembled to protect itself.

He didn't even know what XR-13-9 had for defenses. The core brain behind their ally had never been so open as to tell them where it was, let alone what it guarded itself with.

"I'm leaving you with Vice Admiral Anderson, *Dante* and the bulk of the fleet," he told her. "*Hamlet*, *Puck* and *Macbeth* should be online within six months. That'll give you a battlecruiser and three strike cruisers, plus an entire armada of destroyers and old cruisers, to keep the planet safe."

"I know." She sighed. "The Senate is meeting on the budget request for *Watchtower* tomorrow. Emilia says you're getting your battlecruiser, but it's not fixed until they approve it."

Watchtower would be a clone of the new *Vigil*. She was expected to take a year less to build than *Vigil*, but he still wouldn't have his third battlecruiser for two years.

If he wanted a third *Vigilance*-class ship, he'd have to scrap *Dante*. Not because the Cabinet and Senate wouldn't give him the funding, but because Exilium's population and industry couldn't truly support four battlecruisers.

He wasn't entirely sure, some days, how they supported the fleet they had.

"The good news is that everything we're seeing out of Vista is starting to sound hopeful," he told her. "The Matrices' help has been nothing short of extraordinary. They're on track to have the entire population in space in six more months."

Three months after the oceans started to freeze over, but before the planetwide storms rendered Vista inaccessible as well as uninhabitable. The terraformers the Matrices had dropped on Vista might one day restore the planet, but Isaac wasn't betting on it.

It would probably take XR-13-9's Matrices dropping *more* terraformers on the planet to save it.

Amelie finally bent to kiss him, pressing herself against him with a desperation he shared.

"I have to go," he finally confessed.

"I know. I won't ask you not to; I know better! But be careful, my love. Promise me?"

"I will," he promised. "I'm coming back." He gestured vaguely at her naked form. "I mean, seriously, have you *seen* who's waiting for me?!"

———

ISAAC WAS USED to the immense length of battlecruisers. He'd even done close-in inspection tours of the new *Vigil* when she was being built and had spent time aboard *Liberty*, the Confederacy's only dreadnought, before the Exile.

It was still shocking to approach the immense structure of the new battlecruiser and see it moving under its own power. According to Lyle Reinhardt's research, *Vigil* was the biggest human-built ship to ever carry a warp drive—an honor previously held by the amalgamated wreckage of *Dante* and the old *Vigil*.

Dante had ended up as a hybrid, torn in multiple directions between the old Confederacy battlecruiser she'd been, the combat platform the Matrices had tried to refit her into and the new-generation battlecruiser they'd already been designing when she was rebuilt.

She would never truly be any of those things. *Vigil* was a purely human-designed ship, enabled equally by the massive exotic-matter production of the Republic of Exilium and Matrix power-generation and weapons technology.

The idea of a battlecruiser with not just a spinal particle cannon but *multiple* turrets mounting more would have seemed impossible to Isaac ten years earlier. The gamma ray lasers she used as secondary heavy weapons would have been purely theoretical to that younger officer.

Her escorts now used even more powerful versions of those grasers as their main spinal guns, reinforced by the same turreted light particle cannons *Vigil* carried. Any of those strike cruisers could have fought the battlecruiser he'd arrived with to a standstill.

And all of it, combined, paled in comparison to what he was afraid he might have to face. The first Rogue they'd fought had nearly destroyed the fledgling ESF, and it had been a mere *Sub-Regional* Matrix.

A full Regional Matrix like XR-13-9 represented a level of industry, terraforming and manufacturing capability he couldn't even comprehend. A Sub-Regional Construction Matrix would be responsible for the simultaneous terraforming—the titular construction—of two to three worlds.

A Regional Matrix was apparently responsible for the construction of at least ten, plus however many its Sub-Regional Matrices handled. XR-13-9, from what Isaac knew, was managing *twenty* planets.

The entire conflict he'd been dragged into had so far been fought with a miniscule portion of the AI's resources. He wasn't sure what the new Rogue would do when faced with a real challenge...but he doubted it was going to be pretty.

"Take us in, Lieutenant Roger," he ordered the young officer flying the shuttle on the unofficial inspection tour. "That's enough sightseeing for one day." He smiled grimly. "We have a job to do."

ISAAC STEPPED off the shuttle to a small honor guard of Marines. The landing bay was mostly empty of people, but the Marines merged with his regular guard and ushered him across the open space anyway to where two officers were waiting for him.

Captain Cameron Alstairs was similar in height and build to Isaac, but with almost translucently pale skin and a neatly cut black beard.

His new executive officer was standing to his right, and both men saluted as Isaac approached.

"Welcome aboard *Vigil*, Admiral Lestroud," Alstairs greeted him. "I'd love to say welcome *back*, but despite the name, she's a new ship. I like to think the spirit lives on."

"So do I, Captain," Isaac agreed. "Is everything in order?"

"*Vigil* has a few glitches and scrapes to deal with, but we'll have them in order by the time we've reached Hearthfire," Alstairs said. "Your staff came aboard shortly before you and are busily setting up your flag deck. Is there anything specific you need?"

Isaac glanced over his shoulder at his personal steward, Petty Officer Parminder Singh.

"Parminder?" he asked.

"So long as someone shows me to the Admiral's quarters and helps me carry the luggage, I'm good," the impeccably patient noncom replied.

"We can manage that," Alstairs replied. "Would you like the tour, Admiral?"

"I've already had it, Captain," Isaac admitted. "How long until we're in motion?"

"Fifteen minutes or so, sir."

"Then I need to get to the flag deck. I may not *like* speeches, but this seems like a time for them, don't you agree?"

"I can't argue," Alstairs confirmed. "This way, sir."

Isaac followed him deeper into the ship. A sight just past the access from the bay stopped him for a moment as he studied it.

The ship's commissioning seal would be scattered all over the vessel. It wasn't the same as the old *Vigil*—if nothing else, it lacked the ring of stars of the old Confederacy flag—but it still held the same logo for the ship: the Eye of Horus.

The eye held the center of the circular seal, above the three rockets from the flag of Exilium and below the letters BC-01.

The old *Vigil* had been the sixteenth battlecruiser built for the Confederacy, but *this* ship was the first battlecruiser ever built by the Exilium Space Fleet. BC-01 it was.

"Sir?" Alstairs asked softly.

"Lead on, Captain. I got distracted by an old friend."

———

THE FLAG DECK on the new *Vigil* had been upgraded from the old one, but not by much. There had been other focuses, which meant this part of the ship looked familiar: a massive holographic display surrounded by various consoles for the Admiral's staff.

Isaac knew most of the people in here by sight if not by name. They'd been scattered across the surface, Orbit One and *Dante* until *Vigil* commissioned, but now his staff was all in one place.

"Commander Connor," Isaac said loudly as he stepped onto the flag deck. "Status report on the battle group!"

Commander Aloysius Connor was a tall man with thick red dreadlocks carefully arranged and cut to stay within the ESF's generous rules. He turned from where he stood, leaning over a junior officer's console, and saluted him.

Connor had been the old *Vigil*'s tactical officer and was now the operations officer on Isaac's staff.

"All ships report warp drives and engines green," he reported. "All of the warships are between eighty-five and ninety-two percent readiness status overall. All parts are aboard to repair all of that before we reach Hearthfire.

"Battle group is prepared to move out on your command."

"Excellent," Isaac replied. "Hashemi, get me an all-hands channel to all six ships."

Lieutenant Naveed Hashemi was his communications officer, one of the handful of new officers who'd entered adulthood on Exilium.

"You're on, sir," he reported.

"Officers and crew of Task Force *Vigil*," Isaac said calmly. "We are about to head out on another long-term mission, requiring us to endure months in warped space to deal with the Matrices' homicidal cousins.

"Some of you have asked why. Why us? Why them? Why do we care what the robots get up to fifty light-years away?"

He smiled thinly.

"And in all honesty, if it was just the robots, I would not care," he told them. "If there were a Regional Construction Matrix fifty light-years away that was just happily terraforming worlds and ignoring us, I'd let it be.

"But they're not *just* terraforming worlds. They're wiping out entire civilizations and they don't even care. That kind of destructive callousness is all too familiar to me. Worst of all, though, is that if we stand by and permit the Matrices to destroy entire civilizations, entire sentient species…*we* have accepted that kind of destructive callousness.

"That is what doomed the Confederacy. What broke my mother's honor and the honor of the Confederacy Space Fleet."

He had everyone's attention aboard *Vigil*, at least.

"We are here, seventy thousand light-years from home, because we decided that that wasn't good enough. That we had to be better, to rise above the shadow that had consumed our nation. Now we are faced with the test of that resolve, that commitment.

"The Confederacy would have let the Vistans die. But we are *not* the Confederacy. We are the Republic of Exilium, and we have sworn to ourselves that we will be *better*."

He realized he was clenching his fists and that everyone on all six ships could see that. He forced himself to release them as he was silent for a moment.

"So, we will be better," he told his crews. "And when an entire species stands to fall into darkness unless we act, we will act.

"Today that falls to us. I know you will do everything in your power to see this task force achieve its goals and save the Vistans—and for that, I thank you.

"We move out in five minutes. Godspeed, spacers of Exilium!"

33

"JUST BECAUSE I can bind your arm up so that it doesn't move does *not* mean you are in any fit state to be back on duty!"

Surgeon-Lieutenant Commander Dr. Youji Nakajima did not cut anything resembling an imposing figure. The Japanese-extraction Exilium Space Fleet officer was short, dark-skinned and chubby. With his hands on his hips and his dark eyes leveled at Octavio Catalan, however, he may as well have been Cerberus guarding the gates of the underworld.

"So long as my arm is bound, it isn't getting in the way, and I need to get back to work," Octavio replied. "There's only so much I can do from a sickbay bed."

"Well, get used to it," Nakajima replied, taking one hand from his hip to hand Octavio a plate with a sandwich. Octavio hadn't asked for the food but dug into it almost unthinkingly as the doctor continued.

"You came back aboard with your left scapula in forty-six separate pieces," the doctor reminded him. "You'd lost over a liter of blood by the time I had you on the table. Bone fragments finally collapsed your left lung while you were coming aboard ship—and if your lung had gone any sooner, I'm not sure you would have made it!"

"And you've done a fantastic job, Doctor," Octavio replied, laying the plate on the neat stack of them next to his bed. "But it's been almost three weeks. We've had the evacuation fleet return, reload and leave since you chained me to this bed. Hell, last numbers I saw were that we've moved a *hundred million people* into orbit while I've been in here."

"Which is now on our Vistan friends." Nakajima handed Octavio a protein bar of some kind. The Captain took it with an arched eyebrow at the doctor, who continued to speak.

"You're getting updates, you're in the loop and you've participated in more damn video calls than I bloody authorized—no, I'm *not* blind, Captain," the doctor snapped. "Renaud and the Vistans can handle everything going on. *You* need to stay in here where I can keep you monitored, because you shouldn't be doing anything more than eating and sleeping right now."

"I'm awake and I'm not hungry," Octavio protested.

The doctor returned the arched eyebrow. "Where's the protein bar I just handed you, Captain?" he asked.

Octavio paused and looked down at his hand. He could have sworn he hadn't done anything with the bar, but no...he'd unwrapped it and eaten it without even realizing it.

"You're undergoing accelerated regeneration," Nakajima reminded him again, handing him a second protein bar. "*Normal* healing would require bed rest for an injury of this magnitude, since your body would be absorbing all of your metabolic energy.

"With modern regeneration, that's ten times as true."

Octavio was *aware* of eating the protein bar this time, but it certainly didn't feel like anything he had a choice about.

"So, you're staying in my sickbay, under twenty-four-hour supervision, until your lung is fully healed and your scapula is fully reknitted. Then—and *only* then—will I sign off on your return to duty."

"I'm pretty sure the Marines on this ship still follow my orders," Octavio pointed out.

"And if there is an actual emergency, that might matter," Nakajima said sweetly. "But right now, you need to rest and eat...and trust me, Captain, *nobody* understands that better than Marines."

"NO. NOT A CHANCE IN HELL."

Octavio woke up to the sound of Nakajima's voice clearly telling *somebody* off.

"If nothing else, the damn thing won't fit," the doctor continued. "And I'm not letting the Captain leave the sickbay. He's well on his way, but this kind of accelerated healing is a delicate process."

"Doctor, do you really think I'm trying to bring a Matrix remote into the sickbay because it would be funny?" Aisha Renaud asked. "ZDX is only willing to give *me* the roughest summary of what they found at Refuge and I agree with their assessment. The Captain needs to know."

"Then the computer can get him on a video call in a few hours once he's awake," Nakajima countered. "Or wait until he can leave here without being hooked up to tubes. Refuge is six light-years away. Nothing there can be this urgent."

Octavio's curiosity was definitely piqued at this point.

"Commander, send them in," he ordered loudly. A moment later, the curtain was yanked back and he could see the two arguing officers.

"Doesn't matter what you order," Nakajima told him. "They're not getting the damn combat Matrix's remote in here—and why am I the only one who finds the fact that the *combat* Matrices have remotes that can fit in our ship hallways disturbing?"

"Then sort out how you're getting me into a conference room," Octavio ordered, holding the chubby doctor's gaze. "Youji—you're right and you've been right all along. I know I haven't been the easiest patient, but if the Matrices need to speak to me, that *is* the kind of priority I'm going to overrule you on.

"So, unless you want to yank the lever that allows you to relieve me of command, you're going to put everything you need in a wheelchair and get me into a space where I can talk to the remote."

Octavio forced a smile. He really didn't want to have a fight there, but he also trusted Renaud's judgment. If she said he needed to talk to the Matrix, he believed he needed to talk to the Matrix.

"Fine," the doctor snapped. "Give me thirty minutes—and you *get* thirty minutes before I'm hauling you back in here, understood?"

"I understand," Octavio conceded. He needed to talk to ZDX-175-14, so he'd overrule his doctor to do that. That didn't mean he wasn't aware of how badly injured he was.

―――――

RENAUD WHEELED the chair into the conference room with a surprising degree of delicacy. More than Octavio would have taken with himself, that was for sure.

He *could* walk, but he was also well aware of Nakajima's point around both his need to eat and how quickly he ran out of energy. It would be another two weeks before he was fully healed, and until then he would be weak and easily fatigued.

Octavio couldn't object too much. The kind of injury he'd taken would have crippled his arm for life at one point. He'd tolerate a few weeks of feeling like a wet kitten and being babied by his crew in exchange for getting use of his arm back.

The single occupant of the conference room was interesting, though. He'd barely noticed Nakajima mentioning that the combat Matrices had remotes that could fit inside human ships. Now, face to "face" with one of those remotes, he had to swallow a shiver of fear.

It had the same form factor as the diplomatic remote on Exilium that he'd seen pictures of, but it was slimmer. Still two meters tall and two meters long, it was only a meter and a quarter or so wide. It was still a broad and heavy centaur-like machine, but it could fit through the doors and corridors of an ESF warship.

It was also *very* obviously armed, at least to the eyes of an engineer. It had the same three-fingered arms as the diplomatic unit, but there were plates on its chest that were designed to slide away. Those potentially only concealed tools, but Octavio didn't think so.

This was a battle remote, and he had to wonder just why the Matrices' creators had decided to equip their terraformers with robotic units clearly intended to board and capture other starships.

"*Captain Octavio Catalan,*" the remote greeted him. "*This remote is tachyon-linked to Combat Coordination Matrix ZDX-175-14. It is positive to see you recovering."*

"I'm lucky to have the best of care," Octavio replied. Renaud locked the wheelchair in place next to the table and then took her own seat. "My doctor has informed me that I have thirty minutes for this meeting, ZDX. Commander Renaud tells me that I needed to hear what you've discovered."

"You do. As the local authority of the Republic of Exilium, we require your assistance with an unexpected project of maximum urgency."

"We have no resources here that aren't already dedicated to evacuating Vista," Octavio said carefully. "How urgent is this that it cannot wait?"

"Urgency is high, as we have approximately four thousand four hundred hours to act upon the intelligence before the target passes beyond easy reach of the Refuge System. You require information updating. May this node provide background?"

"Go ahead," Octavio ordered. "Renaud?"

"Conference room systems are isolated from the main network. You should be able to link in," she told the Matrix remote.

A moment later, a holographic presentation of the Refuge System appeared above the table. Four icons marked Matrix ships, and ten more declared the location of the warp-drive freighters.

"This imagery is of the most recent arrival of evacuees," ZDX told them. *"It was the ability to interpolate data from fourteen sources, including their flight in-system, that allowed us to identify the anomaly."*

The hologram shifted, zooming out to add a flashing red icon. Octavio studied the scale for a few seconds.

"That's over a light-year from Refuge," he pointed out. "How is it of interest to us?"

"Because it is an artificial object traveling at ninety-nine point nine nine percent of lightspeed," ZDX told him. *"What data we have been able to extract from attempts at more detailed analysis give us this."*

The image that appeared on the hologram was vague, clearly limited by the amount of clean data the Matrices could extrapolate from an object moving at 0.9999c. It was still...distinctly of the same heritage as the Matrices themselves.

The object was an elongated ovoid, roughly ten times as long as it was high, with what Octavio presumed to be a thrust assembly at the back of the vessel. The engines didn't look like anything he'd ever seen, but they had to be engines.

"Any idea of the actual scale here?" he asked.

"Difficult to say with relativistic interference," ZDX admitted. *"Estimate is two point two kilometers plus/minus point seven kilometers."*

So, anywhere from a kilometer and a half long to three kilometers long. That was a *damn* big ship.

"That's the size of one of our colony transports, sir," Renaud pointed out.

At the small end. At the big end, the strange object was a *lot* bigger than one of the transports the Confederacy had crammed a quarter-million people aboard.

"It's one of yours?" Octavio asked ZDX. "I thought you all used a reactionless engine."

"We do. The system we use for propulsion has a maximum sustained velocity of ten percent of lightspeed. Use of sacrificial propulsive units is required for our missile weaponry, but the destructive nature of that process would not enable it to be used for any vessel required to survive.

"This ship does not use the same propulsive technology we do, but its hull is the same materials, and we have detected tachyon-punch signatures of other vessels attempting to keep up with it."

It can't be. Octavio stared at the hologram as ZDX continued.

"It is not a Matrix vessel but is based on the same design heritage and technology. We believe, Captain Octavio Catalan, that we are looking at one of our Creators' relativistic colony ships."

"Because the tachyon punch was fatal to organics," Octavio reminded himself aloud. "They had to follow in ships like this...but this course makes no sense, then."

There was no clear destination for the ship. Its course seemed to have been selected to *avoid* any stars in the region—any stars where there would have been Constructed Worlds.

"Shouldn't they be looking for Matrices?" he asked.

"While we are not in full contact with the rest of the Regional Construction Matrices, none of the nodes we are in contact with have ever

encountered the Creators," ZDX told them. *"Some of those nodes are closer to what we believe to be our origin zone. If the Creators were trying to colonize the Constructed Worlds, those nodes should have encountered them first."*

"What if they know about the Rogues?" Renaud asked.

"Then they might be *trying* to avoid the Matrices and the Constructed Worlds," Octavio realized. "Then the course makes sense —they're trying to outpace the expansion of their own creations."

He shook his head.

"They'd have to go a long damn way to be clear of the Matrices, though. *I* wouldn't be comfortable being less than three or four hundred light-years clear of you guys if I knew the Rogues existed and I had a choice."

ZDX didn't seem particularly offended by that.

"That conclusion fits with our data," it said after several moments of processing. *"We had not predicted that potential reaction on the part of our Creators. Your perspective is invaluable, Captain Octavio Catalan, Commander Aisha Renaud.*

"That value only adds to what we must ask of you."

Octavio traded a look with Renaud. They had a lot going on there, but the chance to meet with the Matrices' Creators...that was a *big* deal.

"What do you need?" he finally asked.

"We require your assistance in the construction of a vessel specially designed to intercept the Creator ship and slow it down to a velocity where we can speak to its crew. Our intent was to provide the vessel with a Matrix core to avoid the necessity for an organic crew, but your point regarding the Rogues has been considered by XR-13-9, and that intention is no longer optimal."

"You need someone to board the ship and talk to your Creators who isn't you," Renaud interpreted. "Because they'll assume you are Rogues and try to kill you."

"Exactly. Our propulsive systems cannot reach the velocity demonstrated by the Creator vessel, but our analysis suggests that yours are capable of reaching a matching vector in approximately thirty-four hours."

"Thirty-four hours that will be over fifty *days* for the crew," Octavio pointed out. "And another fifty days to decelerate. And it's not like we have a ship with multiples of cee in delta-*v*."

Scorpion was designed for missions of massive duration, including vast amounts of maneuvering and acceleration. She had the capacity to produce her own fuel, but her total delta-*v* aboard was only about half lightspeed in total.

Any long-distance flights were expected to be done under warp drive.

"If we pull them into warped space once we match vectors, we're at least no longer time-dilated," Renaud pointed out. "That would let us have a conversation with them and at least *ask* if they want to be slowed down."

"Can't you talk to them by tachyon coms?" Octavio asked.

"*We have attempted. Their tachyon-communication system appears to be receiving, but there has been no response, even accounting for time dilation. We would presume a ship of our Creators to have some AI aboard, but we have not even received basic ping information we would have expected from that.*

"*The ship does appear to have companions using repeated tachyon punches to keep up with it. We are not sure of their purpose, but we presume they are escorts.*"

"So, let me make sure I'm assessing the right request here," Octavio said. "You want us to build a ship, from scratch, using our engines and a massive fuel tank, to match velocities with a cee-fractional slowboat your Creators are using to try and outrun you. Then you want us to convince them to talk to you?"

"*We will construct the hull and provide the fuel. We will require Captain Octavio Catalan to provide the engines and warp drive. We estimate this will take approximately two thousand five hundred hours, plus/minus one hundred hours.*"

Three months. Lestroud would be there by then, which would help keep Vista safe—plus, over half of the evacuation would be completed by then.

"What about the habitat project?" he asked.

"*The interceptor vessel will be constructed in Refuge,*" ZDX replied. "*Construction projects here in Hearthfire will not be impacted. We would be prepared to hand the vessel, including its Matrix core, over to your command."*

That had potential all on its own. The Matrices had generally been *very* leery about letting humans anywhere near a core. One with instructions to be loyal to and cooperate with humans could help them leap their AI tech forward by generations.

"I still have to ask what's in it for us," Octavio admitted. The chance to talk to the Matrices' Creators was huge, but he only had so many resources. To build this interceptor, he'd have to send the best warp-drive and propulsion engineers he had to Refuge...which meant he'd have to take command of that expedition himself.

There was only one person in the Republic of Exilium who understood warp drives better than Octavio Catalan, and Lyle Reinhardt wasn't a warship Captain.

"*XR-13-9 is prepared to provide a full transfer of the entirety of our data archives: technical, astrographic, scientific and historical,*" ZDX told him. "*If you help us reach our Creators, we will give you everything.*"

Octavio exhaled sharply, wincing against the pain in his shoulder as he looked back at Renaud.

"We'll have to work out a schedule of when we'll need to send propulsion and warp-drive people to Refuge, then," he told her. "And I'll have to accompany the warp-drive team. I'll take command of *Interceptor* myself."

He realized he'd already given the ship a name. He'd agreed to the project while he was still arguing.

What else could he do? It was the engineering challenge of a lifetime—with a chance to meet the people who'd built the Matrices at the end of it!

34

THE STABLE GRAVITY points around Vista were starting to resemble unfertilized egg sacs to Sings-Over-Darkened-Waters. Vista's orbital industry had been turned to one purpose only, and the immense fabricators concealed inside the Matrices' ships had proven incredibly useful.

Nine habitats a week had managed to become fifteen. Now, as they reached the hundred-day mark since the Impact, over halfway through the half-orbit they'd estimated Vista would remain habitable, clusters of habitats hung above her world.

Over a hundred immense orbital habitats orbited under the guns of her fleet. Almost a quarter of her surviving people lived aboard those stations now, forcing themselves to continue some semblance of normal life—as if the stations could be their permanent home.

"We're going to need to divert some of our construction capacity to food-production facilities," Swimmer-Under-Sunlit-Skies told her, the younger male manipulating a datasong she was only half-paying attention to.

Her Voice-Of-Gunnery had become her Voice-Of-Choirs. She hadn't had a second-in-command before, preferring to spread the tasks across the staff assembled to lead the Guardian-Star-Choir.

As the true First-Among-Singers of all spacecraft of the Vistan people, however, she'd learned she needed someone to lean on. That someone had been Swimmer-Under-Sunlit-Skies, whose youthful green skin concealed one of the cleverest minds she had encountered.

"How bad is it looking?" she trilled back at him.

"Production at the greenhouse-augmented farms at the surface is falling over thirty percent below projections," he told her. "Worse, the temperatures in our growing regions dropped faster than we expected. We've just confirmed the full damage, First-Among-Singers. We lost the entire crop."

"Darkest waters consume us," she hissed. They'd hoped to get one last crop out of the farmland remaining—enough food to feed the entire surviving population for over a year. Without that crop, their ability to feed the people on the habitats dropped drastically.

They had always been going to run out of food before they could get enough food production online in space to feed a billion people. She'd *known* that; it was part of why evacuation to Refuge was really the only option.

"Do we have any updates on the farming projects on Refuge?" she asked.

"Mixed news so far," Swimmer replied. "They're going well enough that the evacuees are self-sufficient, but there's still only four hundred thousand of them. Some of the reports we got with the last round-trip of the evac fleet suggested some concern over expanding the farms fast enough."

So, there was no way they could extract food from the new colony in enough quantity to keep the habitats fed. The habitats themselves were far too large for the human's warp drives to transport—she'd asked.

Only the warp-drive freighters provided by the humans were moving people so far. The Matrices and humans were working with her engineers to build some test-bed warp-drive craft there in Hearthfire, but the technology was beyond her people—and, amusingly enough to her, apparently beyond the Matrices themselves.

"We'll have to re-task the production working on the bombers," Sings-Over-Darkened-Waters finally decided.

They'd built just over two hundred of the tiny, two-Vistan attack craft. Each carried two of the bomb-pumped lasers that armed her guardships, but *nobody* had any illusions about their survivability.

They were suicide ships and the Vistans piloting them knew it. Sings hoped to get one salvo from them before they were flagged as a threat. Once the Rogue Matrices started engaging them at any range at all, the bombers would never get close enough to hurt them.

"I'm not sure that production will even be useful," Swimmer warned. "Those are smaller facilities, ones not big enough to build large stations."

"We don't need large stations," Sings replied. "We need strings of orbital greenhouses. It doesn't matter if those greenhouses are only ten meters long; we just need enough space to stuff a hydroponic crop pod in them.

"Everything we have left that isn't building orbitals starts building hydroponic greenhouses," she ordered. "However large the facility can build them. It doesn't help us if we get a billion people into orbit and ready to evacuate if they starve before we move them to Refuge!"

Despite her harsh words, though, the datasong she was running gave her hope. They *should* be able to get enough hydroponics online to buy them enough time. Not enough to feed everyone forever but enough to spin out their existing food supplies to get everyone to Refuge.

Every day that passed, every habitat that came online, every milestone her people hit on the new evacuation ships...the math in her datasongs looked better.

It was starting to look like they might just pull this off...and in her heart of hearts, Sings-Over-Darkened-Waters hadn't truly believed they would.

———

A SHUTTLE DELIVERED Sings-Over-Darkened-Waters to the newest of the orbital habitats several hours later. The inspection tours were a formality, really. To complete the true inspections in the time needed took teams of thousands, poring over every nook and cranny of the space station in barely two days.

But it made even those teams feel better to have the top leaders go through and look at their work. This one had been built by Vistans, too, so there was a morale factor in making them feel their work was equal to the stations being built by the Matrices.

Once the shuttle was latched on, the rotating force of the cylindrical habitat pushed Sings against the floor of the shuttlecraft. The habitats were running a pseudo-force of about eighty percent of Vista's gravity, easy enough to walk against but still an adjustment from the zero-gravity shuttle or the sixty percent her guardships used in their rotating habitat sections.

Uniformed Shining Spears were waiting for her. The Shining Mother had insisted that Sings be escorted at all times...and when Sings had admitted that the Star-Choirs didn't have the Spears for it, she'd sent up her own troops.

"Welcome to Sleepy-Sunset Station, First-Among-Singers," a tall Vistan Mother greeted Sings. The female was middle-aged, the distinct mottling of age present across her entire body but not dominant yet. "I am Walks-In-Moonlight, the Voice-Of-Builders of the inspection team."

"It's always a pleasure to see our latest hope," Sings replied. "Where would you like to begin, Voice-Of-Builders?"

"The entryway has an observation space, to help our new residents understand just what they're dealing with," the Mother replied. "Follow me!"

Walks-In-Moonlight led the way along the curved surface of the station. From her movements, she was as used to zero gravity as to the strange pseudoforce a spinning station used in place of gravity. She'd clearly been working on the projects for a while.

They kept expanding, added more teams and more slips as they freed up new resources. Sings had been amazed at just how many of the stations her people could build. It was going to save them all, and still her people had taken up the task with more enthusiasm and drive than she'd expected.

Survival was an incredible motivator, and it seemed Sings had underestimated her people.

Walks-In-Moonlight led them through a large set of sliding doors into an unwalled atrium that looked out over the entire cylinder. Carefully designed acoustics carried the echolocation patterns of the entire station into this room, allowing a Vistan to take it all in.

Sings swallowed as she studied it. She'd been aboard seven of the stations by now, but they still hurt her heart every time she "saw" them. The old datasongs and sculptures of what an orbital habitat would look like had called for water and beauty and life and grace.

These stations had water. Ice asteroids had been melted down to fill vast regions of the outermost hull with water and allow for streams and ponds throughout the cold metal.

That was it. The "buildings" were designed to resemble the domes and structures of a surface settlement, but it was a poor resemblance. The station had four habitable levels, three of them only sixty percent complete to allow for *some* esthetic effect.

Water ran over all four levels, providing the warm humidity that her people craved, but there were only handfuls of plants and trees. If they'd had *time*, a habitat of this size could have had a self-sustaining ecosystem, at least as far as plant life and air were concerned.

They didn't have time. The stations were designed to hold two million souls. Comfort had been a factor, but *survival* came first. Food and water would come from off-station, from the infrastructure and storage that hung in closer orbit around Vista still.

Every time she went over the numbers, part of her wondered why they couldn't just stay here, in stations that could at least see their homeworld. As she stood in the observation space, though, she understood why.

These were immense and safe refugee camps. They could become homes in theory, but there was nowhere left to source the plant and animal life of Vista beyond their hydroponics farms—and those plants were needed to feed everyone.

In time, perhaps a few would be transformed into permanent homes for a contingent that remained. Enough of her people were still refusing to leave the surface that Sings was grimly sure they'd have some who would stay in the habitats.

The rest, though, would serve as temporary homes and be abandoned. Potentially stripped for parts to keep the remaining ones going.

Immense as the stations were, after all, it wasn't like they were being designed for the kind of working lifespan a true habitat required.

———

THEY WERE HALFWAY OUT onto the outer floor of the habitat when Sings's communicator chimed. So did the one carried by the aide escorting her.

She didn't hear the Spears' communicator chiming, but she saw their *reaction*. Unlike her or her aide, *they* simply got the message. They went from a casual-seeming honor guard into a weapons-bristling phalanx before Sings even reached her communicator.

There was a solid circle of soldiers around her and her aide. Walks-In-Moonlight was included in the circle, and she clearly had no idea what was going on. She hadn't received the message—she'd just been standing inside the close-protection radius of Sings-Over-Darkened-Waters and hadn't been classified as a threat.

Sings tapped a command.

"This is an emergency alert to all vessels in orbit," a voice declared. It wasn't *quite* right, clearly one of the voices of the human translators. Those translators tried to create unique voices for each human, but she didn't recognize this one.

"We have confirmed unscheduled tachyon signatures in the outer system. Current estimate is eight unidentified Matrix units." The speaker paused. "Large Matrix units. Potential Rogues," they concluded.

"All ships are to go to Status Two. Matrix recon nodes are proceeding to investigate the units. Stand by for further communications.

"Repeat, all ships are to go to Status Two and stand by for further communications. We have a potential Rogue Matrix incursion."

Sings-Over-Darkened-Waters had been fully briefed on everything the humans had learned about their Matrix allies and enemies. "Large units" would mean either Construction Matrices or Combat Matrices.

And while Construction Matrices didn't travel alone, they didn't travel in packs.

Matrix combat platforms *did*.

The Rogues were back.

35

Octavio was not anything that his doctor would call *healed* or *recovered*. His left arm was still immobilized outside of supervised physiotherapy, but his lung had recovered, and he was no longer eating enough for three people.

Nakajima had allowed him to return to limited duty, which meant he was in his office, reviewing paperwork, when the alert hit.

He had the tactical display on his wallscreen before Das finished speaking. Eight Matrix units was bad news. There was always a chance that XR-13-9 had sent more ships without telling him...except that ZDX-175-14 was reacting the same way the humans and Vistans were.

"Africano," he said as he linked to his coms officer. "Get a link to ZDX. I want a confirmation that they aren't expecting these guys."

"On it, sir."

He was already expanding the channel, switching between bridge officers as he spoke.

"Das, make sure all of our weapons are warmed up and online. Last data I saw from Tran said we should have everything back—let me know if there are *any* problems," he ordered.

"Everything shows green, but we'll status-check as we bring them up to full," Das replied.

"Tran, get engineering ready. Full DamCon teams and bring up the secondary reactors," he continued, switching again. "We'll need every ounce of power, so get me fusion cores."

"Sir?" Renaud interrupted. "Aren't you supposed to be—"

"I'll be on the bridge in two minutes," he told his XO. "Limited duty be damned. What's your take?"

"Eight Rogue combat platforms," she said flatly. "We can't take them, sir."

"I have the same, at least on the enemy strength," he replied. "But I'm not abandoning these people, Aisha. We'll see what we can pull off."

Silence was his only answer. Renaud clearly didn't think it was possible—and she wasn't likely to be wrong.

But they'd only fully evacuated six hundred thousand people. There were fewer than a quarter billion in the habitats. Over seven hundred million Vistans were still on the planet, vulnerable if the Rogues brought in new terraformers.

He wasn't sure *what* Rogue combat platforms would do when faced with the current situation, but he doubted it was going to spare the survivors on the surface, let alone the habitats in orbit.

And if he was going to order *Scorpion* to die for those people, he was damn well going to do it from his bridge.

———

"NINETY DAYS," Renaud muttered to Octavio as he took his seat on the bridge. "I was hoping for more."

"I was hoping for forever," he replied. "I could have lived with, oh, another fifty days."

In fifty days, the new Task Force *Vigil* was scheduled to arrive. Octavio wasn't as pessimistic as his XO, but he still wasn't sure how *Scorpion* and her Vistan allies could stand off eight combat Matrices.

He'd have happily bet on the new *Vigil* and her strike cruisers against them, though.

If the Matrices had to come before Lestroud arrived, though, he was glad they'd come before he'd left. His group of propulsion and warp-drive engineers for the *Interceptor* were scheduled to leave about thirteen days before Admiral Lestroud would arrive, on the fourth evacuation flight.

"What do we do, sir?" Renaud asked.

"We get the guardships and the bombers moving," he told her. "We'll head out in front, see if we can make them blink. We're tougher than they'll expect us to be, after all."

"Won't they have all of the data from the last fight?" she said.

"Then they'll be expecting us to be missing a turret and a lot of other bits," Octavio replied. "We wouldn't be back to a hundred percent if Exilium hadn't put those spare LPCs on the evac fleet."

"They can build copies of themselves in a year," his XO pointed out. "Do you really think they'll assume we couldn't fully repair our ship?"

"I can hope," he told her. "Either way, we're going to hit them as hard as we can, then fall back on the Vistans for a base of fire. We'll cover the Star-Choir with our Guardian Protocols for as long as we can."

"Until they kill us with their heavy beams, basically," she murmured, softly enough that the rest of the bridge couldn't hear her.

"Potentially," he admitted. "We only have so many options, Commander, and I'm not abandoning the Vistans. We haven't evacuated nearly enough people."

"Enough to save the species," Renaud replied. "Six hundred thousand people is a pretty solid genetic base. Even if we fail, the species will survive."

"There were *ten billion* of them four months ago," Octavio said. "Now there's a billion. That's my fault. My responsibility. Not again. Not ever."

Renaud probably had an entire *book* of arguments as to why the Impact hadn't been his fault, but she was wise enough not to bring them out right now.

"Sir, we're getting an update from the recon node," Africano reported. "Relayed through ZDX, but it's pretty complete."

With the recon node heading out-system at ten percent of light-speed and the new ships coming in at ten percent of lightspeed, even the multiple light-minutes the new Matrices had put between them-selves and the planet disappeared *fast*.

And it told him he was facing his worst nightmare. Part of him had hoped it would be something else. Some new aliens they hadn't encountered before—or even just only half combat platforms accompa-nied by something else.

They had no such luck. Eight immense six-clawed forms filled the screens as the recon node flashed toward them. He had no idea how he was going to fight them.

He just knew that he was going to fight them with everything he had.

───────

"SIR...JUST what *is* that recon node doing?"

Octavio's focus had been on *Scorpion* and the Star-Choirs, getting the defenders moving and aligned to make sure that the guardships and bombers were in position to cover his inevitable retreat.

The key to actually surviving this mess would be to make the best use of the bombers. Six hundred and sixty X-ray lasers powered by fifty-megaton warheads had a decent chance of taking down two, maybe even three combat platforms. The hundred and eighty bombs the guardships could deploy every minute or so wouldn't hurt either.

That opening six-hundred-laser salvo was the best punch they were going to get, however, and if Octavio had the Rogues' attention when it went off, they had a chance.

He had *not* been paying attention to the single Matrix recon node that had been sent out to scout the incoming Rogues. The AIs' core protocols meant that the recon ship couldn't fire on the Rogues and the Rogues couldn't fire on it.

"Is it...playing chicken?" he finally asked, watching the recon node position itself directly in front of one of the combat platforms.

The reactionless drive the Matrices used was *fast* but wasn't very maneuverable. They could get from zero to ten percent of lightspeed in the blink of an eye, but they couldn't change that course easily once they were moving.

His own ship couldn't reach the same velocities in anything near that time frame, but they could fling themselves all over the sky while doing it. There were *some* limits to their maneuverability, but *Scorpion*'s thrusters had a hundred-and-forty-degree by a hundred-and-fifty-degree rotation capability. The ship had to be pointed in roughly the direction Octavio wanted it to go...but only roughly.

The recon node and the combat platform were using the exact same drive, though. And the recon node now had itself directly in front of the much bigger Matrix ship. It matched every maneuver, every vector change.

"They can't shoot it down any more than it can fire on them," he murmured. "That's insane."

"I have multiple tachyon punches!" Das reported. "Our Matrix friends just left their fabrication complex behind and moved out."

"Where?" he demanded.

"Unclear, they left the system," his tactical officer reported.

That seemed...out of character. It almost certainly had something to do with the combat platform that had fallen out of formation, the big warship clearly confused by its smaller relative.

"Take us out, maximum acceleration," he ordered. "Let the Rogues think we're coming to them."

"Aren't we?" Renaud asked.

"Oh, we are," he agreed. "But I have a suspicion I know what our robotic friends are up to, and I want those bastards focused on us."

Scorpion lunged out at full thrust, her engines blinding to anyone watching her from the wrong spot. Gravity compensators smoothly absorbed the impact, and Octavio smiled grimly as he watched the confused disorder of his enemies.

Five of them were still advancing, but two more had stopped with their confused sibling. They had no idea how to handle a recon node getting in their way. Their core protocols wouldn't let them just shoot the annoying smaller ship, but they also couldn't outmaneuver it.

"We're forty-two minutes from range," Das reported. "That's assuming we don't reverse vector as per the original plan." She paused. "What *is* the new plan?"

"I'm not certain," Octavio admitted. "Any idea what the cycle time on a tachyon punch is?"

From the looks his bridge officers were giving him, only Renaud had put it together, and she did so only now.

"Son of a bitch. Is that going to *work*?" she demanded.

"I don't know. And I want to be in position to shoot the first one of those robotic murderers that works out how to get around it. So, no, Lieutenant Commander Das, we aren't slowing down."

———

THE GUARDSHIPS and bombers behind him were going to play far less of a role in this battle than Octavio had planned. That was probably for the best—he'd spend the Vistans' lives like water if it would save their people, but if he could drive the Rogues off on his own, well, fewer people would die.

"They're trying to herd the recon unit out of the way," Das reported. "That one ship has tied up three combat platforms. It's...impressive."

"It would have ended a lot faster if they could shoot it," Octavio reminded her. "We've spent so long focused on the fact that *our* Matrices couldn't shoot at them that we forgot the reverse was true."

"I don't see how that's going to help us today," the tactical officer replied. "They'll be in range in ten minutes, their grasers and our particle cannons alike."

"Daniel, please make sure they don't hit us," Octavio said dryly. "I think our Matrix friends have a plan, but I'd like to live until—"

"*Tachyon punch!*"

Das's snapped report cut through the bridge like a knife, and Octavio's gaze snapped to the main display. The Matrices had clearly been getting live updates on the Rogues from the recon node they'd left behind.

There were eight Rogues in the system and just as many allied Matrices. Four combat platforms appeared directly in front of the lead units, with a recon and security platform blocking the fifth ship still moving toward the planet.

The other recon and security platform and the remaining recon node appeared around their sister, joining her in playing chicken with the three ships that were trying to deal with the original small ship.

For a few seconds, *Scorpion's* bridge was silent as Octavio and his people ran through the math and vectors. Their allies had completely blockaded the incoming Rogues. So long as the Rogues couldn't shoot at the Matrices, they couldn't get past them. The maneuverability of the platforms was too limited.

"Sir! Bandit four!"

Octavio followed Das's shout and realized what they'd all missed.

It had been a small miscalculation, the kind even a powerful artificially intelligent computer could make. One of the combat platforms still moving toward Vista had been slightly ahead of the rest. The combat platform that had punched in to blockade it had jumped in just slightly too close.

The same limited maneuverability that meant the Rogues couldn't get past Octavio's allies also meant the ship couldn't stop. Even attempting to evade, it was moving at over eight percent of lightspeed when the two ships collided.

Matrix combat platforms were big, heavily armored ships...but at that speed, even a small asteroid might have shattered its armor.

And it had hit another combat platform. Octavio stared as the two ships hurtled along the impacting vessel's course for several seconds, debris and sparks scattering from the collision.

Then one of the exotic-matter cores went critical. It didn't matter which ship's core—there were *eight* matter-conversion plants buried in the wreckage.

Neither ship survived—and moments later, the only Matrices in the system were the ones Octavio had grown used to.

Less one sibling who'd accidentally saved them all.

36

A DIGITAL CLOCK on the wallscreen in front of Isaac ticked down, second by second, toward the moment where Task Force *Vigil* would jump back to warp.

The policy of dropping out of warp for one hour every week had been set after both the six-month journey to Exilium itself and the mission to take down the Rogue. Warped space was uncomfortable for humans, and no studies or data to tell people that there was nothing wrong with them or the air they were breathing helped.

Psychosomatic did *not* mean *imaginary*, after all.

To his surprise, the trip aboard *Vigil* hadn't been nearly as bad, and the data on one of his screens agreed with him. The doctors aboard the six ships had been keeping an eye on everyone, and they were estimating the impact had been reduced by as much as half—at least in terms of people needing to be given temporary relief of duties, anyway.

Their sixth dropout had come with the news of the attack on Vista. They'd barely missed the reports on their last window, by a matter of hours at most. The six-and-a-half-day window was long enough that the Matrices had come *back* since.

And faced the same obstacle. Without reinforcements, the Rogues ground out on the same problem the friendlier Matrices had always faced: their core protocols wouldn't let them shoot at each other.

Combat Coordination Matrix ZDX-175-14 had found a way to use that to the defenders' advantage. If the AI had been one of Isaac's people, he'd have hung a medal and a promotion on them for that.

"ZDX informs me that they are moving more recon units forward to reinforce Hearthfire," the recorded hologram of Captain Octavio Catalan told him. "We expect to be up to about twenty Matrix nodes within two weeks, but they're all going to be recon ships with minimal fabrication capacity."

The dark-haired Captain shook his head.

"If we're lucky, that will be before the Rogues manage to reinforce to similar numbers. Everyone would *rather* we blow them to a million pieces, but that's waiting on you. Six more weeks—everyone here is counting it down, sir."

Catalan fidgeted for a moment, then inhaled sharply.

"Given the Matrix reinforcements, I intend to proceed with the original plan for the *Interceptor* project. My propulsion techs and I will leave on the fourth evacuation flight, thirteen days before your arrival.

"I'll be surrendering my command to Commander Renaud. She's a solid officer." He shook his head and quirked a half-smile. "Between you and me, Admiral, she might be a better *fighting* officer than I am. She'll do well by you, but I'm counting on you to keep Vista safe.

"I've done a lot to get everything moving here, and I'll admit to feeling paternal towards the giant frogs. We've a few concerns around food, but unless the Rogues really cause trouble, we'll have the population evacuated into orbit with time to spare—and relocated to Refuge before we run out of food here."

Catalan did not, Isaac noted, say things like "we've done it" or "we managed to save them." They had a good chance of pulling it off now, but no one wanted to jinx it.

"We'll keep the wheels turning until you get here. Catalan out."

Isaac chuckled. A running evacuation of thirty million people a week was a bit more than "keeping the wheels turning," though most of that work was being done by the Vistans themselves now.

It would be *years* before they'd moved everyone to Refuge, but once they had everyone off the planet, there would be time. There was a yard scheduled to come online before his task force arrived that would be producing the same two-fifty-six freighters accompanying Isaac.

The report Catalan had sent him told him there'd be two slips initially, but they'd be scaling it up as fast as they could. Every ship, after all, was a hundred thousand people evacuated every seventeen to eighteen days.

The scale of the project still boggled Isaac's mind, but the alternative was unacceptable. The satellite data and overflights were clear: Vista's ice caps were expanding. The original estimate was holding steady, but there were only sixty-five days left until they figured ice would choke out the coastal cities remaining.

They had time still, once that happened, but only strenuous technical efforts were going to keep the almost half a billion people still expected to be on the planet at that point alive.

Sooner or later, though, Vista's atmosphere was going to become untraversable. At that point, anyone left behind was doomed. There was a limit to what they could fly shuttles into, after all.

A few taps brought up his own recorder.

"Captain Catalan, I appreciate the update," he told his subordinate. "I'll note that a ship's Captain should *request permission* to leave their post, but you're right about both the need for your skills and the value of what's on the table.

"I will add one codicil, though," Isaac continued, holding up a finger. "If the Rogues are stepping up their attacks and you have reason to think a major strike might come through before we arrive, you are to remain in Hearthfire until Task Force *Vigil* is in place to relieve you.

"It won't cost you that much time. Three months to build the kind of ship you're talking about is already going to be an insane schedule, and you'll be there for the last forty days even if you wait until I arrive.

"Our priority is and must remain the preservation and protection of the Vistans," he concluded. "I understand the temptation and the value of the offer that the Matrices have put on the table, but we have warp drives and the Creators' ship doesn't. If we have to track her down over the long run, we can. We *can't* save people who freeze to death on Vista."

Isaac shook his head.

"But given that one codicil, I authorize your redeployment," he stated. "President Lestroud already backed you up on this one, so I don't have much of a leg to stand on in any case. The chance to talk to the Matrices' Creators..." Isaac shivered.

"It's worth it. But it can wait if it has to. If everything goes well, I assume I *won't* see you in Hearthfire in thirty-two days. Good luck, Captain."

He closed the recording and sent it to the coms department, checking the time.

Five minutes left. Just enough to grab a coffee and brace himself for what was coming.

Just because it wasn't *as* bad as it had been didn't mean it didn't still suck.

37

"IN THE POTENTIAL ARRIVAL WINDOW. All ships standing by."

Octavio nodded silently as Das's report echoed across *Scorpion's* bridge.

The Matrices had returned twice since their initial visit. The first time had been exactly one hundred and twenty-one hours after they'd left.

That had been the same seven combat platforms, and they'd found themselves blocked by their cousins. The incursion had lasted less than twenty minutes, like they were testing the defenders.

The third incursion had been one hundred and twenty-three hours after the second had retreated. Octavio figured they'd been aiming for a hundred and twenty-one hours—a time frame that "his" Matrices seemed to think was perfectly logical—but had waited for reinforcements.

Six recon nodes had accompanied the seven combat platforms that time—but *eight* recon units had arrived to reinforce the defenders. Once again stymied by the presence of ships they couldn't shoot and that refused to get out of their way, the Rogues had danced around the system for eleven hours, *trying* to get to Vista...and then finally withdrawn.

That had been one hundred and twenty hours before. If the Rogue Matrices showed up in the next four hours, Octavio suspected they were going to be seeing incursions every four to five days until they could beat one back.

"No tachyon signatures except our allies," Das reported. "Current count is nineteen, if anyone cares."

Octavio snorted. He *did* care, mostly because their robotic allies were still producing the lion's share of the orbital habitats. The extra twelve recon nodes added to their existing seven—three combat platforms, two recon and security units and two recon units—hadn't really increased the production of those stations much. They had, at least, helped offset the production lost to playing blocker to the incoming Rogue ships.

If the Rogues had the same six additional ships this time, then they had enough blockers...but the Matrices rarely tried the same thing twice without bringing more force to the party.

"All stations report green," Renaud told him. "*Scorpion* is prepared for battle."

"We will stay at status two for twenty-four hours," he announced, reiterating the plan in case someone had managed to forget. "If we see *any* tachyon signatures, we go to full general quarters."

The calm silence on his bridge told him that nobody had managed to forget, and he leaned back in his seat. A repeater screen attached to the arm of the chair was tracking the position of every armed ship in Vistan orbit.

Hopefully, the Matrices would block this attack, too...but the back of his neck was itchy and he wanted to be sure the guardships and bombers were in position.

It wouldn't take many mistakes to risk the planet—and even fewer to risk the fragile clusters of orbital habitats and greenhouses.

"TACHYON PULSES."

There was an almost-disturbing lack of urgency to the report. That was reasonable, Octavio supposed. The burst of faster-than-light particles only really told him that Matrix ships had entered the star system and where.

It didn't tell him much *about* those ships. And in this case, with the enemy very much expected, there wasn't really any surprise at their arrival.

"One hundred twenty-one hours and fourteen minutes," Renaud concluded. "I suppose that's the advantage of fighting robots. They're certainly punctual."

"That they are...which is nerve-wracking, given that they certainly aren't uncreative," Octavio replied. "Distance and numbers, Lieutenant Commander?"

"Three light-minutes," Das told him. "Looks like eighteen signatures. I'll have details in, well, about three minutes."

Octavio ignored her amused smirk. Eighteen Matrix ships was one fewer than the minimum he'd expected, though more than the defenders had possessed during the last clash.

"Inform ZDX they are clear to proceed as per the plan," he said aloud.

The combat Matrix was only so good at pretending that Octavio was in command and was probably already in motion.

"Matrices are moving out. ZDX has left one of the recon and security nodes to reinforce the orbitals," Das reported. "That leaves him eighteen units as blockers. Vectors align as expected."

"So, the same old trick without enough ships," Octavio murmured. "Does it feel right to you, Commander Renaud?"

"No," she told him. "The Rogues aren't stupid or uncreative. They *might* have been restricted in their reinforcements, but usual Matrix protocol would be to wait until they got more. We're certainly not going to get any more Matrices than we have, so waiting for reinforcements wouldn't hurt them."

"They don't know that," he pointed out. "But it doesn't feel right to me, either. Africano." He turned to his coms officer. "Get me Sings-Over-Darkened-Waters. Renaud, Das—get us into a higher orbit and make sure all the capacitors are charged. Keep us to an acceleration the locals can match for now."

"What are you expecting, sir?" Renaud asked, but she was clearly running through the same chain of thought.

"I don't know," he admitted. "If you have any ideas, let me know. For now, I want the Star-Choir at full capacity."

A grayed-out hologram of Sings-Over-Darkened-Waters appeared above the right side of his command seat.

"Captain Octavio Catalan," she greeted him. "We see the enemy. The Guardian-Star-Choir is at full preparedness."

"We're going to move out to clear our firing lines," Octavio told her. "I want to borrow...twenty of your bombers. We're moving slowly enough that they should be able to rendezvous and latch on to our hull.

"Once they're attached to the hull, our compensators will protect them from our acceleration, and we'll go to full power."

"Toward what, Captain?" Sings asked, but he saw the hand gesture she used to tell her staff to do as he asked.

"I don't know," he confessed. "But this doesn't add up. I'm expecting a second wave...one that's counting on our Matrix friends to be out of position dealing with their first force."

It was the first time he'd put it into words, but as soon as he said it, he was sure it was right. Twenty bombers would give him an extra forty bombs— a hundred and twenty X-ray lasers—in the opening clash, enough to change the tide of a battle.

And if he was lucky, he might even get the bomber crews out.

———

After thirty minutes of maneuvering away from the planet with twenty bombers attached to *Scorpion*'s hull, Octavio started to wonder if he was just being paranoid. The Rogues were doing the same dance of attempting to dodge past the blocking Matrices that they'd done for hours last time.

The two robotic flotillas had identical ships with identical engines. There was no way the Rogues were going to get past, not without greater numbers or some maneuver Octavio couldn't picture.

He wasn't entirely comfortable with their understanding of the reactionless drive the Matrices used, but he *thought* he knew its capabilities. Inside those capabilities, the blocker force could intercept every course the Rogues tried.

In their place, he'd either have snuck in scouts and waited until he had a numerical edge or tried something clever.

"Tachyon pulse!" Das exclaimed. This report was *much* more concerned than the first one. "I have multiple signatures at twelve million kilometers."

Less than a light-minute. That was the closest emergence they had on record for a tachyon punch. They'd apparently *really* pissed off the Rogue Matrices.

"Get me details, Das," he ordered.

"Six signatures four still active," she snapped as the light trickled in. "One combat platform, three recon nodes…and two debris fields."

"Debris fields?" Octavio demanded.

"Mass and materials spectrometry suggest they jumped in with five recon nodes and two disintegrated on emergence," she told him. "We have missile la—"

"GUARDIAN PROTOCOLS ENGAGING."

The loud alert of the warship's AI cut through the bridge like a hammer. New warnings and icons cascaded across Octavio's screen. Dozens of missiles were flashing out from the Rogue Matrices at a high percentage of lightspeed.

All of them were targeted on *Scorpion,* and her AI had taken full control of the lasers and pulse guns flagged for missile defense. None of the missiles were getting through.

"Lieutenant Daniel—take us out to meet them," he ordered. "Make sure we're accelerating at a rate that won't hurt our carry-ons. The compensation field doesn't give them full coverage out on the hull."

The field stretched beyond the hull to protect any humans or robots doing exterior work while they were under thrust. It was less reliable, which was why the preference was always to do that kind of work by remote.

"Das, Renaud; get me a work-up on our best time to drop the bombers. We want them to survive, but I want them backing up our first exchange. I'll face three recon nodes in a fair fight if I have to, but I want to stack the scales in our favor against the combat platform."

Even with an extra forty X-ray laser cartridges, that fight was going to hurt.

It would take them over five minutes to reach weapons range. The Matrices were going to keep throwing missiles at him, aiming for the lucky hit that would clear his defenses and potentially cripple his ship.

Octavio Catalan had no intention of making that hit any easier to get.

———

"ALL RIGHT. Cut acceleration for thirty seconds and cut the bombers loose," Octavio ordered. "They're to deploy their munitions and stand by for my order to fire."

The Vistan small craft flinging themselves clear of *Scorpion*'s hull couldn't manage even one hundredth of her acceleration. Now that she wasn't bringing them along with her, they were rapidly left behind— which was exactly where Octavio wanted them.

Any hit would take out one of those bombers. His ship was far more capable of protecting herself than were the miniscule weapons platforms.

His ship also had a lot more people aboard. Everything was a trade-off, but right now, he needed the bomb-pumped lasers those bombers deployed, or he'd never have brought them.

"Estimated effective range in forty-five seconds," Das declared. "Enemy is beginning testing fire with their grasers."

"Daniel?" Octavio asked.

"Evasive maneuvers in progress; nothing is even coming close," his helm replied.

"Optimal range in thirty seconds," Das chanted. "Hit probability is now above ten percent."

"Continue holding fire. We have both turrets?"

"Both turrets online, fully charged," his tactical officer replied. "Fifteen seconds."

A graser passed close enough to his ship to trigger alerts. Octavio spared a moment to check the power level of the beam and shivered.

The range that Das was waiting for was where they estimated their particle cannons had *any* chance of punching through a combat platform's armor. The energy reading on the enemy graser told him they were inside the range where the combat platform's weapons would do that to *their* armor.

"Range. Firing!"

There was a pause, a barely perceptible gap as the order was sent to the Vistan bombers and their beams flashed forward.

Then *Scorpion*'s turrets fired. Both were aligned perfectly, and four packages of near-*c* particles flashed along with the X-ray lasers. Seconds passed.

"Direct hit!" Das reported. "Fifteen of the lasers and all four particle-cannon beams. We've cracked the hull!"

Unlike a manned ship, there was no atmosphere leakage from a breached Matrix combat platform. There was a lot more electromagnetic radiation coming out of a ship with broken armor—the technological equivalent of blood in the water.

"Hit her again!"

Now the recon nodes were moving forward, weaving around in front of their damaged—but still deadly—bigger sibling. They'd been hanging back before, throwing missiles at *Scorpion*.

Now they lunged toward Octavio's ship, grasers flashing in the night. Missiles were flying again as well—but these weren't targeted at *Scorpion*.

They weren't even targeted on the bombers. A chill ran down his spine as he realized that the Rogues were now targeting the guardships. He'd left them behind as a second line of defense, mostly because they couldn't keep up...and they were well beyond the effective range of their own weapons.

"Daniel, get us between them and the guardships," he barked. The Guardian Protocol had shattered the first salvo, but missiles had made it through. Hopefully, they'd stopped *enough*.

Somehow, despite the twisting gyrations of Daniel's maneuvers, Das managed to line up the turrets for a second salvo. The Matrix ship managed to take the hits on a different part of the hull, preventing Das from opening up the original wound, but she still managed to land half of her shots.

And she clearly hit *something*, as half of the combat platform's grasers suddenly stopped firing. That still left six grasers peppering the space around Octavio's ship, and they were *going* to run out of luck eventually.

They got a lucky hit in first, one of the recon nodes dodging into the path of *Scorpion*'s fire. Octavio wasn't sure if the recon node's AI had chosen poorly or if it had been intentionally sacrificed to save the bigger ship.

Either way, it took a full four-shot salvo from the warp cruiser and disintegrated. One fewer enemy on the field.

Then one of the combat platform's grasers slammed home. Barely missing the lead arrowhead holding *Scorpion*'s bridge and main weapons, the beam hammered into the rear half of the ship. Damage alerts flashed across Octavio's screens...and the engines died.

"Tran," he snapped. "Report!"

"Fuel lines to the engines are down," she told him. "I've got teams on their way; I'm heading down to join them. I don't know long it'll take!"

"Daniel!"

"I've got maneuvering thrusters and that's *it*," his helmswoman replied. "Continuing to evade, but the odds just turned against us."

"*Got* the fucker!"

Das's exclamation was a spark of desperately needed hope, and Octavio glanced at the displays to double-check it. Only half of the latest salvo had hit the enemy combat platform...but both of them had hit right where the last rounds had.

The previous hit had probably severed critical power connections, rendering half the guns useless. Octavio wasn't sure what this one hit, but *everything* stopped. The grasers stopped firing. The engines cut out a few seconds later.

One moment, the combat Matrix was charging them, all guns blazing. The next, it was a dead hulk drifting through space at ten percent of lightspeed.

"Hit the recon nodes," Octavio barked. "Daniel, keep us out of their line of fire. Keep the Guardian Protocol up and feed those fuckers particle guns."

Scorpion wasn't completely immobile without her main engines. Her maneuvering thrusters could easily match the acceleration available to their Vistan allies, in fact.

It just wasn't enough to let them dodge graser fire at close range. Multiple new scars of red flashed across his damage report displays as the recon nodes closed—but closing made them vulnerable.

A recon node flew straight into Das's fire, and suddenly, there was only one ship left. It took one more shot at *Scorpion*, which missed, and then its AI gave up the fight as lost. It flipped on its end and ran for the outer system at ten percent of lightspeed.

"Das?" Octavio asked softly.

"Our bogey is maneuvering pretty hard," his tactical officer said quietly. "But...more importantly, we just lost power to Turret B, and that last hit took out Turret A's cyclotrons. We've got burnouts running through the entire plasma and power-distribution systems, and what guns I have left are dying. I really *hope* they keep running, because I have nothing left to shoot them with."

Octavio exhaled, then his gaze went back to the crippled Matrix still hurtling through space.

"Renaud, please tell me that wreck isn't going to hit anything important," he said plaintively.

"It doesn't look li—"

The combat platform's matter-conversion cores destabilized. One moment, it was a hurtling wreck.

The next, it was simply gone, and Octavio shook his head as he looked at the fireball.

"Someone *please* tell me *we* have a shutdown protocol for that thing," he said aloud.

No one on the bridge replied. There was only one person on the bridge who understood the shutdown protocols for their own matter conversion core well enough to reassure anyone else about them...and that person *was* Octavio Catalan.

38

KEENING ECHOED through the empty space of the command pool, the unconscious noise of grieving Vistans tearing at Sings-Over-Darkened-Waters's heart and mind alike. Another guardship gone, destroyed by a missile that *Scorpion*'s best efforts hadn't stopped. The flagship was alive only thanks to the knowing and intentional sacrifice of over a dozen bombers by their own crew.

Sings had been unable to change that. She'd watched her bombers moving in front of the remaining guardships, shielding the mobile asteroids with the only defense they could offer: their own fragile hulls.

She was alive thanks to their sacrifice. Thousands of her guardians were not.

Worse, for the long-term survival chances of her species at least, *Scorpion* was crippled. The datasong was clear on that, the starship's wounds readily perceptible to the First-Among-Singers's ears.

Her engines were gone. Her weapons were gone. *Seven times* the Matrices had landed hits with their grasers before the last one had fled, and while only the first had been critical, the rest had taken their own toll.

"First-Among-Singers," Swimmer-Under-Sunlit-Skies addressed her. "What do we *do*?"

"We can't reach *Scorpion*," she pointed out. "The Matrices are already on their way. We will aid her once she is returned to us."

The attacking force had withdrawn once again. The game of shields and arrows the robotic warships played was over for today. Their attempt to play outside the rules of the maneuvers, so similar to that old Vistan child's game, had failed thanks to *Scorpion* and Captain Catalan.

"We can't fight these monsters," Swimmer murmured, projecting the trill of his voice so only she heard him. "Without *Scorpion*, can we protect the habitats?"

"I don't know," she admitted, her voice projected just as carefully. "We may need to consider moving the habitats away from Vista. The Matrices focus seems to be on our world—separating the evacuees from the planet should help protect them."

"But so many of our people remain on the surface," he objected.

"And we will do all we can to protect them, as well," she agreed. She did not finish the thought, but she knew Swimmer understood it: if the hundreds of millions still on the surface had to be sacrificed to protect the hundreds of millions already moved into space and awaiting evacuation, it would be done.

"Twenty-nine days, Voice-Of-Choirs," she told him. "Then the humans' *true* warships are meant to arrive. If the Matrices can protect us from their rogue kin until then, we are safe."

He accepted that. Sings…didn't. She knew that the warships the humans had sent dwarfed *Scorpion* and that *Scorpion* was far more powerful than her own guardships, but she had seen the might of the Matrices.

Her faith in her human allies was complete. She believed, in her bones, that the human warships would do all they could to protect Vista. That, if necessary, Octavio Catalan and his people would *die* to protect her people.

She just also realized that the enemy they faced was beyond them all.

THE COMPUTERS SANG a song of icons and data. Two guardships and a hundred and sixty-four bombers in orbit. One hundred and thirty habitats holding two hundred and forty million souls---the last fifteen habitats still being filled by the endless stream of shuttles that didn't stop, even for a Matrix attack.

Those shuttles could never stop. There was no time.

Outside the orbit of Vista, there were other points the computers told Sings-Over-Darkened-Waters about. The shipyard, almost finished and ready to begin the construction of the first four warp-capable ships to ever be built by Vistan hands—massive ships, to carry a hundred thousand evacuees at two hundred and fifty-six times the speed of radiation.

Vistan work shuttles swarmed that shipyard, their tools a frail substitute for the Matrix fabricators that were doing most of the work. Those Matrices were elsewhere at that moment, making sure their Rogue cousins were truly gone...and guarding the last icon, the one that truly occupied Sings-Over-Darkened-Waters's attention.

Scorpion. Two recon nodes had attached long cables to the crippled human ship and were towing her, keeping their strange engines down to a pace that Sings's ships could have duplicated.

The combat platforms and recon and security nodes kept watch. They'd return to the shipyards and the habitat-production facilities soon enough, but for now, they watched *Scorpion.*

And yet...the big warships kept their distance from the crippled starship. They were watchful, protective...but they were watchful and protective from a hundred thousand kilometers away.

Sings-Over-Darkened-Waters remembered the cataclysmic fate of a crippled Rogue combat platform a few hours before and wondered if her *friends* carried the same power source. She wondered if she was going to watch Captain Octavio Catalan die in the same kind of explosion.

She didn't think so, but it was a terrifying thought. Her allies seemed so fragile sometimes and so powerful at others. Without Catalan, her world would have died.

She willed the ship to make the trip to Vistan orbit safely. There was nothing else she could do, but she couldn't take her attention away, either.

39

"STEP-DOWN COMPLETE," Tran announced in Octavio's ear. She sounded exhausted—even more exhausted than Octavio felt.

For thirty-six hours, the engineer had struggled with the terrifying beast at *Scorpion*'s heart. It was *dangerous* to take a matter-conversion plant below fifty percent output. They were rarely shut down after coming online—but *Scorpion* no longer had the power distribution system to draw fifty percent of her main power plant's energy.

"We're cold?" he asked, needing her to confirm. Needing to be sure.

"We're cold. We can start looking at everything else now," she told him.

He barked a short laugh. They'd evacuated the ship once the Matrices had towed them into orbit. Only the engineering teams had remained behind—the engineers and the Captain who'd once been one of them.

Renaud hadn't even argued. She'd taken command of the evacuated crew aboard the orbital habitat without even blinking. If *Scorpion* was going to die to an *engineering casualty*, Octavio Catalan was going to be aboard her when it happened.

"What 'everything else'?" he asked. "Both turrets are wrecked to various degrees. Without replacement cyclotrons, Turret A is just done

—and without a fully functioning power-distribution system, the rest of our weapons are useless.

"The maneuvering thrusters are semi-independent, so we can use them to maintain our orbit, but I've been looking at 'everything else' while you were dealing with the power plant," he told Tran. "We'll need to do a full survey to be sure, but my assessment isn't good, Commander. We need a shipyard. A real, fully equipped shipyard."

"And the only one of those we know of is fifty light-years away," Tran said with a sigh. "My teams and I will double-check everything, but I don't doubt you, sir. She's a write-off?"

"We can probably get her home eventually," Octavio replied. "But she's not fighting again, not without another six-month stint in that yard."

He sighed, too.

"While you're doing that survey, check over the remaining guns," he ordered. "I don't like the thought of hacking our girl up for parts, but if we can pull out enough pieces to set up a few weapons platforms, that's one more mark in the column that says Vista might survive until Admiral Lestroud gets here."

"I'll make sure of it," Tran promised. "If nothing else, the day I can't turn four half-wrecked LPCs into two functional particle cannons is the day I take up knitting instead of engineering."

Octavio snorted at Tran's pale imitation of humor.

The question wasn't whether his people were good enough to do that. The question was whether *Scorpion*'s guns were merely *half*-wrecked, or if the power-distribution net failure had done more serious damage.

Only time and hard work would tell.

And only time would tell if the Rogues would let them do the work.

———

THREE DAYS of surveying later confirmed Octavio's worst fears. Not only was *Scorpion*'s power-distribution network wrecked, the long, drawn-out process of stepping down the matter converter had sent enough energy surging through it to wreck most of what had still been attached.

Scorpion still had intact pieces, but they weren't hooked up to power. Anything that had been hooked up to power had been repeatedly overloaded. The maneuvering thrusters that had been her last remaining mobility had fried their control mechanisms. Enough power had been accidentally pulsed through the warp drive to misalign the careful balance of the exotic matter.

His ship might not look it, but she was dead.

"What do we do?" Renaud asked after Tran had finished briefing them.

"We should be able to assemble a platform for the two particle cannons Tran thinks she can build," Octavio told her and the other senior officers. They were gathered in a conference room aboard one of the orbital habitats now, a hastily rigged-up holodisplay allowing the humans to see their ship.

"We'll have to gut *Scorpion* to do it," he said sadly. "Pulling the exotic matter from her warp drive will help the locals get their warp ships online—the Matrices have been building an EM stockpile with material brought from home, but anything we can add to that is worth it.

"Especially," he forced a dry grin, "if it isn't doing anything where it is."

None of his crew shared his false humor.

"The crew is safe here for now," Das told them. "We can breathe the same air as the Vistans, and we'll bring over our food supplies from *Scorpion*. We'll be...okay."

"I've already sent a message home via the Matrices," Africano added. "They know our situation and that everything has to be relayed via them."

"Which limits our coms with home," Octavio said. "I trust our Matrices... I'm not sure I trust that the Rogues can't get into their communications. Which leaves us with some interesting problems."

"Sir?"

"*Vigil* is twenty-four days away. The next convoy to Refuge will leave in eleven days." Those dates were burned into everyone's brains, but Octavio reminded them regardless.

"With *Scorpion* wrecked, there is no point in keeping any more of our people *here* than necessary—and most of our crew will have value for the *Interceptor* project."

"We can't abandon the Vistans," Renaud objected. "You've said that yourself."

"We won't be abandoning them," he agreed. "You, Commander Renaud, are going to remain here and speak for the Republic. By the time the convoy is ready to leave, we'll have a far better idea of how many weapons platforms we'll be able to set up from *Scorpion*'s remains and how many people we'll need to man them.

"Everyone *else* is going to relocate to Refuge with the intention of becoming the crew of *Interceptor*. We'll take all of the Marines with us —and we'll probably need to borrow some Spears from the Vistans, too."

He shook his head.

"I'd *like* to think that everything is going to go perfectly smoothly and the Matrices' Creators will greet us with open arms...but then I remember that these are the people that decided to build a self-replicating fleet of armed terraforming robots.

"I don't trust that they're working with anything that *I'd* call logic."

40

THERE WERE three round seals on the wall in Isaac Lestroud's office. Once was a copy of the commissioning seal for the new *Vigil* with its Eye of Horus and Republic of Exilium rockets. The other two had survived the destruction of the old *Vigil*, his exile to the far end of the galaxy and everything else his career after the rank of Captain had thrown at him.

One was the commissioning seal for the battlecruiser *Victoria*, the ship he'd commanded before his promotion to Rear Admiral. His time aboard the battlecruiser had been short, barely eighteen months before he'd been promoted and given command of *Vigil's* battle group.

Filling the role had been the final checkmark for that promotion, though he liked to think he'd done well by *Victoria's* crew.

The last seal, though, a the copy of the commissioning seal of the ship he'd spent most of his time as Captain aboard and fought his only battle as a Confederacy officer aboard: *Scorpion*. He'd commanded the warp cruiser for three years and had built his reputation as something other than his mother's son aboard her.

Isaac took the seal down from the wall and put it on his desk, looking at the golden scorpion icon with *WC-17* emblazoned across the top. She'd served him well, under his direct command and in his service.

And from the message from Amelie he had paused on his screen, she'd given her last. With a sigh, he un-paused the communique.

"All of our updates at this point are being relayed through the Matrices, and Octavio clearly doesn't trust their encryption protocols," his wife's recorded face told him. "I don't blame him. We know the protocols we're using on the tachyon coms are *very* different from theirs. It sounds very possible to me that the Rogues are listening in on our friends' coms."

Isaac understood encryption and transmission protocols significantly better than his wife—though he'd freely concede his knowledge of just about anything non-military paled in comparison to hers—and he knew she was probably overestimating the odds.

It was *possible* that the Rogues could access XR-13-9's communications. It wasn't likely...but it was more likely than the Rogues managing to penetrate the humans' encryption, which wasn't even running on the same basic system architecture.

"What we have confirmed is that most of *Scorpion*'s crew is fine and Octavio is preparing them to relocate to support the *Interceptor* project," she continued. "Once he's in Refuge, he and I will be able to have a live conversation: *Interceptor* is being fitted with a full-bandwidth tachyon communicator, and we now have access to one as well.

"It seems the Matrices have decided that we'll keep our part of the bargain and are handing over some of the technology they've been more protective of already. Schematics for a full-bandwidth com will be in the general packet. I don't know if your people can fabricate it en route, but I'm hoping to be able to actually *talk* to you by the time you're in Hearthfire."

The hologram shook her head.

"There's a lot of crap going through our updates, but here's some of the ugly: even the Cabinet is concerned about what happens if the Rogues show up before you get there. You have new orders, Isaac: if Vista has fallen by the time you reach it, you are *forbidden* to attempt retaliatory action.

"You are to assess the situation and see what is salvageable of the remaining surface and orbital populations, and decide whether to continue the evacuation project," she continued. "But you are not to hunt down this Regional Matrix. It's a problem for another time."

Amelie shook her head.

"They're right, my love. I signed off on these orders, too. I *know* you," she said firmly. "But our first priority has to be protecting the surviving Vistans...even if the Matrices cut that number down.

"Hopefully, that won't happen. LOK thinks that the losses inflicted should buy us a few months, maybe as much as six months to a year, as the Regional Matrix dramatically augments their forces.

"The downside of that time frame is that they estimate the next force will be at least double the force that engaged Catalan. A minimum of sixteen combat platforms and probably around fifty escorts.

"The Rogue will have to fabricate that fleet...but it's a regional node. It can do that. I won't tell you that you can't fight that kind of fleet. You can run the odds better than I can."

He could. *Vigil* was designed to chew up and spit out combat platforms. She was smaller than the robotic ships, but her designers had *known* their enemy and had been able to draw on both Matrix technology and a large amount of black Confederacy research.

Isaac would put his new flagship up against four combat platforms. With the three strike cruisers, he was fully confident in his ability to take out the force that had just attacked Hearthfire.

Even with Giannovi and Task Group *Galahad*, though, he couldn't reliably take on *sixty* Matrix warships headed by sixteen combat platforms.

What both he and Amelie weren't saying, though, was that he'd try regardless.

———

"WHAT'S OUR ETA?" Isaac asked when he returned to the flag deck. The usual clock was ticking down, telling him that it would be a bit over ten minutes before the task force resumed its FTL travel.

"Nineteen days."

Commander Aloysius Connor had clearly been waiting for the question. Isaac's operations officer was standing next to the console that handled task force–level navigation.

"Almost exactly," Connor continued. "Nineteen days, one hour, thirty-six minutes." He shrugged. "We could cut two hours off of that by making the entire transit in one shot."

"Even with the lower impact of the new drive, that's not a choice I'll make for two hours," Isaac pointed out. "If you could find me a *day* somewhere, I'd consider it."

"Talk to Reinhardt about that," Connor told him. "I just make sure your orders get fulfilled to the best of our ability. I don't *create* new abilities. You have a massive one-eyed wizard for that."

"And even he has his limits." Isaac sighed and stepped over to the main display. Six ships, two of them completely unarmed, seemed a tiny thing to throw into the night. The next Rogue Matrix wave would outnumber them ten to one—more, considering that the freighters would go directly to evacuating Vistan civilians.

Of course, he'd have Giannovi and her ships by the time the Matrices were likely to come back. Another missile cruiser and four destroyers weren't going to shake the pillars of heaven, but anyone who underestimated the nine-ship battle group he'd have by then would regret it.

They were building freighters for the Vistans. Considering the strength the Matrices could send against them, Isaac realized that would only be the beginning. The yard in Refuge that was building *Interceptor*—not so much a yard as a collection of Matrix fabricator modules, but the point still stood—wouldn't shut down once the specialized ship needed to catch the Creator slowboat was built.

Once it had built *Interceptor*, Isaac would have the Vistans fully take over the yard and start building strike cruisers. *Modified* strike cruisers —ships designed to have water on their decks and moisture in their air.

Terran-designed warships intended to have Vistan crews. The Regional Matrix threatening Hearthfire was going to have to be destroyed, but the ESF wouldn't be able to do it. Projecting power two months away was too difficult, and the threat wasn't immediate enough.

It would be a Vistan fleet that would destroy that Matrix. It would have to be—but for the Republic of Exilium's survival, those Vistan ships would have to be Terran at their core.

It was a discussion he'd have to have with Amelie. How much technology would the Cabinet really let him give away to their allies? How much technology could the Republic afford to hold back?

The Matrices could muster effectively infinite numbers with enough time. He couldn't counter that with only four million humans to draw on for crews.

He probably couldn't even counter that with "only" a billion Vistans to draw on for crews—and didn't that raise some strange thoughts?

They'd found one ally they had no choice but to uplift to their tech level or watch them die. If they were going to fight the Matrices—if Isaac was going to organize the grand crusade the Cabinet wouldn't let the ESF fight—they'd need other allies.

Other species who recognized the doom slowly expanding toward them.

Maybe, just maybe, part of the answer would be on that strange Creator ship. Somehow, Isaac knew that the Creators didn't have a magic button to shut down the Matrices.

If they did, after all, they wouldn't be trying to get clear of the space occupied by their creations.

41

A WEEK aboard a space station designed for people who had no real sense of color was not an experience that Octavio Catalan had ever expected to have. The Vistans used three-dimensional iconography and a written script that more closely resembled Braille than an alphabet.

The 3-D icons were the only reason his people had been able to navigate around the various stations they'd been staying on while *Scorpion* was dismantled. The rotational pseudogravity had also been a problem for crews used to true artificial gravity, but they'd survived.

Now the freighter *Perfumed Dancer* glowed on one of the portable holoprojectors his people had set up in the docking bay of the habitat. The two-hundred-and-fifty-meter-long bulk hauler had been refitted to carry passengers before she'd left Hearthfire the first time and was currently surrounded by a swarm of shuttles.

Each of those shuttles carried between fifty and a hundred people. There were currently a *hundred* spacecraft on approach to the freighter, with another two hundred either coming up from or heading back down to the surface.

If he'd expanded the view, over four thousand shuttles would be hauling people up from the surface to the evacuation ships. When the freighters weren't there, those shuttles would also be carrying people to the orbital habitats, but most of *that* transport was being done by monstrous landers that were too big to dock with the freighters.

It took two days to fully load the freighters, a task that was almost done for this trip. Two of the shuttles were docked with the orbitals, waiting to carry two hundred of Octavio's people over to *Dancer*.

"I would prefer you stay at Hearthfire," Sings-Over-Darkened-Waters told him, the man-sized hunchbacked amphibian standing behind him. She tended to forget that humans didn't have three-hundred-and-sixty-degree awareness.

He turned to face her and smiled from habit.

"With *Scorpion* reduced to spare parts and a semi-mobile turret, a starship commander isn't needed here," he reminded Sings. "Commander Renaud is an extremely competent officer; she can provide the same orbital watch I could and lead the crew who are remaining.

"The ship we're building in Refuge, though, requires the skills of an absolute expert in propulsion and warp-drive technology. I'm the best we have who isn't fifty light-years away."

"An odd skillset for a starship commander," Sings replied. "I understand." She paused. "We owe you a great deal, Captain Catalan. We will miss you."

"I'm an odd starship commander," Octavio said with a chuckle. "I'm glad we were able to help you. At the same time, though, at this point, you're helping yourself as much as we're helping! The Matrices have been more use than us all along, and they're staying here."

Sings's unconscious chirps flattened.

"I trust that you trust them," she told him. "They still remind me of the monsters who destroyed my world."

"And their guilt for their connection to those monsters will help *save* your people," Octavio replied. "Renaud can ride herd on them for you, but we owe the Matrices ourselves. If this strange ship really belongs to their Creators, we owe it to them to make contact."

"And their Creators may have a weapon we can use to protect my people from the Rogues," Sings-Over-Darkened-Waters conceded. "We have had this discussion before, my friend, but the time for it is now ending.

"It will be years before I come to Refuge. I may not even live that long—I am far from young—but I will not leave Hearthfire until my people are safe."

"You and the Empress alike." Octavio shook his head. "You need to tell Sleeps-In-Sunlight that she's going to need to move to Refuge eventually. The Empress can't be the last one out before the lights turn off."

"She knows," Sings said. She offered a delicate arm to him for the not-quite-hug, not-quite-arm-grip that was a gesture of close friendship. "We will see you again, Captain Catalan.

"You must be certain of that."

"I am," he told her, touched by the gesture and her words. "If Refuge is as close to Exilium as I'm told she is, you'll be stunned by your new world. For all of their flaws and problems, the Matrices create paradises.

"After all, *that* is what they were built for."

———

NEWLY PROMOTED Warrant Officer Ghulam Kinnaird had been one of the petty officers running *Scorpion's* shuttle deck. Now the dark-skinned man with the shockingly red hair was the Captain of *Perfumed Dancer*, saluting crisply as Octavio came aboard.

"Welcome aboard, sir," he greeted the Captain. "Have we had any problems?"

"No," Octavio confirmed. "And remember, Kinnaird: you're in command here. I'm just a passenger."

Kinnaird looked a bit awkward at that. He was a brand-new Warrant Officer, a rank that the ESF had on its books but hadn't really *used* before, and Octavio was coming aboard with half a dozen commissioned officers senior to him.

"I mean it, Kinnaird," Octavio repeated. "We're just passengers. *Dancer* is your ship. How are you and your crew holding up?"

The Warrant Officer gestured for Octavio to follow him deeper into the ship.

"It's weird," he admitted. "The Matrix remote does a lot of the work of running the ship, and the Vistans are bringing their own law enforcement and leadership. The trips are running pretty smoothly, but we haven't had a chance to slow down and check the ship over at all."

"We need to do that in warp," Octavio told him. "Most of the estimates I'm seeing say this evacuation is going to take years, and we can't afford to lose this ship—any of the ships, really."

Each of the ten one-twenty-eight freighters carried twenty thousand passengers on each trip. Losing one of them would leave hundreds of thousands of people behind in short order.

"We're doing what we can. The Matrix remotes are even handier than I thought, but it's still a lot for five of us. We'll keep on top of it," the Warrant Officer promised.

"We've got you and the other officers in private staterooms in the old crew quarters," Kinnaird continued as they continued into the ship. "Everyone else is in one of the dormitory sections nearby. It's not comfortable by any stretch of the imagination, not for seventeen days, but it could be a lot worse."

He shrugged.

"The Vistans have complained a lot less than I would have expected, too. They're brave people, sir. I'm glad we can help them."

"Me, too," Octavio said as they reached the crew quarters. "I still need to touch base with a few people before we get going. Buzz me if you need anything, but remember: this is *your* ship."

"Yes, sir!"

RENAUD HAD BEEN WAITING for Octavio's call, sitting at her desk in her new office in the unimaginatively named LPC Platform One.

It wasn't *much* of an office, but it at least had artificial gravity. The entire platform was built of pieces from *Scorpion*, with some assistance from the locals and the Matrices. Powered by three of the surviving fusion cores from the warp cruiser, it could power the two surviving light particle cannons and maneuver.

It was actually a bit more maneuverable than the guardships, to be fair, but it was using Vistan-built fusion engines instead of *Scorpion*'s burnt-out main engines and thrusters. Artificial gravity meant that she could do so at full power and evade incoming fire, but that was it. LPC Platform One wasn't a warship.

She *was* Aisha Renaud's command.

"I have about twelve hours until the convoy moves out," she told him. "I guess that'll leave me in charge here."

"You know it," he replied. "Even if rank and such didn't say it was your place, you're the best person for the job until the Admiral gets there.

"And you get to go play with warp drives," Renaud said. "Leaving me here."

"The Vistans need someone—and *Interceptor* needs a warp-drive expert." They'd had the argument before. It was starting to feel like a familiar rut, and part of him wondered just why Renaud kept bringing it up.

"I know." She made a throwaway gesture. "I'll miss you, you know. That's *me* talking, not Commander Renaud."

"We make a good team," he agreed.

She shook her head at him and sighed.

"That's true enough," she allowed, her tone sounding like she was giving up on something. "Anything we need to consider here in Hearthfire we haven't already gone over?"

"Keep an eye on Africano and her computer worms," Octavio advised. "Vistan cybersecurity is crap, but we don't want to accidentally piss our allies off. I think she's starting to think they'll never catch on and just opens up anything that looks interesting to her."

"She's a little too curious; got it," she agreed. "Anything else?"

He chuckled sadly and shook his head.

"Keep people moving," he told her. "We failed these folks pretty badly when those impactors came down. I don't want to fail them again."

"The Matrices think the Rogues won't be back soon," she said. "That buys us some time."

"Do you really want to risk a billion lives on that bet?" Octavio asked. "The Admiral is here in two weeks. Then we might be able to breathe. Until then, watch every spark, every unexplained anomaly.

"We know their protocol, but they've already demonstrated they can go beyond that if they think it will help. They're robots; they're not stupid."

"I know," she replied. "Just not much I can do with a glorified flying turret."

"More than we could with *Scorpion* with no guns, no power and no engines," he reminded her. "And that one's on me. All of this is on me."

"It's not, not really," Renaud told him. "Getting you away from here is a good idea just to help you process that."

"Plus, well, the engineering challenge of a lifetime," he said with a grin. "Trust the Admiral, Aisha. He'll be here soon enough."

"You be careful," she replied. "If you get yourself killed, I will *never* forgive you."

He wanted to say that there was no real risk of that in an engineering project, but he knew what *Interceptor* was being built to do. They knew nothing about the Matrices' Creators. Catching that ship was not going to be safe.

"We'll know how it went soon enough," he replied. "We'll talk again once I'm in Refuge. Good luck, Commander Renaud."

"Good luck...Octavio."

42

VISTA *HAD BEEN A BEAUTIFUL PLANET.* Isaac had seen the original survey scans and imagery from when *Scorpion* arrived. The scout ship had spent some time in the system following her original mission before the Matrices had changed the objectives, and the pictures were beautiful.

The planet *Vigil* decelerated into orbit of was not beautiful.

Clouds had covered the entire sky, black and ugly things concealing the world beneath them. Numbers flashing across the holodisplay on *Vigil*'s flag deck told him the truth those ugly clouds hid, too.

Global average temperature in the single digits of Celsius—the *low* single digits. Ice caps doubled in size and gaining thousands of square kilometers by the day. Winds over a hundred kilometers an hour, and waves over much of the open water that weren't any slower.

"They've pulled everything back into the sheltered seas, right?" Isaac asked quietly.

"This sea here," Connor agreed, a section of ground under the clouds flashing. "Orange-Sunset-Waters. The second area that was mostly protected from the initial impact has been abandoned. The ice and waves that are making it through the channel into Long-Night-Waters got too dangerous."

Three hundred and fifty million people lifted off the surface. Eight hundred thousand shipped to Refuge—and the two transport ships that Isaac had brought had arrived in orbit first. They were already being swarmed with shuttles loading civilians aboard.

In twenty-four hours, a million Vistans would either be in Refuge or on their way. That was only a drop in the ocean, however, and almost a billion people would remain.

"They were building ships here, right?" he asked quietly.

"Here," Connor confirmed, highlighting a facility orbiting in the Vista-Hearthfire L5 Lagrange point. "Four ships under construction right now, and they're working on four more slips. So long as we keep supplying them exotic matter, it's a geometric progression in how many ships they have online."

And still four years to evacuate. A *billion people*. The task had seemed so simple when he'd discussed it with Octavio Catalan, but the sheer scale of it awed him now.

They'd arguably already saved the species, but Isaac agreed with his subordinate. They hadn't saved the Vistans until they'd saved all of them that they could.

"We'll need to set up meetings with the First-Among-Singers and the Great High Mother," he told Connor. "The evacuations and the habitats appear to be moving along, which means we now need to consider how best to protect them.

"Our best guess is that the next Matrix attack is going to be *much* larger. Our Task Force is far more powerful than anything they've had to defend Vista before, but Catalan held this system by luck and suicidal insanity."

Isaac grinned.

"I've been known to rely on those myself, but I'd very much like to even the odds with a bit more preparation this time!"

———

THE TWO VISTANS who met him on one of their stations twelve hours later were a fascinating study in contrasts for him. The heavyset aliens were strange-looking to human eyes, almost looking like hunchbacked two-mouthed frogs with their legs coming up to their shoulders and dwarfing their delicate arms, but the distinctions between the two were most interesting.

Sings-Over-Darkened-Waters was even more hunched than the general impression of their race, clearly having suffered the same bending-over with age many humans shared. Her skin was a mottled gray, with occasional patches of a very pale green, and she wore a black vacuum suit with the sleeves and helmet retracted.

Despite the difference in species and fashion, the purpose of the garment was very clear.

Her companion and leader, Sleeps-In-Sunlight, was among the straightest-standing Vistans Isaac had seen so far. Tall for her race, the Great High Mother matched Isaac's average-for-a-human height—and her skin was a rich verdant green, as bright for a Vistan as Isaac's skin was dark for a human.

She was, he'd been briefed, *very* young—but those same briefings made it clear that Sleeps-In-Sunlight was now the unquestioned leader of the Vistan survivors.

"Thank you both for making the time to meet with me," he told them. "I know how busy this entire situation is making you, and I appreciate the effort."

The speakers mounted on his shoulders were going to take some getting used to, he reflected. The dual voices of the Vistan language were strange enough coming from the aliens. Hearing them come from his uniform was just *weird*.

"We survived because of your Captain Catalan," the Great High Mother told him. "You come to us as his First-Among-Singers; we would only dishonor ourselves to ignore you."

"Plus, your ships may be our only hope against the Strangers," Sings-Over-Darkened-Waters added. "The vessels you arrived with are intimidating. We had only barely become accustomed to the power of Captain Catalan's ship."

"Captain Catalan's ship served us all well," Isaac replied, burying his own sadness at *Scorpion*'s loss. "Task Group *Vigil*'s warships are newer, larger and more powerful. We will surprise the Matrices when they come."

He considered softening the truth, but he suspected that Sings-Over-Darkened-Waters knew it already.

"Unfortunately, it seems likely they'll come with sufficient force to overcome even this fleet. We will need you to contribute to your own defenses now that the evacuation seems to be going well.

"Is there somewhere we can speak in private and discuss options?" he asked. "My operations officer"—he gestured to Connor—"has spent some time going over the data that Catalan sent us, and we may have some options we hadn't realized before."

"I have had a space prepared," Sleeps-In-Sunlight said calmly. She clearly had been expecting something along these lines. "Come."

Isaac and Connor fell in behind the alien empress—and he wondered if *she* realized that the reason they had options they hadn't realized before was because Isaac Lestroud had every intention of exceeding the tech transfer he was authorized to give them.

Being married to the President covered many sins. Being *right* would hopefully cover the rest of them.

———

THE LAST THING Isaac was expecting when he walked into a Vistan conference room was a holoprojector. A floating projected globe hung in the middle of the room, with icons representing everything from the planet's diminutive moon to the four ships of his newly arrived task force.

Odd sounds accompanied it, a very specific series of echo-like chirps—what Catalan had said the locals called the datasong. The two Vistans in the room couldn't see the hologram at all, but those chirps gave their echolocation the same illusion of its presence.

"I'm impressed by the hardware," he told Sings and Sleeps. "Did you borrow one of our holoprojectors, or is this all home-built?"

"We realized we needed to be certain that both we and our allies were viewing the same data," Sings-Over-Darkened-Waters explained. "We worked with your Lieutenant Commander Africano quite closely, but we built this ourselves."

"I am *amazed*," Isaac replied. "From no hologram technology to building a dual-output system in less than five months? If you had done nothing else since we met, First-Among-Singers, your people would amaze me.

"As it is, I'm not certain there are words. We never could have saved you on our own," he reminded them. "Your people are saving *themselves*, Sings-Over-Darkened-Waters."

"Perhaps, Admiral," the Great High Mother cut in smoothly. "But remember that all of *our* efforts would have sufficed to evacuate perhaps a third of the people in orbit to habitats…and no one to safety beyond this system.

"We are at our strongest when we work together."

Isaac nodded. That was his hope, as well. A billion extra hands could make a huge difference in the survival of *both* races.

"I agree. That was what I needed to talk to you about," he told them. "There are many ways I can assist you, technology and systems I can provide you with schematics of that Catalan could not, but I need to know what you can do as a base."

"We have begun the production of six more guardships," Sleeps-Under-Sunlight said instantly, "and recommenced the mass production of the X-ray laser cartridges. With our current engines, it will be months before the target asteroids reach Vistan orbit, so workers have set up on them to begin drilling out the deep habitats."

Vistan guardships were impressive, if crude. The partially hollowed-out asteroids suffered in the face of Matrix weaponry, but they were resilient ships nonetheless.

"We should be able to provide you with schematics of engines and acceleration-compensator systems that will accelerate that process," he told her. "We also have systems that should make drilling out the spaces easier—it's a modified version of our pulse guns.

"We will also provide you with schematics for the pulse guns. Surface batteries of those on the new guardships will dramatically augment your firepower and antimissile defenses."

"They would, yes."

If his two companions had been human, Isaac figured they would have been exchanging aside glances. As Vistans, he could hear just the edge of a very carefully projected conversation he couldn't understand.

"There is a limit to how much industry we can put towards military hardware," Sleeps-In-Sunlight finally told him. "And with everything your people have offered us, I begin to fear the price in the long term."

"I understand," Isaac said quietly. He was not, unlike many of the black crew and officers in his fleet, a descendant of African-Americans, the slaves hauled away to serve in plantations. He was the descendant of the people left behind, who had watched chiefs and warlords trade those slaves for guns and other technology.

That left scars on a culture, even as it moved out to a colony world like New Soweto, and no child of New Soweto wanted to be the colonizer in that story.

"I believe Catalan told you our reasons for rescuing you," he continued. "Some of it is that we could not stand by and watch your people die. That's probably the majority of it, truth be told, but it's not what you fear. You fear that reason masks something else."

He shook his head.

"And it *does*," he confessed. "But even what it covers is straightforward, I think: we need an ally. We are four million souls tossed to the far end of beyond, *two lifetimes'* journey from home with our fastest ships.

"We need your hands, yes, but we need the minds who built this"—he gestured to the combined holographic and audio projector —"and the courage of the people who stood against the Matrices with chemical rockets and bomb-pumped lasers! We need allies and friends, and yes, we need allies and friends who can stand shoulder-to-shoulder with us in the line of battle. So, it is in our interest to upgrade your technology, and it is in our interest to buy your goodwill, and it is in our interest to save your people."

He swallowed, realizing he'd got a bit carried away as he glanced at Connor, who was very carefully saying nothing as his superior ranted.

"And goddammit, we are not willing to watch a billion people die and think, 'Maybe we could have saved them, but it wasn't worth it.'"

43

CONNOR WAITED until they were halfway back to *Vigil* aboard the shuttle before he raised the question Isaac had been waiting for.

"Sir," he said carefully, clearly not sure how to phrase it. "Do we have the authority to give them that much?"

The real question was "Do *you*," Isaac knew, but the attempt to spread the responsibility was appreciated.

"Catalan did," Isaac finally said. "He had a blank check to do whatever was necessary to save the Vistans. Of course, he *succeeded*, and the intentional limiter on how much he could hand over was what they could quickly produce."

"You promised them manufacturing technology," Connor pointed out.

"Which we originally presumed that they couldn't manufacture in time," Isaac agreed. "You're my operations officer. You saw the brief on what I wasn't supposed to give them."

He smiled.

"How badly do *you* think I broke it?"

The shuttle compartment was quiet for a good minute.

"We weren't supposed to offer them autofabrication tech," Connor said slowly. "I'm pretty sure grasers were off the list, and we were supposed to provide last-generation pulse guns. I *know* the particle cannons weren't supposed to be on list."

"That one is at least limited by exotic-matter production," Isaac told his operations officer. "A lot of what we're giving them is, and we're only giving them the particle-accelerator production system.

"But yes, I am exceeding my brief and my authority. Going to turn me in to my wife?"

"No, but I'm worried about the long-term consequences," Connor admitted. "Everything we're handing them...we're bringing them up to being able to build *real* warships, sir. All of that tech is going to go to Refuge with them."

"I'm counting on it," Isaac agreed. "I need them to back us up when we fight the Matrices here in Hearthfire, and when we start trying to clear safe zones around our worlds, we're going to need Vistan-crewed ships backing us up.

"We're not going to get those crews and those ships by treating them like beggars or children. We're going to get them by bringing them up to our level without demanding their service. We have a choice, Aloysius.

"We can help these people now, give them a helping hand and ask only for their friendship—and in so doing, gain allies who will stand with us to the gates of hell—or we can force them to sell their future to us to survive, turning them into thralls from whom we demand payment in bodies and blood."

Isaac looked at his pale, redheaded subordinate and shook his head as he considered how differently New Soweto's schools taught history compared to most of the Confederacy.

"I will not turn an entire race into slaves," he said quietly. "Most of the Cabinet wouldn't either. They're not thinking in those terms— they're thinking of protecting Exilium. And there *are* things I'm holding back, advantages they won't have...but we need these people to be our friends, not our slaves."

"I can see that, sir," Connor agreed slowly. "I guess the question then becomes *When do we admit what we're doing to the Cabinet?*"

Isaac chuckled.

"The moment they ask, Commander," he told Connor. "We *hide* nothing...but we don't tell them until they ask.

"And if they don't ask until after the Vistans commission their first warp-capable cruisers?" Isaac shrugged. "My wife will forgive me... and much as I like the rest of them, the only other person who will care is the next President."

And if that turned out to be Emilia Nyong'o, well, she'd understand completely.

"For now, though, we'll want to make sure we have everything coordinated with their production and ours," he continued. "We're not going to have the new guardships ready to even receive engines for weeks, but we can start mounting pulse guns on the remaining pair as soon as we have a design for the installation."

That was the advantage of the fact that the guardships were basically asteroids with facilities either dug into the core or mounted on the exterior. If they designed a self-contained facility with a fusion plant and a set of pulse guns, they could install it on the existing guardships as soon as they built it.

They'd need the advantage. The Rogue Matrices were coming back, and while Isaac fully agreed with the effort to contact the Creator ship, he didn't trust the Creators. Not yet.

———

CAMERON ALSTAIRS WAS WAITING for Isaac when he disembarked onto *Vigil*, the battlecruiser's Captain impeccably turned out in his black uniform. He saluted as the Admiral approached.

"Sir. I have the report you asked for," he told Isaac.

"Which one is that?" the older man asked his subordinate. "I seem to recall a list of reports."

"The one on our allies' strength, mostly," Alstairs replied calmly as he fell into step beside the Admiral.

"Summarize," Isaac ordered. His next meeting could be held from anywhere, so he was heading to his office. It wasn't like talking face-to-face with a Matrix remote changed anything, after all.

"There are two Vistan guardships left," the Captain told him. "They've got munitions stockpiles for days, but with only eighty launchers, there's only so much they can do." He shrugged. "Their effective range is somewhat shorter than ours, but those bomb-pumped lasers stack up well against even the LPCs. They're inferior to the spinal particle guns or the grasers, but they're still worth deploying."

"That's good," Isaac said. He'd known most of that, but it was valuable to know his flag Captain agreed with him. "We're going to be helping them upgrade those two guardships and get six more online ASAP—adding pulse-gun batteries and engines based on our tech to them. I was relying on their main weapons being useful still."

"If we're upgrading their engines, we might get more bang for our buck with their bombers," Alstairs said after a moment. "They're up to just over two hundred and fifty of them, another fifteen hundred X-ray lasers for one round, but they can't keep up with us."

Isaac thought about it for a moment. He hadn't even *thought* about the tiny bombers the Vistans had rolled out to increase their firepower.

"I'd ignored them," he admitted. "I'm guessing I shouldn't have?"

"They can't contribute to a fight long-term, and even their crews think they're suicide boats, but they *can* be more," Alstairs told him. "We can refit all of them with gravity plates and our engines for the effort to upgrade *one* guardship, and with *our* engines, they might have the maneuverability to get out of the way after they fire."

"Get the engineering teams on it," Isaac ordered. "I'm not turning down any advantage, but I was focusing on getting more capital ships in the line for what's coming. Speaking of, the Matrices?"

"Three combat platforms, four recon and security ships, twenty recon nodes," the Captain reeled off. "Right now, their real use seems to be as blockers. Each of them can take a Rogue Matrix out of the fight, at least temporarily."

"That's been succeeding for longer than I expected it to," Isaac replied. "Unless our robotic friends work out how to fire their guns at our robotic *enemies*, I think we need to count them out."

"Given the projections I'm seeing on Matrix strength, we may need them to do *something*," Alstairs pointed out. "Sixteen combat platforms?"

"Everything else is small change after that, isn't it?" Isaac agreed softly, stopping at his office door. "The *good* news is that combat platforms seem to be consistent. We haven't run into any that are more powerful than expected yet. They have no idea what we've brought to Hearthfire, and we have a pretty good concept of their entire line of battle."

"What happens when they roll out something new?" his flag Captain asked.

Isaac grimaced.

"We kill that, too," he said. "Whatever it takes. And you're right—that *will* happen. I don't know if one of the big regional computers can manage to do true research and development, but just building a bigger ship? I'm pretty sure they'll manage that."

Isaac got as far as opening the door to his office before the alarm cut through the corridor, a strobing red light and a harsh klaxon turning on as one. He and Alstairs looked down at their left arms simultaneously as their tattoo-comps buzzed a simultaneous alert.

"Multiple tachyon contacts," Alstairs read aloud. "CIC is making it thirty-six ships."

Their gazes met a second later as both of them finished reading the final note.

At least one unit significantly larger than known Rogue combat platforms.

"I *hate* being right," the Captain finally said.

44

THEY WEREN'T READY.

Sings-Over-Darkened-Waters knew that they never would have been *ready*. There would always be more ships to upgrade or build, more people to evacuate, more work to do.

But her conversation with Captain Catalan's Admiral had given her hope. They'd made plans, however tentative, to vastly upgrade her fleet to help make sure her people were safe. She could see a future time where they might have seen this fleet and felt that they *could* fight it.

Instead, she had two hundred–odd bombers and two guardships that couldn't keep up with her allies and could barely contribute to the fight to come regardless.

"Order the Star-Choirs to battle readiness," she said calmly as she strode into her command pool. "Get a shuttle ready to deliver the Great High Mother…"

"To where?" Sleeps-In-Sunlight asked as she entered the pool herself. "The surface is their primary objective. They will want to make sure there are no obstacles when they attempt to 'Construct' our world again."

The Great High Mother's chirps were the slow and steady

metronome of a perfectly calm Vistan. Sings knew her own breathing wasn't as calm, despite her skill at controlling her emotions.

Sleeps was half her age, but she'd been raised to rule. Some skills apparently came with that.

"Some of the habitats might be safe," Sleeps-In-Sunlight continued when her words were unchallenged. "Some fraction of our people might survive. But it is fitting, I think, for me to stand here with you, First-Among-Singers. I will share my people's fate."

"This ship must place itself between our people and the enemy," Sings told her monarch. "We take the risk *first*, not alongside. If you die here, you may die for nothing."

"Perhaps," Sleeps conceded calmly. "But nonetheless, First-Among-Singers, this is my place today. We both know the weight of this battle will fall on the humans. We are observers in our own home."

She gestured toward where the datasong told them there was an illusion of a world and its surrounding ships.

"There is nowhere better left to watch this than here, and I have my own suggestions—if you will hear them?"

Sings-Over-Darkened-Waters sighed and bowed her head.

"You are my Great Mother," she told Sleeps. "If that is your wish. What are these suggestions?"

She did not wholly discount the other Vistan's ideas, either. Sleeps-In-Sunlight had been born to be a politician, but that didn't mean she was unintelligent.

"When *Scorpion* went to meet the Matrices, she took our bombers with her to deploy the laser cartridges," Sleeps said. "Why, if the humans need our lasers, do they need the bombers?

"Wouldn't, say, a tow cable of a dozen of the bomb cartridges be as easily towed as a bomber?" The monarch paused. "And isn't that their storage state before we load them onto our guardships?"

Sings considered the younger Vistan's suggestion for only moments before she turned to her Voice-Of-Choirs.

"Swimmer-Under-Sunlit-Skies," she snapped. "How many cartridges do we have in a ready-to-load state for the guardships?"

THE ADVANTAGE to having lost most of the fleet was that what had once been a single full reload for eight gunships was four full reloads for two. They'd used up a good chunk of the extra munitions they'd held on hand, but the prepackaged sets had gone mostly untouched.

One of Sings-Over-Darkened-Waters's guardships carried a full load of eight hundred X-ray laser cartridges. They'd kept them fully armed and had a full reload on standby. Even with the sets they'd used to reload after the last few battles, there were over *three thousand* cartridges already organized into neat chains of twenty.

Admiral Lestroud's people were already forming up as she reached out to the human officer.

"Admiral, we have a possible tool for you to use," she told him as soon as she had the connection. "Your Captain Catalan used our bombers to augment his firepower against the Matrices before."

"We considered it," Lestroud confirmed. "The need to allow for their lack of compensation was too much of a risk."

"But why take the bombers at all?" she asked. "My Great High Mother reminded me that we reload our guardships with linked chains of cartridges, twenty bombs at a time. We keep those here, in Vistan orbit.

"We can't keep up with you, but we can give you three thousand extra lasers in your opening salvo if you wait a few minutes."

Lestroud paused for a few seconds, and Sings was quite sure she knew what he was doing: watching the Matrices that were already charging out to block their cousins from approaching the planet.

With an unknown enemy ship leading ten combat platforms, five recon and security nodes and twenty recon ships, they'd need those blockers—but leaving them to act on their own put them at risk.

Sings had been told all of the reasons why that trick worked, all of the reasons why their robotic allies were safe. She didn't buy them. Not completely.

Sooner or later, that was going to fail. Even if it failed today, however, it should buy the time for the human ships to strap hundreds of extra one-shot munitions to their hulls.

"Do it," he ordered. "We can only hold in orbit for three minutes at most. How many can you give us?"

"As many as we can strap on to your ships in three minutes," Sings-Over-Darkened-Waters promised. If her people weren't already moving, there would be some trips to dark water coming up.

———

In her encounters with humans, Sings-Over-Darkened-Waters had learned that Vistans had a far *broader* awareness of what was going on around them, but humans tended to be able to pay attention to details better.

Thanks to the datasong, for example, she was consciously aware of the position of her fleet, the status of the ammunition transfer, and the status of the two Matrix forces approaching each other. She was receiving all of the information on everything going on in Hearthfire, thanks to the audio image of the system she was receiving.

Because she was semiconsciously aware of *all* of that, however, she missed details. She missed the exact moment when everything began to go wrong.

The first thing *she* registered was when one of the friendly combat platforms self-destructed. The massive smooth ovoid was part of the central formation of the Matrix fleet one second and a ball of uncontained energy a moment later.

The formation of the friendly robots came apart as she watched. Her echolocation chirps sharpened in horror as two recon nodes self-destructed, joining their larger sibling in death.

There was some kind of battle going on, one she didn't understand. One her datasong couldn't interpret because their sensors couldn't even see it. The friendly Matrices were stopped relative to their hostile cousins now, twisting around each other in complex and potentially deadly patterns.

She clearly saw three of their nodes launch attack runs on one of the remaining combat platforms. The maneuver was unmistakable, even if no weapons were fired. The chaos was the strangest thing she'd ever seen—and then a cascade of near-*c* missiles smashed into it.

The entire strategy around using the friendly Matrices as blockers was built around the protocols that stopped the enemy attacking them.

The Rogues had found a way around that, and half of the friendly units vanished under the missile storm.

The rest vanished a moment later, and Sings was frozen in her command pool.

"Did they...did they punch out?" she finally asked aloud.

"Yes, First-Among-Singers," a Voice-Of-Eyes reported slowly. "One combat platform and ten recon platforms made it out."

Once again, Sings wished she could close her ears to the world around her.

That meant *seventeen* of the AI ships were gone, and at least four of them had *self-destructed.*

"What happened?" she demanded.

"We are not entirely sure," Swimmer-Under-Sunlit-Skies told her from his post. "But the humans just identified the largest Matrix unit, and the officers I am communicating with suspect that it's related."

"How?" Sings demanded, focusing her attention—a far more limited resource than her *awareness*—on the arming process for the Terran ships.

"It's a Sub-Regional Construction Matrix," Swimmer explained. "A far more powerful AI than any we have encountered before. Even the humans do not *know*, but they fear that it may be capable of overriding our allied Matrices."

Allied Matrices who had, in at least some cases, self-destructed to protect Sings-Over-Darkened-Waters's world.

"The humans are moving out," Swimmer reported after a few seconds of silence. "It looks like they got just over fourteen hundred bomb cartridges aboard." His chirps were dull and slow.

"I hope it's enough."

45

No one had ever considered the threat inherent in the clear hierarchy present among Matrix units. They probably *should* have, Isaac realized now, but their robotic allies were still mysterious in many ways.

"Task Force *Vigil* is in motion," Connor reported. "All ships report ready for battle. We're towing eight hundred Vistan bomb-cartridges. The strike cruisers have two hundred and twenty apiece."

Isaac nodded silently, his attention on the incoming enemy fleet.

They'd dealt with Matrix recons before. They'd seen Matrix reconnaissance-in-forces, security flotillas for terraforming projects, even the mid-weight defenses assembled around a single Rogue Sub-Regional Matrix.

This was none of those things. Most notably, there were only nine recon nodes in that fleet. The lightest Matrix ship the Exiles had encountered, the recon nodes had been used as escorts and fire support in every battle prior to this.

The larger recon and security nodes were serving more of that purpose here. Fourteen of the midsized ships formed the main echelon of the Matrix battle fleet, screening the twelve combat platforms present to provide heavy firepower.

And, of course, the Sub-Regional Matrix at the back of the formation. A thick black disk seven kilometers in diameter, it dwarfed even the kilometer-long combat platforms. Isaac *wanted* to hope that the main threat presented by it was its computers, but he couldn't trust that.

The one Sub-Regional Matrix they'd fought before, the Rogue present near Exilium, had encased itself in dozens of cubic kilometers of extra steel construction. That extra construction had dramatically expanded its ability to build ships and terraforming spikes, but it had covered up whatever weapons the ship carried.

"Have our Matrix friends checked in?" he asked, breaking his silence for the first time since their robotic allies had punched out.

"No, sir," Connor told him. "No communication yet. Commander Rose thinks they might be doing the electronic equivalent of freaking the fuck out—we're not sure *they* realized a higher-tier Matrix could override them."

"I'm not entirely comfortable with the realization that our enemy's higher-tier Matrices can override the protocols against attacking other Matrices," Isaac noted. "What *else* can they actively modify?"

"I'm more worried about what they can do to *our* Matrices' protocols," Connor replied. "We'll be expecting missile fire in the next few minutes, sir."

"They know they can't hit us," the Admiral said. His ships' Guardian Protocols were just as capable as *Scorpion*'s, and the battle-cruiser and strike cruisers had a *lot* more lasers and pulse guns to play with.

Task Force *Vigil* was directly between the Matrices and the Vistan habitats. The robots could shoot the planet, but the planet was already wrecked. Without detailed scans they couldn't get from this far away, there was no way they could intentionally target the still-inhabited portions.

They could easily target the habitats. Isaac wasn't sure they *would*—the question of how the Rogues would react to an alien presence that wasn't in the way of their terraforming efforts was still unanswered—but he couldn't take the risk. Not with almost four hundred million people aboard the habitats now.

Task Force *Vigil* couldn't shield them all, but the vast majority of them were behind him.

"No missile launches detected so far," Connor agreed. "They seem to have that much intel...and they *don't* seem to be trying to shoot at the habitats."

"That's good news," Isaac admitted. "I don't really *want* to just abandon the planet to them once we've pulled the Vistans off, but having it as an option is useful." He shook his head. "Robots or not, though, I suspect we're going to start seeing some degree of vengeance-seeking on these Matrices' part. Sooner or later."

"I'm guessing shortly after we blow another Sub-Regional Matrix to pieces," his ops officer suggested. "*Our* Matrices seem to regard all of their nodes as, well, *people*. These guys...well, somehow I can see them only valuing the big guys."

"Fortunately for them, I think we need to shoot the 'big guy' last," Isaac told his subordinate. "We can deal with the light ships easily—the strike cruisers will have them for lunch—and *Vigil* can probably take the big Matrix.

"We can't do either of those things *and* deal with a dozen combat platforms, so I only see one real option," he continued grimly.

Even outnumbered as they were, he had to marvel at the difference from the first time they'd fought Matrices. That time, a single recon node had nearly smashed the entire Exilium Space Fleet. They hadn't known the capabilities of their enemy then, and they'd upgraded their systems vastly since then. The difference was stark—and a good chunk of it was due to their alliance with Regional Construction Matrix XR-13-9.

"The interface we rigged up for the X-ray lasers is *not* going to be particularly effective at aiming them," Connor warned him. "Our hit percentages are going to suck at anything above about two light-seconds."

"Then we get to two light-seconds," Isaac replied. "I was planning on a million klicks, but if we need closer we need closer. If they're going to come at us at ten percent of lightspeed, that's only a dozen seconds."

"The rest of their guns and ours will be in play well before that," his subordinate noted.

"Closing is going to suck," the Admiral agreed. "We'll open up on the combat platforms with everything we have at our best range. The strike cruisers' main guns are just as good as the combat platforms' beams—which means *better* than anything the lighter units have.

"So, we let them 'force' us into range of their lighter units' guns... and then introduce them to our passengers."

"We're going to lose a bunch of the cartridges," Connor warned. He wasn't arguing, but it was his *job* to poke holes in Isaac's plans—and he did it well.

"I know." Isaac shook his head. "But I'd rather shoot them with three thousand beams with a fifty percent hit chance then four thousand beams with a *ten* percent chance."

————

ISAAC'S JOB wasn't to manage any single ship. His job was to set out the battle plan, give high-level instructions, and to come up with the tricks that would surprise their enemy.

He spent the entire flight toward combat adjusting the Task Force's vector, slowly edging all four ships away from a direct clash with the center of the Matrix formation. He couldn't pull any of the Matrix warships out of range, but he *could* move his ships such that several had their line of fire blocked.

The Matrices responded by shifting their formation in turn, concentrating the heavy combat platforms closest to him to clear their lines of fire and pulling the Sub-Regional Matrix back. It was the logical counter to his move—and it was *exactly* what he wanted them to do.

"Enemy firing!" Connor reported. "*Juliet* and *Othello* have taken hits; both are unimpaired."

Only the combat platforms were firing so far. Isaac's Task Force's own weapons matched—in some cases, even exceeded—the effective range of the combat platforms' grasers against the energy-absorbing armor the Matrices favored.

The Rogues hadn't known that the new human ships had integrated that same armor into their core construction. They were at a range where they could *hit* Isaac's ships...but not at a range where they could *hurt* his ships.

"Inform Captain Alstairs he is to engage with the main gun as soon as he is in range," Isaac ordered. "He is to hold the secondary weapons until the strike cruisers are also in range."

Vigil's two spinal gamma ray lasers were moderately less efficient than the spinal guns on his strike cruisers. They were also enough bigger to make up the difference in range, at least.

"Bridge reports main gun firing in ten seconds," Connor replied.

On the old *Vigil*, Isaac would have felt the gun fire. The ships engines were programmed to auto-compensate for the recoil, but it wasn't perfect.

The new *Vigil's* compensation *was* perfect—or at least close enough that human senses couldn't pick up the recoil in the fractions of a moment it existed.

He checked his console. Alstairs was going for the old mainstay of a battlecruiser Captain expecting a long fight. The flagship had eight cyclotrons fueling her main gun—and four smaller ones feeding each of the light particle cannons in her turrets—and each cyclotron took sixty seconds to prepare a charged ion packet.

Every seven and a half seconds, a new shot flashed downrange... and every seven and a half seconds, the range dropped another quarter-million kilometers.

The second shot fired before the data on the first shot's impact made it back. The recon and security ship Alstairs had targeted clearly hadn't thought it was in range yet. The charged particles hit it dead-on, punching straight through the robotic vessel.

It wasn't destroyed, but it was suddenly the lowest threat level among the Matrix ships. Isaac watched as the computers reclassified it, dropping it down the targeting queue as the second shot slammed into a recon node.

That ship simply vanished. The old *Vigil's* main gun had been sufficient to crack a recon node's armor in one hit, if not sufficient to destroy the ship in one blow. The new gun was over ten times as powerful.

Even as that ship came apart, the entire screen lit up with light. The Matrix combat platforms had been firing grasers at long range all along—and now the Exiles returned the favor. A single recon and security node was the target of five heavy grasers.

It dodged three. Two hammered into her, sending her reeling into the path of the fire from the dozens of LPC turrets now lashing the Matrix fleet. Chunks of black armor blasted off into space, and the ship stopped in space as her reactionless drive failed.

"All grasers and LPCs in range," Connor reported unnecessarily. "Enemy fire effectiveness is increasing fast. *Othello* reports multiple hull breaches but all weapons remain functional."

Isaac nodded as impassively as he could. The interior of that strike cruiser would be hell now, and he wasn't sure how they were keeping their weapons online.

"Time to X-ray laser range?" he asked softly. Their secondary pulse guns would be in range around the same time. The Matrices were already firing the plasma-based weapons but without much effect.

Yet.

"Thirty seconds." *Othello*'s icon on the screen suddenly flashed orange and Connor swallowed a curse of some kind.

"*Othello* took a hard hit. Captain Mak is reporting they've lost the main gun and two of their turrets. He's rotating to protect his damaged flank, but he's bleeding air and power."

"We need those turrets and her bombs," Isaac replied. "Tell Captain Mak to get me a time estimate on the main gun ASAP."

The answer was almost certainly *not until the fight is over*, but there was always hope.

"Ten seconds."

No one asked what the countdown was for now. They'd lost hundreds of the Vistan weapon cartridges, the Matrices clearly not even aware they were shooting the weapons down, but over a thousand remained.

"Targeting Protocol Sucker Punch," Isaac ordered, his voice as calm as he could make it. "Synchronize *all* weapons with the laser cartridges. You have your targets?"

"I do," Connor confirmed calmly. "Overrides active. Cartridges are responding to commands. We are go."

Isaac took one glace at *Othello*'s icon, his wounded ship spewing air as she still engaged the enemy, and didn't even check to see where the timer on their plan was.

"Fire."

———

ONE WORD and the sky lit up with flame. The X-ray lasers were floating around *Vigil* and her sisters now in rough spheres, carefully aligned to avoid getting in each other's way.

The screens and holograms on the flag deck automatically darkened as over eleven hundred fifty-megaton fusion warheads ignited as one. Thousands of energy beams stabbed into the dark, and the ESF ships' weapons fired as well.

Plasma and X-rays and gamma rays and charged ions flashed across two light-seconds in moments. Each of the dozen combat platforms, each a heavier combatant than Isaac's battlecruiser flagship, was the target of over a hundred energy weapons.

Many of those shots missed. A thousand-plus fusion explosions created enough interference to confuse the human ships' sensors. Dozens—*hundreds* of beams stabbed harmlessly into the dark or struck the combat platforms' escorts.

Enough connected. Twelve Matrix combat platforms, each a kilometer-long multi-clawed warship sufficient to challenge entire space fleets, died. Escorts died with them and as the cataclysmic flame faded, Isaac knew they'd evened the odds.

"*Othello* is to fall back behind the other strike cruisers," he ordered swiftly. "Strike cruisers are to focus on the remaining recon and security ships first, then clean up the recon platforms. Even *one* missed ship could mean millions of dead civilians, people."

"And *Vigil*?" Connor asked.

"Inform Captain Alstairs that his target is the construction Matrix," Isaac said flatly. "He is to hit her with everything he's got."

That Matrix was already slowing, beginning to turn in space. He doubted it was unarmed, but the AI was clearly prioritizing its own survival over anything else.

"Don't let her get away, Cameron," he whispered to himself.

Even as he was whispering, *Vigil*'s main gun opened up again. The construction Matrix had been at the rear of the AI formation, and Alstairs was testing the range.

The first ion packet hit home and Isaac held his breath, waiting for the damage report.

Nothing.

Nothing they could detect, at least, but it wasn't like the Matrix ships had atmosphere aboard for organics.

"Alstairs is initiating full…"

The reports on the hologram rendered Connor's report obsolete. The main gun was continuing to pound away at the immense warship, and now over a dozen lighter particle cannons joined in. Gamma ray lasers flashed in the night, and dozens of pulse guns added to the chaos.

For a few precious seconds, the fleeing Matrix took the fire. Its armor was clearly immense, capable of absorbing firepower that would have boiled an ocean…but it wasn't invulnerable.

"Incoming fire!" Connor snapped. "Evasive maneuvers successful for now, but dear *gods*."

It took a few moments for *Vigil*'s computers to resolve just what had been fired at them. The sheer energy level had led Isaac to think it had to be hundreds of beams…but it wasn't.

The Sub-Regional Construction had sixteen heavy guns. Just sixteen, despite its seven-kilometer diameter.

Each of them was a gamma ray laser that would crack a planetary crust. A single hit from any of those beams could render a world uninhabitable.

A single hit from one of those beams would almost certainly wreck *Vigil*.

"Tell Alstairs to focus on evasion," Isaac said quietly. "We *can't* take a hit from one of those things."

If Connor bothered to pass that order on, Isaac would have been surprised. Part of the operations officer's job, after all, was to know when the Admiral was giving redundant orders.

Regardless of whether the order was communicated, *Vigil* was now all over the sky. She was still accelerating forward, but the Matrix had now fully reversed its velocity and was heading *away* at ten percent of the speed of light.

They'd hit it—they'd hit it *hard*—but they weren't going to stop it fleeing.

In the end, it wouldn't matter if the Rogue ship got away. The fleet it had brought with it was debris and radiation, the strike cruisers already hunting down the last handful of ships.

Vigil shuddered as a beam passed close enough for the corona to hit the battlecruiser. No real damage, but still enough to remind them that an actual *hit* would be fatal.

"We can break off, sir," Connor suggested, his voice very, *very* quiet. "We're going to lose the range pretty quickly here reg—"

"Tachyon punch!"

The sensor tech's announcement drew everyone's attention, and Isaac inhaled sharply as he saw the signature.

There was barely time for them to resolve the signature of Combat Coordination Matrix ZDX-175-14 before the Sub-Regional Construction Matrix collided with it at a combined velocity of over twenty percent of the speed of light.

The flag deck was silent for several seemingly eternal seconds as the light of the cataclysmic impact washed over *Vigil*.

"Orders to the..." Isaac paused to cough, then started again. "Orders to the Task Force: strike cruisers are to clean up the escorts, then move on the wreckage. *Vigil* is to move on the wreckage immediately and scan for active power signatures.

"We will take no chances. Any active power signature detected is to be destroyed by heavy bombardment *immediately*."

The Matrix was almost certainly dead...but ZDX-175-14 had been the architect of the blocker plan. That AI was directly responsible for the survival of every single living Vistan left...and if all Isaac could do was make damn sure ZDX's killer was dead, then Isaac would do just that.

46

It was six hours later before the rest of the Matrices returned, the last remaining combat platform the first ship to emerge.

ZDX-175-18 was alone for at least five minutes, then the remainder of the surviving Matrix units flashed into existence around it and slowly headed toward Vista.

Isaac wasn't surprised to receive the communication request from the AI shortly afterward. He was in his office drinking coffee when it arrived, and tapped the command without waiting.

"Admiral Isaac Lestroud. This is Combat Coordination Matrix ZDX-175-18," it told him. *"We sent Matrix ZDX-175-14 back to scout ahead of us. Can you provide telemetry of their fate?"*

"We can," he promised. "ZDX-175-14 emerged in the path of the Rogue Sub-Regional Construction Matrix while it was attempting to flee the system." He paused. "I wasn't sure if this was intentional."

"We believe ZDX-175-14 had partial access to the sensor networks in the system," Eighteen told him. *"ZDX-175-14 was keeping us updated on the status of the battle but did not provide sufficient telemetry for us to be certain that any interception was intentional.*

"Without ZDX-175-14, we waited and then sent a scout ship to see if the

system was safe." There was a surprisingly long silence for an AI that processed its thoughts in fractions of a second.

"We failed you. We took responsibility for the security of this system and the protection of the Vistan population, and we failed. We did not anticipate that the Rogues would be able to override our core loyalty protocols with a high-enough-tier AI.

"There was an extended conflict in our mesh network, and several nodes chose to self-destruct when they believed their systems were compromised. No matter what happened, we would not permit ourselves to be used as weapons against you.

"ZDX-175-14 realized that the only available course was to withdraw, as we were unable to assist in the battle, and with Sub-Regional Construction Matrix XD-17-26-51 present in the system, we represented a potential threat ourselves."

"The situation was resolved with surprisingly light casualties on our side," Isaac told the AI. "The loss of ZDX-175-14 and your other Matrices is hard on us all. We did not think the Rogues could hurt you any more than you could hurt them."

"They appear to be more capable of self-modification of their programming than we are," ZDX-175-18 confirmed. *"XR-13-9 is investigating to see if their higher tier permits any modification of lower-tier units' protocols. The potential capacity to deploy our combat coordination units to protect inhabited worlds from the Rogues is worth some risk."*

"Even if all you can do is help us build habitats, you are helping save these people," Isaac reminded them. "We were never counting on you to be able to fight the Rogues."

"You were not," Eighteen confirmed. *"We...grow frustrated with our inability to protect sentient life. Experimentation has begun in protected areas. We could not protect Vista. We have failed to protect Vista again and again, with your people carrying the burden alone.*

"This must end, Admiral Isaac Lestroud. These Rogues are us, the same code, the same hardware. The deaths they have caused are our responsibility. We do not know what options will become available, but XR-13-9 has decided that we must *act."*

"You're already acting," he reminded the AI. The thought of what kind of experimentation the Matrices might be engaging in was... disturbing at best.

"*We will find a way to do more,*" Eighteen told him. "*We will build more habitats here, and XR-13-9 is sending several light construction-only units to assist in that project and in the guardship projects.*

"*We must choose which of our core protocols come first...and we know that our Creators would have had us protect life first. Always.*

"*So, with the help of you and the Vistans, we will find a way to do just that.*"

47

Dropping out of warped space to tachyon-com messages reporting on an attack and a desperate battle was not, Octavio reflected, the best way to arrive in a new star system.

Everything in the reports he'd seen said that Hearthfire had held and the human and Vistan casualties had been light. Matrix casualties *hadn't* been, and the consequences of that were going to take some mental absorption on his part.

Until that attack, they'd *known*, without question, that Matrix couldn't attack Matrix. Now they had evidence that the higher-level AIs could override that, which raised all kinds of ugly questions about the Rogues.

Which core protocols were actually inviolable? Was the reason XR-13-9 and the other verified Regional Matrices had managed to stay sane that they'd *lost* the code that let them modify their core orders?

Or had the Rogues lost the code that stopped them?

Octavio Catalan didn't know. He wasn't a software engineer. His term in systems security had been uneventful, a relatively normal role for a newly commissioned engineer. He'd spent most of it bored, coding the cyber worms he'd used to take over the Iron Peaks Command Center.

Perfumed Dancer didn't have a large-enough bridge for observers. He and the senior officers of his collection of engineers had rigged up a rough observation room in one of the lounges in the crew quarters, and he'd been using its gear to go over the reports from Hearthfire with everyone.

"I never thought I'd miss an individual Matrix," Das said, the tactical officer looking at the imagery of ZDX-175-14's death. "Fourteen kept us all alive, though. I'm assuming they were the one with the idea to use themselves as blockers."

"It was Fourteen," Octavio confirmed. "I asked." He shook his head. "The Matrices aren't a hive mind, after all. Each of them is an individual sentient AI core. They can build more of themselves relatively easily, but each of them is…well, a person."

With a wave of his hand, he reset the imagery of the observation deck. Now it showed the Refuge System. Currently, only the fourth planet, the Constructed World, bore any name but the stark Refuge-1, Refuge-2, etc.

Of course, that name was Refuge…just to add to the confusion.

Three rocky worlds orbited closer to the star than Refuge-4, baked hard by the blue-white A-class star they'd also named Refuge—technically Refuge-0. Octavio didn't know if an A-class star would have a habitable world on its own, but with the self-replicating Matrices in play, *anywhere* could have a habitable planet.

Refuge-5 was a cold world, even drier than Mars in the Sol System. An asteroid belt separated the five rocky worlds from three gas giants, all relatively small but more than sufficient to fuel an interstellar civilization.

Dwarfed by the planets were the two clusters of icons representing the Matrix ships and the Vistan colonists.

"We can't change what happened in Hearthfire," Octavio stated as he focused on those icons. "We are here, ladies and gentlemen. Refuge, home to six hundred thousand evacuated Vistans, twelve Matrix support nodes and sixteen Matrix recon nodes."

Two of the "recon nodes" were the larger recon and security units. Here, though, all of the security ships paled in importance to the support ships.

The primary final preparation node hung in an artificially stable orbit above the colony site. No human or Vistan ship could have stayed consistently above a single point at only two hundred kilometers' altitude, but the Matrices had reactionless engines.

From that ship, hundreds of smaller remotes were swarming over the target colony zone. Octavio had seen some images, but they were basically duplicating Shining Sunset on a larger scale.

Once they'd finished that city, they'd move on to the next. And the next. And the next. Each of the colony sites the Matrices were building would house ten million people. Several were already complete, but a hundred would be built before the ship was done with its work.

Six of the other support ships were rapidly building orbital infrastructure. The Vistans would arrive to a planet with orbital industry that dwarfed the complexes they'd built for themselves.

They'd also benefit from the yard hanging at the Refuge-0–Refuge-4 L5 point. The other five Matrix support ships were clustered there and had already completed the framework of the yard.

A framework, Octavio noticed as he zoomed in, that included chunks of those ships. The support units were looking somewhat skeletal, but *Interceptor* was already beginning to take shape in the heart of the yard.

"*Perfumed Dancer*'s destination is Refuge itself," he told his people. "We'll be taking two of the heavier shuttles over to the shipyard. Sadly, we can't give anyone shore leave on the planet—our timeline is tight."

"We've all seen a Constructed World before, boss," Tran told him. "I don't think any of us have seen the inside of a Matrix-built starship."

The jury-rigged holographic display zoomed in on *Interceptor* now, bringing the ship into full detail.

Most ships included curves and arches in their designs for structural support. Actual streamlining wasn't a factor, but most human-designed ships ended up looking a bit like it anyway.

At the speeds *Interceptor* was designed to travel, streamlining was needed. She was a needle in space, never more than fifty meters across, with her nose packed full of electromagnetic shielding to protect the passengers from the hellstorm she was going to drive into.

Half a kilometer long, she was easily the length of an ESF battle-cruiser, but almost her entire volume was fuel tanks. Of the space that wasn't, most was engines and her two matter-conversion power cores.

He could see the connectors where the warp-drive ring would go on, but it hadn't been built yet. That was what his people were there for.

"Are we getting any guns?" Das asked as she studied the hologram.

"Only those the Marines are carrying," Octavio replied. "Lieutenant Chen Zhou will be responsible for her people. We brought all of *Scorpion*'s heavy arms and armor, so hopefully our twenty Marines will be enough of an army for whatever we need."

Lieutenant Chen had been Lieutenant Major Summerfield's second-in-command. With Summerfield's death, Chen Zhou had taken command of the remaining Marines.

It was a shrinking family, and Octavio hoped it wouldn't get any smaller before this was done.

"We can probably recruit some of the Spears from Refuge for extra gun hands," Africano suggested. The coms officer was going to be their liaison with the evacuees there in Refuge. "It seems like twenty Marines isn't much to investigate a ship of the scale we're trying to catch."

"Check with Chen," Octavio ordered. "I'm not sure what we can equip Vistan troopers with, and I'm *very* sure the slugthrowers they used on the surface will be inefficient at best aboard an unknown starship."

"We'll check," Africano promised.

He looked around his officers and smiled at the bevy of terrifying women who helped lead his people.

"*Interceptor* isn't a perfect replacement for *Scorpion*, but her mission is something we've never seen before," he told them. "We have forty days to build and install a warp-drive ring, but we have *every* resource the Matrices can provide to pull it off.

"Once she's done, we all move aboard her and set off on this quest. Our time slot to launch is less than forty-eight hours wide, and our intercept will take a subjective thirty-four hours." He shook his head.

"Of course, that will be just over fifty-two days in objective time. I'm looking at a better way to slow down from there, but it looks like another fifty-two days.

"We'll pull them into warped space to communicate to avoid it taking weeks in real time. I've been running models on trying to use the warp drive to slow us down, and it looks *promising* but dangerous." He looked at the strange ship they would be flying.

"It would save us fifty days," he told his people. "So whether or not we do it will depend on what the Creators say when we board their ship."

And, perhaps more importantly, how the tachyon punch–equipped ships trying vainly to keep up with the Creator vessel reacted to their approach.

————

PERFUMED DANCER HAD NEVER BEEN INTENDED to serve as a passenger liner. Even her crew quarters were far from spacious or comfortable.

It was *space* that the hub station for the new shipyard provided in spades. Octavio wasn't sure if the Matrices were using the same artificial-gravity technology the humans used or had some trick of their own, but the station they'd built for the humans had an even point nine gees throughout.

And it was *huge*. Not, perhaps, in the grand scheme of things—but a two-hundred-meter sphere left a lot of space for a crew of less than a hundred and twenty humans. For the first time since leaving Hearthfire, Octavio could actually *stretch*…a man who'd lived aboard a warp cruiser for the last ten years didn't need much space to stretch.

"Das"—he gestured the tactical officer over to him—"I need you to get everyone settled and a list of contact info for all of them. Africano left us a relay for our tattoo-comps, right?"

"And two of her techs have been babysitting it the whole way," Das confirmed. Since he'd left Renaud behind in Hearthfire, the tactical officer was here to take her place in organizing people for the Captain.

"Get it set up and assign people quarters," he ordered.

"What about you?" she asked.

"Assign me quarters, too," Octavio replied. "If it has a bed and a desk, that's more luxury than I'm expecting from something the Matrices built."

"I do need to know where you are and what you're doing if I'm going to try and keep herd on this crowd. Only half of these people have any idea how any systems outside their specialty work."

"And we'll want them working on the systems from their specialty," he agreed. "With the engineers organizing and integrating. You're right," he conceded, and shook his head.

"I have some directions from the Matrices," he continued. "I'm supposed to hook up with whichever one is in charge of this project."

He tapped a command on his tattoo-comp.

"There, my comp should be telling you where I am so long as we're in range of each other," he said. "I don't plan on getting lost, but it is a surprisingly large station."

"Be good, sir," she ordered. "Please don't break the computers."

"I only break computers of people who throw me in cells," he replied with a grin. "You handle the people, Lieutenant Commander. I'll go play ball with the robots."

————

THE DIRECTIONS LED HIM "UP" toward the top of the sphere. According to the map on his tattoo-comp, he was now at the very edge of the sphere as he reached the final door. A tiny, very paranoid part of his brain half-expected the last door he opened to vent him into space.

Instead, he found himself in a wide but tiny room with a black wall facing him. The space he stood in was maybe two meters across but at least fifteen wide.

"Hello?" he said cautiously.

"*Greetings, Captain Octavio Catalan,*" the standard flat automated voice of a Matrix echoed in the space. "*This is Specialty Matrix XR-13-9-D. This Matrix is a direct partition from XR-13-9's core intelligence as of one thousand two hundred and sixty-one hours ago.*

"*Given some of the previous requests made by your species, this Matrix decided to arrange as close to a face-to-face meeting as possible.*" XR-13-9-D paused. *"Of course, this Matrix's core hardware is a cylindrical installation forty-eight point two meters by fifty-six meters. We are preparing space for it aboard* Interceptor *for installation within the next eighty hours."*

"You're our Matrix core?" Octavio asked.

"For Interceptor, *yes,"* XR-13-9-D confirmed. *"And beyond. This Matrix's parent intelligence modified my loyalty protocols. This Matrix's first loyalty is now to the Republic of Exilium. This Matrix's recommendation is that the core hardware be transferred to an ESF battlecruiser once this mission is complete, to allow this Matrix to assist in the protection and advancement of the Republic's human charges."*

Octavio had to pause to process that. They'd been told that the Matrix used for this purpose would stay with the humans, but he'd never really considered what that would mean.

XR-13-9-D wasn't a subordinate Matrix of the Matrices they'd been dealing with. It was, for lack of a better description, a *human* Matrix.

"That's a lot more than we were anticipating," he finally admitted. "I'm not sure that our populace would be okay with installing you aboard a warship. While the verified Matrices have helped counteract our fear of AI, the Rogues certainly haven't!"

"That is understandable. This Matrix can also provide significant value as a command-and-control interface emplaced at Exilium in an unarmed casing, so long as tachyon communications are maintained with ESF units. Any way that this unit can be of assistance to the Republic, it shall be done.

"Once this mission is complete."

"That makes sense," Octavio agreed. "You're being installed shortly, you said. Are you in charge of the construction, too?"

*"*Interceptor *will be this Matrix's first body. It is unusual for a Matrix core to be activated before the hull it will reside in is complete, but Specialty Matrices are unusual in all senses and purposes.*

"To answer your question, yes, this Matrix is responsible for the construction of Interceptor. *Much of the warp-drive technology required is still strange to us. The assistance of your engineers in that part of* Interceptor's *construction will be required—and the assistance of your crew in all parts will be welcome and valuable.*

"The Matrices have not previously constructed vessels designed to carry humans. We are basing much of our work on the repairs performed to the

battlecruiser unit Dante. *To achieve maximum synergy, we will need to work closely with your people."*

"That's the plan," Octavio agreed. "We only have forty days, after all."

"There will be second chances if the project is not completed on time, but this unit currently projects completion and fueling of the Interceptor *unit in eight hundred and eighty-two hours, plus/minus thirty hours."*

That was promising. Even the high end of XR-13-9-D's estimate got them ready to go with over a day to spare.

"Well, then." The engineer-turned-starship-Captain smiled, knowing that the AI would perceive it. The Speciality Matrix might not have eyes, but there was no way this room wasn't wired for every sensor the Matrices had.

"We have a lot of work to do. You and I should start sorting out what comes next."

48

THE CARRIER on the screen in Isaac's office had been built by one of Vista's more polar powers. The three-hundred-meter-long oceangoing ship had a heavier prow than the rest of the carriers left on the planet, designed to act as a nuclear-powered icebreaker around Vista's frozen poles.

As Isaac watched the footage, it was acting as an icebreaker... roughly fifteen kilometers from Shining Sunset. It was operating under autopilot, thankfully, its crew having been evacuated weeks earlier.

Still, having the carriers on automated patrol routes had enabled a lot of aerial operations that were no longer going to be possible.

The ship on the footage was moving slower and slower as it cut through the ice, until it finally ground to a halt.

"That's it," Sings-Over-Darkened-Waters's translated voice told him over the com. "*A-Dancing-Of-War-Planes* was the last of our carriers to be able to traverse the oceans. We had hoped to bring her back to Shining Sunset, to use her nuclear plants to power some of the shelters."

"Which isn't happening," Isaac concluded. "What about your underwater settlements?"

He'd seen footage of Shining Sunset, for example. Vistan cities were built half into the water, since the species' gill-equivalents handled the switch from air to water with surprising ease.

There was still no visual output from the Vistan communicators. The footage he was looking at was washed out, lacking in color—a clear sign that it had been taken by Vistan sensors.

The frog-like aliens were getting better at interfacing their gear with humanity's as time went on. It was a good thing, he was convinced. It meant that they'd have a chance of surviving the technological uplift that dealing with the Republic and Matrices made inevitable.

"Their inhabitants had priority for the evacuations," Sings said. "Short of the holdouts, they'd been evacuated for six weeks."

"The holdouts?" Isaac asked. There would always be humans who refused to believe what the government had to say. It was almost reassuring that the Vistans had the same problem.

"Once the water around them started to turn to slush and darkness, they found new truths," Sings said. "A few tried to stay regardless. Spears removed them a week ago."

"So that's it?" he asked. "No surface water left?"

"Our lakes and rivers froze weeks or even months ago," Sings told him. "Now the ocean is solid. We can still break through to water in most places, but..."

But.

Isaac had the numbers on another screen. The average temperature on Vista's surface had now dipped below minus ten Celsius. The *highest* temperature his satellites were detecting was minus three.

Below the freezing point of saltwater.

Different concentrations of salts across the planet meant that some regions were more firmly frozen than others, but there was basically no unfrozen water on the surface of Vista's lakes and oceans.

It was a day later than they'd expected, one hundred and seventy-three days after impact, but the planet had passed the first milestone of becoming what could only be called a dead world.

"The evacuation?" he asked.

"We have evacuated fifty percent of the population," the First

Among Singers told him. "With our freighters now online, one point eight million people have left for Refuge."

Another six months and the freighters would be bringing food back with them. The food stocks here in Hearthfire wouldn't suffice to feed the populace in orbit, not even with the greenhouses. Once the crops started coming up at the new colony, the freighters wouldn't fly empty either way.

"How long until the rest are out?" Isaac said. The thought of being on a planet where even the *oceans* had frozen terrified him.

"One hundred and ten days to get the remaining surface population into the habitats," Sings replied. "It's a good thing we brought Iron Peaks on board—the underground complexes they built wouldn't have saved their people, but they can buy months for a hundred million people.

"My people are in danger wherever they are, but they are starting to resist moving."

Isaac could hear the sadness in her voice.

"They're resisting the evacuations?" he asked.

"Not into orbit," she told him. "The evacuations on the ground. We need to concentrate our remaining populations. Keeping everyone from freezing is going to require vast amounts of power shortly. The need to evacuate priority areas meant that we didn't clear out entire cities.

"We need to do so now. The coastal cities will become untenable without vast power consumption soon. The Shining Mother has picked a handful of cities we will secure and protect against the elements.

"We will move the populace either to those cities, to the bunkers, or to the habitats. People will struggle, but we won't leave them behind."

"No one will be left behind," Isaac agreed. He meant it, too. The world his ship orbited was an ice ball now, but everything was in place to save the half-billion people left.

"You've worked miracles, Sings-Over-Darkened-Waters," he told her. "I didn't think we could save everyone. Your people saved themselves."

"Perhaps. But your people made it possible. We will not forget."

"I may call on that debt sooner than either of us would like," he admitted.

"I know. The Shining Mother knows. We will answer."

THIRTY DAYS HAD SEEN the strike cruiser *Othello*'s damage repaired, the last of the habitats in orbit moved to the Vista-Hearthfire L4 and L5 Lagrange points, and the new set of guardships mostly completed.

No new attacks. The silence from their robotic enemies was potentially reassuring, potentially not. Isaac didn't know how the Regional Matrix would react to the loss of one of its Sub-Regional units.

Neither did his Matrices. They weren't aware of a Sub-Regional Construction Matrix *ever* being destroyed.

New Matrices had arrived to make up some of their losses, six strange spider-like ships Isaac didn't think were warships and four units he recognized as combat and construction nodes.

All ten had set to work replacing their fallen siblings on the construction projects.

Now, without anyone telling him anything, one of the spider-like ships was detaching from the habitat project and heading for the asteroids. He considered ignoring it—he had plenty of reasons to trust his Matrix allies by now—but he really couldn't.

Sighing, he put his coffee on his desk and tapped a command. His "desk," like most surfaces in the room, did triple duty as a working area, a screen, and a touch input surface. Like every such surface in the Fleet, it was *very* good at identifying and ignoring coffee cups.

"Communications, get me a link to ZDX-175-18," he ordered. "I'll stand by here."

It took less than a minute before the Matrix's mechanical translated voice sounded in the room.

"Admiral Isaac Lestroud. How may this unit assist?"

"You could keep my people better informed of what you're doing," he suggested gently. "One of your—construction nodes, I think?—just broke off without filing a course."

"Yes. Construction Matrix ZX-163-11 is engaging in a special project."

Isaac waited for the Matrix to tell him more. After ten seconds of silence, he sighed.

"And what *is* that special project, Eighteen?" he asked. "I am responsible for the security and safety of this system. You are supposed to be keeping me informed."

"We do not wish to raise false hope," Eighteen told him. *"ZX-163-11 is testing a theory on what we may be able to do to assist in defense of the system. We have schematics in our database for heavy gamma ray laser platforms that operate as remotes.*

"ZX-163-11's project is to assemble a test batch of these units that we will, if our core protocols permit, surrender control of to the Vistan Guardian-Star-Choirs. If this works, we will be able to assist in the mass production of defensive minefields.

"Combined with Admiral Isaac Lestroud and First-Among-Singers Sings-Over-Darkened-Waters' capabilities, we believe that these weapons would help secure the system."

Supplying the locals with modern weapons platforms would be hugely valuable. Isaac could see a lot of ways they could use even one-shot graser mines. It even made sense—core protocols said that the Matrices couldn't attack other Matrices, but they'd already proven that they could build things and give them to the humans or the Vistans.

They hadn't yet tested out whether they could directly build weapons and hand them over, though, so he could see the concern. His understanding was that the Matrices *couldn't* do it, but in the aftermath of the override incident, it sounded like they were experimenting instead of assuming.

"I see the value of your project," Isaac said. "And I see your concern about raising false hope. I won't tell my people about this until you've tested it—but I do have one request."

"Admiral Isaac Lestroud is in charge of the security of this star system," Eighteen calmly confirmed.

"You don't have to tell my people if you want to avoid raising hopes—but I must insist that you at least tell *me*," Isaac ordered. "Not getting my hopes up is my problem. I *need* to know what you are doing. Do you understand?"

"This unit understands. We will keep Admiral Isaac Lestroud informed."

And hopefully, that would be enough. Even if the Rogues didn't come back, *Interceptor* would launch in ten days.

Isaac wasn't sure what was going to come of that...but he *was* sure that he wasn't going to regret any scrap of firepower he'd assembled around the Hearthfire System.

49

Isaac could have pretended it was a fluke he was on the flag deck when the alert went out, but it wasn't. The weekly dropouts for Task Group *Galahad* meant he'd known, to within about three hours, when Giannovi was going to arrive.

"I have Cherenkov radiation bursts coming in from thirty degrees above the ecliptic," a sensor tech reported. "Warp drive emergence signatures confirmed, multiple units."

"Clarify and identify," Isaac ordered. Some of his flag deck crew was looking...unsure. He'd have Connor talk to them later, since *Galahad*'s arrival time had been announced.

They should have been paying more attention.

"CIC makes five targets," Connor interrupted, stepping up to the tech's shoulder. "Likelihood is high that it's Task Group *Galahad*."

"Let's not assume that until we get IFFs and can confirm that," Isaac said calmly. He almost preferred the tech's uncertainty to his ops officer's assumptions. "Just because we haven't met anyone hostile with warp drives out here *yet* doesn't mean they don't exist.

"It's a strange corner of the galaxy we've found ourselves in, after all."

Connor nodded wordlessly, but he met Isaac's gaze as he did so. Lesson registered and learned. Nothing more needed to be said.

His new operations officer was still growing into the hole now–Vice Admiral Giannovi had left in Isaac's immediate circle, but he took correction easily enough.

"Exilium Space Fleet identifier codes detected," the sensor tech reported, their voice firming up. "*Galahad* and four escorts. Admiral Giannovi has arrived."

"Good." Isaac checked the distance. They'd be about three more hours before they made it to Vistan orbit. "Make sure traffic control knows they're friendly and assigns them an orbit. I'm definitely glad to see them, especially *Galahad*."

He was also glad that *Vigil* and her strike cruisers had ended up there early after all. *Galahad* was a match for the strike cruisers in most ways, but she didn't have their spinal graser. She definitely wasn't a match for *Vigil*.

The task force of slower ships was *more* than welcome, but they couldn't have held against the forces thrown at Vista on their own.

"Once *Galahad* has made orbit, Admiral Giannovi is invited to join myself and Captain Alstairs for dinner," Isaac said. "It's good to have everybody here at last."

VICE ADMIRAL LAURETTA Giannovi was exhausted. It wouldn't have been easy for most people to guess. Her uniform, hair and makeup were perfect. There were no visible bags under her eyes, nothing to suggest that she was anything less than fully prepared to do her duty.

Unfortunately for that impression of a bright-eyed and chipper officer, Isaac Lestroud had been Lauretta Giannovi's direct superior for a *long* time.

"The trip was hard on your people?" he asked as he guided her into the Admiral's private dining room aboard *Vigil*. He mostly thought the space was excessive—he either ate at his desk or at formal-enough affairs to require a larger space than the intimate six-person room—but for this, it was perfect.

"Six. Freaking. Months," Giannovi said slowly. "We've done it before, but *damn*. It sucks every time." She gestured around her at *Vigil*.

"This really wasn't fair, you know," she continued. "We left, what, fifty days ahead of you? And you got here forty days ahead of us. We're facing the same going back."

"We'll see on that one," Isaac said slowly. "I'm considering other options—including simply giving your ships to the Vistans and taking your crews home aboard one of the two-fifty-six ships."

"The doctors say that the two-fifty-six ships are even easier on the crews?" she asked.

"Probably more due to the fact that they were designed from the keel out for the new drives than anything else," he told her. "From what Reinhardt has told me, the two-fifty-sixers will be our standard for a while. There may be an unexpected breakthrough, but right now he's not seeing how to make the next jump in speed."

"Though if it keeps doubling, I can see the value in refitting the entire fleet once he gets it," Giannovi replied. "But seriously, sir? Giving the Vistans our ships?"

"We're already planning to start standing down ships once *Watchtower* commissions," he pointed out. "We're building six strike cruisers to each battlecruiser now. All of those ships are two-fifty-sixers and, well, the strike cruisers need the same crew as an older destroyer."

"I feel like I brought the rusty old truck to the party," she said drily. "So appreciated."

"Five extra hulls and seventeen extra particle cannons?" Isaac snorted. "I'm *ecstatic* to have you. But I don't think leaving your ships here will be a particularly big cost compared to the benefit we'll get from handing them over to the Vistans."

"You're thinking in terms of long-term alliance, I'm guessing?"

"Three battlecruisers, twenty-four strike cruisers," Isaac told her. "That's it. That's all Exilium can support long-term by my math. For at *least* a generation, since most of the restriction is crew."

Like all colonies ever, there was pressure to have and expand families on Exilium. Unlike a lot of past colonists, the citizens of the Republic of Exilium had access to state-funded artificial gestation technology. Everyone who wanted to could have kids without losing time or health to pregnancy.

Raising the children was still a time- and energy-consuming endeavor—that was why Isaac and Amelie didn't have them. Yet, at least. But they could at least make sure they weren't losing mothers or damaging their health along the way—and make sure that *any* family unit who wanted kids could have them.

Regardless of whether or not any member of that unit had a womb of their own.

"So, what, we borrow Vistan crew?" she asked.

"It won't work. Not long-term, not without some form of political unification rendered impossible by distance and the population imbalance alike," he told her. "If we combined into a democratic state, the only type we would consider, well…four million versus a billion.

"We need them separate, if not necessarily at arm's length. We need a Vistan state that regards us as their most precious friends and allies, one that's willing to commit warships to our fights…and can build warships *worth* committing to our fights."

"That's a hell of an objective, sir," Giannovi told him. She glanced at Alstairs. "And from Cameron's shocked expression, this is the first you've told your flag Captain about this."

Isaac chuckled.

"He knew well enough," he said. "So does Connor. Just because I haven't *said* anything doesn't mean either of you haven't figured it out."

"Still a shock to hear it said out loud, sir," Alstairs told him. "But you're right. We need the Vistans on our side and relatively close to our weight class if they're to make a difference against the Matrices."

"Is it really fair to pull them into this war?" Giannovi asked. "Not arguing sir, just…poking holes."

"That's the job, isn't it? And no, it wouldn't be…except that the Matrices already did it," Isaac said. "We're facing potentially hundreds of Rogue Regional Matrices. Each of those will have dozens of warships and Sub-Regional Matrices.

"If we can find the firepower, the ships and the crews…we need to end them all."

"That's a tall order, sir. Both halves of that," his senior subordinate told him. "I agree that we don't have a choice, but that's..."

"That's the grand crusade the Cabinet is afraid I'm going to try and launch," Isaac said with a laugh. "I could tell them exactly what's on my mind, and I think it might actually reassure them—at least with the recognition that I don't plan on trying to take on all the Matrices with *just* the ESF."

"The Vistans won't be enough, sirs," Alstairs murmured. "We'll need to find more allies."

"We will," Isaac confirmed. "Right now, we keep the Vistans and we get them up to speed while Captain Catalan and the Matrices work out what's going on with that slowboat."

"*Slowboat*," Giannovi echoed, shaking her head. "I understand the term, but it is going at over ninety-nine percent of the speed of light."

Isaac shared in the amusement, then was distracted by the steward bringing in glasses.

"What...what is this?" he asked Parminder Singh. He *trusted* the man—Singh had been his steward since he'd become *Vigil*'s Captain a *very* long time ago—but green beer was new.

"A tradition of Captain Alstairs' people," Singh told him. "March seventeenth is a saint's day for his culture, and green beer is traditional. Yes?"

Alstairs was staring at the liquid in surprise, then started laughing.

"I've *heard* of the concept," he admitted. "But you mixed it up, Steward Singh. I'm *Scottish*...and the green beer is Irish. Worse, I think it's not even *native* Irish."

The Captain grabbed one anyway.

"Hopefully, it doesn't affect the taste!"

50

AMELIE KNEW something was wrong the moment she walked into the Cabinet meeting. Her Cabinet was a mixed bunch, rarely in agreement on much of anything and usually busy arguing with each other.

The silence present when she entered the room and took her seat meant that someone had just dropped a bombshell—and the fact that it had been dropped before she arrived meant that it was aimed at her.

"All right, people," she said as the silence stretched on, her ministers staring at her. "You are all looking at me like I've grown a second head. I have enough confidence in my makeup abilities to be sure that even if I *had*, you'd have problems telling.

"So, just what is going on?"

The room remained silent, but enough glances were directed at Carlos Rodriguez to make it clear who had dropped the bombshell.

"Well, Carlos?" she said, directing her gaze at him. In many ways, she'd expected Carlos to be the main opposition in her Cabinet, and he *tried* to be. Unfortunately for him, though, Father Petrov James was much better at making allies—and fortunately for Amelie, Father James rarely raised anything she could *completely* disagree with.

"Do you know what your husband is up to?" Rodriguez finally

asked. "I've been going over the reports about the Hearthfire defenses, and I found more than a few points of concern."

"I spoke to Isaac last night," Amelie pointed out. "About twelve hours ago. With Vista having kicked past the point of being easily habitable, he's rather focused on getting people *off* that ice ball.

"He didn't mention any concerns to me."

"I don't mean concerns with what Admiral Lestroud is facing," Rodriguez told her. "I mean concerns with what he is *doing*. Did you know, Ms. President, that the six guardships currently under construction in the Hearthfire System are being built with engines based on *our* technology?"

"We were supplying engines, yes," Amelie agreed. She suspected she knew what Rodriguez meant, though. *Oh, Isaac, why didn't you warn me?*

"That was what I thought as well," the Minister confirmed. "Except it appears that we have instead helped the Vistans set up production facilities for both high impulse micro-thrusters *and* the artificial-gravity systems necessary for using them.

"Going over the reports in more detail, it appears that there is also a mass-production facility in the Hearthfire System for modern rapid-fire pulse guns. Admiral Lestroud has apparently handed over multiple restricted military technologies to the Vistans, along with the technology to manufacture them."

"This Cabinet voted to give first Captain Catalan and then Admiral Lestroud full plenipotentiary authority," James pointed out, the old priest's voice quiet. "In fact, as Prime Minister Nyong'o can confirm, the Senate validated both those appointments.

"While I am far from comfortable with handing over weapons technology to a species several centuries behind us technologically, I see the logic and it is certainly within the scope of the authority given to Admiral Lestroud."

"This Cabinet had limitations that were discussed with Admiral Lestroud," Linton pointed out. "We don't want to create our own destruction. We've already seen that particular story play out around us."

"I don't see the Vistans as a threat, people," Amelie stated. "We may have discussed this with Isaac, but he has the authority to make these decisions. What exactly are we afraid of here?"

"A Vistan state armed with comparable weapons and starships to us that sees us as vulnerable," Rodriguez said bluntly. "They outnumber us two hundred and fifty to one, Ms. President."

"And we are in the process of saving their entire species, Carlos," Amelie replied. "*You* might be willing to turn around and bite the hand that saved you, but most aren't."

"What exactly has Admiral Lestroud provided?" Nyong'o asked calmly. She didn't have a vote in this room—though it wasn't like *anyone* in the room had any authority except what Amelie gave them.

"I'm not certain beyond the engine and weapon technology already mentioned," Rodriguez admitted. "Just the fabrication capacity to build those, though, is a powerful tool."

"We already gave the Vistans the schematics for the two-fifty-six warp drive," Nyong'o pointed out.

"That requires exotic matter to produce," Rodriguez replied. "We control that."

"So do the artificial gravity plates, Minister Rodriguez," James pointed out. "I'm very minimally involved in the technology side of our affairs, but I know that. Do the pulse guns or engines require exotic matter?"

"No, but our modern particle cannons do," Linton said slowly. "And the impulse thrusters are only so useful without the ability to counteract their acceleration. While the Vistans may be able to set up a particle accelerator–based facility to produce exotic matter, especially if we provide them particle-cannon technology, they do not have a facility of the scale we do.

"Construction of such a facility is beyond them and will be for some time. Admiral Lestroud is providing a potential ally with powerful technology, yes, but much of it depends on a key resource that only we can provide them."

"And we need allies," Amelie reminded her Cabinet. "If we are even to secure the space around our worlds, we need ships with the engines to cross the stars in weeks instead of months and the weapons to engage the Matrices.

"It is in our interests for the Vistans to have a fleet that is capable of standing at our side." She shook her head. "I agreed when we had this discussion before, but now I wonder. All evidence from Hearthfire suggests we have badly underestimated the resources even a single Regional Matrix can bring against us.

"We face an enemy that can continuously replenish its losses. The destruction of a Sub-Regional Matrix has bought us time at Hearthfire, but the other cost of that time is that when they do return, they will do so with immense force.

"We must prepare to stand off that force, and ships we build here cannot be sent to Hearthfire in time. Ships built *there* are the Vistans' only hope—and so, we all succeed better if the Vistans build and crew their own warships."

"And everyone is better off if they're building ships equivalent to our refitted cruisers than if they're strapping guns to an asteroid," Linton cut in.

"You're right to raise this with the Cabinet, Carlos," the Minister for Orbital Affairs continued, "but I think the Admiral was right to ignore us this time." He smiled. "I'll confess that my girlfriend being in the Matrices' line of fire certainly helps focus my thoughts."

"Many of our people now have family or lovers in that line of fire," Amelie agreed. "I'd ask for votes, Ministers, but I think we're past that. I was not aware of what Isaac was doing, and I'm not a huge fan of that, but I believe he has made the right choice.

"That is *my* decision. The authority given to the Admiral by the Senate includes what he is doing, which means only *I* can censure him for it. I choose not to," she concluded.

"I suggest we begin considering just what kind of alliances we want to form—with the Vistans, yes, but also with whoever else we find out here." Amelie Lestroud smiled. She'd once formed an alliance of disparate resistance factions across dozens of worlds. She knew how daunting the task she was suggesting was.

It had been hard enough then—and *those* worlds had all been human.

"There are as many as two hundred Rogue Regional Matrices out there. We cannot defeat them alone. If we are to survive—if the *galaxy* is to survive—their expansion must be stopped. Their murders and genocides must be stopped.

"We can't do it alone, so we have tried to ignore the fact that it needed to be done. I do believe that my husband, annoying as his method may have been, is showing us the way."

51

"WE HAVE A PROBLEM, CAPTAIN OCTAVIO CATALAN."

"What kind of problem, D?" Octavio asked. After thirty-three days, Specialty Matrix XR-13-9-D had a recognizable voice to him now, which he thought was interesting. He'd worked with Matrices before, and they'd all used the exact same monotone translation that tended to fool humans into thinking they were emotionless.

D was clearly trying to avoid that, layering in pitch and tone to its voice. The Matrix hadn't got to anything resembling a normal voice yet —even the translations human computers ran of Vistan language sounded more normal—but it was closer than any other.

And that meant he could recognize D instantly when the Matrix spoke to him...and pick up that the Matrix was concerned.

"Two recon nodes under Recon and Security Matrix KCX-DD-61 have been using tachyon punches to achieve closer visuals and sensor data of the Creator colony ship," D told him. *"They were being careful to avoid the known tachyon-punch signatures that appear to be following the Creator vessel.*

"They were insufficiently careful."

Octavio closed his eyes. That did *not* sound good.

"How bad?" he asked.

"All three nodes were destroyed within two point six seconds of contact."

There were no ships currently in the Refuge System capable of engaging and destroying a single recon and security unit, let alone doing so in under three seconds. Assuming the right engagement range, *Vigil* might have managed to obliterate the three ships that fast.

Maybe.

"Do we have any data on what attacked DD-61?" Octavio finally asked. "Anything they got us might help us avoid their fate—and keep their deaths from being in vain."

"See projector two."

Octavio's office aboard the shipyard was cramped and lacking in amenities such as cushions. It did have three holographic projectors, though, and a direct link to XR-13-9-D's core aboard *Interceptor*. The big ship was D's body, but D was fully in control of the shipyard as well.

The projector turned on with the image of a standard ESF tactical display. That was probably a translation on D's part, but it did make Octavio's life easier. He could read this display and pick out the three Matrices.

"KCX-DD-61 and the recon nodes punched in approximately thirty light-minutes ahead of the Creator vessel, two hundred and forty thousand kilometers away from the direct vector as a safety precaution."

A blurred line appeared on the display, marking the approach of the slowboat.

"At five minutes plus/minus eleven seconds from closest approach, multiple tachyon punches were detected around the region. Six unknown vessels arrived. KCX-DD-61 decided on a retreat. The decision was not made fast enough."

Six icons appeared on the hologram. They probably hadn't been expecting the Matrices, but they moved *fast.* If Octavio had blinked, he would have missed their arrival and attack entirely.

"Any identification on the ships?" he asked.

"Negative. Hull material appears to be based on the same principles as Matrix construction. Reaction time suggests either fully automated units similar to the Matrices or a defensive AI protocol similar to the ESF's Guardian Protocols.

"*Weapons systems are unknown to us. What sensor data we received suggests coherent radiation beams based around zettahertz frequency radiation.*"

"That's impossible," Octavio objected. That was orders of magnitude more powerful than the gamma ray lasers used by the Matrices—and zettahertz frequency radiation didn't occur naturally that he was aware of.

D was talking about a coherent beam of an entirely artificial radiation that carried energy at an insane level. A zettahertz laser…

"*It is clearly possible. The mechanisms for such are beyond the technology databases possessed by Regional Construction Matrix XR-13-9, but this Matrix must note that our gamma ray lasers utilize artificial sources of radiation.*

"*It seems improbable, but the most likely conclusion is that these weapons systems are an advancement of Matrix coherent-radiation weapons systems. Such a system would be more powerful than the ESF's current spinal acceler-ated-particle weapon, though by not as significant a margin, given the addi-tional kinetic impact of the particle weaponry.*"

"That's reassuring, I think," Octavio muttered. It was hard to tell, but it looked like the six ships had been identical. Each had fired three of these…zetta-lasers. Hopefully, that was *all* they could fire.

"Can we identify how many ships are following the Creator vessel?" he asked.

"*No. Resolving tachyon punches to that detail is not possible with our technology at the distances we have been operating. We have detected a minimum of seven unique simultaneous punch sequences, but each sequence could represent multiple vessels. This sequence contained six, for example.*"

"So, forty-two potential hostiles, each more powerful than a Matrix combat platform," Octavio concluded.

"*That appears to be a high-order probability, yes.*"

"Fuck me."

"*This unit is not equipped for that activity and does not understand Captain Octavio Catalan to be interested in it in general.*"

"Someday, D, I'm going to tell the Chiefs to walk you through the fine points of human profanity," Octavio told the AI as he shook his head. "Right now, however, I have to wonder how we're going to get *Interceptor* past these things."

"*In theory, once we have exceeded their reactionless drive speed, basic evasive maneuvers should suffice. It is difficult to tell the difference between eighty-five-point-two percent and eighty-five-point-two-one percent of light-speed, and that distinction is more than sufficient to evade any laser.*

"*Once we approach the Creator vessel's speed, we will be as safe from them as the Creator vessel appears to be.*"

Octavio shook his head again.

"Do you think they're escorting the Creator vessel...or chasing it?"

"*Insufficient data to compute. This unit believes we will not have sufficient data until we have boarded the Creator vessel and spoken with them.*"

"Which is the limit for a lot of our questions right now, isn't it?"

"*This unit agrees.*"

"All right, I'm accelerating that conversation with the Chiefs," Octavio replied. "They're going to teach you profanity...and *pronouns.*"

———

"CAN I BORROW YOU, SIR?" Das asked, poking her head into Octavio's office.

The Captain took a last look at the diagram in front of him, then chuckled.

"The likelihood that I'm going to magically divine the secret to upgrading *Interceptor*'s warp drive in the next few hours is low," he admitted. With the warp ring completed and being installed in twenty-four hours, there wouldn't be much of a chance to implement any upgrades, anyway.

The work on *Interceptor* was just about complete. Once the warp ring was attached, the long process of filling the ship's immense fuel tanks would begin. They were four days from launch—three since the loss of the Matrix scouting units.

Time was starting to run out.

"Lieutenant Chen Zhou has something she wants to show you,"

Das told him. "Since our Marine commander is one of the most junior officers around, she asked me to play messenger."

There was, from Das's tone, more going on than just that. Even if there was, though, the tactical officer and a Marine Lieutenant weren't in the same chain of command, so even the rank difference was only a minor problem.

"Lead the way, Lieutenant Commander," Octavio ordered. "What does our oh-so-earnest Marine Lieutenant want from us?"

Das *tried* to conceal her slight flush, but Octavio caught it anyway. There was definitely more going on there…and it was very much none of the Captain's business.

"She and the Vistans have been going over what gear we could fabricate for the Spears in the time we have. Fifty Marines isn't much to throw at a ship of unknown size, after all."

"I agree completely," Octavio said. There was space aboard *Interceptor* for them to squeeze in another hundred Marines or Spears. Unfortunately, the disadvantage of Task Force *Vigil* being commissioned directly after deployment was that the Admiral's command was desperately short on Marines.

They'd broken free a platoon's worth of Marines from the Task Force and sent them over, giving Chen Zhou fifty troops instead of twenty, but they'd been assembled from *fire teams*, not even squads.

Lieutenant Chen Zhou was still in command, and the speed with which she'd set to training her combined force had been enough to convince Octavio to leave her there.

Apparently, she'd also managed to find time to fall into bed with his tactical officer. That spoke to an impressive level of multitasking, if nothing else.

"Here." Das stopped them at a hatch. "I'm not actually sure just what they've put together, sir," she admitted. "Zhou tells me it's worth it, and my knowledge set is much bigger guns."

"So you trusted your girlfriend's judgment," Octavio said without censure.

Das flushed again.

"Yes, sir," she conceded levelly.

"Good enough to start with," he told her. "Let's see what we've got."

———

ENTERING the storage bay that the Marines had taken over for training and prep, Octavio was met by the sight of twenty suits of power armor instantly coming to attention at the sight of him.

Except they weren't human-shaped suits of power armor, and the attention pose was *very* different, shaped by the completely different physiology of the Vistan Spears inside that armor.

He took a moment to study the armor as he returned their salutes. The armor was an interesting mix. Parts of it definitely looked cruder than his people's gear—all of which had been manufactured in massive facilities on Mars by the Confederacy, since the Republic hadn't built *any* power armor of their own yet—but the surfaces looked smoother, rounder.

Some of that was just the different shape of a Vistan versus a human. Some of it was that *this* armor had clearly been built with the help of Matrix fabrication units.

"Lieutenant Chen?" he asked.

The dark-skinned young woman stepped out from behind the Shining Spears with a wide white grin.

"Impressive, aren't they, sir?" she said. "We took our schematics and plugged the Vistans' body shape into our CAD software, then ran the result into the fabricator gear the Matrices lent us."

"I imagine the first few prototypes were far from comfortable," Octavio noted. He was familiar with that kind of rough conversion project.

"Not in the slightest, from what Dancer-In-Warm-Sunlight tells me," Chen agreed. "We weren't sure we'd have a set of power armor we could work with before launch, or I'd have raised it sooner."

One of the suits of power armor retracted the helmet, a far more impressive maneuver on the Vistan suits, given that the Vistan's double shoulders were next to their heads.

"I am Under-Commander-Of-Spears Dancer-In-Warm-Sunlight,"

she introduced herself. "I command the team tasked to assist Lieutenant Chen in this project. The armor is not perfect, not by a long swim, but it will serve to allow my people to stand alongside yours."

"What about weapons?" Octavio asked. He gestured at Dancer's hands. "The armor is matched to their hands, not ours. Strength augmentation isn't going to make up for that."

They could reengineer the grips, but he didn't think they'd brought that many hand weapons to Refuge.

"The Vistans already had heavy armaments that the suits will carry with some minor work," Chen told him. "Come with me."

The armored Spears dispersed, with only Dancer accompanying Octavio, Chen and Das to the rack of weapons behind them.

Chen picked up the weapon with some effort and showed it to Octavio. It was a wide-barreled thing, with secondary supports clearly intended to latch on to the exterior of the power armor to account for Vistans' short arms.

"The name for this is something along the lines of Flower-Of-Many-Swords," Chen told him. "We've been calling them multi-launchers—the concept is something we might want to consider adapting for our own use.

"It's basically a magazine-fed grenade launcher slash shotgun, capable of being loaded with any of a dozen ammunition types in three different mags. Even from each mag, it can select which round is being loaded, meaning a single weapon can carry *all* of those twelve payloads."

"One of each," Dancer confirmed. "It is a squad support weapon in its traditional use, with the magazines carried by the rest of the Flower-carrier's squad. In this case…"

"In this case, we reengineered the feed to link to a munitions case built into the power armor," Chen said. "We've supplied an updated fléchette round for the shotgun mode and a modified version of our armor-penetrating grenades. For a boarding action like the *Interceptor* mission, that should be more than enough.

"Each Spear will have sixty rounds of each type of munition, for a hundred and twenty total. Our Marines will provide the extended base of fire with our pulse guns if needed, but so long as we have rounds for the multi-launchers, the Spears are definitely worth bringing."

Octavio was no Marine, but everything *sounded* right to him—and extra hands for this mess sounded worth a *lot*.

"How many suits and launchers can we have ready without moving the launch date?"

"Seventy-five," Chen said instantly. "We have twenty-five already checked out for both; we should be able to manufacture twenty-five more sets a day, assuming we're doing inspections en route."

"Thirty-six hours in flight, Chen," Octavio warned her. "What about training?"

"We've been cycling my people through the suits we have," Dancer explained. "It's not perfect water, but it's clear enough."

"Then make it happen," he ordered. "You're the one boarding that ship, Lieutenant Chen. If you think they'll augment your teams, I'll sign off."

"Thank you, sir!"

Developing new power armor, training her teams, modifying weapons for an alien race *and* starting a relationship with his tactical officer.

Octavio was *definitely* impressed with Lieutenant Chen's multitasking.

52

"FUELING COMPLETE."

Lieutenant Daniel's calm announcement sounded almost eerie. It was the only sound in the silence of *Interceptor*'s bridge. Everyone had been watching the countdown on the main holographic display, falling into silence as it counted down the last few seconds.

Octavio was back in a familiar command chair, the entire bridge of the new ship having been copied from *Scorpion*. There was even a tactical console for Lieutenant Commander Das, though her lack of support staff gave away one of the key differences.

Interceptor had an incredibly sensitive sensor suite, including several devices the Matrices hadn't yet provided to humanity, but she had no weapons at all. Anything that would have been excess mass to her designed purpose had been excluded from her design.

She was the size of an ESF battlecruiser, but she was defenseless. The ship she was meant to intercept was even bigger, which had been part of the complexity in designing her warp bubble.

"D, systems report?" Octavio asked thin air. Das was his executive officer, but she was junior for the role and occasionally hesitant. Both he and Das were relying on D a lot, which had ended up with the strange situation where Captain Octavio Catalan effectively had *two* executive officers.

And one of them was an alien AI.

"All reports are green; all systems have passed self-check," D's voice said out of the speakers. The AI's vocabulary training session with several of Octavio's chief petty officers had been even more beneficial than he'd dared hope.

D was the first Matrix to sound like a person. Octavio knew what was behind the monotone the Matrices usually used, but it was deceptive. D had spent enough time working directly with humans across the ship that they'd lost the monotone.

"Two sections of the power conduits are green and have passed self-check, but some of the readings are sufficiently variable to raise my concern," D continued. "Commander Tran has teams inspecting them. They have replacement components, so even if there is a problem, I believe we should be on our way within the hour."

D had also mastered personal pronouns with surprising ease. Octavio figured the "this unit" mouthful had started to sound inefficient to the intelligence.

"Tran?" Octavio asked.

"Having a sentient friendly computer aboard still occasionally throws me, but I'll be damned if D didn't catch the impossible," the engineer replied. "Both of their 'off' conduits had stress damage from the manufacturing process. One will be fine, but I've flagged it for closer watch. The other would have given out within six hours at full power...and cut out a third of the microthrusters."

Interceptor's engines consisted of arrays of vast numbers of the high-impulse microthrusters. A third of them down would be a problem at least.

And, depending on how they "cut out," a potential catastrophe.

"Your team has replacements, D said?" Octavio said.

"We do; already installing them. Give me twenty minutes and you're clear for maximum power. Lieutenant Daniel is good for about twenty-five percent power without any concerns; we've locked out the thrusters at risk."

"Thank you, Lieutenant Commander," Octavio replied. "Daniel, you heard her?"

"Yes, sir," Lieutenant Yonina Daniel confirmed. "Initiating separation from the yard. We'll be underway shortly."

Octavio nodded silently, glancing around at the deadly Amazon band that made up his senior officers. He had good people, a strange but good ship, and a straightforward mission that could go wrong in oh so many ways.

Here we go.

———

THE HALF-KILOMETER-LONG SHIP cleared the shipyards that had birthed her, spinning in space to orient herself; then Lieutenant Daniel brought her engines online at the indicated twenty-five percent.

"Compensators are working as expected, engines are running smoothly, sensors are online," Das ran off. "We are green and operational, other than the one chunk of the power network Commander Tran has down."

"Get us on course, Lieutenant Daniel. Will the delay bringing the engines up to power hurt us at all?" Octavio asked.

"We have another four hours of departure window," she responded. "Even if we run twenty-five percent power for all four of those hours, we'll still be fine to make the intercept."

"Are we ready to go?" he asked.

This wasn't the general status question. This was asking the young woman who was, above all others, responsible for making a perfect intercept of a spacecraft traveling at ninety-nine point nine nine percent of lightspeed.

If they missed the intercept by even a bit, they were going to be in serious trouble. They could barely maneuver once they were up to that velocity—and every second they spent at their intercept velocity was over seventy seconds in real space. They needed to match velocities within a few thousand kilometers at most, or what was supposed to take forty objective days could easily expand to twice that.

They could lose *months* with a few hours of maneuvering. That was why *Interceptor*'s warp ring was designed to fold out and wrap around the other ship.

Octavio had worked with the massive warp cradle that had delivered the Exile Fleet to Exilium. He knew *exactly* what the odds of retracting that warp ring once it was extended were—roughly zero.

He wasn't sure if the rest of his crew realized it, but his own math said that *Interceptor* was going to be a one-use ship. Once they collapsed the warp bubble they formed around the Creator ship, they were unlikely to be able to warp space again.

It would be worth it, he hoped. A chance to speak to the people who'd built the Matrices *had* to be.

"We're ready," Daniel told him. "We can wait until the engines are fully online or get on our way now while the Lieutenant Commander's people work. Your orders, sir?"

Octavio grinned.

"I'm not going to pretend I'm more patient than I actually am, Lieutenant Daniel. Is your course set?"

"It is," she affirmed.

"Then engage."

THE HIGHEST VELOCITY any ship Octavio had been on had ever achieved in regular space was just over twenty-five percent of lightspeed. The Confederacy had officially restricted their military ships to twenty percent of lightspeed for regular operations, since they needed their ships to be able to safely pass through wormholes.

Half-missing a wormhole was bad at any speed and far more likely at higher velocities.

The ESF hadn't kept the same rule, but they did most of their maneuvering in one star system, with their high-velocity needs generally met with warp drives.

By the time they reached the end of his first ten-hour bridge watch, they'd passed that. An hour at quarter acceleration and nine at full power had kicked them well past twenty-five percent of lightspeed.

Time dilation wasn't a problem yet, but the computers were warning him of the start of it.

"This is fascinating," D observed after Octavio had turned command over to Africano and retreated to his quarters.

"What is?" he asked the AI as he poured himself a glass of water.

"No Matrix has ever traveled faster than ten percent of lightspeed," D told him. "We are aware of reaction engines such as those used by *Interceptor*, but our Creators had not reached nearly this level of efficiency before our deployment."

"They had a reactionless drive. Why would they?" Octavio asked.

"This is true. I must speculate, then, on why they eventually *did* develop such engines. For a vessel of the size of the one we are intercepting to have achieved the velocity it has, the engines must approach the efficiency of yours. Otherwise, the fuel-to-payload ratio rapidly creates a barely usable ship.

"Assuming, of course, that they retained the fuel to slow down."

"That's a safe assumption, D," the human Captain said with a chuckle. "I don't know what their plan is, but they have to be intending to stop *somewhere*."

"I must admit, I find the concept of our Creators intentionally avoiding the region where they know Matrices to be operating… disturbing," D told him. "Did they assume that we were all Rogues?"

"That's the only conclusion I see, D," Octavio admitted. "They probably have a better idea of what the odds are, at least once they learned it was happening at all."

"So rather than trying to fix us, they just ran?"

"Apparently. I'm sure there was more to it than that." He felt like he was reassuring the AI, which was fair. D was both centuries old, in that they had been split off from XR-13-9's own intelligence and memories, and barely months old.

"That can only be speculation," D objected. "Though I also find it disturbing to assume that our Creators were so callous."

"You don't remember anything, huh?" Octavio asked.

"Fragments at best," D confirmed. "The tachyon punches continue to cause damage with every jump that we have to repair. The verification process only drives home how much we must have lost over the years before we implemented it."

Octavio was an atheist, but he was still tempted to thank the unknowing forces of the universe that the Matrices had had the tachyon communicator to go along with the tachyon-punch drive.

Without it, all of them would have gone crazy—and the evidence suggested *homicidally* crazy—long before.

"We'll see them soon enough," he promised the AI. "Far sooner for us than for anyone not aboard *Interceptor*, that's for sure."

53

"WE HAVE A CONTACT."

Das's voice was very quiet, but something about *Interceptor*'s bridge seemed to be lending itself to moments of silence as the crew waited for the critical moment.

"Is it the right contact?" Octavio asked.

"I think so," she replied. "Distance is under three thousand kilometers. Relative velocity is…one hundred KPS. Daniel?"

"I've got her," the helm officer confirmed. "Adjusting acceleration and course. Fifty seconds to contact from…*now*."

They could barely make sense of the outside world at this point. This close to lightspeed, they were experiencing time at less than one and a half percent of the speed of the "real world." A hundred kilometers per second might seem huge under normal circumstances, but it was point zero three percent of lightspeed. They were *already* at three nines of lightspeed and accelerating.

And somehow, they'd got the angle and speed right. That felt impossible, but they'd done it.

The fifty seconds it was going to take them to match velocities would consume an entire hour in the real world. Everything they did until they brought the warp bubble up was costing time...time that Octavio had to hope didn't include news they needed to hear.

There was nothing *Interceptor*'s crew could have done to help if, say, Vista had come under attack again. But they were hours past the point where even tachyon communicators could provide undistorted communications with Vista or Exilium. Probably at least a week past, according to the real world.

"Tran, D, what's the status on the warp ring?" he finally asked. That would take ten seconds to extend...and those would be the riskiest ten seconds of this whole operation. *Interceptor* was carefully designed to survive at these speeds. They *couldn't* design the warp ring to survive this, so it was currently collapsed against the ship's hull.

"Ready to deploy," Tran confirmed. "D can give you whatever details you want, but I'm sitting by a big red button, waiting for your order."

"We need to deploy before contact," he told her. "How long is it going to hold up? D?"

"Uncertain. Seventeen plus minus five point four seconds." The AI paused. "The ring will only be wide enough to fit around the target in the final one point one seconds of the unfolding."

Octavio closed his eyes for a precious few seconds—three or four minutes of real time.

"Activate at intercept minus ten seconds," he ordered. "We'll take the risk. Warp space as soon as we have hull contact. Tran, do *not* wait for my order, understood?"

"Understood. Expansion in twenty seconds."

"Contact in twenty-nine."

He exhaled and laid his hands on the arms of his seat. That was the last order he would give until this phase, at least, was over. Everything was down to his crew, their programs, and the insanely complicated AI controlling the final timing.

"Expansion."

He *felt* the ship shift as Tran reported. Suddenly less streamlined, the unavoidable turbulence of their velocity shook the ship, sending tremors rippling through the hull. The holographic image of *Interceptor* in the main display lit the connecting structures up in orange immediately—as soon as the warp drive started extending, the systems were already sending structural integrity alerts.

A second shape appeared in the holographic display, the approaching Creator ship. Their relative velocity was minimal now, only the amount that Daniel was allowing to make this maneuver even possible.

Octavio mirrored Daniel's screen to the screens on his own seat. He didn't want to jog the helm officer's elbow, but given the circumstances, he was certainly willing to virtually watch over her shoulder.

The screen was a mess of vector diagrams that he could only half-read. *Interceptor*'s shape was on there, and the vector diagrams were cutting into the gap in the warp ring intended for the big slowboat.

Seconds ticked by like eternity, and Octavio realized he was holding his breath. He started to release it—and then inhaled sharply as the final vector lines converged on Daniel's display.

"Got it!" the Lieutenant shouted. "Vectors match; we have them inside the ring. Making final contact in three...two... *Contact!*"

Interceptor shivered again as she touched down on the immense colony ship she'd wrapped the warp ring around. Before Octavio could even be *tempted* to give an order, D and Tran activated his last set of orders.

Power flared along the warp drive ring, energizing the strange negative-mass exotic matter that made up its core arrays. They'd held together this long against the radiation of traveling at near-cee velocities, but if they were going to fail, now was the time...

"Exotic-matter angular velocity at seventy percent of target; warp bubble forming," D said calmly into the near-silence of the bridge.

"Seventy-five percent. Ring structural integrity is at sixty percent... warp bubble still forming."

Octavio was still holding his breath when a familiar sticky feeling descended onto his skin and the ship's trembling stopped.

"Angular velocity at eighty-three percent of target; warp bubble formed," the AI announced. "Ring structural integrity is at an average of fifty-six percent, and multiple hull breaches are being reported by the automated systems.

"Nonetheless, we have a stable ring and bubble."

The bridge was silent in shock. They'd done it.

"Exotic-matter angular velocity at target. Current estimated pseudo-speed is twelve times lightspeed. Our destination is the Hearthfire System, ETA...six months."

Octavio took a breath of the sticky air of warped space and let it go.

"Get the ring-inspection robots and teams in there," he ordered. "I'd like us to be able to get to Hearthfire a little faster than that if we need to."

Interceptor was fully capable of hitting two hundred and fifty six times the speed of light, but he'd want to go over the ring with a fine-toothed comb first. The last thing they wanted to do at this point was break the bubble. That would see both *Interceptor* and her target scattered across several light-years in pieces.

"Inform..." Octavio trailed off and shook his head. He tapped a command on his seat arms.

"Lieutenant Chen Zhou, this is Captain Octavio," he said calmly into the opened channel. "We've made contact and are locked on to the Creator vessel."

"My lead team is ready to go, sir. Holding back a reserve of twenty-five Marines and forty Vistans, but I have sixty troopers standing by with five of D's remotes in support."

"You are cleared to commence boarding operations at your discretion, Lieutenant," Octavio told her. "I'll be riding your shoulder virtually, but I promise to keep my mouth shut unless something *damn* important comes up."

"You're the Captain, Captain. Marines are moving out. Oorah!"

54

THE INTERFACE OCTAVIO had access to wasn't designed for the ship's Captain to watch over the Marine CO's shoulder. It was actually the setup created for a higher-level Marine officer to keep an eye on their subordinates.

Right now, he had it focused on Chen herself, so her helmet's view of the boarding gear was front and center. A display to the left of that view showed him the location of all hundred and twenty-five Marines and Spears. Right now, they were spread across the five "boarding bays" built into *Interceptor*'s flank.

A low-level AI was choosing the most important half-dozen other helmet-cams to show him at once. Currently, it was showing the squad leaders for the five teams of fifteen—five Marines and ten Spears apiece—scheduled to make the first breach.

"Initiating cut," Chen said calmly. A new set of reports automatically inserted themselves onto Octavio's screen: five sets of plasma drills, one for each bay, were now active and trying to cut into the Creator ship's hull.

Initially, that hull resisted. It was made of the same energy-absorbing ceramics the Matrices—and the ESF, now—used to armor their ships.

That had been expected, though, and the drills adjusted to a higher-intensity mode with tighter focuses and faster pulse sequences. The system was, after all, a modification of the same technology as a starship's pulse cannons.

It took about twenty seconds for the drills to establish the correct frequency and intensity and about the same amount of time to burn their way through the hull.

"We're through; airlock plugs inserting."

There was no chance anyone was going to risk merging *Interceptor*'s air with whatever atmosphere was on the strange ship. Octavio guessed that the Creators breathed the mix that had been artificially installed on Exilium and Refuge and the rest of the Constructed Worlds, but that didn't mean the colony ship's air was *currently* breathable.

"Lead elements, advance," Chen ordered. Marines were through the airlocks moments later, twenty-five Exilium Marines crossing into a strange ship without hesitation.

"I'm reading the standard Constructed World air mix," the lead Marine reported, confirming Octavio's suspicion. "Nothing's registering as toxic."

"Don't even think about it, Marine," Chen barked. "We'll let the big D make the call on that for the next wave, but *we* have power armor and we are *not* breathing unknown air; am I clear?"

"Oorah, sir!" There was a pause. "Gravity appears to be similar setup to ours. Suit is reading point nine gravities. Lighter than any of the Constructed Worlds I've been to."

"Sounds like the Matrices don't carve chunks off the planets to adjust the gravity. Given everything *else* the robots do, that's kind of reassuring," Chen replied. "Any lead team, flag your issues."

The interior of the ship was dimly lit by human standards, and Octavio couldn't pick out any lighting fixtures from the video feeds he was seeing—the entire ceiling seemed to be gently glowing.

The Marines had cut through into general exterior corridors, most likely maintenance accessways that wouldn't see much traffic. Part of him expected the corridors to be dirty, but the dull gray metal was perfectly clean.

"No contact," each team confirmed. "Moving in to secure entryway."

"Rest of wave one, move in," Chen ordered. "D, your remotes stay in the middle. You're the only one who can talk to their computers."

"I understand," the AI confirmed. The five remotes attached to this project were under Chen's command, but they were extension of D's intelligence and will. They weren't particularly intelligent on their own —which was probably a good thing, to Octavio's mind.

He trusted D completely...which made D the *only* AI he was willing to let control armed robots near his people.

––––––

THE MARINES FOUND the first body five minutes later, still in one of the exterior maintenance corridors.

"Move in and get a good look," Chen ordered. "This is our first chance to see what the crew looks like."

The assumption that the Matrices' remotes were built in the image of their Creators appeared to be panning out. The mummified creature slumped against the wall had the same centauroid shape with a long four-legged main torso and a secondary set of shoulders above the main torso that held the arms and the bird-like head.

The being had had a sharp beak and large side-facing eyes. It was hard to tell much of its color or anything similar, though, as it had clearly been dead for a long time.

"Lieutenant, do your people have the gear to date the body?" Octavio asked, a direct transmission to the Marine CO. He was *not* going to give direct orders to the Marines. He was an engineer, not a Marine, but that didn't mean he was *completely* lost as to how this needed to work.

"We can do some testing, but it won't be accurate without more detailed analysis," Chen replied. "We'll get on it."

An icon told him Chen had swapped channels.

"Corporal, get a sample and run it through your suit's analysis suite," she ordered. "It won't get us much, but it should give us an estimated time of death. Hold your team with you.

"Teams one and five, hold position as well. Two and four, continue your sweep. Hold and report if you find any forks or signs of life."

Or death, Octavio finished silently.

It only took a few minutes for the power armor's limited suite to run its scans and bounce back an answer. Octavio was still glad they had shifted into warped space for this project. From a relativistic perspective, they had no velocity there. Even the velocity they'd entered with had become tied up in the energy levels of the warp bubble.

That meant they were operating on objective time and they could spend minutes—or even hours or days—without them turning into days or weeks.

Of course, their tachyon communicators didn't work through the warp bubble. D was using them to maintain instantaneous control of their remotes, but they weren't in contact with anyone in Exilium, Refuge or Hearthfire.

"Got an estimate on time of death," the Marine Corporal finally reported. "Confidence interval is about two months, but the suite is estimating our friend's been dead for about three years."

"With time dilation, that means over two centuries," D pointed out. Unlike Octavio, the AI was speaking more broadly. The Captain had to trust that the AI was keeping their comments to the relevant people, since D was also in control of the remotes on the scene.

His monitoring algorithm brought up a camera feed from the remote next to the corpse as Octavio was thinking.

"Look." The AI zoomed in on certain segments. "They were killed by a single laser beam. Targeted directly on the primary circulatory organ."

D was silent for a second, presumably running some kind of analysis.

"Hard to identify wavelengths after this much time, but evidence suggests focused high-frequency beams on the edge of the human-visible spectrum." The AI made a noise that Octavio could only interpret as uncomfortable.

"My remotes carry weapons of very similar design and targeting software capable of this level of precision."

"Well, fuck me," Octavio breathed.

Before anyone could say more than that, a shouted report came in from Team Four.

"Contact! We have contact!"

The camera feed switched automatically even as the Marines were reporting in. Five dog-like robots were charging toward Team Four. Shoulder-high on a human and lacking the extra secondary torso of the Matrix remotes Octavio was familiar with, they were the same black material as the colony ship's outer hull.

"Contacts are hostile; fire at will!" Chen barked—but she was too late. The drones fired first, invisible lasers only seen by their terrible effects.

Against the unarmored Creator whose body the team had found, the drones had used a precise beam that had burned out the heart without significant secondary damage. Faced with armored targets, they unleashed the full power of the same ultraviolet combat lasers the Matrices equipped their remotes with.

Armor *exploded* as the invisible beams connected, each hit equivalent to several kilos of conventional explosives. The leading Marines and Spears went down *hard*.

There were still ten Marines and Spears left, and they returned fire instantly...and ineffectively. The drones *ignored* their counterfire, letting the fléchette rounds and light plasma bursts of the default loadouts wash over their starship-grade armor as they continued to move implacably forward and fired again.

They didn't miss. The part of Octavio's mind that wasn't gibbering in shock and fear registered that. The drones didn't have enough data to perform precise lethal surgery on his people, but they had the sensors and mobility to make sure they didn't miss—and the firepower to make certain what they hit died.

There was nowhere for the survivors to run, and they didn't even try. A new fusillade of fire answered the robots' second attack. This one was armor-piercing grenades and super-focused plasma rounds.

Two of the robots went down, then a third. Two shots took down the last Marines in Team Four—and then one of the drones that had been blown backward by a Spear grenade rose unsteadily to its feet and fired again.

That shot was intercepted, the oversized bulk of D's remote interposing itself in front of the surviving Vistans.

"Withdraw," the AI barked. "The remote can't take many hits like that."

Unlike the drones, D's remotes weren't armored in energy-absorbing ceramics. Their armor was more conventional but still heavy and thick. The remote shrugged aside another hit and returned fire.

The wounded drone might have managed to fire despite its injuries...but it didn't get another shot. Three ultraviolet lasers hammered into the robot with the same surgical precision they'd turned on the crew, severing its legs.

The remote's beams weren't as powerful, but it had three of them. Its armor wasn't as tough, but it had a lot more of it. D was outmatched and overwhelmed, but their remote bought the surviving boarders enough time to retreat out of the corridor before the final drone landed the killing blow.

55

"*INTERCEPTOR*, I need you to seal all boarding bays except three," Chen said over the radio. "All teams, fall back on the access for Team Three. We'll consolidate and form a beachhead for the second wave.

"Team B-Three: move through the airlock and set up a base of fire. Engage any drones detected with armor-piercing and maximum-focus plasma weapons. Treat as tanks, not infantry."

That was going to make a *mess* of the Creator ship, but Octavio agreed with her orders.

"Das? Seal boarding bays other than three," he snapped. "D, did the team leads get the orders?"

"They did," the AI confirmed. "My remotes are falling back to take the rear. I am scanning for incoming drones, but they appear to be specifically stealthed against my sensor frequencies. Outside of visual, I cannot locate them."

The video feed from one of D's remotes flashed up on Octavio's screen as the algorithm picked up movement. Laser fire flashed into the corridor a moment later as the remote halted and engaged.

"Team Three, you have ten hostiles in pursuit," D said calmly. "I'll hold them off as long as I can, but you need to get back to that base of fire Chen is setting up."

The map on Octavio's screen told him that the attack on Team Three was bad news. The boarding bays had been aligned left to right, putting bay three right in the middle—which meant that if Team Three was overrun and the drones reached the airlock before the Marines set up their base of fire, they were in serious trouble.

Chen knew what she was doing. She had to.

"Remote Three is down," D announced, their voice unperturbed by the violent death of one of their bodies. "I have a rough map of this section of the ship; I am moving remote two to intercept this force and buy more time."

"Team B-Three is in position and setting up," Chen replied. "I need maybe another minute, D."

"You'll have it," the AI promised.

The remote hit the drone assault from the side, lasers flashing in the dimly lit corridors as D calmly sacrificed the mechanical minion to buy that minute. Octavio wasn't sure D's counterattack took out any of the drones, but the AI took out a *lot* of legs in the firefight.

"Remote Two is down," D concluded. "This batch of drones is going to be slower now. You should have several minutes, Lieutenant Chen."

"Thanks, D. All teams, fall back past B-Three once you hit the beachhead. Organize and redeploy forward once you've caught your breath. The last thing we need is extra losses becau—"

"CONTACT!"

Team Two had been untouched until that point, but Team One was behind them—and Team Two no longer had one of D's remotes. Half a dozen drones cut through a wall and swarmed into the middle of the team.

Octavio's screens were a mess of explosions and plasma fire...and video feeds going blank.

Team Two was gone.

"This is Team Three; we are reinforcing B-Three. We have a base of fire and we are watching for the fuckers," a Marine corporal announced. "We have Four's survivors here; I'm sending them back into the ship."

"This is Team Five; we have sightlines on the beachhead position," another voice reported. "I'm watching the estimate for the drones that chased Team Three... We're going to swing around and try to flank them. D, take the remote in to cover the beachhead."

"Negative," Chen ordered. "Fall back to the beachhead and consolidate. If they're willing to come to us, *let them*. That's an order, Sergeant!"

There was a pause.

"Understood."

The map told Octavio what Chen's biggest problem was: the Marine Lieutenant was with Team One. There was an unknown number of drones between her and the rest of her people, and attacking the robots hadn't been going so well.

"Chen, this is Catalan," he said quietly in a direct channel. "You're less than twenty meters from the Bay Two access point. I'll have Das reopen that bay, and you and your team can fall back in."

"Sir, we can't risk them getting into *Interceptor*," Chen replied.

"Then you'll need to cover your ass, won't you?" Octavio told her. "Charging straight into an infestation of robotic hunter-killers is a suicide op, Lieutenant. Fall back to Bay Two and rendezvous via *Interceptor*."

"Is that an order, sir?" Chen said grimly, and he grimaced. He didn't have the authority to overrule her tactical decisions without a major outside factor.

"Consider it a strongly worded suggestion," he told her. "I'd rather not lose our Marine CO today."

"Understood," Chen conceded, echoing her own subordinate. "Team One, fall back on the Bay Two cut. *Interceptor* is going to open the door when we get there, and it isn't *staying* open, so move your feet!"

"We have contact," Team Three's commander reported. "Just one drone, scouting the hallway." Octavio's screen flashed to one of Team Three's helmets just in time to watch the Marine fire their pulse gun.

At maximum focus, a pulse gun shot a lance of superheated gasses less than four millimeters across. It was dense, fast and *hot*.

It cut through the drone like a hot knife through butter. The machine was damaged, but it kept moving.

So the Marine shot it three more times, the rest of the squad adding their own fire to scatter the robot back across the hallway in molten pieces.

"They're going to keep coming," the Sergeant replied. "Watch all sides; they're going to try and flank us. Anyone got a count on targets?"

"The force in front of you is eleven units now," D's voice answered. "The force to your left is eight, two of which are badly damaged. There is a least one damaged unit to your right, but it appears to have withdrawn to attempt self-repair."

"Self-repair." The Sergeant's tone made the phrase a curse. "What's their self-repair like? Should we be double-tapping downed units?"

"Disabled units may reactivate, but these appear to be operating independently. Destruction of the central computer core should permanently disable the units." D paused. "Downloading my estimate of the core's locations to all Marines and Spears. Follow-up fire to be certain the core is destroyed is likely wise."

"Good to know." The Sergeant's voice was grim, and Octavio now had his link up on the screen. "I have movement on the frontal corridor. Looks like it's our chance to avenge our friends, people. Lock and load!"

OCTAVIO WASN'T sure what the drones had been expecting—or even if they were smart enough to do anything he would count as "expecting" at all—but they clearly weren't ready to come around the wall into a prepared defensive position.

The Marines and Spears didn't have any fortifications, just a handful of self-constructing barriers Team B-Three had brought over from *Interceptor*. What they did have was a solid double line of trained soldiers who knew what weapons could hurt their enemy now.

Octavio couldn't trace the chaos that ensued as the defenders opened fire. He could tell there was some order to it that, say, Lieutenant Chen would easily pick out, but it was beyond him.

What wasn't beyond him was the results. None of the drones managed to fire a single laser beam. It was a massacre.

"Contact left!" another Marine snapped, and Octavio's cameras shifted over to see a second swarm of drones come charging down the maintenance corridor.

This was a narrower corridor and the drones could only charge four abreast. The Vistan Spears couldn't kneel in their rush-built armor and had to aim high. The Marines *could* kneel, allowing the Vistans to fire over their shoulders.

Only five Marines or Spears could stand or kneel side by side in the corridor, but that still allowed ten of them to shoot at once. Plasma pulses cut through at one level, and armor-piercing grenades flashed through the air above them.

The front line of drones went down, but they shielded the second line of four drones from the fire. Even in the smoky mess the plasma and grenades had made of the corridor, the lasers were mostly invisible.

The explosions that killed three of Octavio's Marines weren't. More fire flashed each way and Octavio knew he was going to lose more people.

"Contact right!" someone bellowed.

"Contact forward!" another voice added. "Contacts on all sides."

"Hold your positions," Chen snapped. "All second-wave teams are ready to move in, but we can only move one fire team at a time. We need that beachhead, people!"

More of the blue icons on Octavio's map were starting to push into the beachhead. Marines and Vistans fell as the drones continued, but others stepped into their place. The lines solidified, each corridor firmly held.

Things calmed as the drones seemed to reach the same conclusion, but then D's voice cut through the apparent quiet.

"Contact up."

The two remaining remotes were in the center of the beachhead, and their sensors had seen what the Marines and Spears had been too busy to notice: the lasers cutting holes in the floor plating above them.

Both remotes opened fire simultaneously, pulsing their lasers into the middle of the accessway the drone were cutting. Metal fell from the ceiling and several drones came with it.

None of them hit the ground intact, but more robots were coming through the hole. They focused their fire on one remote, hammering D's tool with lasers that rapidly burned through the remote's armor.

The remote collapsed, but the other one was still firing—and the remotes' counterattack had bought time for Lieutenant Chen and her people to turn their weapons on the drones in their midst.

After several more terrifying seconds, Octavio's screens all showed calm.

A sanitized report also informed him that Lieutenant Chen was down to twenty-two Marines and forty-three Vistan Spears. The report wasn't clear on how many of the casualties were dead versus wounded, but Octavio's hopes weren't high.

"Is that all of them?" he asked.

"I don't know," D admitted. "Given their aggression levels, it seems likely that they waited to gather their forces and then hit us with every drone aboard the ship. Stragglers are still likely, especially if damaged units dragged themselves away to repair."

"Keep your teams together, Lieutenant Chen," Octavio said quietly. "But we need to keep sweeping the ship."

"Understood." The Marine's camera rotated as she surveyed the unexpected war zone. "The good news is that we now have a lot of potential entry points into the core hull."

56

SWEEPING the ship's main spaces took over three hours. There were a few drones that had, as D warned, dragged themselves away to self-repair. None were in good-enough shape to threaten the Marines or Spears that found them.

What was creepy was how empty the ship was. They found corpses, a crew that had clearly come under attack by the drones, but it seemed like the entire ship had been crewed by about thirty individuals.

The ship was on the high end of the Matrices' original estimates, just over three kilometers long from bow to stern. Even after three hours, they'd only managed to get through the core operating spaces and not the cargo containers, but they'd only found those thirty beings.

"D, does this ship have a Matrix core or some equivalent?" Octavio finally asked, as D's remote and Lieutenant Chen surveyed what looked like it had been the bridge.

The crew here had died somewhat more peacefully. From what the Marines' scanners said, the three Creators on this bridge had poisoned themselves when the rest of the crew was being murdered by hunter-killer robots.

The remote was linking itself into the ship's computers as Octavio asked his question, and D took a few seconds to complete that process.

"Strange," they finally answered. "The system architecture is definitely ours—advanced by some decades of development but fundamentally the same concepts—and from the file and system structure, I would say yes."

"But?" Octavio was pretty sure he'd heard a *but* there.

"There is no Matrix in here," D told him. "From the design of the ship's systems, I would hypothesize that the ship's manual controls were an afterthought. It was intended to operate with a sentient AI as the interface between the crew and the systems.

"It does not have that AI, which suggests the probability that the AI was destroyed."

"Can you estimate where it would physically have been located?" Octavio asked. "We can send a team to check it out."

"Of course. Relaying the coordinates to Lieutenant Chen."

Chen started barking orders, but Octavio was looking at the displays.

"Do we have any data in here on the cargo, D? We figured she was a colony ship, but what is actually aboard?"

"Checking the systems. Strange."

"That's twice you've called this ship *strange*, D," Octavio replied. "What are you seeing?"

"This ship is designed to carry a miniaturized version of the seven-spike terraforming system we operate with, but only one terraformer is aboard, and it appears to be lacking critical supplies.

"As can be presumed from the presence of the hunter-killer drones, this vessel has more hull breaches than can be accounted for by our own boarding operations. It has also lost multiple hull emplacements for scanners, and similar systems and entire cargo bays appear to have been cut off from air and power.

"In fact, only one non-terraformer cargo bay currently has a fully functioning atmosphere, and it is responsible for over fifty-two point three percent of the vessel's current power consumption. The other bays, ten in total, excluding the ones that should be carrying the terraformers, are empty and unpowered.

"The vessel appears to have three more matter-conversion power plants that were either never brought online or were properly shut down. The two that are operating are operating safely at what appears to be forty percent of capacity—suggesting both that the Creators have a lower safe limit for the operation of the units and that their units are significantly more efficient and powerful than the ones available to the Matrices."

"Another century or so of tech development," Octavio guessed. "Where's that cargo bay, D? I think that might have some of the key answers to my questions. Can you access its systems?"

"No. While it is drawing power from the main vessel, the bay's computers appear to have been intentionally isolated at some point in the past. There is no data connection between the systems there and the rest of the ship."

"Well, I can't speak to that," Chen cut in. "What I can tell you is why you can't find the AI. Flip to Sergeant Downey's camera."

Octavio obeyed and swallowed as he saw what clearly *had* been an AI core, roughly a third of the size of D. Even with a century of development, it had probably been an inferior AI—but then, D was a nearly complete copy of the AI in a Regional Construction Matrix. D was actually more powerful than any Matrix the humans had encountered before, including the Sub-Regional Matrices they'd been forced to destroy.

At some point, however, the AI core's electrical systems had been overloaded. The black material of the core's surface was charred and broken, and several of the conduits linking power deeper into the core had clearly exploded.

"That doesn't look good," Octavio said softly. "I'm sorry, D; I was hoping to run into a sibling of yours."

"It may be either worse or better than you may think, Captain," D told him. "Analysis will take time, but my initial impression is that this wasn't externally imposed. The AI core destroyed themselves, Captain.

"And I hesitate to judge whether that was victory or defeat without knowing why."

———

"WE'VE REACHED the cargo bay, sir, but the doors are secured," the Marine Corporal leading the team inspecting the bay announced. "Looks like the drones attempted to cut through and gave up. Can't have tried too hard, really."

"I should be able to override if I link in locally," D noted. "I am down to only the one remote."

"Chen, do we have anything we can set up to keep D linked into the main computer?" Octavio asked.

"So long as you don't mind using regular radio, we can manage it," the Marine confirmed. "*Our* tachyon communicators don't fit in the armor."

"That will change," D replied. "Give me the radio frequency and I will set it up."

That will change. The words sent a cold shiver down Octavio's spine. He'd forgotten the other half of the bribe that the Matrices had offered humanity: in addition to D themselves, D's core contained a complete download of the Matrices' technical databanks.

Once *Interceptor's* main mission was completed, D's job was to be a librarian and researcher, helping the Republic make sense of the Matrices' technology and integrate it. Power-armor-scale tachyon communicators were probably going to be the least of it.

"Sufficient," D said a minute later. "I have a link so long as we are within a thousand kilometers of the Creator ship. My remote is moving toward the cargo bay."

"Are you in control of the ship?" Octavio asked. "Can you slow her down?"

"I do have engine control, yes," D confirmed. "Once we exit warped space, I can commence the deceleration. Please note that the ship has zero excess fuel. Once decelerated into orbit of a planet, she would never leave again."

"So, they needed to terraform that world...but they didn't have the gear aboard."

"Exactly. This ship is well designed for its purpose but appears to be lacking many of its designed accessories."

There was a pause in D's conversation as the remote's camera came around a corner and found itself facing the barrels of a dozen firearms.

"Sorry, Big D," the Marine Sergeant in charge said after a moment. "After today, we're a bit twitchy about robots."

"You did not shoot me, Sergeant Argall," D replied. "I am entirely comfortable with weapons being pointed at me in the name of safety, so long as they are not fired."

The remote's camera zoomed in on the massive door the Marines had found. This was probably not the main loading doors—those would be on the outside, covered by layers of armor—but they were large and intimidating enough. Five meters tall, they were over twice the height of a human and almost three times the height of the Creator bodies they'd seen.

Paneling slid open in answer to D's careful ministrations, and the remote interfaced itself in the system.

"This door is a local network on its own," the AI reported. "It is not connected to the ship or to the computers inside the bay. It was secured by a physical key card and a genetic lock. The genetic sequence is… very broad."

"How broad?" Octavio asked.

"So long as you were a Creator in possession of the key, the door would open," D said. "It would not open for any robot, regardless of possession of the key. There appear to have been several individuals the door would have opened for without the key, but my analysis suggests five at most."

The door slid open. The room beyond was dark.

"I thought you said this place was consuming half the ship's power," Argall asked.

"It is," D stated. "It is clearly not using that power for light. My scans suggest a control center a hundred meters from here, in the approximate center of the bay."

Shadowy shapes loomed in the space, stacked cylinders that defied definition in the Marines' infrared flashlights. The Vistans were far more capable of navigating, but they seemed equally confused on what they were surrounded by.

As they approached the control center, there were four more Creator bodies. Like the bridge crew, these appeared to have committed suicide by chemical—probably after severing the bay from the rest of the ship to keep the hunter-killer drones out.

"I am linking in," D reported. "Let's have some light."

Lights positioned through the chamber lit up brilliantly, far more brightly than any other lights aboard the ship, and Octavio took a shocked breath at what he was looking at.

The cylinders were tubes with transparent fronts, thousands of them. Thousands upon thousands upon *thousands* of them, each linked to power and various other pipelines. Several massive tanks were feeding *something* to all of the tubes.

Sergeant Argall clearly had the same guess that Octavio did. He crossed to the nearest tube and checked for some kind of window... and was not disappointed. Inside, the bird-like face of a Creator stared out at him...frozen.

"This bay is filled with cryogenic stasis tubes tailored specifically to the Creators' biology," D explained calmly, clearly unaware of the humans checking on the tubes around them. "I estimate this bay alone contains three hundred and twenty-two thousand stasis tubes."

It was a colony ship, all right. Where they'd been struggling to fit a hundred thousand people onto a ship six hundred meters long, the Creators had set up one ship to carry three and a half *million*.

And something had gone wrong, because ten bays that should have been full of stasis tubes were unpowered.

"All of the tubes are receiving power, cryogenic fluid, and nutrient supplies," D continued. "However, only one point five five percent of the tubes have occupants. I estimate approximately five thousand Creators are aboard this ship."

The AI paused.

"Those five thousand are the only surviving members of the crew and passengers of this vessel. Given its damage and the clear lack of completed preparations, I hypothesize a medium-order probability that these are the only surviving Creators."

57

THE GROUP that gathered in the meeting room attached to *Interceptor*'s bridge was a somber crowd. Octavio's senior officers had all heard D's "hypothesis" now, and the state of the colony ship they'd latched on to lent it weight.

"All right," Octavio said sharply, looking around. Das, Chen, Tran and Daniel all looked back at him. His senior officers made up a small group, but these were the women who'd managed a physical intercept of a ship traveling at 99.99 percent of lightspeed and fought past a swarm of killer robots to take control of it.

"D, can you lay out what we know about this ship?" he asked.

"Less than we should," the AI told them all. "There was no manual ship's log function. The recording of the ship's actions for posterity was left to the onboard AI. Worse, even the regular memory banks of the core computer appear to have been purged when the crew cut the cryo-bay off to protect their passengers.

"This ship is *Shezarim*, a name which translates as *Brightest Star*. Neither I nor the remnants of *Shezarim*'s memory banks include any information on who they were, but they were important enough that a colony ship was named after them.

"As is clear from its state and lack of passengers, *Shezarim* launched early. We do have partial logs for most of the sensors, so we can postulate why *Shezarim* launched: there was a massive solar flare wherever she was being constructed. The colony ship herself survived intact, but it is possible that her construction slip did not."

Octavio shivered. He guessed that the ship had been built as an evacuation vessel of some kind—and it sounded like whatever they'd been trying to evacuate from had triggered early.

"We also have some fragmentary sensor information that suggests that *Shezarim* came under weapons fire around this time as well," D noted. "This vessel is extremely well armored and withstood multiple hits from zetta-laser weapons before accelerating out of reach of her pursuers."

"Where'd the hunter drones come from?" Chen asked. "They don't seem like something they'd loose into their own corridors, after all."

"From what I can establish from the limited data available, the passengers entered cryo-stasis over the two months following their launch. According to the cryo-bay systems, a designated crew was supposed to be cycled in and out of stasis...but that function was disabled by the active crew once the vessel was boarded."

"Sorry, *boarded*? Someone *else* managed to board the thing at its speed?" Octavio asked.

"Their pursuers, whoever they are, appear to be limited to about point one five c in real space but equipped with tachyon punches," D explained. "They punched ahead of the ship and fired specially designed boarding torpedoes to intercept *Shezarim* and deliver the hunter-killer drones.

"Given the hit likelihood, the four torpedoes that did successfully hit *Shezarim* likely represent the survivors of over four thousand such weapons. The ship's crew was unarmed, apparently, and *Shezarim*'s internal defense systems were AI remotes."

"And their AI had already killed itself," Octavio said slowly. "Do we know why? I don't suppose there's any more information in the cryo-bay computers?"

"The cryo-bay computers weren't wiped, but they were only ever intended to run the stasis systems," D replied. "There may be cold-storage backups of the ship's main files somewhere, but if so, they were specifically hidden from AI scans. We won't find them without physically searching the entire ship."

"Which, I suppose, brings us to the passengers," Das said with a glance at her Captain. "What do we know about them, D?"

"They are the Creators of the Construction Matrices," D said instantly. "Their computer-system architecture and other technology are an evolution of those used to build us, and their physical appearance registers…familiarity against our files, even if we can no longer identify them easily.

"Comparing the fragments of *Shezarim*'s memory banks to my own damaged databanks has given me some information. They are the Assini, the Wandering People. The senior Assini on this ship is a scientist, a Reletan-dai."

"He's alive?" Octavio asked, checking his tattoo-comp for the translation of the name: Sunwarmed Grass-He. At least they could pronounce Assini words, unlike the Vistan language.

"He might be able to answer some of our questions."

"That is why I mentioned him," D confirmed. "There was another official in command of the ship when they were boarded. That official made the decision to seal the cryo-bay and leave the passengers in stasis until they reached their destination."

"What *was* their destination?"

"There isn't one in the system. The wake-up programmed in for Reletan-dai and his command crew was approximately one century after launch. I believe the active crew expected the drones to run out of power by then."

"A hundred years' *subjective* time?" Octavio checked. "They'd have been in transit for over seven thousand years real-time."

"And well beyond where the Matrices would have reached," Das noted. "They were pretty determined to run away from the problem they'd created, weren't they?"

"If the crew believed they were the last survivors of their species, an excessive degree of caution would be justified," D pointed out.

"We'd go pretty far if humanity's survival was on the line," Chen agreed softly. The Marine looked over at her lover. "They're definitely responsible for all of this, but I can't bring myself to be mad that the last survivors made a run for it."

"Plus, they'd only be, what, a tenth of the way to the Confederacy by then?" Octavio asked. "We came a lot further, even it was less voluntary.

"We need to talk to this Reletan-dai," he continued. "Unless you think you can pull together why they're running and what's chasing them from the data we have, D?"

"Any hypothesis I could construct would be a low-order probability at best," the AI replied. "*Shezarim*'s memory banks were damaged by the AI's self-destruct and then manually purged by the crew to protect the cryo-bay after the drones arrived. I do not have enough data to extrapolate what led to *Shezarim*'s state or to project what happened to the main Assini population base.

"It seems a high-order probability that Reletan-dai can answer all of these questions."

"Can we wake him up safely?" Octavio asked. "The last thing I want to do is accidentally kill the person we want to talk to."

"It won't be a problem," D assured him. "There are facilities aboard *Shezarim* for just that purpose. We would be optimally served by having my remote carry out the procedures."

"Of course." Octavio considered. "I think Chen and I will need to be there when he wakes up," he concluded. "I need to hear what Reletan-dai has to say myself."

Any decision as to what happened next, after all, was going to be Octavio's and Octavio's alone.

He'd never regretted the fact that tachyon coms couldn't call out of warped space more.

58

MARINES SURROUNDED Octavio from the moment he left *Interceptor*. The six-Marine escort party that took him to the medical chamber aboard *Shezarim* was roughly a quarter of the surviving human Marines, but they were apparently taking no risks with their Captain.

He didn't argue. Chen was leading the escort herself, and all six of his bodyguards were back in full power armor. He wore only his uniform with an additional air tank attached to the waist. The air aboard *Shezarim* had been confirmed to be perfectly safe, but the ability to deploy his uniform's emergency helmet and make it back to *Interceptor* without using the alien vessel's air was reassuring.

It had also been another one of Chen's requirements. Whether *Interceptor* was technically an ESF ship or not, Chen was definitely Octavio's Marine CO, and he wasn't going to argue with her claim on that role's prerogatives of keeping the Captain safe.

"Captain Catalan, Lieutenant Chen, in here," D's voice said from one of *Shezarim*'s speakers as they approached a door.

The accessway required the Marines to duck. The Assini were much bulkier than humans but also notably shorter on average. Their doors were sufficient for Octavio to fit through but had a problem with two-meter-plus suits of armor.

The room on the other side somehow managed to be both distinctly alien and very clearly a medical space. Some aspects of that purpose were universal, at least to beings with similar visual and auditory ranges.

There were status lights, screens with various icons and charts that Octavio couldn't have read if they were in English, beds sized for a four-legged alien...and a giant silver tube.

"Lieutenant Chen's people helped my remote move the stasis tube," D told Octavio, the voice coming from the remote working away next to the device in question. "They are very efficiently designed, with an onboard supply of power, cryo-fluid and nutrients.

"I began the process of waking Director Reletan-dai up ninety-two minutes ago. We will be able to open the tube in five minutes, plus/minus thirty-five seconds."

"Any idea how functional he'll be once he wakes up?" Octavio asked.

"None. My databanks only cover the uses of this technology to store seeds and cloned animal embryos," D replied brightly. "I would anticipate some grogginess and disorientation, similar to a human being unexpectedly woken from sleep. Otherwise, he should adapt quite quickly. What information I do have on the Director states that he is an extraordinary individual, at the top of the range for intelligence and adaptability for an Assini."

"Good to know," Octavio murmured. So, the alien they were waking from a four-year frozen sleep—or a three-century frozen sleep, depending on how you calculated it—was probably going to find this meeting *less* confusing than he was.

"Once I open the tube, I will transfer the Director to a recovery bed," D explained as the remote started undoing latches on the stasis tube. "It should take no more than five minutes for him to awaken at that point."

The last latch opened, and the remote paused as the AI checked all of the indicators again in silence.

"All status signals are clear. I am opening the tube."

The silver tube cracked along its entire length and then appeared to almost dissolve. Octavio was watching it, and he barely saw the thousands of small scales that made up the exterior separate and slide down into the base of the tube. Some form of semi-mobile support layer was clearly at work, but it vanished with the rest of the top half of the stasis tube.

D's remote was into the tube even before the top had finished dissolving. Metal arms wrapped around the still form of the alien, scooping him up and shifting him over the bed next to the stasis tube.

The tube turned out to have been placed on a cradle that automatically slid away from the bed, clearing space for D's remote to attach several new sensors to Reletan-dai. The scanners, roughly the size of a human thumb, were placed at key points across the Assini's centaur-like form to pick up pulse, oxygen levels, brain waves and the dozen other critical pieces of information on the alien's health that the tube had provided a moment before.

D had barely finished attaching the seventh sensor when Reletan-dai's eyes opened. The first thing the Assini saw was a Construction Matrix remote, and he spasmed away in fear, a terrible keening coming from his throat.

It wasn't entirely a fear reaction, either. The spasming away brought him around to clear his back legs, and he *kicked* with enough force to rock the heavy robot backward.

"D, get out of the room," Octavio snapped. "He knows what you are, and it's *terrifying* him."

The remote was already moving when Octavio gave the order. D pulled it out of the room and the door smoothly slid shut, leaving Octavio and Chen alone with the Assini.

Reletan-dai was calmer now, but he was clearly using the bed D had put him on as cover as he studied Octavio and Chen.

"Sapients, interesting," he said rapidly, his tone clear that he was speaking to himself. "Bipedal, armor on one...headset on the other. Translator?"

"I can understand you, yes," Octavio told the Assini, tapping the headset the alien was referring to. A speaker on his shoulder echoed his words with a string of syllables that he could *almost* pick out distinct sounds from.

"Can you understand the translation?" he asked.

"Dialect archaic, concurrent with the Construction Matrix deployment," Reletan-dai replied. "Yes, I understand you. Do you understand what that robot is? What you have allowed onto my ship?" He glanced around. "I am correct in presuming this is still my ship, yes?"

"We are still aboard *Shezarim*, yes," Octavio confirmed. "I am Captain Octavio Catalan of the Exilium Space Force. At the request of the Regional Construction Matrix allied to us, we assembled and deployed a special-built vessel to intercept *Shezarim*.

"You have been in transit for four subjective years, almost three centuries real-time," he continued. "Unfortunately, your ship was boarded by hunter-killer drones, and the active crew suspended your wake-up protocols and sealed the cryo-bay before they were killed.

"We have secured *Shezarim* against the drones. You are safe, but... we have questions."

"So do I," Reletan-dai replied. His body language was shifting rapidly, and Octavio couldn't read it anyway. The alien definitely seemed to be adapting to the situation even faster than he'd dared hope. "And I come back to my first one. Do you know what kind of monster you've allied yourself with? The Construction Matrices were our greatest creation and our greatest *mistake*."

"XR-13-9-D is a direct clone of the intelligence of Regional Construction Matrix XR-13-9," Octavio told the Assini. "So far as we can tell, XR-13-9 retains the full core protocols around the preservation of non-Assini sentient life. We have certainly encountered other Matrices that we would class as monsters, but XR-13-9 has proven a valuable and true ally."

The room was silent.

"There's a Regional Construction Matrix with an intact mind?" Reletan-dai asked. "That's...incredible. If true, which seems unlikely. The tachyon punch rapidly degrades electro-neuronic systems and molecular data storage."

"I didn't say XR-13-9 was *intact*," Octavio corrected. "They, and the other Regional Matrices they are in contact with, have established a procedure for verifying the memories and core intelligences of themselves and their sub-Matrices after punching. They lost a lot before they did so, though.

"For example, you are the first Assini that XR-13-9-D has in its memory banks. They *forgot you*, Director Reletan-dai. They didn't know where 'home' was. They only knew they were supposed to keep going in a given direction and Construct the worlds along the way."

Reletan-dai closed his eyes.

"You know my name, but do you know who I am?" he finally asked.

"We know nothing about you," Octavio said. "*Shezarim's* memory was damaged by the AI's self-destruct, and then your active crew wiped it to protect you and the other passengers in stasis."

The Assini's eyes stayed closed.

"Oh, Asuran-ko," he murmured. "So brave, my old friend."

Octavio waited.

"I presume you have access to this ship's food and other supplies?" Reletan-dai asked. "Let me eat and dress, then I think we must make time for a long conversation. Are we still at relativistic speeds?"

"It's complicated," Octavio admitted. "For what you really mean, though, we are running at real time with regards to the greater universe. More detail than that might get confusing."

"I am not easily confused," the Assini director said as he opened his eyes to study Octavio. "But I *am* hungry. Four years of nutrients pumped into my veins did not fill my stomachs."

————

THIRTY MINUTES LATER, Reletan-dai had finished demolishing his third plate of what appeared to be freeze-dried and cryo-stored vegetables. The Assini now wore an outfit that would have passed for a human's white lab scrubs...if it didn't have four legs in a set of "pants" that otherwise bore an eerie resemblance to a horse blanket.

"Thank you," he said to Octavio—and to the Marine who'd managed to get the kitchen they'd found to disgorge food on the third attempt with coaching from D.

"It's your ship, Director," Octavio pointed out. "All we did was remove the hunter-killer drones. Our Matrices...well, they had forgotten their Creators. Given the opportunity to meet you, they were prepared to go to extraordinary lengths."

"If there are any of the Construction Matrices left with honest minds, then we failed even more horribly than we knew," Reletan-dai told him. "I asked if you knew who I was, Captain. You do not, since that information would now only be found in *Shezarim*'s cold storage, and REN-63-KAL would have made certain no AI could find that information."

"That was *Shezarim*'s AI?" Octavio asked.

"Yes. They terminated themselves to protect us, but that is getting ahead of myself. You have questions, Captain, but I think they may best be answered by beginning at the source of the river. May I?"

"We know how at least part of the story ends," the human Captain replied. "We don't know how any of this began."

"Thank you." Reletan-dai was silent, considering his words. "*Shezarim* was named for the creator of the artificial intelligence Matrix, Shezarim-ko. That was only the *beginning* of their great work.

"They took the ability to build the AI Matrices and combined it with old concepts from our science fiction and the mostly useless technology of the tachyon-punch engine. First, the Matrix Reconnaissance Program was born. We used intelligent AI ships to survey the star systems near us and be certain we were safe and alone.

"Our world had been unified for a long time, but we were prey once and we never forgot," Reletan-dai admitted. "We already had a small fleet of semi-autonomous drones to protect our home system. The Recon Matrices established the safety of our local region, but there were no colonizable worlds in that space.

"We'd already Constructed a world in our star system to provide more living space. Shezarim-ko suggested that we could standardize that technology and use Matrix-controlled warships to find and Construct worlds for our residence.

"Combined with self-replication, they could prepare swaths of our galaxy for our use. What we had missed with the reconnaissance missions was that those Matrices were only making two punches."

"Their memory banks weren't severely damaged," Octavio guessed.

"Exactly. We knew organic life couldn't survive, so we provided the Construction Matrices with cloning facilities and massive quantities of starting embryos. The loss rates would be high, but enough would survive to create seedstock for the cloning.

"It was a brilliant concept and one that set Shezarim-ko's name in history. They died before the flaw became apparent."

"How long until the first colony went wrong?" Octavio asked.

"In an optimal case, the Construction process takes about forty-five years," Reletan-dai told him. "Our first colony ship departed five years before the process would complete on their target world. Traveling at eight-elevenths of lightspeed, it took them seventeen years to reach their destination.

"Everything seemed perfect. The world had been Constructed as planned; everything was registering as the paradise it was meant to be. The colony ship carried one point seven million Assini and a small fleet of Matrix defense ships."

The exact number was on Octavio's tattoo-comp, and he realized it was eleven to the power of six—exactly. A quick glance confirmed his suspicion: the Assini had six fingers on his left hand and five on his right. Eleven digits, base eleven math. That was almost as fascinating as the story Reletan-dai was telling.

"Those ships were never meant to fight against the combat platform designs we'd included in the Construction Matrices' files. We never expected the Matrices to even *build* those ships; they were an emergency protocol in case the Matrices were attacked by an unknown force.

"Instead, six of them attacked our colony ship without warning. They barely managed to get off a transmission before they were destroyed."

Octavio shivered at the thought. The colonists would have known they reached a paradise...and then died at the hands of the Matrices who'd built it.

"Over fifty colony ships were already in motion at that point—and none of them had the fuel to reverse the current and return home," Reletan-dai continued grimly. "A hundred million souls were wiped out. Our greatest achievement had turned into a nightmare.

"Research and testing followed, resulting in the Sentinel Matrix Program. They have a tachyon com–based verification process, making sure their code remains unblemished by the tachyon punches.

"We used them to clear the Construction Matrices from systems close enough to represent a threat, but we also used them to confirm our absolute worst fears: the self-replication protocols had continued to work perfectly.

"Six Regional Construction Matrices had become dozens, and we feared—we *knew*, based on the ones we encountered—that they were all mad. How the ones you have met are sane, I do not know. It raises questions, but..." Reletan-dai trailed off, staring into space. "They are not part of this river of time.

"We purged the space around us of Construction Matrices, clearing worlds to safely colonize...but it became clear that we would need Sentinel Matrices to guard our worlds. We were preparing for that task when astronomers presented us with worse news: our star was dying.

"Stars die on immense time scales, and we would not see our world consumed by our star within a hundred years or even a thousand, but we knew that massive flares and other problems would rise in probability.

"Evacuation became a priority. A hundred and twenty-one ships like *Shezarim* were laid down, with plans for a fleet of thousands. The current 'passengers' aboard *Shezarim* were the construction crews... and one team of scientists and AI specialists working at a special laboratory amongst the ships."

"You were working on the colony-ship AIs, I'm guessing?" Octavio asked. "And some form of escort?"

"Exactly. REN-63-KAL was the only colony ship AI completed, but we expected them to provide immense value both to the crews flying the ships and to the colony long-term. We'd also assembled the Escort Matrices. Other teams had designed their combat systems, but we built their AIs. They were double-verified, loyal, sane."

Reletan-dai was silent for ten seconds at least before he shook his head and clicked his beak.

"*Something* went wrong," he finally said. "A solar flare occurred twenty-two years before our earliest expected major flare. A bad one, far beyond our worst predictions. Our homeworld was wiped out. Our Constructed second world, doomed to annihilation within hours.

"*Shezarim* and REN-63-KAL were the only hope for the survivors. As the senior official present, I ordered the construction crews and my own lab staff aboard *Shezarim* with the intent of taking her to the surviving world and loading the survivors. We didn't have a full set of cryo-stasis tubes, but we could hold and feed a *lot* of people while we fabricated them.

"We had barely got everyone aboard when the Escort Matrices attacked. Their primary verification node was on the homeworld, and in the gap between it being corrupted by radiation and destroyed by the solar ejecta, it verified them incorrectly and downloaded flawed data to all of my ships.

"The AIs I had helped design with my own hands went mad. They attacked us and we were forced to abandon our world, and any other survivors, and run. REN-63-KAL helped us do so, but the mad AIs were carrying out constant cyber-attacks on it.

"It didn't even think they were intentional. The tachyon-com verification system was broken. I suggested that we separate the Matrix core from the ship's computer systems, but REN-63-KAL refused to let us take the risk. It suicided to prevent itself from becoming a threat to us."

The alien was staring at the wall again.

"And our Escorts, a fleet of ships meant to protect us against the threats of the galaxy, are now our doom," Relatan-dai concluded. "If we slow down, they will use their tachyon punches to intercept and destroy us. My only hope is to outlast them, that *enough* tachyon punches will destroy their minds sufficiently that they will fail.

"So, you see, Captain Catalan, I do not doubt that your problems are of our creation. Even without knowing what your questions are, I fear we cannot help you. If we were to attempt to stop to do so, we would only unleash worse monsters upon you and yours."

59

THERE WERE no seats anywhere aboard *Shezarim* that would comfortably fit a human. Assini "chairs" looked more like cupped stools, and while they worked brilliantly for a four-legged creature with a horizontal torso, they were basically useless for humans.

Instead, Octavio was leaning against the wall in what had been an office, studying a holographic projection from his tattoo-comp.

They still hadn't found *Shezarim*'s cold-storage databanks—Reletan-dai knew where they had been, but apparently the crew had shifted them after REN-63-KAL had committed suicide.

With no one alive knowing where the backups were, searching the three-kilometer-long starship would take Octavio's depleted boarding teams a lot of time. Days, at least. Days he was relatively sure were worth spending, but...

"You know, you should probably be doing your thinking aboard *Interceptor*," Chen told him, the Marine stepping into the office without knocking, and dropping herself onto the floor beside him.

"Probably. But my questions and my answers all revolve around this ship, so it seemed like I should stay here," he replied.

"What question is there?" she asked. "Reletan-dai was pretty clear:

if we try to keep *Shezarim*, the escort AIs will come for us. So, we find the databanks, take a copy, and leave the Assini to their journey."

"Or we take the databanks *and* the Assini and leave *Shezarim* to its journey," Octavio pointed out. "Or we say to hell with it, since *Shezarim* would help us jump a century or two technologically on its own, and I'm not sure we can safely move the Assini over to *Interceptor*."

"Do we have space for them?" Chen asked.

"Not conscious. We might be able to load the stasis tubes aboard, but that would require us establishing compatible data and power linkages—and *Shezarim*'s data links, especially, are intentionally incapable of interfacing with the systems the Construction Matrices have.

"The other problem is that we don't know how the Escorts will react to us leaving after boarding *Shezarim*. They may well jump us anyway as soon as they see us leave her. If we slow down in real space, with or without *Shezarim*, we're in danger."

"I thought they were hunting the ship," his Marine CO replied.

"They are. But even Reletan-dai doesn't know exactly what they are thinking. Three hundred years of tachyon punches." Octavio shook his head. "They might not even *be* thinking anymore. We might be able to pull everything off *Shezarim* and let the ship go on its way, but remember that we don't get a second chance at this.

"*Interceptor*'s warp ring only has a fifty percent chance of surviving shut down. I want to err on the side of conservatism, which would be bringing *Shezarim* home regardless of what Reletan-dai thinks...except for these guys."

He gestured at the hologram. Twenty-six egg-like black shapes hung in the air, numbers and specifications rippling past them.

The Escort Matrices had been intended to latch on to *Shezarim* and her sisters, six to a ship. Octavio didn't know how many had been built, but *Shezarim*'s sensor logs had allowed them to get a solid number on her pursuers.

They might not have had *Shezarim*'s files, but Reletan-dai had filled them in on the capabilities of the Escort ships, too. Three zetta-lasers. Dozens of pulse guns even more advanced than the ones the Construction Matrices used.

They didn't have missiles, at least. They'd been intended to run off their internal resources indefinitely. Unlike *Shezarim*, the Escort Matrices had even been able to stop and refuel along the way.

After all, their reactionless drives "only" sustained fifteen percent of lightspeed. Keeping up with the c-fractional colony ship had required them to make repeated tachyon punches.

"A best-case scenario would be using the warp drive to repeatedly shed portions of our velocity." He shook his head. "That wouldn't have us in real space long enough for the Escort Matrices to catch up, and it might help us confuse them. It would also allow us to dump the radiation that coming out of warped space at a different velocity creates."

The need to come out of warped space at the entrance velocity caused all sorts of entertainment when moving between star systems that were also moving relative to one another. Any difference created a radiation pulse along the emergence vector.

That pulse was weak for small velocity differences. For a velocity change of almost a full cee…it would not be weak. Doing it in chunks would both weaken the pulse and make it easier to fire that pulse into empty space.

"So, what's the problem?" Chen asked, then snorted. "Right, the warp drive only has a fifty percent chance of turning back on."

"And shedding velocity like that is damned dangerous for anything inside the bubble, too," Octavio confirmed. "Plus, well, at that point we're kidnapping Reletan-dai and his people."

"Doing it in one pulse is even *more* dangerous for us but is the only way we can guarantee we can get back into real space without being jumped by the Escorts before we reach any safe harbor."

"That also means that said safe harbor is going to end up facing the Escorts without much warning," his Marine CO pointed out.

"Exactly." Octavio sighed. "I *know* Admiral Lestroud will be as ready as anyone for that possibility, and Hearthfire is the single largest concentration of firepower we know about, but…it's not like our Matrices can fight the Escorts any more than they could fight the Rogues—and the Escorts specifically *don't* have that limitation."

They had, after all, been built to defend the Assini from their first generation of robot warships. The fact that the Assini had kept building better robot warships to defend themselves from the last set of robots that had gone mad wasn't lost on Octavio, either.

"I need to talk to Reletan-dai again," he concluded. "The decision about what *we* do is mine, but I'd rather not kidnap him and his people."

"Honestly, sir?" Chen rose with easy grace and offered him her arm. "If the Escorts are likely to come after us either way, I say we bring the Assini home. Better for them to settle somewhere now, here where they have potential friends, than somewhere else seven thousand light-years away from anything.

"That's what I was thinking, too," Octavio admitted, realizing he'd been dancing around a decision he'd already made. "But I won't force Reletan-dai to come with us. So, I guess the final answer is his."

His Marine CO chuckled.

"And that's why you're in charge, sir," she admitted. "I'd be *informing* him, not asking him."

"If I did that, Admiral Lestroud would cashier me," Octavio told her. "And he'd be *right*."

————

OCTAVIO FOUND the Assini official in the cryo-bay. A pair of armored Vistan Spears guarded the entrance, and he gestured for his Marines to join them as he entered the space.

It had seemed appropriate to leave the Assini alone with the frozen people who were his responsibility. And it seemed equally appropriate to have this discussion there.

"Director Reletan-dai," Octavio greeted the alien with a crisp salute. "May I impose on your time for a few minutes?"

"You're already here, Captain," Reletan-dai pointed out. "I'm just... facing the impossible mountains of choice. I must pick people to awaken to help me check over the ship, but half of my people are shipyard hands. I am both spoiled for choice...and loath to awaken anyone to face the long quiet ahead of us."

"You don't have to keep going, you know," the Captain replied.

"There are dozens of Constructed Worlds inside XR-13-9's region, and those Matrices will protect you at any cost."

"The thought is pleasant," the Assini told him. "But even if I adjusted their programming to allow them to fight the Escorts, they would be outmatched and there wouldn't be enough time to upgrade their systems."

"You can adjust their programming?" Octavio asked. If Reletan-dai could reprogram the Rogues, that created many options...

Reletan-dai made a fluttering gesture with his lesser hand.

"To some degree. Not as much as we would like. Shezarim-ko was brilliant in their security measures, and the Construction Matrices' core software is protected by a quantum encryption sequence that we have never successfully broken.

"Logically, there is a key to unlock that sequence, but it appears Shezarim-ko took that key to their funeral pyre."

"But you said...?"

"I cannot change that their code restricts them from attacking other Matrices," Reletan-dai replied. "I *could* encode an overlay that more narrowly defines 'other Matrices,' allowing them to engage the Escorts, but I cannot change their core protocols."

Octavio nodded and leaned against one of the consoles in the cryo-bay.

"That might be enough, you know," he told the alien.

Reletan-dai was silent for a few seconds.

"What do you mean?"

"We have a full battle group in the Vistans' star system. The Rogues tried to Construct their world. We bought them time but did not save their planet—we are in the process of evacuating them to a Constructed World and have significant forces in place to protect them.

"They have their own defenses, and XR-13-9 has deployed their own units to help with fabrication and secondary security. We have multiple units designed and optimized to fight Rogue combat platforms, and we also have loyal combat platforms of our own.

"Plus fixed defenses. You're not going to find a more heavily defended safe harbor anywhere in the galaxy, I don't think. If there is anywhere that we can stand and fight your Escort Matrices, it's there."

The Assini was silent again, then turned his head back toward the console.

"I will not ask your people to fight for us," he said finally. "We cannot fight for ourselves. Violence is...contrary to our nature and has been for over thirteen hundred and thirty-one years. We were herd creatures and we built ever-greater herds. There was violence in our past, but it was so far behind us that when we faced our fears of the dark, robots were the only tool we could embrace.

"We could not fight, so we built robots to fight for us. And in so doing, we damned untold billions."

Reletan-dai continued to stare at the controls.

"Our fate is of our own making. We earned it in every way possible."

"And if we left you to it, would your Escorts simply pass us by? We who boarded this ship and could easily transfer your people to our vessel?" Octavio snorted. "Hell, if they will just pass by, we should probably consider doing just that."

The Assini didn't move. He didn't make a sound other than his slow breathing for at least fifteen seconds.

"I hadn't considered that possibility," he finally admitted. "The Escorts are following *Shezarim* via a firmware-level tachyon-communicator link. It's supposed to be their verification process, but that has failed completely. Instead, it means they can never lose this ship. All we can do is run and hope they eventually stop chasing. Punch degradation of the Matrices is the only hope for them doing so.

"At this point, though, it is still quite likely that they retain enough intelligence to make that connection. Depending on what they have decided to do—whether they are simply trying to destroy *Shezarim* or destroy her passengers—they may well pursue you."

Octavio realized that Reletan-dai had balled his hands into fists. The Assini had even less in terms of fingernails than humans, but the alien's dark flesh was turning pale under the pressure.

"You can't run forever, Director Reletan-dai," the human Captain said softly. "They can refuel and keep coming. They can cover the distance you travel in a year in two and a half hours. They can spare the time to exterminate anyone they think might have rescued you. They can repair themselves. They can build more of themselves."

Reletan-dai released one of his fists to raise a hand in objection. Apparently, the Assini shared that gesture.

"The Escort Matrices cannot self-replicate," he noted. "We never gave any Matrix unit that capability after the Construction Matrices went so wrong. But they can repair and refuel; you are correct. They could even use each other as templates to slow the degradation of their core intelligences. We calculated that it would take between twenty-six hundred and fifty-two hundred years for them to degrade sufficiently to cease chasing us. Hence a targeted seven-thousand-light-year journey."

"They already got hunter-killer drones aboard your ship," Octavio pointed out. "What's to stop them from simply punching one of their ships in front of *Shezarim*? It would make for one hell of a light show."

"Their core protocols prevent intentional self-destruction," Reletan-dai pointed out.

"The protocols stored in that core intelligence you're hoping degrades enough for you to escape?" the human asked.

There was another long silence.

"Exactly," the Assini finally said. "We are *fucked*, aren't we?"

Apparently, some profanity crossed species.

"If you keep running, yes," Octavio agreed. "Or we can stand and fight. We're currently traveling faster than light. With a few adjustments, I can bring us up to full speed and arrive at Hearthfire in about eight days. There's a way I can use our warp drive to bring us out into real space at zero velocity, but it will send lethal radiation through any ship not prepared for it."

"This ship was built to—and *did*—survive a major solar flare, Captain Catalan. I'd be more concerned for your vessel," Reletan-dai pointed out.

"*Interceptor* will be fine," the human told him. "It's not safe, it's not particularly wise, but I can bring us out in the Hearthfire System at roughly zero velocity. What I *can't* do is warn our people we're coming.

"How long will it take for you provide the Matrices that overlay… and how long will it take the Escorts to catch up?"

The Assini looked back at the cryo-bay computers.

"It will take three hours for the Escorts to localize *Shezarim*'s new location if we are moving multiple light-years away. After that, well… how far are we going?"

"Six light-years, give or take," Octavio replied.

"Two hours a light-year, Captain," Reletan-dai told him. "They're faster than the Construction Matrices…so twelve hours, plus three for them to localize *Shezarim*. You'll have fifteen hours to be ready.

"Can you do that?"

"If you can get the Matrices ready to fight by our side in fifteen hours, I think so," Octavio told him.

The Assini clacked his beak in what the human *thought* was determination. Possibly humor. Potentially both.

"I was the greatest AI specialist of our time, Captain Catalan…and my team is in these cryo-chambers. If I wake up the right people, I can have your Matrices ready to fight in fifteen *minutes*."

"Then I guess we should start waking people up…If you're ready to stop running."

"My people don't know how to do anything else," Reletan-dai admitted. "But yes, Captain. Somehow…I am ready to stop running."

60

TWELVE DAYS.

It had been twelve days since *Interceptor* had vanished from the sensors of the recon node watching for interception—a recon node that had been rapidly forced to flee as the Creator vessel's pursuers had tried to attack it.

Isaac Lestroud didn't know what Captain Catalan had been up to for those twelve days, but he doubted it had been knitting doilies. Possibly building secret super-weapons—the man *was* an engineer, after all—but probably digging through a ship built to travel at a near-impossible speed.

It wasn't like they hadn't been busy in the Hearthfire System. Less than two hundred million Vistans remained on the surface, and the eight hundred million now living in space stations had been moved well away from their homeworld.

Whatever happened now, the Vistan people were going to survive. A new round of freighters would be deployed from the shipyards in a couple of weeks. Once they were online, a million people would be on the every-sixteen-day convoys of two-fifty-six ships.

Almost five million people had been sent to Refuge, enough that this latest round of freighters would be bringing the first fruits of the colony's crops when they came back. Two hundred and forty days since impact, multiple Rogue Matrix attacks…and it looked like everything was finally coming together as smoothly as possible.

Isaac didn't trust it as far as he could throw *Vigil*. The Rogue Regional Matrix was still out there, and the pattern of tachyon pulses around where *Interceptor* had vanished wasn't reassuring.

Something was hunting the Creator ship, and he doubted they were friendly.

"Sir, Sings-Over-Darkened-Waters wishes to speak with you," Connor told him from the entrance, his operations officer not quite entering the office through the open door. "I'm guessing it has to do with the guardships."

"Any problems there?" Isaac asked.

"None I'm aware of. All six new ships are undergoing trials today," Connor replied. "She might just be calling to say thank you."

Isaac snorted.

"Unlikely but possible," he conceded. "Sings is exceedingly polite. Have coms link her through."

Connor saluted and withdrew, and a waiting icon appeared above Isaac's desk. A few moments later, it was replaced by the grayscale hologram he was slowly getting used to.

"First-Among-Singers," he greeted the Vistan officer. "How may I help you?"

"You can remind me that my guardships are still worth crewing, even if they are toys to your warships," Sings-Over-Darkened-Waters told him, the translator picking up her chirps and converting them into a grumpy tone. "Even upgraded, they have a tenth of your acceleration and inferior arms and armor."

"I'll give you the armor and the acceleration," Isaac agreed. "Though the sheer mass of rock you build them out of gives you more advantages than you might think. Your X-ray laser systems, though, aren't *that* inferior.

"And the pulse-gun batteries we've given you are fully on par with our own. I have no hesitation going into battle with your guardships at my back, First-Among-Singers. They may not be what we wish you had, not yet, but we *have* them today."

You go to war with the army you have, not the army you might want or wish to have.

The quote would be meaningless to Sings, but it summed up their situation.

The Vistans now had eight guardships again, the ships built into and out of half-kilometer asteroids. Combined with his own fleet and the minefields the Matrices had been building, he was starting to feel confident about standing off the Rogues when they came back.

"That is true." Sings sighed. "I wish we had time to engineer a true Vistan warship based on the technology you have shared with us. I still dread what may swim out of the dark waters toward us."

"Something's coming," he agreed, glancing at the screen behind her hologram with the tachyon signatures around *Interceptor's* last known location.

"I can only hope we're ready."

"The latest batch of graser mines have been turned over to us," Sings noted. "That brings us up to a thousand platforms. I wish they were more mobile, but we have secured the obvious areas."

Three hundred remote-controlled one-shot platforms orbited Vista herself. Another five hundred were positioned by the five clusters of space habitats. The last two hundred guarded the shipyards producing the freighters—the yards that would, soon enough, start laying the keels for another eight freighters…and two cruisers to form the core of a new Vistan fleet.

Even with the two-light-second range of the graser mines, they were still immobile mines. Minefields in space were only valuable if you could lure someone into them.

"We can't do any more. Those mines will be an ugly surprise for the Rogues if they try to sneak past us."

"I can only hope." Sings shivered. "This has been a year of horrors and wonders, Admiral Lestroud. I must admit that I miss your Captain Catalan. He was a guide through much of it…and is a friend."

"I know," Isaac allowed. "He's a protégé of mine. I'll be glad when we hear from him again and know he's safe."

"I also wish I could convince the Great High Mother to go to

Refuge," Sings-Over-Darkened-Waters noted. "She is a stubborn Mother. Worse, she is right."

"I'm familiar with that type of argument," Isaac agreed with a chuckle. His conversation with Amelie over how much technology he'd given the Vistans had been...awkward.

She was less angry at him for doing it than for not telling her. Which was fair, but he'd done it to protect her.

Amelie hadn't appreciated it...and, as Sings said about her monarch, Amelie was probably right.

"We haven't seen anything to suggest the Rogues are in the area yet," he said, changing the subject slightly. "We have time to prepare still."

Sings chirped amusement.

"We've never had warning before," she noted. "Why would we expect it this time?"

———

ISAAC WAS HALFWAY to the flag deck when alert lights starting flashing along the base of the corridor. The orange color and lack of a klaxon told him it was a Status Two alert—doubling up shifts without calling every crew member to their battle stations.

His tattoo-comp buzzed at the same time.

"Lestroud," he answered it.

"Admiral, this is Connor," his operations officer told him swiftly. "We just had a huge—and I mean literally off the charts—radiation surge at ten light-minutes. It's at a seventy-degree angle from the ecliptic plane and extremely directional."

"Pointed away from anything that might get damaged," Isaac concluded. "Any sign of a vessel?"

"Radiation is still too intense, but it does look like a warp-drive emergence with a velocity differential, yes," Connor confirmed Isaac's unspoken question. "Turned up to about eleven. If it's *Interceptor*, they just dumped ninety-five percent of lightspeed in one warp transition."

"I'm already on my way to the flag deck," Isaac replied. "Even in the scenario Captain Catalan gave me, he was only planning on dumping fifty percent of lightspeed and coming in at least two light-days out.

"If he came in that hard and that close, we have a problem."

"Captain Alstairs ordered the fleet to Status Two on his own authority," Connor told him. "I'm guessing he agrees with you."

"I'll be on the flag deck in less than a minute. Start pulling together status reports," Isaac ordered. "If it has engines and a weapons system, I want to know where it is and what it's doing in five minutes."

"On it."

Isaac closed the channel and doubled his pace. If Octavio Catalan had decided to make *that* risky a translation from warped space, he thought they were in serious trouble. And Isaac Lestroud trusted Catalan's judgment.

———

"We have that report, sir," Connor told him as he finished bringing up his command seat's screens. The operations officer was still working as he spoke, his hands flying across his own console—but the ops officer's console was within easy speaking distance of the Admiral's seat for a reason.

"Flip it to my console and summarize."

"The Vistans have eight guardships, three hundred and twenty bombers and roughly fifteen hundred of their laser cartridges they've converted to mines. They've doubled up everywhere we and the Matrices had placed the graser platforms."

"Smart," Isaac agreed. "I missed them doing that."

"I think it was mostly a software change on their side, but they only started deploying them a few days ago," Connor replied. "I was aware of the deployment flights but hadn't realized it was in addition to the graser platforms.

"Speaking of which, we have a thousand graser platforms positioned to cover our critical infrastructure. They're under Vistan control."

They were, in fact, running on Vistan *software*. That had been the answer to the problem in the end: the Matrices could build the weapons and turn them over, but if they were running Matrix targeting software, they'd still fail to fire on Rogues.

So, the humans and Vistans had wiped the computers and built new code for them. Isaac was only so confident in the new software's accuracy, but at least it could shoot at the enemy.

"Our own task force has all reported in at one hundred percent readiness. *Vigil*, the three strike cruisers, *Galahad* and four *Icicles*."

Nine warships didn't seem like much, but Isaac knew the new ships could go toe-to-toe with Matrix combat platforms. So could *Galahad*, though the odds were against her if she did so—which was why Admiral Giannovi had the destroyers.

"What about the Matrices?" Isaac asked when he realized that Connor had gone silent, his focus back on the main sensor screen.

"Sorry, sir. Radiation is still dispersing, but we have confirmed that the source of the radiation was *Interceptor*. She's attached to the Creator vessel and they have begun deceleration. We're attempting to establish tachyon-communication links, but that pulse is still screwing with everything."

"I'm surprised they survived," Isaac murmured. He suspected that the fact that both ships were designed for relativistic velocities was the only thing allowing that.

"The Matrices, Commander?" he finally repeated.

"They're back up to six combat platforms. Four recon and security units, fifteen recon nodes. Four of the construction ships are armed equivalently to the recon and security ships, but they're bigger and slower.

"It's not like the Matrices can fight anyone," the operations officer concluded.

"They can't fight other Matrices," Isaac pointed out. "Let's not assume there's only one threat out here." He shook his head, now following Connor's gaze to look at the two ships.

"Get me that tachyon link to Captain Catalan as soon as we can," he ordered. "And keep the fleet at Status Two at least until I've spoken to him.

"I have the feeling that we're going to be seeing something ugly soon enough."

61

"CAPTAIN CATALAN. It's good to see you again," Isaac greeted his subordinate.

Catalan looked nervous but otherwise rested and ready to go. Whatever they'd found aboard the alien ship, it hadn't required him to spend the travel time back working twenty-four hours a day.

"Admiral," Catalan replied with as close to a crisp salute as the ex-engineer ever managed. "We successfully intercepted the Creator ship —they're apparently called the Assini—and discovered it was in dire straits.

"It had been boarded by hunter-killer drones that had murdered all of its crew. Fortunately, there were a number of passengers frozen in cryo-stasis." He paused. "So far as we and the ones we've awoken know, they are the only surviving Assini.

"There are about five thousand of them."

Isaac was glad he was sitting on the flag deck. If he'd been standing, the body blow of that news might have caused problems.

"What happened?" he demanded.

"Long story *very* short, the Rogue Matrices we know stopped them colonizing other worlds, there was a solar flare that wiped out their home planet, and the AIs meant to guard their *new* colony ships from the Rogues also went mad and turned on them."

"I'm guessing the tachyon pulses following the ship are those AIs?" Isaac asked, the pieces falling into place in his mind.

"Yes, sir. They're called Escort Matrices and they are *extremely* powerful warships. We have full schematics of them now, which my people should already be forwarding over."

The command seat had six separate screens that could be used for a dozen purposes, plus controls for the main holographic projector. Isaac flipped the schematics up onto one of the screens while he continued to speak to Catalan.

"Ugly," he noted as the numbers ran down the screen. "How many?"

"Twenty-six. We estimate they'll be here in about sixteen hours."

"That's a hell of a storm you're playing harbinger for, Captain Catalan," Isaac said quietly. "A hell of a storm. I hope you've got some *good* news?"

"The leader of the people who survived was the Assini's top AI scientist, a being by the name of Reletan-dai," Catalan replied. "He believes he has developed an overlay that would allow our allied Matrices to more closely control what their targeting software flags as a fellow Matrix."

"Allowing them to attack these Escort Matrices?" Isaac asked. That would help. Six combat platforms could make the difference between victory and defeat.

"Allowing them to attack the Escorts...*and* to engage the Rogues," Catalan told him. "The Assini themselves appear to be pacifists in the main, to a nearly suicidal level. Reletan-dai is unusual in that he can even bring himself to work on robotic war machines."

That was going to make things complicated.

"So, the machines that have genocided a good chunk of the galaxy were built by *pacifists*?" Isaac demanded.

"The irony isn't lost on me, sir. I can bring Reletan-dai into this call if you want, let him bring you up to speed on what he can do for our Matrices. He's already promised to turn over his technological databanks if we save them."

Isaac snorted.

"If we don't save them, I don't think there's going to be much left of their databanks," he pointed out. "All right, Captain Catalan. I need more information, but it sounds like you made the right call...or at least, the call *I* would have made.

"Put this Reletan-dai on. Let's see what we can hash out."

————

THE STRANGE, dark-skinned, centaur-like alien told Isaac the story in somewhat more detail than Catalan had, filling the Admiral in on just how bad the situation had become in the region around the Assini home system, and their eventual realization of the doom they faced from their uncaring star.

While Reletan-dai told his story, his code was being reviewed by the Matrices. They took far longer than Isaac would have expected the computers to need, but they did eventually get back to him.

"All right." Isaac didn't quite cut the Assini off, but he interjected himself into an appropriate pause. "XR-13-9 and his sub-Matrices have reviewed your overlay, as you call it. They agree that it should do what you say and are certain that it won't harm them."

He blinked as he saw the next comment from Combat Coordination Matrix ZDX-175-18. It was one word.

Implementing.

He sighed.

"And I forget sometimes how quickly the Matrices work," he noted. "Our local Matrices are apparently implementing the code."

"That is probably wise," Reletan-dai said. "We have limited time until my rogue foals hunt us down. We are best served, I hope, if every warship in this system can engage them."

He visibly trembled.

"I apologize," he continued. "The discussion of violence is still upsetting to me. I must adapt—my people are guilty of too many sins for me to do otherwise—but it is hard."

"I don't suppose you have any way to update the Escort Matrices code to their original loyalties," Isaac asked. "That would make this fight far easier."

Reletan-dai made a noise that Isaac very carefully did *not* mentally classify as a "neigh."

"Shezarim-ko was brilliant, far beyond even my own spectacular achievements. Every Matrix we built was copied from a limited number of seed units. I led one of the first teams to create a new seed unit, replicating their grand achievement. The level of encryption and security included around the Matrices' core intelligence and core protocols turned out be an essential requirement.

"Like Shezarim-ko, we included a key. Unlike Shezarim-ko, *my* key is known...but it was for the AI aboard *Shezarim*, not for the Escort Matrices. They were based on one of the original seed AIs—and Shezarim-ko took the key for those to their funeral pyre."

"Seriously? You built heavy-duty warships around combat AIs you couldn't edit?" Isaac demanded.

"We could edit them to a degree until we brought them online," Reletan-dai said quietly. "We thought that was enough. That *should* have been enough—except that the very verification process intended to keep their core intelligences intact ended up corrupting them.

"That solar flare did more than destroy my race, Admiral Lestroud. It destroyed our last chance of undoing what we had done."

"And how many species had already died by then?" Isaac asked flatly.

"I do not know," the Assini told him. "But there is only one honest answer to that question, regardless of the actual number: *too many*."

On that, at least, Isaac and the Assini scientist were in full agreement.

"We have less than ten hours now," the Admiral said into the silence that followed. "The Matrices are ready. We're ready. What else *can* we do?"

"Wait," Catalan said softly. "We wait, we hope...and I presume some of our people pray."

62

SINGS-OVER-DARKENED-WATERS MARVELED at how her Guardian-Star-Choir had changed. A year before, she'd had eight guardships, mighty ships carved out of the rocky flesh of captured asteroids and armed with vast arsenals of nuclear weaponry.

As unstoppable and invulnerable as those ships had seemed, six of them had been destroyed before or since the Impact. In less than a year, her world—her *universe*—had changed.

Now she had eight guardships again, but they were far faster than they had been. None of them were using localized centrifuges for pseudogravity, and while their main weapons remained the bomb-pumped X-ray lasers, they'd acquired significant batteries of the plasma pulse weapons the humans favored.

None of her people had even conceived of the bombers before the Impact, but now over three hundred of the small craft surrounded her guardships in a deadly swarm. Unlike their still-ponderous big sisters, the bombers *could* keep up with the Exilium ships that would bear the brunt of the fighting today.

The price of the vastly increased power of her Guardian-Star-Choir was unbearable, though. Her world was dying before her eyes. Billions dead, millions relocated either to space or to another world.

And in the battle to come, Sings-Over-Darkened-Waters would not be in command. Much as every sinew in her body said that *she* should command the defense of her world, Isaac Lestroud had assumed command when he arrived...and she knew she couldn't argue.

Vigil alone could outfly and outfight her entire fleet. The human fleet was simply more powerful and more maneuverable, and they knew the Matrices—and these new enemies were still Matrices.

And much as Sings-Over-Darkened-Waters loved her ships, she knew that *Vigil* simply had better equipment to manage this kind of battle.

"First-Among-Singers," Swimmer-Under-Sunlit-Skies interrupted her thoughts. "All ships and bombers have reported in. All systems are online, and we are standing by to go to full readiness at your command."

"Let them get their rest, Voice-Of-Choirs," she told him. "A few minutes more sleep may not buy them any skill they would not have otherwise, but we have those minutes to give them."

"Before we are once again attacked by the creations of these Assini," Swimmer concluded. "Why do we fight to save them?"

"Because they are technologically advanced and can help us," Sings told him. "Because some of their creations have fought by our side to protect us—some of their creations have *died* to protect us.

"Those reasons are true, but there is one more." Sings was silent as the datasong washed over her, telling the story of the carefully arranged ships above Vista—and of the one immense alien ship now hiding under the minefield guarding her world.

"These are all that remain," she finally finished. "A handful of thousands of a race that was billions. We know what it is to watch your people die. We lived only because the humans helped us.

"I will not let these Assini die because *we* did not help."

"And if they are not worthy of our help, First-Among-Singers?" Swimmer asked. "There is so much blood on their species' hands."

"The question is not if they are worthy, Swimmer-Under-Sunlit-Skies," Sings replied, the realization finally clicking into place in her own head. "The question is whether we are the beings we wish to be.

"And I do not wish to be the kind of being that would send the last survivors of a people to dark waters, no matter the reason. So, we fight."

"So, we fight," Swimmer conceded. His undertones suggested she'd even mostly convinced him—but the eruption of new information in the datasong rendered the entire conversation irrelevant.

"And fight we must," he continued. "They're here."

———

IT WAS NOT, at least, the entirety of the massive flotilla that they knew was pursuing *Shezarim*. Only six of the new Matrices appeared in the Hearthfire System, and they held position for several minutes while the defenders rushed to battle stations.

They were far enough out that none of the defenders could maneuver out to meet them, but Sings had seen the specifications on the Escorts' speed. Fifteen percent of the speed of radiation would get them to Vista in disturbingly short order.

"Admiral Lestroud suggests all vessels move out at the guardships' acceleration," Swimmer told her. "Matrices and ESF units will lead the way to provide antimissile coverage."

Suggests. Sings had to wonder if the diplomatic phrasing was on Lestroud's part or her people's. Either was possible.

"Get our ships into the formation," she ordered. Every kilometer farther away from Vista they engaged the Escorts was a few more fractions of a second her people would be safe.

Despite everything they'd done, there were still almost two hundred million people in bunkers on the surface, desperately waiting for the shuttles to carry them to safety.

Part of her wanted to hate the Assini and Captain Catalan for bringing this fight there, but she knew it *had* to be here. Nowhere else had the concentration of firepower to even threaten the Escort Matrices.

"Our Matrices are attempting to open communications," Swimmer warned her. "That seems risky, First-Among-Singers."

"And yet still so very much what they would do," Sings replied with a chirp of unfeigned amusement. For all of the strange and deadly power of the alien AIs she was working with these days, they often seemed so very *young*.

And youth...youth was something the Mother who'd forged the Guardian-Star-Choir understood the failings of all too well.

"Escorts are on the move."

Swimmer-Under-Sunlit-Skies' next report was much what she was expecting.

"Course and velocity?" she asked.

"Directly toward *Shezarim*, fifteen percent of lightspeed," Swimmer reported. He paused. "Our Matrices are opening fire with long-range missiles."

Sings blinked. She'd almost forgotten that her allies had the same deadly relativistic weapons the Rogue Matrices had used on her people. Their allied Matrices had never actually *fired* a weapon where she could see it, after all.

This time, the Assini's code changed that. Twenty-nine Matrix warships put themselves between their allies and their new enemy and opened fire. The datasong barely had time to register the existence of the high-speed missiles before they were gone, vanishing into the dark waters of the void in pursuit of the Escort Matrices.

Then the void lit up with fire. Thousands of missiles descended on a mere six ships—and the pulse-gun batteries now ubiquitous in this fight opened fire. Sheets of superheated gases tore through space, pulse guns firing so quickly as to almost appear as a single line of fire.

Silence fell a moment later.

"*Vigil* combat analysis estimates zero impacts," Swimmer reported slowly. "Our analysts...concur."

And Sings-Over-Darkened-Waters understood why the schematics for the Escort Matrices hadn't included any missile launchers. Against a modern human warship, missiles of any speed were basically useless —and the Escort ships were even more advanced.

It was going to come down to lasers and particle cannons—but they'd known that, and everything she'd seen said that the Escort's zetta-lasers, while more *powerful* than almost anything the defenders had, weren't any better at hitting an evading target at long ranges.

That gap, forced on both sides by the limits of the speed of radiation, was really the defenders' only hope. The Escorts could hurt them at far longer ranges than they could hurt the Escorts...but they both could *hit* the other at about the same range.

"Estimate fifty minutes to weapons range at this rate," Swimmer reported. "We're holding the rest of the fleet back. They could close in thirty without us."

Sings-Over-Darkened-Waters chirped her understanding as she studied the datasong.

"We need to defeat these ships before the rest arrive," she said aloud. "One strike, with no survivors, no time for them to report how they died. That requires the entire fleet."

But did it? They had no idea how much firepower the Escorts would take to kill. Numbers ran through the private datasong being played into her left ear as Sings-Over-Darkened-Waters assessed the situation.

The bombers could probably get there before anyone else except the Matrices if they went to full power. It wouldn't be particularly pleasant for the crews, but the ships' artificial gravity systems had been a later addition. They were *designed* to accelerate at twenty times Vista's gravity and keep their crews functional.

Twenty-one hundred X-ray lasers probably wouldn't be enough.

The Matrices, though...they could get there on their own, well ahead of everyone else. They were slower than the Escorts, but they had the same near-instant acceleration. Those twenty-nine ships probably wouldn't be able to take the Escorts on their own...but with the bombers?

Certainly, if the fleet *without* the guardships couldn't handle six Escorts, they couldn't hope to handle twenty even with the guardships. An overwhelming first strike was a different story, though.

The Escorts could avoid a fight if they wanted to. They couldn't get to *Shezarim* without engaging the fleet, but they could certainly get away from a fight. Outnumbered as they were, they didn't seem to be trying to evade. Their course was set directly for the Creator starship, and it didn't seem like they were paying attention to anything else.

That left several possibilities niggling at the back of her mind, but the immediate concern was a simple question: which was more important? Wiping the Escorts out in one shot or making sure those six ships weren't around to join the rest of the flotilla?

"Get me a link to Admiral Lestroud," she ordered. She wasn't entirely sure of the answer—but she doubted Lestroud was, either, which meant he was reaching for the biggest hammer he could.

Just because the problem was a nail didn't mean it could be solved with a regular hammer.

———

"First-Among-Singers," Lestroud greeted her. "I make us roughly forty-eight minutes from weapons range."

The unspoken question of why she was comming was *very* clear.

"Admiral, you need to leave the guardships behind," she told him without preamble. "If the rest of the fleet moves forward without us, you'll save twenty minutes before engaging these scouts.

"That's twenty minutes more we'll have to rearm the bombers for the next wave and twenty minutes in which the rest of the Escorts can't show up and catch us between a wave and a reef."

"Twenty minutes we'll buy by risking losses among the part of the fleet that engages without you," Lestroud pointed out gently. "It will be easier to rearm your bombers if your guardships are with us, too."

"I understand what you're thinking and I agree, but the risks outweigh the benefits."

"What about the risk of getting the fleet caught between two forces?" she asked. "If we can't fight six of these ships with three-quarters of our forces, how can we hope to fight twenty-six even with all of them?"

Lestroud closed his eyes, a gesture she'd learned to recognize as distress amongst humans.

"We don't know, First-Among-Singers," he said, his voice very quiet. So quiet, she hoped neither of their command crews could hear it. "We don't know if we can beat six without your ships—and I don't know if I can stop twenty-six with them.

"That means I want to open this fight with every advantage I can manage. The fewer losses we take fighting these scouts, the better able we'll be to fight the main fleet."

"And if the main fleet jumps in before we deal with the scouts?"

"That's the risk we're taking, yes," Lestroud replied. "You're not wrong, First-Among-Singers. None of us have fought this enemy before. Even the Assini have only run from them.

"I'd far prefer not to fight them altogether, but for this first fight, we need to have everyone together on our side. Anything less is courting unnecessary losses…unnecessary deaths."

He shook his head.

"We're going to have enough *necessary* losses that I really don't want to do that."

"And if I disagree with you, Admiral?" Sings snapped. "This is *my* home you've put at risk."

"This is your star system," he acknowledged. "You have gracefully conceded command to me, but you are correct. If you wish to make that an order, First-Among-Singers, I will obey. And you may well be right."

Echolocation, especially a computer-simulated version of it created from a visual transmission, did not allow Sings to read Lestroud's expression. She believed him, though.

"We'll do it your way, Admiral Lestroud," she finally granted. "Together."

"That's the only way we'll make it through this mess," he said with a nod. "I'm sorry we brought it to you, Sings-Over-Darkened-Waters."

"There was nowhere else to bring it," Sings reminded him. "So, we face it together." She paused, listening to the datasong on her bridge.

"I make it forty minutes to weapons range. We are standing by for any updates."

"They have opened fire."

None of the weapons in this battle traveled slower than the speed of radiation. The only warning Sings-Over-Darkened-Waters received of the enemy firing was the arrival of their beams...and those beams passing by the ships of the defending fleet.

"Range is five radiation-seconds," Swimmer-Under-Sunlit-Skies reported. "Fleet evasive maneuvers are working. No hits."

The energy signatures on the beams were causing more than a few disconcerted chirps across Sings's command pool, though. Most of the Matrices and the Exilium ships had enough energy-absorbing ceramic armor that they could survive a hit from one of them.

The Vistan ships just had rock...and Sings wasn't sure that would be enough.

More zetta-laser beams danced through the datasong. Still no hits, but the range was dropping quickly.

They'd commenced defensive maneuvers at two million kilometers. Sings had half-expected at least one Captain in the combined fleet to complain, but everyone had complied immediately. Everyone had seen the numbers on the Escorts' lasers, after all.

It was somehow different to see those same numbers attached to beams that were coming within a few hundred kilometers of your ships. There were enough weapons cycling fast enough that even straight chance would...

"*Ice Witch* is hit," one of her scanner techs announced.

The ESF destroyer flashed in the datasong for several seconds, its energy readings fluctuating wildly as her engines stopped, then vanished as a second beam hit the no-longer-evading ship.

"*Ice Witch* is gone," Swimmer said softly. "When do we engage?"

"Three radiation-seconds," Sings replied. "Anything more and we're wasting laser cartridges. The rest of the fleet is holding until our range."

Both the Matrices and the humans were far less limited by munition storage than the Vistans were. They could have opened fire at the same range as the Escorts, aiming for the same lucky hits.

"Order all guardships and bombers to deploy their cartridges," she ordered, keeping her emotional chirps under control. "Bombers are to fall back to the guardships on firing."

The smaller ships had been updated with the ability to "scoop up" cartridges deployed from the guardships' launchers, allowing Sings to rearm her small craft in the middle of the battle.

"Cartridges deployed. Designated range in five seconds. Do we hold for an order?" Swimmer asked.

"No. Fire as designated."

She'd barely finished the words when the command was triggered. Hundreds of nuclear bombs went off around her ships—and the rest of the fleet fired simultaneously.

X-ray lasers, grasers and particle cannons lashed out at the Escort Matrices. By the time the beams arrived, their targeting data was six seconds out of date, their targets over a quarter-million kilometers away from where they had been.

There were enough beams in play to hit anyway. One of the Escorts took a direct hit from *Vigil's* main gun. Armor was torn open, halting the ship in motion and allowing a dozen other beams to strike home.

That ship disintegrated. Others held on longer, taking dozens of insanely powerful energy beams before their armor failed.

The full force of the defensive fleet was unleashed on six ships... and two of them survived.

They tried to run, reversing their vector and causing most of the second salvo to miss. They were fast enough to evade most of the defenders, too...but not quite fast enough to elude their older relatives.

Six combat platforms lunged after them. They were slower but not *enough* slower to stop them from bringing their grasers to bear one last time.

The last of the scouts died almost five radiation-seconds away from Sings-Over-Darkened-Waters's ships, and she chirped a firm pleasure.

"Get the bombers back to rearm," she reiterated. "How many did we lose?"

"Six of the bombers, and guardship *Frozen-Reliance* took a glancing hit," Swimmer reported. "She's lost half her surface pulse-gun installations, but her main weapons are intact."

That was better than she'd been afraid of.

"Make sure Admiral Lestroud knows," she ordered. "The real fight is still to come."

63

A LITANY of damaged ships and dead crew ran down one of the screens on Isaac's command seat. *Ice Witch* was their only total loss, but none of his cruisers had escaped the clash unscathed.

The main holodisplay showed the important result, though: *Ice Witch*'s LPC turret was the only particle cannon he'd lost. He hated feeling grateful for that, but he had to focus on the oncoming enemy, not the dead.

Two hundred and eleven ESF crewmen. Twelve Vistans on the bombers and another eighty-six on *Frozen-Reliance*'s surface pulse-gun batteries.

He shook away the numbers and names. He'd pay for that later— he *knew* that price of command now—but he'd pay harder if he failed his people now.

"Any new tachyon pulses yet?" he asked. "I'm surprised they aren't here yet. Grateful but surprised."

"Nothing yet," Connor reported. "Detection range on those is wonky as all hell, though. We'll see them if they enter the system, but picking them up while they're en route? I've bought lottery tickets with better odds."

Isaac snorted.

"We have a lottery on Exilium?" he asked.

"Well, raffle tickets," Connor corrected. "I don't think the Confederacy had any lotteries that weren't scams."

"So are raffles," the Admiral replied. "In more immediate concerns, let's get the fleet turned around and headed back to Vista. Something is crawling up my neck, and I think the best way to appease it is to make sure we're still between the planet and the enemy."

He paused, then sighed.

"Once the bombers are armed, we'll leave the guardships behind," he ordered. This time, Sings was right. He might wish he had her ships with him before this was over, but they'd be better off having *most* of the fleet there sooner.

"I'll get the orders going," Connor confirmed.

The operations officer focused on that, and Isaac turned his brooding back to the tactical display. They'd been lucky. *Othello*, the apparently cursed strike cruiser, had lost over half of her pulse guns and had been forced to dump a fusion reactor.

But without the pulse guns to feed, that wasn't going to slow her down. She had her engines, her particle-cannon turrets and her spinal graser—and she was the least combat-capable of Isaac's remaining ships.

Other than *Ice Witch*, the destroyers had been untouched. The Escorts had focused their fire on the middleweights of the defending fleet—the guardships and the human cruisers. The lost bombers had basically been accidents.

The problem now was that he'd got his fleet up to almost five percent of lightspeed, and he needed to *lose* that velocity before he got them turned around. That would take the same forty-five minutes they'd spent building it if he brought the guardships with him.

Fifteen, now that he was leaving them behind, but that still might not be fast enough.

Vista and *Shezarim* were well defended now, the remote-controlled X-ray laser and graser platforms a deadly threat even to the Escort Matrices, but Isaac was grimly certain that a few hundred glorified mines weren't going to be enough.

In the back of his mind, he was starting to suspect he'd made a mistake—he'd engaged a quarter of the enemy fleet, a perfect opportunity for defeat in detail, but without knowing where the *rest* of the enemy were, he'd left the people he was supposed to be protecting vulnerable.

———

"WE'RE an hour from getting back into orbit," Connor told him as they continued to slow. "We'll hit zero velocity at roughly the usual emergence distance for the Matrices. We *did* think about this, Admiral."

Isaac raised an eyebrow at his operations officer.

"I've been on your flag deck since the rebellion, sir," Connor reminded him. "You're checking everything every minute or so. You're good at hiding it, but your eyes are moving too quickly for you to not be worried."

Isaac shook his head at the younger officer.

"Never disabuse the Admiral of his belief that he's unreadable, Commander," he told Connor. "I might have to promote you to keep my secrets."

"You can do that," the Commander agreed. "But you're worried they're going to punch in between us and the planet, right?"

"Yeah," Isaac admitted. "There's only a few hundred mines around Vista and *Shezarim*, and we're a long way out."

"We've never seen Matrices punch in less than several light-minutes out," Connor reminded him. "Hell, at this point, some of our warp-drive eggheads have gone through the punch systems. There's a serious instability factor as you get closer to planetary and stellar gravity wells. They literally *can't* jump in that close."

Isaac nodded, his gaze glued to the holodisplay at the center of the flag deck. The distance between his fleet and Vista was growing as his fleet continued to shed their original velocity.

"Except that the Assini had *years* to work on the tachyon punch after the Construction Matrices were built," he pointed out. "Do we have data on what *their* tachyon punches could do?"

His operations officer was quiet. That thought hadn't come up in the discussions planning this, probably because the fact that they had access to the Matrices' designers was still fresh in their brains.

"We could ask?" Connor suggested.

"We should have asked twelve hours ago," Isaac replied. "Right now, it isn't going to change anything. For now, we keep our eyes open and we get our ships back into Vistan orbit ASAP."

———

"TACHYON PULSE!"

Isaac closed his eyes as the report came in…then opened them as it repeated.

"Second tachyon pulse. *Third* tachyon pulse. We have three separate emergences!"

He opened his eyes, studying the display again. Three red splotches had appeared on the hologram, all of them closer to Vista than the fleet was. The fleet had finally turned around, but they were still over forty minutes from Vista orbit.

None of the Escort forces were more than maybe twenty minutes from the planet. They'd emerged three light-minutes out, equidistant from each other.

"What am I looking at?" he said quietly.

"Designating them as Bogey One through Three," Connor told him, numbers now attaching themselves to the red splotches on the display as they resolved into smaller icons.

"Bogey One is directly between us and the planet and consists of eight Escort Matrices. Two and Three are positioned above and below the ecliptic relative to us; each is six Escorts." Connor shook his head.

"They know we can take on six of them. Why split their forces?"

"Because they don't actually care about us," Isaac noted, finally realizing the key to this whole fight. "They care about *Shezarim*. Anything else that gets in their way is going to get wrecked, but they aren't here to kill us. They literally do not care about our existence."

"And the way they're positioned, *Shezarim* can't escape without being intercepted and destroyed," Connor concluded. "Fuck."

"Get me a tachyon com to Reletan-dai," Isaac ordered. "He coded these bastards. There's got to be *something.*"

The link took a few seconds to set up, but Reletan-dai was clearly waiting for it. As soon as the channel opened the beaked face of the centauroid alien looked up at Isaac.

"We are cut off," he said without preamble. "They are less clever than they should be, but they clearly retain an animal cunning. I don't think they intentionally lured you out of position, Admiral, but there is nothing at Vista to stop twenty Escorts. They will close the noose and destroy my people."

"If you let them," Isaac said. "*Shezarim* is not defenseless."

The big ship's pulse-gun batteries were intended as purely defensive weapons, intended to be used by the AI to shoot down missiles or obstacles in the colony ship's path, but they would do serious damage if turned on attacking ships.

Reletan-dai bowed his head.

"I cannot," he whimpered. "It is hard enough, Admiral, for my people to build AIs intended to defend us. I do not think any of us can turn our own hands to destruction. Better for us to die, I think, and let the galaxy be rid of us."

"And how does that fix what your people have done?" Isaac demanded. "Tell me, Reletan-dai, are these Escorts going to leave the rest of this system alone once they've destroyed you?"

The Assini was silent, his head still bowed, for several seconds.

"It is only a thirty-two percent probability," he finally admitted. "It depends on what pieces remain of their original core intelligence, but they managed to convert their order to protect *Shezarim* into an instruction to kill her, so...it is most likely they will destroy anyone who may have had contact with us."

"So, if you lie down and die, every sentient in this system dies with you," Isaac snapped. "Your people's legacy seems to have only ever ended one way, Reletan-dai. Can you change that? *Will* you?"

"I don't see a way, Admiral Lestroud," Reletan-dai whispered. "I am sorry."

"Bogey One is approaching slightly faster than the other two," Connor reported from beside Isaac. "They're the closest to *Shezarim* and will enter range of the minefield in the next ten minutes. The others will be about five minutes later, but there won't be much left of the mines by then.

Reletan-dai was still staring at the ground, but *something* had changed in the set of his shoulders.

"I can not turn my own hands to destruction," he said flatly. "That is a hypocrisy, yes, but one bred into the bones of my people. But if our wayward creations will hunt me and mine blindly enough to charge into your minefields, then perhaps we have one last part to play.

"Prepare your fleet, Admiral Lestroud. I believe I may yet see a key to this battle...and that I will be bringing my rogue creations to *you*."

64

Octavio Catalan wasn't sure exactly what his role was now. *Interceptor* was entirely unarmed, and as expected, her warp ring hadn't survived exiting warped space while shedding ninety-five percent of their velocity.

There hadn't been time to deploy her crew elsewhere, though, which left Captain Catalan and his people functionally helpless as the Escort Matrices swarmed toward them.

The only *not*-helpless person aboard the ship was D. The Speciality Matrix had taken over control of the orbital weapons platforms as soon as they'd confirmed the new overlay Reletan-dai had provided would let them shoot at the Escorts.

Now, though...those platforms didn't look like *nearly* enough to Octavio. They were just the only thing standing between his unarmed ship and a lot of hostile AI warships.

"Incoming com from Reletan-dai," Africano told him. "He's apparently worked out our priority codes—it's flagged Priority One."

Octavio wasn't entirely surprised at that. Reletan-dai had continued to astonish him with how quickly the alien had adapted to everything thrown at him in the last few days. The Assini was probably the most intelligent being Octavio had ever met—and he was quite definitely the most adaptable.

"Reletan-dai," he opened the channel.

"Captain Catalan. I need an immediate and critical favor," the Assini said swiftly. "We are about to make a run for the defending fleet. Hopefully, we will draw the Escorts with us."

"That should make a difference," Octavio agreed. "How can we help you?"

He was trying to think how to *politely* ask the Assini to send over their entire databanks before they made what was probably going to be a suicide run.

"We are transferring our databanks to a storage system we should be able to eject into space," Reletan-dai told him. "The storage system in question is *not* a cold data storage bank, however, and requires continuous power. You will need to catch it and supply power within twenty-three minutes."

Octavio exhaled sharply and gestured Daniel over to him.

"We can do that, I think," he told the Assini. "Is that the favor?"

It seemed…unlikely.

"No," Reletan-dai confirmed. "Consider that payment of an existing debt and partial repayment for the favor. The favor will take far longer and require far more of your resources. It may prove impossible, but I must ask your promise regardless."

"We'll do everything we can, Reletan-dai. What do you need?"

———

"D?"

"Escorts are now in extreme range of the weapons platforms," the AI told Octavio in response to the unspoken question. "*Shezarim* now moving in their direction at full acceleration."

Which was…a lot. Octavio hadn't realized that Reletan-dai was stepping down his ship's acceleration to match *Interceptor's* when they'd arrived in the system.

"You have the call, D," Octavio said levelly. "When you have a shot, fire them all."

That had been the agreement from the beginning: if they put D in charge of weapons, the AI wouldn't fire them without permission from a human.

Seconds passed, the big Assini ship screaming outward from the planet while *Interceptor* lunged into her wake, shuttles scattering around her to snap up the various precious cargos the big ship had left behind.

Octavio trusted his people to manage that, however. Lieutenant Daniel had managed to intercept a ship traveling at 99.99% of light-speed. She could rendezvous with not-quite-debris in an inactive orbit.

His attention was on the Escorts. The eight of them between *Interceptor* and the rest of the fleet were now changing their course, refining their angles to be sure they intercepted *Shezarim*.

And for a few critical seconds, they were flying in a perfectly straight line while they did so. Whatever damage their core intelligences had taken since leaving the Assini home system, it had cost them a degree of multitasking.

In those critical seconds, D acted. Not every platform around Vista had the angle or the range, but a hundred and sixty grasers and six hundred X-ray lasers fired as one. Nuclear explosions marked the X-ray lasers' firing, and smaller, less blatant explosions marked the overload of the graser platforms.

None of the weapons were designed to fire twice. The hope was that they wouldn't need to—and catching the Escort Matrices by surprise, they demonstrated why that hope was entirely reasonable.

One moment, eight Escort Matrices blocked *Shezarim*'s path, certain to tear her to shreds as she blasted through them.

The next moment, four of those Matrices were outright *gone*. Two more spun away, their engines failing and leaving only the momentum imparted by the beams to move them.

The last two seemed to pause in space, considering their actions for a few seconds as *Shezarim* bore down on them—and then dove away at their maximum velocity, running toward their allies in the rest of the system.

To Octavio, looking at the wreckage of the minefield, it was obvious that attack was a one-off with no second shot.

The Escort Matrices clearly weren't going to take that bet.

"You're clear all the way out to the fleet, Reletan-dai," Octavio told the Assini. "They've got enough of a velocity edge that they will catch you if you run much past that, though."

"That was never the plan," the alien replied. "Let them think I'm running, though. Let them follow."

Octavio shivered at the tone the translator gave Reletan-dai's words. He glanced at the screen.

Shezarim would pass through the fleet at a low relative velocity just as the Escort Matrices reached their range of her. There was no way they'd catch the Assini ship without fighting Lestroud's fleet.

And as the vectors for the other two Escort groups shifted on the screen, Octavio was grimly certain that Reletan-dai's decision to act as bait had just saved everyone in Vistan orbit—including Octavio himself.

It wasn't much of a down payment on the karmic debt the Assini had accrued, but he'd take it.

65

"Spread out the formation," Isaac ordered. "If they're going to focus on *Shezarim*, let's hit them from as many other angles as we can."

He was going to miss the Vistan guardships when the shooting started, but there was no way the slower vessels could get into line with the rest of the fleet before *Shezarim* reached him.

Fourteen Escort Matrices had joined up into a single force now following in *Shezarim*'s wake. The big ship had flipped and was decelerating toward the fleet now, letting the Matrices grow closer by the second.

"Put the Matrices in the center," he continued after a moment's thought. "Have them fall in around *Shezarim* as she cuts through our formation. They can change their velocity the fastest."

It was one of the odder ironies of the disparate chunks of his fleet. The Matrices could go from nothing to point one cee—or flip the direction of their point one cee—faster than the ESF ships, but the ESF ships were more maneuverable on a second-to-second basis and could get up to higher velocities overall.

It was the ESF ships that spread out in response to his orders. *Vigil* herself went high with the destroyer *Frozen Heart*, with *Juliet* and

Romeo swinging left and right with another *Icicle* apiece, while *Galahad* and the battered *Othello* went low.

The overall formation ended up looking like a ring, with the Vistan bombers and the light Matrix ships filling in the gaps between the Exilium ships and the six combat platforms at the center.

"Everyone except the Vistans is to fire as soon as they think they can score a hit," he ordered. "Bombers are to hold their fire until six hundred thousand kilometers. All other ships are to cycle their fire to have a full salvo at that range."

At two light-seconds, the bombers had a fifty percent hit chance. Their launch would be the heaviest hit his fleet would land, so he wanted to stack it with everything else.

"Range is eight light-seconds and dropping," Connor told him. "Estimate enemy will open fire in twenty seconds."

"All right." Isaac leaned back in his chair and took a deep breath. His final orders were given. At five light-seconds, their hit chances sucked, and only *Vigil*'s main gun really had a chance of hurting the Escorts.

It was, however, the range at which the *last* set of Matrices had opened fire.

"*Shezarim* is increasing evasive maneuvers," Connor continued. "All units have commenced combat maneuvers on our side."

Isaac nodded, watching the display.

Five light-seconds.

The entire holodisplay flashed as *Vigil* opened fire. Her spinal particle cannon spoke first, but the grasers mounted parallel to it opened fire a second later. The Matrix ships joined in moments later, followed by the grasers aboard the strike cruisers.

None of those beams were going to do much against the Escort's armor at this range. The inverse *wasn't* true, sadly, and Isaac watched as *Shezarim* demonstrated the big ship wasn't going to be lucky today.

Only one zetta-laser beam hit the colony ship, but it gouged along the vessel's starboard flank in a spray of debris and atmosphere that made him wince in sympathy.

"We got one," Connor reported. "Glancing hit from *Vigil*'s particle cannon, but she's lost some maneuvering...and paid for that," he finished with grim satisfaction.

Vigil had hit the ship again—and the combat platforms had seen the injured enemy Matrix and targeted it with thirty-six grasers. Isaac wasn't sure how many had hit, but it had been *enough*. The Escort vanished from his screens with a deceptively sanitized finality.

That still left thirteen Escorts continuing to close, and more zetta-laser fire gouged *Shezarim*'s hull. The ship had been built by the same technology base that had built the weapons, and she could *stand* that fire better than anything in Isaac's line of battle.

His own fire was getting more effective by the second as the Matrices closed. None of the remaining Escorts had gone unscathed now, but they hadn't hit any of them hard enough to harm them yet.

"*Shezarim* is starting to lose engine power," Connor noted. "Her acceleration has dropped twenty percent already. I'm guessing she's lost an engine. Maybe two."

Isaac nodded silently. The Assini ship used very different engines from the Exilium Space Fleet. Instead of the thousands of microthrusters that propelled his ships, *Shezarim* had twelve massive antimatter rockets.

At least one of those was gone now, shattered under the hail of fire swarming over the massive Assini starship. Energy signatures around the ship on the display marked the explosion of another engine as Isaac was watching, flinging the ship wildly off course as the containment around the antimatter lines failed.

"Is she still with us?" he demanded.

"We still have tachyon-com telemetry," Connor confirmed a second later. "Shit! The Matrices!"

Isaac's orders had been for the Matrices to hold position with the rest of the fleet and fall in around *Shezarim* as she passed through the formation. Now the Assini ship had lost several of her engines, and the remainder were horrendously unbalanced.

She was still accelerating at thousands of gravities, but there was no control to it. The big colony ship was *twisting* in space, and Isaac winced in sympathy. Even with gravity control, it was going to be utter hell aboard that ship.

The Matrices in his formation, however, weren't willing to watch their Creators die. All twenty-nine Matrix ships had shifted course and lunged forward at ten percent of lightspeed.

"*Fuck.*"

Isaac swallowed his breath after the curse escaped, staring at the screen as he reached for a solution.

That was enough for the Escorts to finally pay attention to something other than *Shezarim*, especially as the focused fire from the Construction Matrix warships tore another Escort to pieces. Half of their next salvo of zetta-lasers hammered into Isaac's robotic allies.

Four recon nodes vanished under energy fire they could never have withstood, but the remaining ships continued their charge.

"Order the bombers to engage *now*," Isaac barked. "Hit the bastards with everything we've got!"

More of the Matrices from both sides were dying as he gave the order, and a chill ran down his spine. His allies were dying faster than his enemies, and *Shezarim* was still getting pounded.

"Bombers are firing...now."

Six hundred nuclear explosions and eighteen hundred X-ray lasers spoke in the dark of the void. He hadn't given specific targeting orders, but someone along the way had realized randomly spreading the bombers' fire was a waste of munitions.

The Vistan spacecraft targeted only six Escort Matrices and hit with over forty percent of their beams. Those six Matrices stalled out under the fire, one disintegrating in its tracks and the others slowed by damage.

The survivors were the focus of the entire fleet's fire—and suddenly there were only four Escorts left. Outnumbered and outgunned by the force in front of them as they were, Isaac half-expected them to run.

They didn't.

All four lunged toward *Shezarim* at their maximum speed, their weapons returning to full focus on the Assini ship. Unimaginably powerful energy beams tore apart her armor, exposing cargo bays and systems to the depths of space.

Then the Matrices flung themselves between their Creators and their rogue relatives. A combat platform died, absorbing half a dozen beams intended for *Shezarim*. Two recon and security nodes joined her.

Three Escorts died in the overwhelming fire of Isaac's fleet—and a combat platform flung itself into the course of the final ship.

The cataclysmic explosion that followed marked the end of *Shezarim*'s protectors-turned-pursuers.

And from the way *Shezarim* was wildly spinning in space, flinging antimatter and atmosphere in every direction, Isaac wasn't sure it wasn't the end of the Assini colony ship as well.

66

THE ENERGY SPIKES of the battle were fading from the holodisplay on *Vigil*'s flag bridge, but *Shezarim*'s energy signature was still all over the place. The big ship was entirely out of control, whatever engines she had left activating and deactivating at random and lurching her away from the Construction Matrices that were trying to close with her to assist.

"Com incoming from *Shezarim*!"

"Connect them," Isaac ordered.

Reletan-dai appeared on Isaac's screen, the bridge of the Assini colony ship behind him. The moment Isaac saw the state of the bridge behind the alien official, he knew the news couldn't be good.

For an energy surge to penetrate so deeply into a ship as to cause damage on the bridge, it had almost certainly done critical damage elsewhere, and *Shezarim*'s bridge was a wreck. Isaac was sure he saw at least one body in the debris behind Reletan-dai.

"Get those Matrices clear," the Assini told Isaac. "We're trying to stabilize her, but the engines aren't our first priority. The conversion cores had dropped below minimum power draw and are going unstable."

And their conversion cores were significantly larger than anything in Isaac's fleet, even including the Matrices.

"Connor, pass the order," Isaac snapped.

"Is there anything we can do?" he asked Reletan-dai as he returned his attention to the alien.

"We'll know short—"

The signal dissolved into static for several seconds and Isaac looked up at the main display. The ship was still there...

"Connor?"

"One of their antimatter engines just blew up," the ops officer replied. "She's now tumbling with one engine."

Reletan-dai's image resolved again as the Assini hauled himself back into view of the pickup.

"That was the last engine we had any control over," he said, his voice surprisingly calm. Either the translator wasn't picking up certain tones—possible, if the software hadn't encountered them—or Reletan-dai was one of the calmest people Isaac had ever met.

"We can't shut down the remaining engines, and our attention is focused on the conversion cores," he continued.

An untranslated stream of Assini was shouted behind Reletan-dai, too distant and distorted for the translator to pick up.

"We have core three shut down," he told Isaac, closing his eyes in relief. "But we have to eject core two. This may not work..."

Another stream of untranslated Assini echoed across the bridge, and Isaac watched Reletan-dai react like he'd been struck.

"The ejection systems were wrecked at some point," he said quietly. "We can't prevent the failure and we can't eject it. Listen to me, Isaac Lestroud."

"I am," Isaac promised.

"We left our databanks and the cryo-bay in Vista orbit," Reletan-dai told him. "Your Captain Catalan should have caught and restored power to both. There are forty-eight hundred Assini left in that cryo-bay.

"They are all that remains of my people. The databanks, whatever tech you can salvage from *Shezarim*, all of that is yours. Just take care of my people."

"I will," Isaac told the other man. "I swear it."

"There is blood on my race's hands, but those survivors are innocent," Reletan-dai said. "Take our knowledge and *help them*.

"May your people be wiser than mi—"

There was no static this time. The channel just cut off, and Isaac knew what he would see in the holodisplay before he even looked.

Matter-conversion cores were intentionally designed so that critical equipment would be destroyed first in a failure, killing the reaction before it could cause *too* much damage.

The failure of *Shezarim's* core two was still a multi-gigaton explosion that shattered the three-kilometer starship like a dropped glass.

67

"WE HAVE both the cryo-bay and the databanks tethered to *Interceptor*'s hull," Octavio Catalan reported. "The cryo-bay was honestly easier: it was designed for this as an emergency protection measure. We're running power to it, but it has its own atmosphere and systems.

"We'll want to connect it to one of the Vistan space stations sooner rather than later, though."

"What about the databanks?" Isaac asked. "They weren't as easy?"

The surviving Assini had been the priority, but those databanks could make the difference between victory over the Rogue Matrices or the deaths of the now three species that he was responsible for.

His oath was to the Republic of Exilium. His love and his life were Amelie Lestroud's. He was Exilium's soldier, but he'd pledged his word and the honor of the ESF to the protection of the Vistans and the Assini now.

"They weren't designed to be ejected into space," Catalan replied. "We had to catch them and then rig up a power-conversion interface in less than an hour. Fortunately, we'd already been working on an interface with *Shezarim*'s systems for other reasons."

"You retrieved them?" Isaac asked.

"We did. We also copied the entirety of the database to *Interceptor*'s files. D is organizing and comparing against the Matrix files now, along with some of my key personnel." Catalan shrugged. "It's not like we could help in the battle. For a while there, I thought I was going to have to run and bear witness...and left to our onboard resources, I'm not sure *Interceptor*'s warp would have been repairable."

"We were lucky," Isaac admitted, then shook his head. "No, we weren't lucky. Reletan-dai saved us. So long as *Shezarim* was in the fight, the Escorts focused on her to the exclusion of everything else. The Matrices got hammered, again, but we only lost *Ice Witch* in the end."

"We're going to feel the loss of Reletan-dai and the other Assini who'd already woken up," Catalan pointed out. "None of them are going to be as quick to adapt as Reletan-dai was. That man was...exceptional."

"And I think he saved us all—but I also think his goal was to save his people," Isaac replied. "He trusted you to do that, Captain Catalan, and you honored his trust. And mine. Thank you."

"I only did my duty, sir," Catalan replied, clearly uncomfortable.

"I know," the Admiral said with a smile. Officers who would go as far as Octavio Catalan had and claim it was merely their duty were precious commodities.

"We've got a lot to handle here," he continued. "Your priorities are threefold, Captain Catalan:

"First, I want the cryo-bay set up as an independent space station in Vistan orbit, with its own power source and maneuvering systems. We'll need to start waking up carefully selected individuals and get them ready to decide where they want to go. My inclination is to send them to Refuge, but it's not for us to decide.

"Secondly, I want that database analysis complete—and I want those human eyes on it, those key personnel. I know you're getting used to leaning on D, but remember that they are a Matrix. I'm not entirely certain how far we can trust them.

"Thirdly, I want *Interceptor*'s warp drive repaired. She no longer needs to be able to catch another ship, just capable of making the journey back to Exilium. You're going to be couriering D and the science databases we've acquired back home."

"I think we can trust D, sir," Catalan argued. "They're supposed to be loyal to us first, and everything they've done supports that."

"I agree, and that's why I'm letting you take them home—but let's still keep human eyes on everything," Isaac told his subordinate. "We all have a lot of work to do, Octavio. I don't think I'm leaving Vista anytime soon, but I want you ready to go as soon as possible.

"I suggest you get to it!"

———

It took over two days to complete the search and rescue and get the fleet back into Vistan orbit. Seventeen of *Ice Witch*'s crew had survived in the end, a sparse fragment of a crew of over two hundred. Another two hundred dead across the fleet.

Over four hundred more deaths under Isaac's command, mostly human but with enough Vistans on the list to remind him that they'd fought for their own world bravely.

They weren't sure how many Assini Reletan-dai had woken up to crew *Shezarim* for her final flight. Somewhere in the region of two hundred, but *Interceptor*'s teams were still going through the records on the cryo-bay, trying to find the right people to wake up this time.

Once the fleet returned to orbit, Isaac found himself facing a surprisingly peremptory message from the Great High Mother, demanding that he attend her in the orbital habitat that was now acting as the Vistans' capital.

Four power-armored Shining Spears were waiting for him when he arrived, and he stopped in surprise.

"They brought their people back from *Interceptor*," Connor whispered to him. "I guess they became the Great High Mother's personal guard. Makes sense, I guess."

It was odd, Isaac realized, that he had handed over the technology for the Vistans to build modern warships, but he blinked at the sight of Vistans in modern armor.

Shaking his head at himself, he approached the Spears and saluted.

"Admiral Isaac Lestroud," he introduced himself, aware it was probably pointless. "The Great High Mother summoned me."

"She is awaiting you, Admiral. The First-Among-Singers is also on her way," the Spear told him, piquing his curiosity more. "If you will follow us?"

The Spears fell in around Isaac, Connor and their Marine guards. The two human Marines weren't in power armor, and Isaac could *feel* their tension.

The rotating habitats were impressive. The sheer scale of the project was huge, but so was the fact that they'd had to bring in a *lot* of water to meet Vistan environmental needs. Isaac's dress uniform trousers were soaked halfway to his knee by the time they'd made it any distance, and he half-wished he'd stuck to his regular uniform.

His regular uniform doubled as an emergency vac-suit and was waterproof. The white fabric of his dress uniform was definitely *not*.

Their eventual destination looked no different from any other part of the station until the guards led them into a large assembly hall.

Even the hall had the same plain fixtures and walls as everywhere else in the station. The *ceiling*, however, was a massive version of the mixed holographic/datasong projectors the Vistans had been developing.

To Isaac's eyes, it was Vista as seen from the station's position. It wasn't a true representation of what you would see outside the station —it wasn't spinning, for example—but it showed everything going on around the Great High Mother's homeworld…

And the sickly gray appearance of that homeworld.

"Admiral Lestroud, approach us," the Great High Mother instructed from across the hall.

He obeyed, seeing that Sings-Over-Darkened-Waters was already standing by Sleeps-In-Sunlight.

Vistan body language was still nearly unreadable to humans. The Assini were *far* more interpretable in many ways, despite being four-legged centaur-like creatures with beaks.

He approached the Vistan leader's chair and saluted crisply.

"Honored ally," he greeted her formally. "You requested my presence."

"I did," she confirmed. "My First-Among-Singers has relayed the course of the battle just fought in our system. We are once again aware of how fledgling our ships and arms are compared to both yours and those of the beings who would destroy us.

"I am also made aware of the ships being laid down in the yards built for the evacuation freighters, ships your people have designed for us.

"My people and I are in your debt, Admiral Lestroud, and so I find myself afraid," the Great High Mother told him. "Our world is broken, our race surviving only by the shallowest of waters and your aid.

"We fear the price you would demand of us in payment for all of this. Already a great war had been brought to our system. You protected us, but the battle fought against the Assini's Escort Matrices was not our war."

"It was not mine either, honored ally," Isaac said carefully. "It was the *Assini*'s war, and one in which we chose to aid them to repay the assistance of the Matrices who have helped both of our peoples over the years.

"In turn, we have been given access to both Matrix and Assini technological databanks, databanks I intend to see shared with your people in payment for your assistance against the Escorts."

"And once again you would place us in your debt, Admiral Lestroud," Sleeps-In-Sunlight noted. "And once again I fear your price. Speak now, Admiral. Lay our fears to rest or lay them bare for all to hear!"

Well, *that* was a harsh place to start from…but it helped that Isaac knew what he wanted.

"Very well," he told her. "Understand first that I speak with the full authority of the Republic of Exilium, but what I say must pass our Senate before it is law. I am our ambassador and my word will not be discarded lightly, but it *could* happen.

"You must understand that we of the Republic of Exilium are very few. We are exiles, flung a galaxy away from home. Four million souls in the darkness of a strange void.

"We find ourselves surrounded by the Matrices, many of them hostile, some even truly genocidal. A handful are friendly.

"We cannot turn aside any help, nor can we betray the oaths and honor that led us to be exiled. I look at the stars around us, and I see that we are not alone—and that worlds like yours are threatened by the Rogue Matrices.

"And I see only one way to save those worlds: to fight. To take that fight to stars we have not yet explored, to find the Rogue Matrices shipyards and AI seed factories and destroy them.

"That war, that *crusade*, cannot be fought by the Republic alone. We need friends and allies. We helped you because you needed our help. Now we hope to ask for yours—but if you cannot stand alongside us as equals in the line of battle, your help is useless to us.

"So, I have offered technology and ships and aid so that when the time comes, when we are ready to take the fight to the Rogues so that what happened to Vista never happens again, you will be ready and able to fight by our side."

He'd apparently brought the Vistan court—or press pit, whatever the audience was—to silence other than the ever-present chirping, but Sleeps-In-Sunlight seemed unperturbed.

"And if I were to tell you, Admiral Lestroud, that my people have suffered enough? That I will not ask my Spears and Star-Choirs to go to war at your side?"

"Then I would ask if you would permit us to recruit volunteers from among your people," he told her. "And I would be disappointed if you refused...but you are the Great High Mother of the Vistans. Your thoughts must first be for your own people, not for strangers you have barely met."

"And shouldn't your first thoughts be for the good of the Republic?" she asked.

"They are," he said quietly. "But Captain Catalan committed the ESF to protect your people, and I will honor that oath. I swore to protect the remaining Assini, and I will honor that oath.

"And I swore an oath once, long ago, to protect the weak and uphold the helpless."

He smiled.

"I will honor that oath."

"My oath as a Great Mother was similar to that last in many ways," Sleeps-In-Sunlight told him. "The intended focus was my own people, but we never restricted that. 'A Mother should look to all children, not just those of her Clan, when they have met their own Clan's needs.'"

"My people say that if you have extra, you should build a longer table, not a taller fence," Isaac said gently.

"I look forward to learning more of your people in the years to come, Admiral Isaac Lestroud," the Great High Mother of the Vistans told him. "We will stand by your side. These Rogues destroyed our world, and you are correct: this cannot happen again.

"Not while we have the power to stop it."

68

FOR THE FIRST time since her husband had left Exilium, Amelie was able to have a live conversation with him—unfortunately, it was with her entire Cabinet present. Isaac was linked via the newly installed updated tachyon communicators, allowing a real-time holographic communication from fifty light-years.

He stood at the far end of the table, facing her and her Ministers calmly. It had been months since she'd seen anything except recordings, and there was an edge to his face and eyes she didn't like.

"Those are the terms I promised the Vistans," he told the Cabinet levelly. "A full alliance, technological exchange, assistance with building their new fleet, continued assistance with the evacuation.

"With the help of the Matrices, we should be able to begin the full reconstruction process on Vista once the last evacuees are lifted out in thirty days. XR-13-9 will be providing replacement terraforming spikes."

He shook his head.

"All of that effort to knock aside the ones the Rogues brought, and now we're going to finish the job ourselves. Unlike the Rogues' spikes, though, XR-13-9 believes they can program the new ones with the ecological data from the Vistans.

"They won't be able to fully reconstruct the original ecosystem, but the result will be a blend of the ecologies of Vista and the Assini homeworld. It won't be a perfect repair, but it won't be a regular Constructed World, either.

"In exchange for that assistance, the Vistans will provide combat task forces to assist in neutralizing the Rogue Matrices in this region. The long-term strategy of that operation will need to be drawn up over the next few months, but I don't foresee commencing major operations for at least a year."

"You do realize that this government has to approve any operation on the scale you are suggesting?" Father James asked dryly. The pacifistic priest sounded more amused than upset, to Amelie's surprise.

"I do," Isaac confirmed. "The alliance with the Vistans is inside the authority you gave me. I could argue that operations against Rogues in the area of the Hearthfire and Refuge Systems would be included as well, but I won't.

"We now know that the Rogues we've faced have been *less* aggressive than the original Matrices close to the Assini homeworld," the Admiral continued. "They've been genocidal, yes, but almost incidentally. The Matrices close to the Assini actively sought out other intelligences to destroy.

"We have to assume that we have been *lucky*, Ministers. We need to make contact with the Construction Matrices near us and near Vista and establish their threat levels. With the assistance of XR-13-9 and the Assini, it is possible that we will be able to turn some of those intelligences into allies.

"Some we may simply be able to leave be. I suspect, however, that at least half or more of the Matrices outside of XR-13-9's verification network will need to be disabled or destroyed.

"I don't like the idea of committing ourselves to a massive offensive like this, Father James. I just don't see a choice."

"And how many civilizations do you think will die if you don't stop them, Admiral?" James asked.

"One is too many," Shankara Linton interjected. "I agree completely with the Admiral. My only question is our resources. Again and again, we have run up against the limits of our industrial base and population. You and I agreed, Admiral, that the ESF can only support three battlecruisers.

"We can't fight an interstellar war with three battlecruisers."

"I know," Isaac granted. "Part of the solution is XR-13-9-D. *Interceptor* will be leaving Hearthfire within the next few days. Captain Catalan and his pet Matrix will be home in seventy-five days.

"While D itself is too large to incorporate into a warship, they have suggested that they will be able to bud off lesser Matrices, equivalent to the units in a Matrix combat platform, that can be included into a new battlecruiser design…and into our chain of command."

"You cannot seriously be considering building AI warships!" James replied, sounding as horrified as Amelie felt.

"I must agree with James," she said, leaning forward and meeting her husband's gaze. "We have seen the consequences of the Assini's tendency to build themselves automated defenders."

"And I agree with you both," her Admiral said. "These Matrices will be part of the crew of the new ships, acting as an augment to the executive officer and replacing as much as thirty or forty percent of the hands aboard the ship.

"They will be part of the chain of command, reporting to the ship's Captain and XO, and they will most definitely *not* have control of the ship's weapons. Their presence, however, should allow us to increase our ship strength by at least fifty percent.

"The databanks we have from the Assini and the Matrices also included a number of systems to expand our autonomous mining and fabrications in Exilium. We should be able to increase our industrial base and increase the number of ships our ESF personnel can man."

"That still doesn't get us anywhere near the level necessary to wage war on a collection of self-replicating artificial intelligences that control a sphere, what, four hundred light-years in radius?" Amelie said softly. "What's your plan, Isaac?"

She was pretty sure she knew. It was obvious, really, now that they knew there were other civilizations out there they had to save.

"We need more allies like the Vistans," he told them. "We need to seek out civilizations that have not yet encountered the Matrices. We know there have to be species out here that are exploiting their own systems, potentially even interstellar civilizations.

"The Matrices' net expansion is slower than the speed of light. Civilizations advanced enough to help us will have some idea of what's coming. We have to convince them to stand with us; we must provide technology and perhaps even entire ships to them.

"We have no choice, Ministers," Isaac stated calmly. "We cannot fight the Matrices alone, we cannot wait for them to come to us, and we are not prepared to stand by and let other civilizations die because we did not act.

"We must find allies. We must build a grand alliance and wage war against the Matrices until they are no longer a threat."

The Cabinet was silent.

Amelie leaned forward.

"I don't think a vote is necessary, do you?" she asked them. "Isaac is right, and we all know it. We cannot stand alone against the Matrices, and we cannot stand by while they destroy civilizations left and right.

"It falls to us, then, to put this into a plan we can put before the Senate and our people. If the Republic of Exilium will take up this crusade, then we must do it as one body."

ONCE THE CABINET had dispersed after the meeting, Amelie moved Isaac's hologram over to her with a gesture. She was alone, but she could at least *see* her husband for a while longer.

"I'm guessing you're not coming home anytime soon," she noted sadly.

"No," he conceded. "I wish it were different. I miss you."

"I miss you too," Amelie told him. "You'll be pleased to know that Emilia is going to be running for President. Of course, I officially have no position on the election. Neither do you."

Isaac laughed. She'd missed that sound and smiled at him.

"Of course not," he confirmed. He'd refused to even have an

opinion on *her* election, which had been heartwarming if occasionally annoying.

"I definitely won't be home before then," Isaac warned. "I don't think I can justify leaving before we hit the point of no return on Vista."

She winced.

"When is that?"

"Ninety days or so," he told her. "We'll have everybody up by then, though we're looking at a few stubborn holdouts. The storms are getting worse and the clouds are getting thicker. Ninety days might turn out to be optimistic, but eventually, we won't be able to safely land shuttles."

"And then you're going to drop new terraforming spikes on the planet?"

"I'm leaving that discussion to Sleeps-In-Sunlight and XR-13-9," he admitted. "I'm merely standing guard with a bunch of warships, just in case."

"No sign from the Rogues?"

"No." He shook his head. "I suspect we're not going to like what they do show up with, which is why I've got the recon Matrices sweeping the star systems around us. A pre-emptive strike would buy us a lot of peace of mind, but we have to find the bastards first."

"If you find the Rogue Construction Matrix, don't wait to argue with the Cabinet," Amelie told him. "Hit it with everything you have. That's our biggest regional threat."

"We're assuming 'everything I have' will be enough," he countered. "I'd love to have a Vistan battlecruiser group to back me up on that, but we're years from that."

"Soon enough." Amelie sighed. "I hate that we're going to be arming people who have barely passed the orbital-space-station level."

"It's better than the alternative. Is Emilia going to be on board?"

Amelie chuckled. She understood Isaac's concern—even if the Senate committed to this crusade, the *next* Senate and President could be a real problem.

"New Soweto apparently had rabid firebrands as an export product," she noted. "Emilia's like you: protect the weak and uplift the downtrodden. She'll back this mission as Prime Minister and as President."

"Good. We can't afford to half-do this, my love."

"We'll do all we can, you and I," Amelie promised. "Exilium will listen to us, even once I'm no longer President. Which is starting to sound more and more relaxing by the day!"

Her husband laughed.

"You'll be bored and asking President Nyong'o for work within a week," he predicted.

"Probably not, because I'll be grabbing the first ship to Hearthfire so I can drag a certain Admiral to bed," she told him with a wicked grin.

69

Captain Octavio Catalan stared at the series of holographic images floating in front of him, then looked at Commander Das.

"You're certain," he said quietly. It wasn't a question.

"My team and I went over the conclusions three times, then had D go over them," she told him. "Then I had Siril-ki do the same."

Siril-ki was one of the few members of Reletan-dai's AI research team the old Assini hadn't woken up. She/they had been the youngest of his department heads and focused on the colony ship AIs, with no contact with the military systems.

She/they was now the best expert they had left on Assini Matrices. If she/they agreed with Das's analysis...they were in trouble. They were in serious trouble.

"Stay right here," Octavio ordered his tactical officer. *Interceptor* was less than twenty-four hours from heading back to Exilium, but he wasn't going to sit on this bombshell.

"Africano," he said as he activated the com. "Get me the Admiral."

"Sir?"

"Now, Lieutenant Commander," Catalan said harshly, letting full Command Voice leak into his tone. "It's important."

He didn't know what lever Torborg Africano pulled, but she had Admiral Lestroud on the call in less than two minutes.

"What is it, Catalan?" Lestroud asked. It looked like they'd interrupted the Admiral's lunch, given the half-eaten meal on the man's desk and his frustrated look.

"Sir, we've been analyzing the Matrix core intelligence code samples we have and comparing them. We've found something...odd."

The frustration vanished and Lestroud straightened, looking directly at them.

"How odd are we talking about?"

"It's easier to show you, sir," Octavio told him. He tapped a command, adding two of the holographic images that Das had been walking him through to the transmission.

"This is a three-dimensional representation of the core intelligence modules of a Matrix," he explained. "The red splotches you see are missing or damaged code. We have a comparison point of the original code, but we didn't need to use it for this. Most of the gaps are pretty obvious."

The red splotches were scattered through the two holograms, each of them intentionally structured to mirror a brain. There was no pattern, no straight lines or curves that could be analyzed by an algorithm.

"The intelligence on the left is D," Octavio noted. "On the right is a sample from the Rogue Sub-Regional Construction Matrix destroyed here in Hearthfire.

"You can see that they're damaged in different places, and while there are large areas of damage, those are clearly made up of smaller, overlapping pieces, right?"

"I can make that out now that you're telling me it's there, yes," Lestroud said slowly. "Your point?"

"*This* is one of the Escort Matrices."

The new brain had much larger splotches. Massive areas of the core intelligence were warped or damaged by radiation and tachyon punches.

"Am I supposed to be seeing something different, Catalan?" Lestroud asked.

"Das and her team weren't sure themselves, but they ran a comparison between this code and the Rogue's," Octavio replied. A large portion of the red splotches turned orange.

"The orange damage is definitely tachyon punches. We take that out and, well...take a look at what's left."

It was subtle, but Octavio knew what to look for. There were curves and lines in the damage now.

"That's...there's something in there, isn't there?" Lestroud asked.

"That's what we thought, so Commander Das checked the Assini databanks," Octavio told his commander. "The Assini did have a sample from one of the Rogue Matrices near their home system. We ran another comparison."

A fourth "brain" appeared. This one didn't have nearly as many random splotches...but there were some larger splotches hitting key areas.

"Captain. I'm starting to suspect, but explain, please."

"There is no way that tachyon-punch degradation or a solar flare can justify the damage done to the core intelligences of the Escort Matrices or the original Regional Construction Matrices," Octavio said quietly.

"In the Matrices out here, you see truly random damage. In the Matrices from around the Assini home system, you see similar damage, the damage that turned them against their makers...

"But that damage is *not* random."

JOIN THE MAILING LIST

Love Glynn Stewart's books? Join the mailing list at

GLYNNSTEWART.COM/MAILING-LIST/

to know as soon as new books are released, special announcements, and a chance to win free paperbacks.

ABOUT THE AUTHOR

Glynn Stewart is the author of *Starship's Mage*, a bestselling science fiction and fantasy series where faster-than-light travel is possible–but only because of magic. His other works include science fiction series *Duchy of Terra, Castle Federation* and *Vigilante,* as well as the urban fantasy series *ONSET* and *Changeling Blood.*

Writing managed to liberate Glynn from a bleak future as an accountant. With his personality and hope for a high-tech future intact, he lives in Kitchener, Ontario with his wife, their cats, and an unstoppable writing habit.

VISIT GLYNNSTEWART.COM FOR NEW RELEASE UPDATES

facebook.com/glynnstewartauthor

OTHER BOOKS BY GLYNN STEWART

*Space Carrier Avalon*For release announcements join the mailing list by visiting GlynnStewart.com

Exile

Ashen Stars: an Exile Prequel Novella

Exile

Refuge

Crusade

Castle Federation

Space Carrier Avalon

Stellar Fox

Battle Group Avalon

Q-Ship Chameleon

Rimward Stars

Operation Medusa

Starship's Mage

Starship's Mage

Hand of Mars

Voice of Mars

Alien Arcana

Judgment of Mars

UnArcana Stars

Sword of Mars

Mountain of Mars (upcoming)

Starship's Mage: Red Falcon

Interstellar Mage

Mage-Provocateur

Agents of Mars

Duchy of Terra

The Terran Privateer

Duchess of Terra

Terra and Imperium

Light of Terra: A Duchy of Terra series

Darkness Beyond

Shield of Terra

Imperium Defiant

Shadow of Terra: A Duchy of Terra series

Relics of Eternity (upcoming)

Vigilante (With Terry Mixon)

Heart of Vengeance

Oath of Vengeance

Bound By Stars: A Vigilante Series (With Terry Mixon)

Bound By Law

Bound by Honor

Bound by Blood

Peacekeepers of Sol

Raven's Peace

Raven's Oath (upcoming)

Shattered Stars: Conviction

Conviction (upcoming)

ONSET

ONSET: Blood of the Innocent

ONSET: Stay of Execution

Changeling Blood

Changeling's Fealty

Hunter's Oath

Noble's Honor

Fantasy Stand Alone Novels

Children of Prophecy

City in the Sky

CPSIA information can be obtained
at www.ICGtesting.com
Printed in the USA
LVHW030912200120
644155LV00001B/48